A BID TO RULE

THE STARS AND GREEN MAGICS
BOOK 3

NOVAE CAELUM

AUTHOR'S NOTE

A Bid to Rule was originally published as *The Seritarchus*, a prequel serial to The Stars and Green Magics series, covering episodes 1-107, the complete book. While it was first intended to be a standalone (and, quite honestly, less than fifty pages), it took on a glorious life of its own. This book changed the course of the main series in many ways, deepening the characters, interweaving new plotlines, and showing me the story I was building toward all along.

So, this book has been renamed *A Bid to Rule*, been given a proper place within the series (Book 3!), and as of this moment is the longest book in the series. It's also a spy novel inside a court intrigue thriller inside a family saga, and I'm deliciously happy with that.

So don't skip this book—so much in here is woven into the story moving forward! I deeply hope you enjoy reading it as much as I enjoyed writing it, and that Homaj, Iata, Zhang, and Jalava will find a happy place in your heart, too.

As far as changes, I made some moderate editing changes from the original serial version, most notably that one of the rival families' last names is now Delor. I combined some chapters, too, and there are now 104 chapters, not 107. I also added my beloved header quotes! These are all new and were not in the original serial.

This book features several characters who use gender neutral pronouns (they/them/their, fae/faer/faerself, e/em/eir, or other neopronouns).

This book, barring the occasional and inspired burst of strong language, is PG-13, with a note that it deals with grief, parental death, and mistreatment among family members.

For detailed content notes, please see:
https://novaecaelum.com/content-notes

1

NEWS

The death of a ruler is a cataclysmic event in the life of a Truthspoken. But also, it's only to be expected.

— ANATHARIE RHIALDEN, SERITARCHUS VIII
AS QUOTED IN *THE CHANGE DIALOGUES*

Homaj Rhialden, second Truthspoken heir to the interstellar Kingdom of Valoris, sat rigid in a wing-back chair in his sitting room. He stared down at the single square of quality card stock in his hands. Creamy paper, the writing cramped and hurried. There was a smudge of dirt near the edge. Or was it possibly blood?

His hands, despite all his efforts, were shaking.

He looked up at the messenger, a young woman who'd introduced herself as Sergeant Vi Zhang of the Palace Guard, she and her pronouns. She wore a maroon and silver uniform, dark bobbed hair framing a heart-shaped face. She couldn't have been much older than he was, maybe mid-twenties at most. She stood stiffly at attention, waiting for him to speak. To react. Anything.

"This—" He cleared his throat. "This is from Commander Tavven's own hand?"

"From the scene, Ser Truthspoken, it was handed off to me at the palace gates. The commander is on their way back to the palace now, and I'm to relay it's their first priority to make sure the palace is secure and you are safe."

Homaj stood, unable to sit still with the storm welling up inside him. "Yes. Fine. I'll go meet them."

He couldn't stay here. Not with the walls too solid, not knowing that just down the hall sat his parents' apartment, which they'd never inhabit again.

"Ser?" the guard said, startled into a less formal address. "Ser, you must stay here. I'm to stay with you, in your quarters. The Seritarchus, your father—"

"Is dead," Homaj said softly.

His hands steadied by his sides, but his insides roiled, and he couldn't gather his thoughts enough to soothe them.

It was what the note had said. The Seritarchus and the Seritarchus Consort were dead, assassinated in an explosion in the city during a tour of one of the city's hospitals. A *hospital*.

And his older sibling, the Truthspoken Heir, wasn't in the palace, and wasn't responding to calls.

And him? Was he safe here, in his sitting room, in the royal residence of Palace Rhialden? Was he, a Truthspoken, ever safe?

He needed focus, a purpose, a direction at which to aim.

Zhang shifted. "Ser—Truthspoken—please stay in your quarters. We have two guards at the doors, and myself, and more on the way. I was the fastest runner. They'll be here shortly."

She was adamant, but not losing her cool. Homaj examined the rank pins on her collar. Yes, sergeant.

"Sergeant Zhang. What is your assessment of my immediate situation?"

She tilted her head, calculating. "Two prime targets down, one missing. The Truthspoken Heir was last seen in a meeting with Lord Xavi Birka, with whom they're known to have casual intimacies. We've been unable to contact Lord Birka as well. Or the Heir's bloodservant, who is also missing. The palace is on lockdown. We are searching and strengthening the perimeters around both the palace and the residence wing. You—you are exactly where you need to be. I advise you to go into your bedroom, which has no windows. We will guard all doors, including the doors into the back passages. You, at least, will absolutely be safe."

She sounded like she knew what she was talking about, but Homaj read uncertainty in her voice. His Truthspoken training in reading people and all their subtle cues left little room for lies.

Not that he thought she was lying to him. Only that she wasn't so sure of events herself.

Because it was logical, if you assassinate the ruler, and possibly the Heir, to take out the only other Truthspoken in existence as well. Which would be him.

"You don't trust the other guards?" he asked.

Could he trust her? If there was even a chance that any of the Palace Guard had a hand in all of this, could he afford to?

She narrowed her eyes, her shoulders shifting uncomfortably in her uniform jacket. "They are the Guard. We are the Guard. We'll protect you."

She also didn't believe that.

Zhang looked down and away before bracing herself and meeting his eyes. She knew he'd seen through that statement, too.

Was this a game, something she was trying to tell him but couldn't say outright?

No, she just couldn't bring herself to say that it might have been someone in the Guard who'd betrayed his family.

Homaj drew in a long breath.

He had to Change. He was dressed, now, in his own court finery—an embroidered blue silk blouse, flowing white trousers. His long black hair was braided in an elaborate, asymmetrical pile, set with tiny diamond and nova heart pins. All flow when he needed...command? He didn't know if he was in command, and he couldn't think it. Not yet. His sibling hadn't been contacted, might be alive, might be fine. Had to be fine.

Adeius. Had to be fine.

His hands were trembling again, and he squeezed his palms tight. What could he do? Who could he be that would most effectively shield him from any attack and allow him to direct the outcome of events? Let him know what the hell was going on?

He started for his bedroom, and Zhang followed.

2

CHANGE

I'm good at Change. I like Change. It's a core part of who I am.

— HOMAJ RHIALDEN, SERITARCHUS IX IN A
PRIVATE LETTER, NEVER SENT; AS QUOTED IN
THE CHANGE DIALOGUES

On the way to the bedroom, they passed through Homaj's prep room, with the closet door open and cosmetics scattered across two separate vanity tables. Then into his bedroom, which didn't feel nearly as safe as it should.

Homaj glanced through the open doorway to his bloodservant's bedroom, adjoining his. "Where's Iata?"

He vaguely knew that his bloodservant, Iata, had gone to take care of the things he usually took care of in managing Homaj's daily life in the palace, but Homaj wasn't in the habit of tracking his bloodservant's daily tasks. Iata managed his life; he didn't feel the need to manage Iata's.

He scowled. Iata should be here right now. Iata should be here when he needed him.

Zhang raised her ring comm and spoke a few quick words in code, wrapped around Iata's name. Homaj quickly translated: Verify Iata's whereabouts.

Zhang listened as the reply came into her earpiece, and it irked Homaj that he couldn't hear that, too.

"Iata's in the kitchen," she said. "Verified."

"Send him up." He wanted his bloodservant now, but the kitchens were in the basement, two floors below where he was standing and under the administrative part of the palace, not the residence. It would be at least ten minutes before Iata made it back. He needed to start his Change, now.

Homaj shut the door to his bedroom, locked it, and moved toward the large, four-poster bed.

"Watch me, Zhang. I will be vulnerable in the trance."

"Ser," she said, startled. "Please wait until the reinforcements have arrived."

"Do you think there's time for that? I don't. This will be a quick Change only. But I must start it now."

He lay down, his thoughts already racing ahead to what he would Change. His facial features, surely. His skin pigmentation. Not his height or overall body shape—there wasn't time for that sort of structural Change. But he'd shift some of the musculature in his legs so his walk would be different. He'd—Adeius, he hated beards, but it would be useful now.

With one last glance at Zhang, who had her pistol out and was facing the door, he sank back into the soft mattress and closed his eyes.

The Change trance came easily to him, and he slipped just below the level of consciousness, his body carrying out the Changes his mind had assigned.

He knew it was only minutes later when he opened his eyes again. The bones of his face ached, his skin feeling taut and prickly. He hadn't had the concentration to block all the pain and discomfort of the Change, especially a quick Change, but he sucked in a breath and diverted his concentration there now, only breathing out again as the discomfort eased.

Zhang looked back, did a double take. "Oh."

Homaj levered himself out of bed, hands already combing through his long hair, gathering it into a bun. He hadn't changed the length or texture, but he had changed the color from black to a dark gold. He stepped into Iata's room, which held a wall mirror—his own was in his prep room, and he didn't want to leave the bedroom just yet.

His features were blockier, brow thick, nose longer. He had a small gap between his front teeth now. His face was paler than his usual tan skin, scattered with freckles. His eyes were wider, though he hadn't changed the color, which was brown. The color mattered far less than reshuffling his features.

His enemies, whoever they were, would be expecting him to Change. It was what Truthspoken did. It was how Truthspoken ruled. They might not be expecting him to Change this fast, though—Truthspoken rarely accomplished a Change in under an hour. But then, he'd always been a prodigy of the one thing he was supposed to be good at.

Homaj finished tying up his hair, smoothed down thick brows and the golden-brown beard.

He was shaky, he needed to eat and replenish his body's reserves after expending so much in a fast Change. He pulled open a drawer in the stand beside his bed, grabbed an energy bar, and tore open the wrapper. He'd have privacy in his own bedroom and prep room, but when he went beyond it, he would be this new person. And this new person would definitely not know how to Change.

"Is it safe to go to the prep room?" he asked. The door would have locked behind them as they'd entered the suite, and it was nearly as secure as his bedroom. But the walls of his bedroom felt more of a fortress just now, one he was suddenly reluctant to leave.

Homaj cleared his throat. He hadn't Changed his voice yet —that was a more delicate Change, but he moved it down in pitch. Burred the edges. "Please, check the prep room." That was better.

Zhang blinked at him, then waved him back, out of sight of the door, and ducked into the prep room. He waited impatiently for her to check the room and the closet.

"Clear," she said.

3

THE UNIFORM

The maroon and silver of a Palace Guard uniform signifies the blood our ancestors shed to reach their new home on Valon, and the stars in which they traveled.

— MUZHARIN IRAL IN "THE SYMBOLOGY OF PALACE RHIALDEN"

Homaj swept past the vanity tables and headed for the closet. No, he needed to strengthen his walk. Not his usual flow. He needed to project more awareness of his body, of the weapon it could become.

His closet, as a Truthspoken, held clothing of every size, every cut, from every gender presentation and economic class. He moved toward the back where there was a rack of maroon and silver uniforms and a box beside them holding an assortment of rank and service pins.

Zhang, half watching him, half watching the closed prep room door that led out to the central hallway of his apartment, frowned. But she didn't comment as he skinned out of his silks and into the lightly armored fabric of a Palace Guard uniform.

He buckled the belt and ran his hands up the front buttons with practiced ease.

"You've worn the uniform before?" Zhang finally asked. Then remembered herself and added, "Ser?"

Homaj didn't have to answer a familiar question like that from a guard. But Adeius, he wasn't that petty. Not now. And he was about to be a guard, he had to function, for a time, as her equal.

"A few times. Not as who I'm about to be, though."

An identity which he was rapidly formulating, with as much plausible backstory as he could. Lt. Karda Reyin, newly detached from the Valon City Municipal Guard, sent to back up Zhang ahead of other reinforcements. Zhang was nominally in charge because of her familiarity with the palace and palace protocol, but as an officer, he was her superior. That would nicely entangle the weird dynamics they were about to face.

He scooped lieutenant's pins and a Municipal Guard experience pin from the box and fixed them to his collar. Then he pulled out a Palace Guard issue ring comm and fit it on his index finger, left hand to keep his firing hand free, and fit the small transparent earplug in his left ear. Glancing at Zhang's pistol, he went to the very back of the closet, keyed a code into a safe door, and retrieved a pistol of identical make, complete with the wear from constant use and cleaning. Which his bloodservant, Iata, did, or one of his own rotation of guards, not himself.

And where were his own guards just now?

But they'd been set to change their monthly shifts today. They would have gone back into rotation, new guards being assigned by Commander Tavven this morning. No guards were supposed to form attachments to the Truthspoken they guarded, not for the two heirs, at least. His father had a steady complement of personal guards, but then, his father didn't have anyone to usurp but himself.

Homaj closed his eyes, briefly, to shut out thoughts of his father. He couldn't go there yet. Not yet.

Zhang watched him, bemused. "Ser?"

"I'm Lt. Karda Reyin." He gave a quick summary of his ad hoc backstory, and when he finished, her face was a little pinched, but she nodded.

"Reyin, then." Zhang surveyed him again, then straightened, relaxed a little, even. As if she was not in the presence of a Truthspoken, but a comrade-in-arms.

Oh. Oh, he liked her.

A knock came on the outer prep room door, then he heard the lock thunk open. Zhang whipped around, pistol up, striding for the closet door.

Homaj made quick steps to press her arm down. "It's Iata, my bloodservant."

She hovered in the entrance to the closet, holding out an arm to bar him from passing. "Do you a hundred percent know that, sir?"

The knob turned.

The knock had been Iata's. But—but as Truthspoken, he should know that anything about a person could be simulated with enough skill and practice. And before he had any other chance to think, the prep room door swung open and Iata strode in, a cooler in each hand.

So the cook had decided the palace lockdown might be awhile and had sent up food. Or, Iata had insisted. Iata would know he'd likely Change.

Iata spotted them just inside the open closet door. Homaj watched him quickly survey them both and their tells to determine which, in fact, was the Truthspoken.

Iata's dark brown eyes met his, and Homaj searched the nuances of his bloodservant's face. Iata was taller than him by a few centimeters, and Homaj hadn't Changed his height. He was just under two years older than Homaj, a whole lot stiffer all around, and lightyears more responsible. Iata had always presented firmly masc, and his long black hair was neatly braided and wound into a knot at the back of his neck, held with two titanium spikes. His extremely expensive bespoke indigo jacket had little ornamentation, but fit him in every angle.

Iata wasn't disheveled. He didn't look frantic or scared. But then, Iata had much of the same training as Homaj did in schooling his emotions off of his face and out of his mannerisms.

Did Iata know what had happened? The news had come to Homaj by Zhang, but had that been in strict confidence? Was the death of the Seritarchus public? No, Homaj didn't think so, or there wouldn't have been the handwritten note. But Iata would certainly know something was wrong—the palace was on lockdown.

Iata's mouth twitched, the tiniest betrayal of distress. Yes. Yes, Iata knew.

"Is the Truthspoken still in his bedroom?" Iata asked.

Homaj's heart slammed into his throat, and for the first time since Zhang had handed him that note in the sitting room, he stopped to consider what he was actually doing. He'd known he'd needed to Change, yes. He'd just had a vicious reminder that Truthspoken were not safe anywhere, especially as themselves. And he'd known that the safest persona to be right now, the one with the best chance at getting actually useful information, was a Palace Guard. Beyond that—

Iata was asking him what he wanted to do. Iata was asking so much with that single question. If he said no, the Truthspoken was not in his bedroom, then Iata would drop the pretense right now. He'd assume Zhang knew Homaj was Truthspoken. He'd break out the coolers, Homaj would eat, and they'd plan their next steps.

Iata, as his bloodservant, had a limited capacity to Change.

He was from a service branch of the royal Rhialden line, a distant cousin to Homaj. Not a full Truthspoken, either in training or ability, but he could enact smaller Changes to himself if needed. He had much more training in body language, accents, and all the little things that could divert attention from one persona to another.

But few people outside the royal family knew that particularly volatile detail about the duties of a bloodservant, and Homaj didn't want to add Zhang to that list just now.

And if he waited for Iata to make the barest possible Change to be unrecognizable, for them both to pass through the palace unnoticed, it would be half an hour at least. Could he afford that time? Could his sibling, if his sibling was still out there?

He was going to find his sibling. He hadn't consciously thought about that, but—yes. Yes, that was what he was going to do. What he'd already been moving toward.

If he didn't wait for Iata to Change himself, Homaj would have to go through the back corridors alone. Search alone. And then what? A lone anonymous guard just now, with absolutely no ties to anyone, no identity in the system, would have little traction. Would invite more suspicion than anything.

Adeius. He was running on adrenaline. He hadn't thought this through.

Homaj glanced at Zhang. He'd had to trust her enough to watch him while he Changed, but did he trust her to take her through the back corridors that wound in and around every room in the palace? No guards went through there but the Guard Commander and occasionally the Seritarchus' personal guards.

He had the gut sense that wasn't what was needed right now, either. Not a back corridor trek, anyway. He had to work his way into a visible group. He needed the safety and resources of others, because he had no idea who'd attacked his family, and there were ways certain people could identify even the most skilled Truthspoken. In a crowd, he could do his best to deflect attention from anything that might give off his Truthspoken nature.

"Yes," he said to Iata, deciding on his accent and interweaving the city cadences with every word. Leaning into this new persona. "The Truthspoken is in his bedroom. I'm Lt. Reyin, this is Sgt. Zhang. We'll be in the hall watching the main door until reinforcements arrive."

Iata hesitated the barest second, then nodded and pointed. "Out, then. I won't have you bothering the Truthspoken."

There were no cameras or microphones in Homaj's prep room or bedroom, but Iata wouldn't know if Zhang was safe or not, and he would have marked the tentative glance Homaj had just given her. Yes, she did know who Homaj was and what was going on, but he wasn't ready to drop all his walls just now.

"It's an emergency, we should be here to guard the Truthspoken," Zhang protested. Was she getting into the spirit of this, or genuinely displeased Iata wasn't more concerned?

Iata's brows rose. "And you will be. In the hallway."

"No, I mean that—"

Homaj touched Zhang's arm. "Sergeant."

He and Iata had just had an entire nuanced conversation, but Zhang would only see they'd had an awkward exchange.

She glanced at him, then her face cleared. She nodded.

"Please let us know if you need anything," he said to Iata, but Iata had already turned away, carrying the coolers into the bedroom.

Homaj's stomach churned. He'd just done a quick Change, and the energy bar hadn't been enough. He really needed to eat a full and hearty meal. But—but. He was in good enough physical condition that it could wait.

And what would Iata do? He should stay here and make it seem as if the Truthspoken was in his bedroom. Maybe, after a time, he could come out and announce that the Truthspoken had gone out through the back corridors—yes, that's what Homaj would do, as it would then allow the guards to disperse. And Homaj could go with them. As Homaj's bloodservant, Iata's highest mandate was to protect Homaj by giving him cover, whatever form that cover might take.

But would Iata do that? He'd certainly follow the logic—but there'd been something in Iata's eyes that Homaj wasn't as sure of as everything else.

Okay. Okay, he needed to recenter.

"Reinforcements?" he asked Zhang as they moved toward the prep room door. "Have they arrived?" None of this was any good if he'd have to try to explain why an unknown guard had just emerged from the Truthspoken's bedroom suite. That would be tricky enough as it was.

She tapped her ring comm and spoke to the guards at the apartment's outer door, then shook her head. "Only Iata has come in."

Okay. Good. He had to get out there and establish himself as Lt. Karda Reyin before the reinforcements arrived. The apartment, of course, was under security surveillance, so that was a risk, but the door to the prep room was in a deliberate blind spot in the apartment's security systems.

It was just possible that he himself as Homaj could have been scared enough just now, and tired of waiting for reinforcements on his own, to go out and bring back another guard through the back corridors. Not likely, and incredibly foolish, but possible. It was even, mostly, in character. Homaj Rhialden wasn't known in the Rhialden Court for making the wisest decisions.

So there was some leeway, and in the state of chaos the palace was in, the sudden appearance of Lt. Karda Reyin might not be as noticeable as it might in the normal everyday. He was used to taking days and weeks to carefully craft and insert his

Truthspoken personas into the daily life around him, but he had been trained to craft on the fly, too. The door guards—he'd find a way to bluff his way past the door guards. His new persona didn't have to hold up indefinitely, just long enough to get him out there and get some answers.

"I'm Lt. Reyin," he reminded Zhang, as he reached for the door.

"Yes, sir." She met his eyes, steady and determined. "I'll vouch for you, sir."

She glanced back after the closed bedroom door. There was a question in her eyes, but she didn't ask it. And Homaj, at least, thought he owed her the answer.

"Yes, he knows who I am. And what's happened."

Zhang nodded tightly.

He didn't say more as they stepped out into the hallway, and she didn't ask. She didn't have the lifetime of training that he did, but she was catching up fast.

4

DEFLECTION

> *The friendly rivalry between the Palace Guard and the Valon City Municipal Guard sometimes escalates to brawls—most often, to their superiors' chagrin, started by members of the Municipal Guard. Those who avoid brawls, however, might find themselves with a chance to transfer to Palace Guard training at some point in their career.*
>
> — VALENTINA MARCH IN "HABITS OF SUCCESSFUL LAW ENFORCEMENT OFFICERS"

Homaj and Zhang took up different positions around the bend in the apartment's central hallway, standing so they covered both the doorway to the prep room and the main apartment doors at the end of the hall. Except for them, there were no other guards in the apartment, and Homaj had never liked having servants around at all hours of the day—they only came in during the middle of the day to clean and change the sheets. So he and Zhang were, in theory, alone, besides Iata in his own bedroom.

And when were Zhang's reinforcements coming again? It had been more than a half hour since she'd arrived with her news.

Well, he could establish himself as Lt. Reyin in the meantime, start leaving a trail of doubt for anyone who might be watching. Very few people had access to the security feeds from his apartment, but he couldn't afford to trust any of them.

"So, Sergeant," he said. "Um, what do you all do for fun around here? After hours, I mean."

Zhang shot him an incredulous look.

He shrugged. "What? I'm new here." He holstered his pistol and shook his arms out, stretching his shoulders before grabbing his pistol again and settling back into a ready pose. None of those motions natural to him. "I mean, I know it's a crisis and all, but afterward, right? Is there a bar somewhere in the palace?"

"Fucking Municipal Guards," Zhang said under her breath, and he relaxed a little. She understood. She got his need to settle into this persona, and she was following him there.

"No, Lieutenant," she said in a tone that was clearly annoyed, "there are no palace bars. You think we get drunk on duty? And we're always on duty here. You should have looked into it more before you signed up."

"What? The pay's a lot better."

"And the chance for promotion, I'm sure."

"That too. And—" He made himself blush. "I met one of the palace guards in a bar—in the city—and after the fourth drink, she told me I should give it a try. I already have the training, I took all the advanced courses to be able to pull diplomatic duty."

Zhang snorted. "Who? Who told you that?"

"Ina Vogret."

"Oh, Adeius. You know Ina likes to lead people on, right? She'd tell you to join because she thinks it's funny?"

He shrugged.

"Did she also mention that fraternization among the Palace Guard is not allowed?"

A brisk knock came from the main doors and they both stiffened, abandoning the riff. He didn't recognize the knock.

"Stay alert," Zhang said as she moved toward the corridor doors. Homaj followed, covering her from the other side of the hall.

"Reinforcements," Zhang said, looking through the peephole.

"Do you know them? Can you vouch for them?"

"I don't know you," she retorted, which was true enough for him as Lt. Reyin. Well, and for him as himself, too. "Yes, I know them." The smallest hesitation. "I vouch for them."

Not all of them, then. Homaj would be on guard.

Zhang tapped a code into the door lock and it clicked open, the new guards coming in with a rush of cooler air.

There were four of them, all in maroon and silver, all with pistols drawn, red lights on the pistols' sides glowing with the warning of their lethal rounds. Bandoliers crossed their chests, holding crowd-control gear.

The new guards nodded at Zhang, and one, a short and stocky androgynous person with pale skin and a neat crop of white-blonde hair, frowned at Homaj.

"Zhang, I don't know this person. Who's the lieutenant?" Homaj had seen them among the Palace Guard before, but he didn't know them well—Jalava, he thought their name was.

Zhang looked back at Homaj, face pinched again. "This is, uh—"

Oh, hell, she didn't remember his name as a guard.

"Lt. Karda Reyin," Homaj said, coming down hard on that Valon City accent. "He and him. Just transferred yesterday from the Municipal Guard. I'm still in training here."

Jalava, junior lieutenant though they were to his own full

lieutenant's pins, narrowed their craggy gaze at him. "And now you just happen to be in the Truthspoken's quarters? Forgive me, sir, but has anyone vetted you?"

"He's been shadowing me all day," Zhang said. "He's got diplomatic training. And please keep your voice down, sir—the Truthspoken's in his bedroom. Reyin and I are watching the door to the bedroom suite."

"I'm in command, Sergeant," Jalava. "I'm senior here— among anyone I trust." Another glance in Homaj's direction. "And I have my orders to see the Truthspoken is safe. I sent the door detail down the corridor to form an extra perimeter check for this section of the residence—you two go outside and take up positions outside the apartment. Municipal Guard, huh?" They studied Homaj. "Are you ready for door detail in a crisis?"

That was the door guards taken care of, then. Homaj wouldn't have to bluff his way past them—depending on where they were stationed, he'd just go the other way around.

"Actually, I'm senior?" Homaj said, raising an apologetic hand.

Zhang grimaced. "Respectfully, sir, you're in training, and we are in a crisis. Please defer. Jalava, sir, the Truthspoken asked me to guard him personally, and I'd like to continue to do so. Sir."

Jalava huffed, rocking back on their polished heels. "Fine. Not as interesting as standing out here, admiring all the scenery, I'm sure. Go."

It was a delay, and Homaj would have to find a way to maneuver the group itself outside if Iata didn't show, or at least get Zhang outside with him and on some mission or other. But for the moment, establishing himself was still the priority. The safety of the group would do no good if they suspected who he really was.

Zhang turned back toward the prep room, Homaj moving

to follow, but then she paused. "Sir, any word from the Commander?"

"Nothing new," Jalava said, their mouth pulling tight. "Tavven will call us when they know more. Our job is to keep the Truthspoken safe and alive."

There was a very soft thump in the direction of the bedroom. With the sound dampening in both bedroom and prep room, that had to have been loud for him to hear out here.

Homaj, nerves spiking, looked at Zhang. They both took off running.

5

OKAY IN THERE

The security measures of Palace Rhialden are a secret as deeply hidden and speculated on as our ancestral origins.

— CHENGUANG S.P., POLITICAL FEED
COMMENTATOR, IN A POST ON THEIR FEED

Zhang swore as she reached the door to the prep room, which of course was locked. She banged on the door. "Truthspoken? Are you okay in there?"

An indistinct voice came from within. Homaj strained to hear any other voices—which shouldn't have been possible. There would be no other voices. The only other way into that room was through the back corridor entrance in his bedroom, and only the Truthspoken and their bloodservants had access to the back corridors. And Commander Tavven. And a few of his father's guards.

Shit.

Another thump. But *were* there intruders? Right now, anything was possible.

And if there weren't intruders, what the hell was Iata doing in there?

Homaj glanced at Zhang, his own rising panic reflected in her eyes, the sourness of her breath as they bent their heads close to the door to listen.

Jalava came up, radiating tension, weapon ready. The other three guards they'd brought with trailed behind them, also alert.

"Well?" Jalava asked.

Homaj held up a hand, still listening. He could reach for the door handle and open it. All the locks into his bedroom suite were both biometric and genetic, but he was Truthspoken. He could Change his palm and only his palm back to his own DNA and unlock the door. Not without giving himself away, though. Lt. Reyin had no business being able to open that door.

Was his secrecy worth Iata's life?

Was it worth his own, if Iata was under attack, and that attack had been meant for Homaj?

Then, he barely had time to step back before the knob turned and the door swung open.

Iata looked out, glaring at Homaj and the assembled guards. He was holding a—Adeius, a truly priceless artisan shirt, one of Homaj's, and he'd been intending to wear that this week—to his upper arm. There was a red blotch on the cream cloth, and a red smudge on Iata's face.

Or rather, not Iata's face.

Homaj stared, his stomach clenching. That hadn't been ten minutes, but Iata had done a quick job of making broad Changes. He'd pushed his features more royal Rhialden, more like Homaj's own.

Homaj's lips drew tight. If Iata was going to Change—and that hadn't exactly been Homaj's plan—he was supposed to Change himself into someone innocuous, someone who could move around the palace with ease, to help the Truthspoken he served. That lie about the Truthspoken still being in the bedroom—that was supposed to be a smokescreen, not a freaking reality. He wasn't supposed to make it look like he was the Truthspoken himself. He wasn't supposed to make himself a target.

And he truly shouldn't have been able to accomplish all that in ten minutes.

Zhang shot a panicked what-the-fuck look to Homaj, who, in character, shot the same look back.

"T-Truthspoken?" he asked. "Is there anyone else in there with you?"

"My bloodservant," Iata snapped. "Who left a cooler on the floor where I could trip on it."

He nailed the accent, and intonation.

"I need some quick heal!" he shouted in the direction of the guards, all of them. "If you've got any—"

Was Homaj that shrill when he was angry?

Homaj took a step back as Iata leveled his gaze on him. "Lieutenant. Give me your quick heal patch."

Homaj patted his uniform jacket inner pockets, but he didn't have any emergency patches, as a guard should. He'd forgotten that detail. Small detail in a dizzying chain of events. But he should have been better than that.

And was quick heal a good idea with a cut like Iata's? Quick heal came laced with stimulants, and Iata already looked a little wild around the edges. But was that actually blood on Iata's arm? Why hadn't he already healed it through Change?

Zhang touched Homaj's arm, but it was Jalava who said, "Truthspoken, you have a medical cabinet in the hall? Like in the Truthspoken Heir's apartment? Forgive me, I haven't been in this apartment before—"

"Yes, yes," Iata said. "Bandages and sealants."

Jalava snapped a finger and sent someone off.

Homaj nodded. "Right." Nodded again. "That's good."

Jalava gave him a flat look, and Homaj shut his mouth. This was quickly spinning out of any kind of control.

Iata grabbed his shoulder. "I need a patch, though. Now."

Homaj blinked, and focus crashed back in on him.

Oh, hell. Iata had Changed far, far too quickly for his ability and skill. There was a danger, when a Truthspoken pushed too far in a Change, too fast, of unbalancing the body's vital systems. A quick heal patch would pump Iata with stimulants, but the smart readers in the patch would identify the imbalances, too, and release the right drugs to correct them. Iata's cut was only a means to get to that end and get him out of danger.

Homaj nodded. He turned and waved to the guards. "I didn't pack my patches today. Forgot. Does anyone have—"

But they already had patches out, and three patches were thrust at him. He took them, tearing open the first with his teeth while he reached for Iata's arm.

"Truthspoken, may I?" he asked.

"Yes—" Iata hissed as Homaj lifted the shirt he'd been using to staunch the blood. The shirt tried to stick to the wound. Was the cut that deep?

No. There was no cut. And this close, Homaj smelled the faintly sweet smell of the makeup he sometimes used to simulate blood, if a specific Truthspoken mission required it. Iata had only ripped the sleeve and liberally poured the fake blood.

Homaj motioned Zhang back and shielded the rest of them from seeing that, too, as he pressed the quick heal patch over the fake wound. He could feel the slightest tremble in Iata's arm as he held it, and that twisted his gut all over again. Iata was always, always in control.

Iata shuddered and leaned against Homaj as the patch took his vitals and began pumping drugs. His skin was clammy, his face pinched.

Homaj shuffled a half step sideways and awkwardly managed to sink Iata down to sit against the hallway wall.

"Another patch," Iata whispered.

"Another patch might kill you. Truthspoken."

He met Iata's eyes. Saw fear and pain mixing with a staunch anger. Iata's lips twitched in a grimace—one of Homaj's gestures. He nodded.

The guard Jalava had sent to the medical cabinet came back with an armful of bandages and ointments, which Zhang scooped up and knelt down beside them on the floor.

"Truthspoken?" she asked, shooting another glance at Homaj.

"Thank you," Iata said, nodding at the bandages. "I'll need that when the patch is done."

"Ser Truthspoken," Jalava said, "we should clear your bedroom. The only person in there is your bloodservant?"

Iata held up a hand. "Yes. This lieutenant and his partner will go in. I cleared them before—I wish to keep visits to my rooms minimal just now."

Zhang stood, and so, reluctantly, did Homaj.

"Jalava, sir, can you keep watch on him?" Zhang asked. "The patch is working."

Jalava didn't look happy about not being able to check the situation for themselves, but they eyed the Truthspoken on the floor and nodded, crouching down where Homaj had just been.

Zhang nodded to Homaj, and they both slipped through the open doorway, back into the prep room.

6

COUNT ME IN

Subterfuge is the highest art form, as the canvas is the mind.

— ANATHARIE RHIALDEN, SERITARCHUS VIII
AS QUOTED IN *THE CHANGE DIALOGUES*

They checked everything in the prep room. They had to. There were no cameras in this room, but the door to the hallway was still partially open, and the guards could see a small way into the room. Homaj didn't want to close the door with Iata's status still uncertain.

The prep room had some drops of red on the pale blue carpet—blood? No, there were matching drops on Iata's vanity table, though he'd stashed the bottle of fake blood away again. On the floor, clothing was strewn in a path to the closet. Iata must have come out, poured some of the fake blood on a cloth, and then gone to change into some of Homaj's clothes, because he hadn't been wearing what Homaj had seen him in ten minutes ago. Adeius. So less than a ten-minute Change. Five?

Homaj's heart beat a little faster.

What had Iata been thinking? Was the shift toward Homaj's features only supposed to be a resemblance, or had Iata been aiming way above his training to try and actually form Homaj's likeness? Iata was a few centimeters taller than Homaj. But— but had he been, in the corridor?

No. No, he hadn't. Adeius, Iata. And he'd tried to do all that quickly. Even Homaj had known not to make that sort of Change quickly, and he had all the training and inborn ability to accomplish it. Iata wasn't a royal Rhialden, and he wasn't trained in much more than the basics of Change. Had he been trying to train himself in private? But no, that wasn't like Iata, he wasn't one to break the rules.

He'd risked his life just now trying to carry out what he saw as his duty. Homaj wouldn't be as much of a target if no one was looking for him, because Iata as Homaj was already there.

The bedroom door was also ajar, and he and Zhang stepped inside without a word. Homaj pulled the door nearly shut behind them. The need to process this was outweighing the need to see to Iata's safety. Iata had the guards, and Jalava seemed competent enough. If they were loyal. *If* they were loyal.

Iata would probably be fine.

There was a heavy, broken vase on the floor. That had to have been the first crash. There were a few shards that could have made the kind of cut Iata was feigning, though the angle would have been weird. Iata hadn't been going for accuracy, though, so much as speed.

And after the Change Iata had just done, it was a wonder he'd thought that far ahead. Homaj knew what a dangerous Change felt like. He'd been pushed there in training before, to know the signs and be able to treat them if he had to. So had Iata, though Iata had more training in what to do if Homaj made a dangerous Change than how to handle his own. Apparently, the part about needing to get to a quick heal patch had stuck. Homaj didn't keep them in his bedroom—he'd never felt the need, with Iata around to go get them from the hall cabinet.

He was going to stock a case in the low cabinet beside the bed.

And there were better drugs in the hallway med cabinet for dealing with an over-Change, too, which if Iata had been tending to Homaj while he was Changing, Iata would have gone to fetch. But since Iata had been alone in this, he couldn't have asked for them himself, and Homaj certainly couldn't have shown his knowledge. Not and not show a vital weakness in the Truthspoken armor, or expose Iata's need. A quick heal patch was effective and also innocuous. No one would question the need to put it over a cut.

They passed from Homaj's bedroom into Iata's, where Iata's trail had begun. The bed was neatly made, as if Iata hadn't just used it to attempt a dangerous Change.

"What happened?" Zhang hissed, glancing back at the series of almost-closed doors. "Is this part of some plan?"

Homaj debated whether to act like it had been. But he'd been reading Zhang since he'd met her, and he decided he needed another ally just now. He'd worry about the consequences of that decision later. After they all survived.

"Change can be dangerous if done too quickly."

She waved a hand like that was a given, though it certainly wasn't.

"Your bloodservant is Truthspoken, too? But I thought—there's only supposed to be three. The ruler, and the Heir, and you—"

Homaj grimaced. So very few people knew the true extent of a bloodservant's abilities and duties. He hadn't wanted to widen that circle, but, well.

"He's not Truthspoken—that's a title given by holy mandate, and yes, there's only three. Legally."

Two now. Maybe...maybe only one, if his sibling wasn't yet alive. And were they? Oh Adeius, were they?

He shoved the thought aside. "Bloodservants have a very limited capacity to Change—and that is a high-level piece of information. I'll have your life if you share it."

Zhang stiffened but nodded. "So—so he tried to Change too fast, is that it, and it made him bleed?"

"Made him sick. He isn't cut. He feigned the cut so he could get a quick heal patch, which can help balance his system again."

"That...was the blood on the vanity," she said. "Ah. It wasn't blood."

"No."

She tilted her head, studying him. "He looked like you. Like you did before you—" She waved at him, at the appearance he wore now. "Close, anyhow."

Homaj glanced around Iata's bedroom, at the neatly made four-poster, the walnut trunk at the foot. The framed shadowbox holos of Iata's favorite flowers from the terrace gardens. Iata loved working in the gardens and took every chance he could to work with the plants. He'd taken those still holos.

Homaj felt his body start to tremble. Had Iata really almost died while on a complete fool's task—a heroically foolish task—of Changing into Homaj so he could be a decoy?

He blinked slowly as he kept turning around, gauging these familiar surroundings. Or, had Iata known that there might only be Homaj left among the royal family, and had he just made an attempt to take over Homaj's life?

But bloodservants were unfailingly loyal. They were raised knowing it was their holy duty, mandated by Adeius and the Adeium, to serve the Truthspoken, their cousins. He knew Iata. He'd grown up with Iata, though Iata was just under two years older. Iata was, in some ways, like a brother. A subservient brother who could never stand on equal footing with him, sure.

But, a brother. More than his older sibling had been. But then, that was part of the bond of Truthspoken with their bloodservants. They had to be close, had to trust. Iata managed his life, and he'd trust no one else with that.

Had he ever done anything to turn Iata against him? Had Iata ever shown signs of ambition?

He didn't think so. But he couldn't discount it, either, could he? Not when his world was still in the process of being upended, and the assassins had yet to be found.

"Do you trust him?" Zhang asked.

Homaj turned back to her. She knew the question was a dangerous one, and she'd still asked it. He didn't know whether to curse or praise Adeius that he had a guard with the cunning to see deeper into Truthspoken plots.

"I do. As much as I can afford to trust anyone just now."

Zhang nodded. "So what's the plan?"

"I think—"

His mind went blank.

And there he was again, that point at which he had to think, and he truly did not want to think right now. But he couldn't plan, could he, without viewing the entire scope of the chaos?

Oh, Adeius, the Seritarchus was gone. And the Seritarchus Consort. His fathers were both, in an instant, gone. Yes, he'd trained for this, he'd prepared for assassination attempts and he'd already outlived a few milder attempts. Truthspoken were not fated to live long and happy lives, not when they stood against a kingdom that secretly wished to see them fall.

Was his older sibling, the Heir, still alive? He hoped so, oh he hoped so. Vatrin hadn't wanted to marry yet—they'd wanted a few good years with their lovers before they took an officially sanctioned spouse, and their father the Seritarchus, after a long and heated argument that had made everyone in the residence wing miserable for weeks, had finally agreed. But because Vatrin hadn't married yet, they hadn't produced their own heirs. And if Vatrin was gone...then Homaj was it, wasn't he? The only Truthspoken left.

Well, save for his aunt, but that hardly counted, did it? There were only ever three officially sanctioned Truthspoken, like he'd told Zhang. When the Truthspoken Heir had their own heirs, and the oldest heir was judged fit to make the choices it would take to rule—usually at twenty, the legal age of adulthood—the second Truthspoken would renounce their position and forswear their ability to Change, as mandated by the Adeium.

Because his father was the Seritarchus, his aunt shouldn't have had to renounce her title until Homaj turned twenty-three years ago. But she'd left when Homaj was eight, after a fight with the Seritarchus. She'd sworn off Change and had left the capital of Valon to wander the worlds. Homaj wasn't even sure if she was still in the kingdom or had gone to live in another nation, though he was fairly certain his father would have known. That did him little good now, though.

Homaj drew in a long breath. He pulled himself back into his own persona, his training in control, then flowed back into the persona of Reyin, the guard.

Whatever else, no matter how bad it was, he had trained for this.

"We have to, first priority, verify if the Heir is alive. When we've verified that, then we can gather resources to protect the Heir."

Zhang shifted uneasily. "And if they're not alive? If you...are the new Heir?"

Homaj fiddled with the rank pins on his collar, straightening them in Iata's mirror.

"Then—then there are ten days before the new ruler chooses his title and style of rule. There are ten days when the new ruler has the legal sanction to hunt down and punish the ones who speeded his ascension to the rulership. Ten days while revenge is considered good and moral, and if he can't manage it in ten days, he's not deserving of it."

Zhang watched him with narrowed calculation. "If it comes to that, sir, count me in."

A warmth, a very small warmth, blossomed in his chest. He wasn't entirely alone in this. He didn't even know where Iata stood, but Zhang—her loyalty, her sincerity—nearly sang to him.

He clapped her on the shoulder and headed for the door. "All clear, Sergeant. Best get back to the Truthspoken."

7

NAMES

A name is an introduction, a gateway to who a person can be.

— ANHE ISHII IN *A HISTORY OF VALORAN TRENDS IN NAMES*

Outside the prep room, the guards had grabbed a delicate wingback chair from the sitting room and brought it into the hall. Iata sat with exhaustion in every line of his body. But he looked up when Zhang and Homaj came out.

"I need to eat," Iata said. "There are coolers with fresh food in the bedroom."

Homaj held up a hand. "I saw them, I'll get it." He couldn't have brought them on his own initiative—Lt. Reyin wouldn't know their necessity.

He detoured back into the bedroom while Zhang spoke with Jalava and the rest of the guards, though leaving them again made him twitch. Yes, Iata had intensive acting training, and some training in direct impersonation techniques, the best training in the kingdom. But, to Homaj's knowledge, he'd never put it to this much of a test before.

Truthspoken were the ones who impersonated people to keep the kingdom in check. When the ruler could be anyone or anywhere, control was constantly established and maintained. But bloodservants were meant to support those roles, and sometimes to make subtle Changes themselves, adopting their own roles.

But could Iata truly impersonate him?

"Got it," Homaj said, holding up one of the coolers as he came back into the hall. He set both down on the floor beside Iata and knelt, breaking the freshness seals. He peered inside.

Jalava looked over, too. "Does this food need tested?"

"Straight from the kitchen," Iata said. "Carried by my bloodservant."

"And the bloodservant? He's absolutely loyal?"

Homaj looked up, but Iata didn't even blink.

"Of course." Iata took the sweet roll and container of slaw Homaj handed him.

"And where's your bloodservant now?" Jalava turned to Zhang. "Did you see him? I heard you verify he was in the kitchens over comm."

"He went out through the back corridors," Iata said. "I sent him to gather more information."

Iata pried off the lid on the slaw. "But I don't know what he'll find on his own. He's not trained as a guard. We must go out and find out what happened to my sibling."

The reasoning was clumsy, leaning too heavily on the fiction that bloodservants were just loyal valets. Anyone who spent any amount of time in the residence would know differently, of course, though most still wouldn't know the full extent of it.

But Jalava's mouth pulled tight. They were certainly buying it.

"We're not going anywhere, Ser Truthspoken."

"I know better where to look for my sibling than any of the guards."

Which was probably true. But Iata wasn't pressing that for his own benefit, but Homaj's. Iata was telling him he wasn't about to let Homaj go out there alone.

Homaj opened his mouth, but Iata held up a hand.

"It might be a long day. Please, everyone, if you haven't eaten in a while, take what you need. I want all of you in your topmost shape. The cook packed these with several meals."

Jalava's expression soured. They looked around at Iata and all the guards, and at the coolers which were giving off a tempting aroma.

"Have you had breakfast?" Iata asked. "All of this happened early today."

"I was about to go off-shift this morning," Jalava admitted, looking down at the coolers. They grimaced. "Okay, but eat in shifts."

They counted out two of their guards and themself to take the first watch. Which left Homaj, Zhang, and another of Jalava's backup, Ehj, a tall man with a healing nick on his upper lip, his hair braided in tight rows.

Homaj sat cross-legged on the floor, pulling out containers, sorting the hot from the cold. Did they have time to eat? Yes, he decided, they had to make the time. For Iata's sake, to give him time to eat more, and for his own—he wasn't thinking as clearly as he should be, and just now, that could get him killed.

He read the labels on each container and handed two more to Iata and set aside two each for everyone else.

And Adeius, no matter how tight his stomach was with tension, he was starving. A Change like he had accomplished should have required a much larger meal than this, and any benefits from the energy bar were long gone.

But Iata needed it more. Some of the vitality was coming

back to Iata's face as he started into his second round, some of the life coming back to his posture. What in the worlds would Homaj have done if he'd lost Iata today, too?

He couldn't think it. Just could not think it.

Iata's hand brushed his arm as he reached for a napkin.

"Sorry," Homaj said, jerking back. "Forgive me, Truthspoken."

Iata made a small shrug. "No matter. Your name is?"

"Uh, Karda Reyin. Lieutenant. I'm...new. Sir. Ser. Truthspoken."

He felt his cheeks heating, exactly at his command, and looked down.

"I'm Vi Zhang," Zhang offered. "She/her. And this is Ehj. That's Jalava, Chadrikour, and Bozde."

Iata made note of all of them. Homaj watched the flick of his eyes as he committed names to memory. Homaj was doing the same for those he didn't know. Neither of them would forget. Training.

"Ser Truthspoken," Zhang said, "forgive me for being blunt, but you're injured. We need to be able to move swiftly and stealthily. We might need to fight."

Iata flexed his shoulders. "The patch helped. I'm good."

Homaj finished his last container and stood, waving one of the others over. "Yes, and we're glad of it, Ser Truthspoken. But you're also still recognizable. If we go out there, some people will know who you are."

"I'm not an amateur," Iata snapped. "Give me ten minutes—"

"I don't think it's a good idea to Change again," Homaj said quickly.

Iata leaned forward, a dangerous gleam in his eyes. "What do you know about Change, Lieutenant?"

Homaj looked down. "Nothing, Ser Truthspoken. I just thought—"

Iata waved a hand. And maybe that was a bit much. Homaj didn't wave that much. But who among these guards would know that?

"In any case," Iata said, "we don't have time for more Change, or the time needed to refuel afterward. And we're out of food. Cosmetics will get me there."

And they would. Iata, like himself, was a master. Iata often applied Homaj's makeup as he prepared for the Truthspoken jobs his father sent him on, though Homaj usually did his own in the day-to-day.

Homaj's meal churned in his gut. He couldn't think about his fathers right now, either.

Jalava came over, tapped Homaj on the arm. "Can you take the main door?"

Zhang looked like she wanted to protest, but she didn't have a good reason why a guard lieutenant shouldn't guard something.

"Sure," Homaj said.

8

THE PERFORMANCE

I crave the performance of a good role. It is immensely fulfilling to become another person for a time, feel what they're feeling, live a life completely outside my own.

— INSAMMAN RHIALDEN (FICTIONALIZED) IN THE BIOPIC *VENORAM IV: THE LIFE OF AN IALORIUS*

Homaj took up where Jalava had been watching, at the hallway's bend toward the apartment's entry. He could see the main double doors, and his heart sped up just a little. Yes, he'd had training in being both a Palace Guard and various branches of the military. Not enough to pull from a lifetime of experience, not yet—his training in most professions had been just deep enough to impersonate someone for an afternoon. It was his earnest hope that was all he'd have to do now.

He knew how to use the pistol in his holster. He knew how to fight hand-to-hand, if it came to that, and likely win. On the other side of those doors was the corridor that ran down the

center of the royal residence wing of the palace. Out there—
was a lot less safe than in here.

Unless someone decided to attack the palace with artillery.
Or bomb the support beams. Or bombard from orbit—

He wrenched his thoughts away from those scenarios and
focused on the conversation just out of sight behind him, which
was falsely cheerful. Jalava was trying to get Iata to tell the
places where the Heir might be, if the Heir had caught wind of
what was happening and gone into hiding.

Iata was having none of it. Good. He knew the value of
keeping his usefulness intact, and none of them knew how
much they could trust the Palace Guard.

When the meal was finished, Iata called Homaj back,
motioned to Zhang, and headed for the prep room.

Homaj didn't like leaving the rest of the guards to roam free
in his apartment, not with Zhang's unease, but he just as surely
didn't want to leave Iata alone. He suspected that feeling was
mutual.

"Close the door, this is private," Iata said, settling himself
before Homaj's vanity table.

Homaj let the door click shut and heard the lock engage. He
hesitated a moment, then touched the control panel beside the
door and turned on the active sound suppression fields. The
prep room and bedroom weren't under surveillance like the
rest of his apartment, and the sound dampening was already
good, but he wasn't about to take any chances.

He turned back to Iata, who now wouldn't meet his eyes.

Yeah, he knew he'd overstepped. Far, far overstepped in
trying to Change toward Homaj. But, that was done. Homaj
didn't have it in him to be angry just now, not when his sibling
might still be out there.

Homaj came around the vanity table, gauging what Iata's
appearance needed, grabbing up jars and opening them. "Let
me, it'll go faster."

Iata's brows twitched in protest, but after a moment, he nodded. Yes, they were both masters at cosmetics, but Homaj was still better at changing the shape of a face, camouflaging with misdirection.

Iata sat still, his eyes closed, while Homaj worked with as much speed as he dared.

Questions flitted through Homaj's thoughts, and admonishments. He didn't ask his questions, though. Not because they weren't alone, but because he wasn't sure he wanted the answers just then. Like, "Did you, oh person who's like a brother to me, just Change so you could try and take my place?" or "Were you stupid enough to try and draw any attack against me on you?"

Okay, yes, he was angry. He just didn't know where or how to direct his anger. He couldn't afford, even here, to lose control.

"Zhang," Homaj said, "can you go into the closet, pull out a Palace Guard uniform in his size?"

"No," Iata said, opening his eyes. "If we produce a magic uniform for me, they'll suspect you also. We'll need to ask one of them to lend me their uniform. Bring out something one of them can wear."

Zhang peered into the closet. "Like what? There's one of everything in here."

Homaj snorted. "To the right, near the back. There's light tactical street gear. That's innocuous enough."

He finished softening Iata's features and penned a sheen of gloss on his lips.

"Egh," Iata said. "I hate the cherry one."

"Too bad. Red liner or blue?"

"Red."

Homaj uncapped the blue.

"That will make me look bruised."

"The red will make you look bereaved."

Iata tightly gripped the chair arms. He looked up. "Homaj, I am bereaved."

It was a plea. A plea for Homaj to understand why Iata had done what he'd done, and what Iata was feeling now. No, Iata hadn't just lost his fathers, but the Seritarchus had trained them both. The Seritarchus had been a big part of both of their lives.

Homaj closed his eyes against his own flood, against the growing tightness in his throat. He'd been trying not to think about the card that still lay on the table in the sitting room, notifying him of a successful assassination.

"Explosives just don't get through like that," Iata went on in a low, heated voice. "Not when the guards are doing their jobs."

"I know," Homaj said.

Well, and that answered that question, didn't it? There was no way Iata could have Changed to try to replace him and have that much emotion quivering in his voice, Truthspoken-trained or not.

Homaj sniffed hard, capped the liner again, and surveyed his work.

Maybe not his finest work, but serviceable.

"Lean more femme?" he asked.

Iata studied himself in the mirror. He nodded.

Homaj grabbed a comb and pulled Iata's long hair back—he'd loosened it from his braid in another of those elusive minutes in which he'd had to Change—twisting it into a high, knotted style more popular with femme presentations just now. More importantly, it was a style Homaj found uncomfortable and pinching, so he never wore it himself. Iata would just have to deal. He secured it all with an array of nondescript black pins that anyone could have used.

Zhang emerged from the closet, holding up an armful of discreetly armored street wear. "I didn't know what size, exactly.

I'm not good at measuring by eye. Half of what I buy doesn't fit me."

Iata stood as Homaj finished the last hair pin. Iata took the bundle from Zhang and sorted it quickly to find what items he wanted, draping them over one arm.

He rolled his shoulders once, and on the relaxation his posture shifted, became more flowing, his movements much broader than Homaj used when he himself was presenting femme—which was good. Every bit of distance they could put between Iata and Homaj was good.

"Name?" Homaj asked.

"Mir," Iata said. "Or, no. Sky?"

"Mir is better. Doesn't stand out."

Iata nodded. "Okay, then, Mir. Mir Shajan." He pitched his voice a little higher, softened the edges. Added an accent that held notes of the rural county outside Valon City.

Zhang had watched Homaj do this before, but she watched Iata do it again now with furrowed brows.

"Okay," Iata said, bobbing his head. "Okay." The only thing he'd done so far to betray that he was nervous.

He truly didn't look at all like Homaj, or himself. Homaj had applied heavier cosmetics, obviously so, though not as obvious on the heavy contouring, and with a deliberate lack of artistry that would absolutely not say "Truthspoken." Slanting femme had been a good choice, too. Iata was masc in his own presentation, but Homaj had seen him do femme before in training, and he did it with excellent ease. And with Iata—always with Iata—the performance would carry the rest.

For Homaj's part, though he wasn't really feeling it anymore, he'd keep pushing his current persona masc. He scratched at the beard, grimaced, shrugged. It was camouflage, that was all.

"Okay," Homaj confirmed. "Let's go."

They made their way back out to the corridor.

9

THE CORRIDOR

> *I don't always take the back corridors. Sometimes I want to walk among the people as myself, not around them.*

> — HOMAJ RHIALDEN, SERITARCHUS IX IN A
> PRIVATE LETTER, NEVER SENT; AS QUOTED IN
> *THE CHANGE DIALOGUES*

It was Jalava whose size best matched Iata's, and an unhappy Jalava, now dressed in discreet tactical gear, surveyed Iata one last time before jerking their head toward the door. "If we're going to do this, best get going, *Lieutenant* Shajan."

Iata shrugged and gave an edged smile, patting Jalava's gun now holstered on his own belt.

Jalava's face puckered.

Adeius, Iata shouldn't bait Jalava. Would Homaj bait them, if he was himself?

Well, yes. Yes, he would.

"Should we take the back corridors?" Zhang asked. "Would that be safer?"

"No," Iata said with tight finality. "Those are reserved for Truthspoken and their bloodservants alone."

There was an uneasy glance among the guards, which Homaj shared with Zhang. But yes, Iata should absolutely have vetoed that suggestion. If the back corridors were compromised, the whole palace would be compromised, if it wasn't already.

"Unless there's no other choice," Iata amended.

"Agreed," Jalava said. "Though we'll go in at the first sign of trouble. I'm not gambling with your life. Agreed?"

They waited for Iata to reluctantly nod, then turned the inner ring on their ring comm, listening through their earpiece.

Homaj tensed. Would Jalava alert someone that their squad was on the move? But they didn't, not even in code. Good.

Homaj didn't like that Iata's stumbling out from the prep room after his botched Change, and then switching clothes just now with Jalava, would be caught on surveillance. His own transformation into a guard was more credible now, with Iata-as-Homaj coming out at just the right time to establish that both Iata and Homaj had been there, and that Iata-as-Homaj had been the one to come out. But that also wouldn't hold up to close scrutiny for anyone who'd seen the surveillance and knew what to look for. There just hadn't been time to properly set up the identity of Reyin and establish the inroads into the palace he normally would have.

And who would have access to the apartment surveillance? His father the Seritarchus would have, and his father's blood-servant, Omari, who helped with the administrative end of ruling the kingdom. And...who would also have been with the Seritarchus at the hospital, he was always near the Seritarchus.

Tavven's note hadn't stated that his father's bloodservant had also been killed, but a bloodservant wouldn't be formally listed alongside a ruler, would they? That he hadn't been named as a survivor was more telling.

Homaj swallowed.

So that left Palace Guard Commander Tavven with the only access left to the apartment surveillance. Possibly one of Tavven's trusted seconds if Tavven was still out and the palace was in a crisis—or maybe not. Would Tavven have remembered, in this crisis, to transfer those permissions?

Could Homaj trust for absolute certainty that no one else had gained access to the system? Or that Commander Tavven themself hadn't been compromised?

He wasn't at all used to mistrusting the Palace Guard's ever-present security.

Jalava waited, listening to their ring comm, then touched their ring again and waved at the door. They'd sent Ehj and Chadrikour to guard the door outside the apartment while Homaj and Zhang had been helping Iata in the prep room, but they'd recalled them back when Iata announced he needed a uniform change.

Now, Jalava waved the pair back out. "Ehj, Chadrikour. Check if we're clear."

Tall Ehj and willowy Chadrikour carefully cracked the door, then opened it wide enough to slip out.

They all waited while the two ran opposite directions down the corridor and came back.

"Clear," Ehj said. Then added, "All the doors are closed. No one in sight. Didn't see the door guards we sent down the corridor earlier, either, or anyone around the bends."

There should always be someone. Doubly so in a crisis. Did Commander Tavven think that sending Zhang and Jalava's four would be enough to guard him? Or was Tavven trying to deflect attention from him, concentrating their guards somewhere else?

Jalava grimaced and made to touch their comm again, then

hesitated. They met Homaj's eyes. "Don't want to announce we're on the move."

Homaj nodded. "We'd do the same in the Municipal Guard. Were the door guards recalled, do you think?"

"I don't know. Everyone, be on guard." Jalava glanced at Iata, who was thumbing the safety off on his borrowed pistol. "Please tell me you know how to use that."

"Of course I know how to use it." Iata glared at Jalava, daring them to defy him.

"This is a bad idea," Jalava said, scrubbing a hand through their short hair.

"And I might not yet be the Heir," Iata said. "If Vatrin's out there, I'm not willing to give anyone else leverage over my sibling. Over the kingdom. We're going."

Yes. *Yes.* With that, Homaj fully agreed.

Jalava took a breath. "Okay. Clear enough."

They filed out into the residence's main corridor.

The air was cooler outside the apartment. Too quiet, everything too still.

Homaj tapped his own comm earpiece on, turning the inner circle on his ring to tune to the main Guard channel. It was mostly quiet, with short bursts of code. No one would risk more, not knowing who or where the enemy was.

From listening and parsing the code, Homaj gathered that the palace was being searched in earnest for his sibling, Vatrin, and those who'd last been seen with them—Vatrin's current lover, Lord Xavi Birka, and Vatrin's bloodservant, Eyras. The status of the second Truthspoken—Homaj—was listed as secure, and Jalava didn't make any move to update that status. All of the residence wing had been searched and cleared twice, though no one yet had cleared the back corridors. The Guard Commander was the only one besides the royal family, the bloodservants, and a few of his father's personal guards who had access there, so Commander Tavven wasn't back yet. And...

either his father's guards weren't back, either, or they were dead, too.

Homaj fought to keep his posture in a normal state of alertness, not the itching, crawling dread that was winding up his spine. A new thought grew and loomed large in his mind: his apartment's internal surveillance was extremely secure, but more people had access to the residence corridor feeds. If anyone saw them come out from the Truthspoken's apartment with different guards than had gone in, that was an exposure, too. He'd been hoping to plant some doubt with the door guards Jalava had sent out to make a checkpoint, but that wasn't an option now.

Well, they were out now. He eyed Iata ahead of him, walking that very fine line between being Homaj and being *Homaj being someone else*. He checked his own posture, his body language, his performance, and subtly shifted what he thought might help push even more distance between them.

If it came to it, if Iata drew fire, would Homaj be able to stand there and let him take it? Even knowing that was part of a bloodservant's purpose, too? Deflection, and support?

And what if whoever came for Homaj came with an explosion, too? Would it matter if Homaj wasn't himself just now, if he was still too close? Should they split up? Should he sacrifice Iata to save himself?

Adeius.

Of the two of them, with the Seritarchus dead, and the Heir possibly dead or compromised, Homaj had the bloodline and training to become the next ruler. He was supposed to be the second heir. But now, he might be up.

Between him and Iata's lives, purely pragmatically, Homaj was far more important than a mere bloodservant.

But, Adeius. Iata was hardly just a bloodservant, he was like a brother, he was a friend. Iata might be the only family Homaj had left in all the worlds. How could he possibly let Iata go to draw fire and escape himself?

He swallowed bile. He should make that choice. He really should make it right now. But instead he moved just a little closer to Iata as they walked down the corridor.

10

THE PASTRY CHEF

Truthspoken take personas and truly live in them. A persona isn't just a role we play, it's a facet of ourselves that we become.

— ANATHARIE RHIALDEN, SERITARCHUS VIII
AS QUOTED IN *THE CHANGE DIALOGUES*

"The Adeium," Iata said as they neared the bend in the central corridor. "Have we searched the Adeium?"

Homaj had been wondering, too, though if his sibling was there, surely Commander Tavven would know. The Adeium, the religious seat of the kingdom, sat across the back courtyard from the palace. He'd spent many, many days there training with the Truthspeaker growing up. He knew the Adeium as well as the palace itself.

If the Truthspoken ruled over the minds of the Kingdom of Valoris, then the Truthspeaker equally ruled over their souls, both in the eyes and will of the god Adeius. Equal in their separate authority, balances to each other. The kingdom might have just lost the Seritarchus, its Truthspoken ruler, but it hadn't yet lost its Truthspeaker.

But was taking refuge with the Truthspeaker even safe in this crisis? If the Seritarchus had been assassinated, was it a stretch to assume the Truthspeaker was in danger as well?

Another thing to worry about.

"Yes, the Adeium was searched," Jalava said tersely. "The Heir isn't there. And we searched the administrative offices, and the guest wing, and the terrace garden, though not the grounds gardens yet, not fully."

Iata was a few steps ahead of Homaj and didn't look back, though Homaj could tell by the tiniest twitch of his head that he wanted to. Iata didn't say what they'd both be thinking— there were places in the Adeium that the speakers could hide a Truthspoken, if they wanted to. If the Truthspoken asked them to. Or even against the Truthspoken's will, for their own safety.

There were other places in the palace that Vatrin might be as well that weren't obvious to the guards.

Jalava held up a hand, and everyone stopped. Homaj kept his pistol down, but stared at the corridor bend just ahead.

Jalava signaled Chadrikour and Bozde and they ran ahead, close to the wall, weapons ready. Homaj tensed as Bozde eased to the edge, extending their pistol past it just enough to get a visual reading on the pistol's tiny screen.

"Clear," Bozde said, and went around the bend. "No one ahead."

"That shouldn't have been clear, either," Jalava said, glancing at Homaj, who they seemed to have adopted as their second, no matter the tangled ranks involved.

Homaj agreed. In a crisis, guards were supposed to checkpoint every defendable point in any area where a Truthspoken was. He didn't know if this was a sign of disorganization or something yet more sinister.

"Where to?" Jalava asked, a soft question, not looking at Iata.

Iata hesitated. Glanced behind him as if looking back the way they'd come, his gaze passing over Homaj's. He jerked his chin the tiniest measure downward. Down exactly toward the palace kitchens.

Homaj waited a heartbeat before dipping his own gaze down, rubbing the back of his neck. Not as blatant as a nod, but Iata would read his body language and know that was his assent. Now wasn't the time to preserve Vatrin's various identities as a Truthspoken, no matter how long they'd taken to build.

"Jalava," Iata asked, "do you know Siv Gladi, the overflow chef?"

"Uh, yeah? Yeah, you mean the one who makes pastries? They bring the extras to Guard H.Q. after a gala. What does that have to do with—"

"Do you know where they are now?"

"No—I mean, I know they work at the palace during the big events." Jalava glanced at the bend in the corridor, where Chadrikour had come back and was waiting, keeping an anxious watch on both corridors.

Homaj grimaced. Wrap this up, Iata. Just say they needed to go to the kitchens.

"I don't think Siv's in the palace, we haven't had a gala this week. Why are you—" Jalava coughed. "Do you mean Siv is—"

"Is an excellent chef," Iata said smoothly. "We should head to the kitchens."

"I'll call it in, we'll search for—"

"No, sir," Zhang broke in, moving past Homaj. "No one else should know until we find them."

"Yeah, that's the point, Sergeant," Jalava said, wheezing as they pounded their chest. "We have to actually find them."

"I mean, I'm new here," Homaj said, "but even I can tell

when the chain of command is thoroughly fucked. You didn't tell anyone we're on the move."

Jalava's fist tightened...and eased again, a wave of pure exasperation. "Okay. Okay, then...the kitchens."

They made it, finally, around the bend in the corridor, then took a sharp left to an auxiliary staircase—also not guarded. What the hell, Commander Tavven? But on the way down, they did meet four of the Palace Guard jogging toward the stairs on the first floor, and then up them as they passed, only giving the barest nods of acknowledgement. One glanced toward Homaj and at the Municipal Guard pin on his collar. Homaj tensed, but the guard looked past him to Jalava, who nodded.

When they reached the basement kitchens, an enormous room with dozens of workstations and several full chef teams, the staff was keeping busy. Palace lockdown didn't mean there were less mouths to feed, apparently, or that those mouths were less hungry. Everyone who'd been in the palace when the lockdown started was still here.

Homaj inhaled stewing carrots in ginger sauce, an array of thickly sliced printed meats, and freshly baked rolls. He snatched a hot roll from a basket and took a bite before one of the cooks could swat him away. And, well, maybe he shouldn't have done that. That wasn't what a guard would do.

But he grinned and turned up the charm on his smile, even while his eyes were scanning everywhere. Looking for Siv Gladi. Or at least, his sibling Vatrin's tells, on whoever they might be.

Vatrin might not have had time to Change much, like Homaj hadn't had time. Could Vatrin accomplish a drastic enough Change to the taller, thinner Siv, if Siv was a genetic signature and form they knew well? Maybe. But then what about their lover, Lord Birka, who was also still missing? Homaj's gut said they'd be together.

Vatrin might be able to do a quick Change on themself, but

they couldn't Change Lord Birka. Only Truthspoken—well, and their bloodservants—could Change. And they'd have little or no cosmetics to work with, not the kind that could shift appearances.

And what about their bloodservant, too? Vatrin's bloodservant, Eyras, could be anywhere, and also anyone as well. Vatrin had never been as close to their bloodservant as Homaj was with Iata, but that didn't mean Eyras wouldn't protect the Heir with her life.

"Hey, we're looking for Siv Gladi," Jalava yelled over the kitchen din. "The pastry chef. Have they been in today? Has anyone seen them?"

11

THE KITCHENS

If you're in the palace and get a chance when they're working, definitely try anything made by Siv Gladi. Just ask any of the staff, they'll know. Adeius, their pastries are fucking heaven.

— ANONYMOUS89446-D7 IN THE CHATSPHERE
I'M AT THE PALACE, NOW WHAT?

Jalava's shouted question hardly made a dent in the noise of the large kitchen, but a short woman with thick dark brows, wearing a brightly patterned apron, dried her hands on a towel. She was a newer chef, one Homaj hadn't spoken to personally before.

"Siv? No, they haven't been in this last week," she said. "Coming in a few days for the next ball, though. Well, or they would have been, at least."

The chef's brows drew sharply together as she must have remembered what was going on. "Is there any word? We've heard something happened to the Seritarchus, but no one's told us more than that."

Jalava shot a look at Iata that said clearly, "This was a waste of time."

"Thank you, Ser," Iata said, making a delicate wave to the chef. "We don't have any more information at this time."

Adeius, Iata, tone down the aristocratic air. Wearing Jalava's uniform and rank pins, he might plausibly be in command of the group, but that was a bit too courtly for a guard. Either Iata's lack of full Truthspoken training was showing through, or Iata was trying to establish another line of misdirection away from Homaj to himself as Homaj.

Knowing Iata, it was probably the latter.

Jalava's face was turning sour. Without knowing the extra layers of what was happening, all they'd see was that their charge was drawing too much attention to himself.

The chef looked bemused. "Well, okay. But why do you want Siv? What did they do?"

"Nothing, Ser," Homaj said.

Iata shot him a look and cut in, "We have a group of VIPs upstairs who are getting restless, we were hoping to bribe them with Siv's pastries."

The chef rolled her eyes. "Ah, yeah. Well—well, we have rolls here. Some sweets in that cabinet over there. But don't take too much—it's between meals. People—" Her voice cracked, and her careful composure was threatening to crack as well. Her whole posture was lined with nervous tension. Maybe she didn't know exactly what was going on, but there wasn't much short of an assassination or a coup that could shut the whole palace down.

"People need consistency in times like these, don't they?" Homaj said gently, finishing what she couldn't.

She turned shining eyes to him. Her name was Hadfen, he thought, or was it Hadden?

His throat closed, and he had to blink hard.

No. No, look away, don't engage with the emotion. He couldn't engage with the emotion, not and still function.

"Thank you," Zhang said, "we'll take the rolls and won't trouble you anymore." She made steering motions toward where the chef had motioned, and she and Ehj hefted a basket of rolls each. Homaj grabbed a stack of disposable plates, knives, and a tub of butter, because he knew the rest would forget and someone would ask.

He snuck another roll in the meantime and was starting to feel more himself again. Iata snuck another roll, too.

"Okay," Jalava said when they were in the corridor again. "Now where?"

Again Iata hesitated. If his thoughts were following the same lines as Homaj, he was thinking about Vatrin's Palace Guard persona. But Vatrin wouldn't be among the guards right now while the whole palace was looking for them, would they?

Not that Homaj and Iata were any indicator of that particular game—but Vatrin had never particularly enjoyed their time spent among the Guard. They always preferred the more personable roles—the staff, the diplomats, the lesser nobility. If Vatrin had Changed and hidden themself among the palace staff, that was much more plausible to Homaj than Vatrin trying to maintain a persona they typically struggled with even under low pressure.

And that still left the question of their lover.

"The Adeium," Iata finally said.

Jalava started to protest, but Iata held up a hand.

"I guarantee you no one has fully searched the Adeium. We'll go there next."

And if Vatrin wasn't there, either?

How much of the palace had been cleared as thoroughly as it should be? And cleared looking for a Truthspoken who didn't necessarily want to be found? The thought of going room to room across hundreds of rooms, looking for just the right tells that Vatrin would be doing their utmost to hide, maybe going through the back corridors—but who knew if even they were safe, and Homaj certainly couldn't enter them as a guard, and couldn't take Zhang, who he was growing reluctant to part with on the principle that he might trust her a little more than anyone else in the palace—

He felt his chest start to constrict and consciously made his thoughts drop, relied on years of training to take him into a light walking Change trance to calm his body's reactions.

If Vatrin wasn't in the Adeium, they'd all assess the situation then and go from there. Either conduct their own thorough search of the palace, which would likely be questioned by Tavven at some point, adding that complication Homaj wanted to avoid for the moment, or branch out toward the city, which... was a much larger field of play.

Homaj's gut, though, was tugging him toward the city. A Truthspoken's greatest defense was their ability to hide among the crowds. And his fathers had been killed in the city, not the palace.

Homaj knew of several safe houses in Valon City where he'd had training or been on various Truthspoken missions— Iata had been to a few with him, too. They both knew where to start looking if it came to it. Some of the houses, too, were known to the Palace Guard and Vatrin would know not to go there. He hoped. Others were known only to the Truthspoken, and not even Iata had been there.

Or Vatrin could have fled the city altogether. Could have fled the world.

And all of this was assuming they were even still alive.

Homaj's stomach clenched, and he had to force another light trance to ease it.

The Adeium, he told himself. First, thoroughly check the Adeium. Assume Vatrin was still alive and somewhere on the planet, in the general vicinity of the palace or the capital, Valon City, across the river.

He couldn't help the feeling, though, that with every minute that passed, his chances of finding his sibling alive were slipping through his hands.

12

THE ENCOUNTER

> *I propose a law that grants the Truthspeaker equal listing with the Truthspoken as the ruler of Valoris, because it's true. And yet, though they're the very living will of Adeius among the stars, the Truthspeaker is often spoken of in the second breath, not the first.*
>
> — COUNT SIMA KAZEMI, FROM *THE COLLECTED SPEECHES OF THE GENERAL ASSEMBLY, FOURTH EDITION*

They trekked back up the service stairs to the first floor, deposited the food with a harassed-looking staffer to distribute among the palace guests, and went out the back delivery doors to the courtyard behind the palace.

The courtyard of Palace Rhialden was nestled in the U of the palace, with the residence wing to the left of the back exit, a separate guest wing building to the right, and an administrative wing as the palace's core. At the open back of the courtyard was the Adeium, jutting up with cream stone and asymmetrical blue steel and glass peaks. The seat of the religion of Adeius, the god of the Kingdom of Valoris.

That was where the Truthspeaker held his office—and though the Truthspoken technically didn't answer to anyone else in the kingdom, they did answer to the Truthspeaker, and by proxy, Adeius themself. And vice versa.

Homaj found himself tensing as their small group of guards approached the massive building. Other palace guards were milling about, questioning speakers draped in gray and indigo robes, depending on their ranks. The guards were questioning anyone in sight, really, which was interesting—they hadn't been actively guarding the royal residence, yet they were out in the courtyard in droves?

If Vatrin had come to the Adeium like Homaj was doing now, out in the open, no matter the disguise, they would have had to cross the courtyard. Someone would have seen something, even if not who they were expecting.

If Vatrin had come through the back corridors and the tunnels that ran beneath the palace, courtyard, and Adeium... well. That would be a bit harder to track.

As they approached the entry gate to the Adeium's own narrow courtyard, one of the gray-robed Adeium speakers glanced toward their group.

Homaj sucked in a breath. Ceorre Gatri, her back straight and poised, a chin-length cut framing her angular dark brown face. She was in training to become the next Truthspeaker, with all the highest forms of evaku training that entailed. The same evaku training in the art of reading people and shifting your own self expression to manipulate them that Homaj had. That was technically illegal for anyone *but* the kingdom's rulers to know, though most nobles had picked up some form of it too.

Ceorre absently scanned the group, then her gaze razored back to Iata, narrowed, then shot to Homaj. All without her expression changing.

Homaj held her gaze for a second longer than he should have, then looked away. Because though Homaj had done a fair amount of training with her, helping her pick out his tells from among dozens of personas, Lt. Karda Reyin wouldn't have met her. So soon from the Municipal Guard, he just wouldn't have had time, and Valon City had its own Adeium with its own speakers. Though not its own Truthspeaker—there was only ever one Truthspeaker.

Ceorre broke from her conversation with a guard and strode over, her gray robes flowing around her as she walked. Around her neck, she wore the heavy silver seal pendant of a Truthspeaker in training—she didn't hold a Truthspeaker's authority yet, but she would. She was as much an heir to the Truthspeaker's position as he was to his father's. More—there was no backup Truthspeaker in training. She wasn't a spare.

Adeius, Ceorre shouldn't be out in the open just now.

Homaj had to resist the urge to survey the courtyard again, take stock of where a sniper might hide. Or—or someone with explosives, or a weapon of any kind—

"May I help you all?" Ceorre asked, making a show of scanning rank pins before focusing on Homaj.

He waved to Jalava. "They're in charge, Ser Speaker. I'm in training."

Jalava cleared their throat, stood a little taller. "Ser Speaker, we'd like to search the Adeium. Will you guide us on this search?"

Ceorre tilted her head. "The Adeium's been searched twice already. Commander Tavven was just through on his way in from the city—they went back to the palace just now. I led that tour myself."

Was that why she was outside the Adeium, in the open just now? Had Homaj just missed Tavven and their senior palace guards? Did he dare ask?

Ceorre's cheek gave the barest twitch. Homaj didn't think

those statements were lies—so what was she trying to convey with them?

"Yes, well—" Jalava glanced toward Iata. "We have some new information. If you could please lead us on the tour again—"

"That would be a waste of my time," Ceorre snapped. "However, if any of you would like to enter the sanctum to pray, I will certainly supervise that."

Did she want to speak with Homaj? Was that what she meant now? But he didn't know how to say that yes, in fact, he wanted to pray without it coming off as clunky. As Lt. Reyin, he was on duty. Religious matters seldom outweighed duty in a crisis. Prayers to Adeius—or any other god, for that matter— seldom produced actionable results.

When no one said anything, Ceorre spread her hands. She glanced around, as if looking for someone else on which to fend off their group. Then she stiffened, a tension around her eyes and a slight bracing of her shoulders that Homaj doubted anyone had noticed but himself.

He followed her gaze to where the Truthspeaker was emerging from the entrance to the Adeium, brown hair braided and wound into a tight knot, his red and violet robes bright in the sunlight. Tall and fit, he'd always been a physically intimidating person, and his scowl now compounded that impression.

Homaj noted the Truthspeaker but watched Ceorre. Her breath had quickened, and he'd bet her pulse had, too. Why? She was the Truthspeaker's protégé. Truthspeaker Aduwel Shin Merna was her teacher. Homaj had never been particularly fond of the Truthspeaker—and the feeling was mutual—but he respected him well enough and trusted his judgment.

Was Ceorre afraid for the Truthspeaker's life? But no, the cues weren't right for that.

The Truthspeaker's eyes caught Homaj's, and after a

moment, his thick brows rose. He'd know Homaj, of course. He'd know Iata. He'd know every Truthspoken and bloodservant on sight in every situation. Aduwel had conducted some of their training in evaku. He was their confessor and confidante. He advised the Seritarchus on how best to balance the kingdom, and his advice was usually sound.

So why did Homaj feel a chill that the Truthspeaker could see him now? That look wasn't safety, wasn't acknowledgement or reassurance. Aduwel could see through the different face and body he wore now to the reality of who he was, and he wasn't looking away. And he should have.

The Truthspeaker had as much evaku as the Seritarchus, but he wasn't reading the situation now. He should be protecting the Truthspoken, not putting Homaj on the spot here, among dozens of guards.

And was that why Ceorre had tensed? What information, what nuance was Homaj missing?

Jalava was frowning at Homaj, confused at the Truthspeaker's attention, but that confusion wouldn't last long, would it?

"Uh, Speaker," Homaj said, and Ceorre turned back. "Yes, thank you, we would like to pray. All of us."

"Of course. Follow me." And she took off at a brisk pace for the entrance to the Adeium, taking as wide a path around the Truthspeaker as she dared.

The Truthspeaker finally looked away, turning to confront two nobles who were lingering near the Adeium gates.

Homaj noted them, noted that they rated the Truthspeaker's attention. Two minor lords only, both, he was fairly sure, from offworld. He would have centered them in his attention if they'd been anything more. Was that turn-away a snub? And if so, what did that mean for him?

"What the hell?" Jalava hissed, coming close to Homaj as they passed through the Adeium gates and into the lapis-tiled courtyard of the Adeium grounds. A veritable garden of overflowing planters were intermixed with small outdoor altars, each bearing an androgynous stone statue of the god. "What happened to my being in charge?"

"I do outrank you," Homaj said quietly. "And didn't you notice the tension? Something is off here. I've been around enough diplomats to know that. Being a Municipal Guard and all. I want to know what's what, don't you?"

Jalava swore under their breath but didn't say anything more as they returned to the head of the group.

In silence, together, they stepped into the entry to the Adeium itself.

13

THE SANCTUM

" *Sometimes I come into the sanctum, often at night when there are few petitioners, and lay down on the floor. I stare up at the constellations above and try to understand how Adeius, who brought humanity safely through our journey through the stars, decided that their entire will should be centered in the focus of four people.*

— CEORRE GATRI, AS QUOTED IN *THE CHANGE DIALOGUES*

Inside the Adeium, the restless sounds of the courtyard cut off to an anxious hush.

"Shoes off," Ceorre said quietly. "And voices down. We are in mourning."

Then someone had released an official statement about the Seritarchus' assassination? Had the Truthspeaker? Had Commander Tavven, or one of the military commanders? Shouldn't Jalava have received word of that over comm? Homaj's own comm was still open, but the channels had been quiet. Tavven must be using a different channel for Guard communications. Damn.

Homaj should know about this. Whoever had released the statement should have at least tried to consult with him, as the next in line if Vatrin was still missing.

Well, and maybe they had tried. Maybe Tavven had sent another runner like Zhang to his apartment, and he hadn't been there. What would Tavven think of that?

The Truthspeaker and Speaker Ceorre now knew where he was. He wasn't completely off the grid. Would they tell Tavven?

Of course they'd tell Tavven.

Homaj paused and removed his shoes at the door, giving them to an attendant speaker acolyte in indigo robes who slipped a tracking clip into each pair, then gave them each a matching chit to claim them again.

The carpet was soft beneath Homaj's socked feet. He padded behind the rest into the sanctum proper, a vaulted space with pillars swirling with raw lapis lazuli, ruby, and jade. Mosaics lined the base of the walls and lacquered wood ran the rest of the way up to an indigo ceiling full of painted stars. The faint scent of astral incense wafted from braziers set around the room.

At the front of the Adeium stood a large hologram, a representation of Adeius, which was a reflection of whoever approached it. It rippled through several variations in features, skin tone, and hair color and texture as they all filed into the open space.

Ceorre led them past several groups in prayer to the far wall, motioning to a rug that had seen better days.

As the others knelt, Homaj took his place on the side closer to the sanctum doors, Zhang beside him. Ceorre was last to kneel down, placing herself carefully in their group's center.

Homaj made the opening gestures of supplication to

Adeius, a tracing of the constellation of the same name as the god, and no one spoke until they'd all done the same.

Then, Jalava said, "Speaker, what's this about? Couldn't you speak in the courtyard?"

"The sanctum is acoustically dampened," she said. "It's very hard to hear what other people are praying for."

Her gaze flicked to Homaj, then settled on Iata. "Truthspoken. You won't find your sibling here, though they did come just before we received word of the assassinations. Perhaps forty minutes before."

Homaj pressed his lips tightly together to stifle the urge to speak, but Iata was quick to the questions: "What did Vatrin say? Did they speak to you? Did they know they were in danger?"

"Yes, and no, they didn't have a defined feel of danger, but a sense of unease. You know, Truthspoken. They read something in the people around them, though they couldn't say what, or from whom."

Homaj did know, and so would Iata. Truthspoken could read a lot from a person, even when the things they were reading and the conclusions they were making weren't obvious. That evaku training didn't go away when they weren't actively using it. It cataloged details in the background, presenting a vague extra sense of the mood around them.

Homaj usually tried to ignore that sense of mood, which was within his court persona as the sharp but apathetic second Truthspoken. If Homaj hadn't been so intent on *not* paying attention to the moods of the palace, he might have picked up on the same unease as his sibling. He might have been able to do something about it.

"Was Lord Birka with them?" Zhang asked. "He's missing, too. And the Heir's bloodservant?"

"Yes, Lord Birka was with them, and Eyras," Ceorre said. "They all came to us."

Homaj went on full alert at Ceorre's slight emphasis on the word "us." Came to *us*. To her and the Truthspeaker. There was absolutely something going on there—Ceorre didn't trust the Truthspeaker, or he'd made a bad move.

But—but the Truthspeaker was always on the side of the Truthspoken. That was most of his purpose, to be a counterbalance to the Truthspoken rule, a direct line to Adeius.

"Where did the Heir go when they left?" Homaj asked hoarsely.

"I can't tell you that, I'm sorry."

Jalava grunted. "Speaker, if you know where they are—and, hell, you know this is the Truthspoken, here." They glanced at Iata. "We need to find the Heir to keep them safe. Keep both Truthspoken safe."

"I can't tell you," Ceorre said slowly, "because I don't know. I was excused from that part of the meeting."

Iata hissed out in frustration. "Then, an idea of where? Another safe house? A place where the Truthspeaker might send them?"

She turned her palms up, clearly not liking any of this. "All I can tell you, Truthspoken, is you might be safer disappearing right now. Go underground. Go deep enough even a Seritarchus would struggle to find you."

Or a Truthspeaker?

But she hadn't said it, and Homaj knew she wouldn't. Whatever she was feeling—whatever he was feeling—there was nothing substantial yet to back it up. And yet, Vatrin had come here on less information, hadn't they?

He ignored the everyday mood of the palace to keep himself sane, to not be consumed by the *muchness* of it all. But he certainly couldn't ignore it now.

14

ENOUGH

Are we prisoners? Are we prisoners of our own control and our own power, when we have to hide in our palaces everything that makes us ourselves?

— HOMAJ RHIALDEN, SERITARCHUS IX IN A
PRIVATE LETTER, NEVER SENT; AS QUOTED IN
THE CHANGE DIALOGUES

"I can't go underground," Iata said to Ceorre. "I'm biding time only. If Vatrin isn't found in the next few hours, I'll have to step up as the next—as the Truthspoken Heir. There can't be a power vacuum here."

And no, he was right, there couldn't be. *Shouldn't* be, unless it had been engineered. There were three Adeium-sanctioned Truthspoken at any given time to allow for fluctuations such as assassinations. And to keep the ever power-hungry high houses from swooping in to make their own claims to power.

Was Ceorre a part of these machinations, pushing the Truthspoken to go underground? No, Homaj thought the fear tensing her posture, tightening her mouth, was sincere. She was genuinely afraid for his life.

He wasn't sure whether to be touched by that or if it drove his own fear deeper.

Zhang let out a soft breath beside him. She met his eyes— oh, she was following this, at least the important parts. She wasn't liking any of it, either.

Ceorre looked up a split second before Homaj felt the shift in the room.

The Truthspeaker had come back into the Adeium and was making his way toward them, trailing a retinue of mostly gray-robed speakers and some of his own guards in their own indigo and gray uniforms.

Homaj's heart began to pound. The Truthspeaker wasn't looking at him now, not yet, but he would, wouldn't he? He was walking with grim determination exactly toward Homaj, and he either hadn't spotted Iata—which Homaj didn't believe—or decided he wasn't going to acknowledge Iata, who was just now doing everything he could to scream "I am Truthspoken!" to anyone who'd be able to see it.

The Truthspeaker stopped, then crouched down beside Homaj at the edge of their group. His scent, heavy with cloves, made Homaj's nostrils flare.

"Come on, son. The Municipal Guard just found Lord Birka's body, shot down in an aircar. We have to assume the worst. Vatrin's either dead or compromised. Either way, you're the Heir now. You'd best get yourself ready to announce your bid to rule. Soonest is best."

Truthspeaker Aduwel stood again, wincing as his knees audibly cracked.

Homaj kept his breathing steady only from years of training in soothing his body's fight-or-flight responses. He concentrated on slowing the flow of blood through his heart and his veins through the barest grasp of a Change trance, even while his ears rang.

Zhang's eyes could spit fire. Ceorre's lips were drawn tight. Jalava—Jalava was looking between Iata and Homaj in bafflement and growing rage.

Fuck. Fuck, the Truthspeaker could have found a way to call him aside, to talk to him without outing him like that. That had been very deliberate, and Homaj wasn't convinced it had been for his benefit. And that shouldn't be the case.

He stood slowly. Zhang rose with him, her look questioning.

"I want you with me," he said to her. Looked around at the other guards. "All of you, with me. You are all, from this moment, my personal guard, until I say otherwise."

"But—but—" Jalava was still slow on the uptake, or maybe too proud to admit they'd been fooled.

Homaj didn't have time for that. Vatrin's lover, Lord Xavi Birka, had been found, and he needed to know where and how, and why he was shot down. He needed to know what was happening out in the city. He needed to find his sibling, because there was still time. There had to be time. Once he made his bid to rule, it could still be contradicted within the mandatory ten provisional days if the Heir showed up and proved to Homaj and the Truthspeaker that they weren't compromised.

But the Truthspeaker himself might be compromised. So what the hell would constitute an acceptable resolution in that case?

He couldn't rule this kingdom. He just could not. He wasn't built for it. Trained, yes, but—but he'd spent the last few years proving to everyone, including himself, that he wasn't someone who should ever be given a kingdom, because he just didn't care.

"Listen," Homaj said in a low voice. Others in the sanctum

were watching now, clued in by the Truthspeaker's retreating presence that something important was happening. "I don't trust anyone. But I trust you a little more than anyone else. Keep me alive until we figure this out, okay?"

He was still speaking in a city accent—he'd continue to speak in a city accent until he Changed back to himself. Which he'd have to do soon. The Truthspeaker wasn't wrong, and neither was Iata. Power in the Kingdom of Valoris couldn't be left in a vacuum. There were too many nobles just waiting to pounce, and that wasn't counting the nations outside their borders.

He'd known that. He'd known that when he'd Changed to the body he wore now and ran out to find Vatrin. He was *desperate* to find Vatrin, so he wouldn't have to rule.

Homaj surveyed the faces around him—Zhang's determination, Jalava's anger, the rest of the guards watching him with a mixture of confusion and resolve. But all of them nodded. All of them, even Ceorre.

When Homaj announced his bid to rule, he would have ten days to figure out what had happened to his parents, and to his sibling, and punish those responsible. He hoped—oh Adeius he hoped Vatrin was still alive. But he had the aching feeling in his gut that this wasn't going to end well.

He had ten days as well to decide which style of rule he would use, and which title accordingly. Would he be the new Melesorie and rule with the force of momentum? Would he be an Ialorius and rule with fluidity and adaptability? Or would he be a Seritarchus like his father, a scion of absolute control?

He'd thought of it before, of course. He'd thought he'd most likely be an Ialorius, if it ever came to it. Vatrin had been leaning hard toward Melesorie, full of projects and reforms. But with the kingdom on such shaky ground, was fluidity what was needed?

He'd never, ever wanted to make that kind of decision.

Didn't these people, with their loyal gazes—he *hoped* their loyal gazes—know he was the absolute last person anyone should want as a ruler?

His eyes stung. And the flood of emotions sat just behind his throat again, pushing hard to come out.

He viciously shoved them back down.

"I'm with you," Ceorre said quietly, a ragged edge to her voice. "Never doubt that. I'll do my own part to keep you safe."

He met her eyes, nodded. He didn't doubt her sincerity, at least, or her quiet rage at the actions of her Truthspeaker. Whether her help would be enough, though, they'd all have to see.

15

THESE GAMES

Anyone who associates with Truthspoken for long—
those who marry them, who befriend them, who guard
them, who work beside them in any capacity—have a
steep and painful learning curve just to function
enough to understand the level on which the Truth-
spoken work.

— ORALA SWIFTWATER, CHAMBERLAIN OF
PALACE RHIALDEN AS QUOTED IN *THE CHANGE*
DIALOGUES

It was a long and mostly silent walk back to the residence
wing.

Jalava, once aware of the actual situation, had proven
adept enough to keep their group's current arrangement. If
anyone asked, Iata was still the Truthspoken. Homaj was
simply a new hire, farther back in their lineup—though court
gossip sped like lightning, and the identity of Lt. Reyin was
already way past compromised.

Zhang stayed close and painfully alert to him. She twitched whenever he so much as sniffed.

When the doors to his apartment were closed, though, and locked behind them, the silence broke.

"Why the hell didn't you tell me who you were?" Jalava demanded. "Why the masquerade among us? We're Palace Guard! We're supposed to protect you, not be a part of your Truthspoken games!"

Iata held up his hands, still using Homaj's gestures. "We can't speak here—"

"And *you*!" Jalava rounded on him. "You're the bloodservant, right? How the hell are you also Truthspoken?"

"He's not," Homaj said. "And the roles of a bloodservant are not for listening ears. We must go into the prep room. There are no cameras or microphones there."

Jalava's face flushed, but after a moment, they thrust out a hand toward the prep room. "After you, Truthspoken."

Jalava's attitude was dangerously insolent, but Homaj was inclined to think they had a right to their anger just now. He read the panic there, too, fueling that anger. Knowing they were caught up in something far more intense than they'd thought. That they could have lost Homaj on their own watch by not knowing who he was.

Homaj waved to Ehj and Bozde, who'd stationed themselves by the main door. "You'd best come in, too. Being one door over won't make the difference here."

They looked at each other, then followed the rest into Homaj's prep room. A private place that was quickly becoming too open and crowded. He'd best make this quick in any case.

Zhang closed the door and locked it like she'd seen Homaj do before.

Iata took the chair at his own vanity table and sank onto it backwards, arms leaning over the back. He looked exhausted.

Homaj turned to Jalava, still keeping his voice and mannerisms as Lt. Reyin. Loose and friendly. He didn't need anyone clamming up just now over his status.

"Are you religious, Jalava? Are any of you very religious?"

Jalava made a face. "Yes, I am, and I get that the Truthspeaker just outed you, and that's not good. I'm not about to follow a sour Truthspeaker blindly, if that's what you're asking, but the thought that a Truthspeaker would go sour is...is..." They grasped at the air. They looked almost as exhausted as Iata. "Do you really think Truthspeaker Aduwel had anything to do with the assassinations?"

Ah, then they had followed all of that, or at least pieced it together on the way back up.

"I don't know. I aim to find out." Homaj held up his hands, his own gesture, and so much an echo of what Iata had been doing that he saw Jalava flinch. "Before you ask more—if we're suspecting the Truthspeaker of being less than loyal, can you still question why I wouldn't want to expose myself to any of you? Zhang knew, and Iata knew. Now, you all know. I'm going to go into my bedroom and Change back to my original appearance. It will take around a half hour—I Changed quickly once today, but it would be too dangerous to attempt a quicker Change again. A half hour is too fast as it is. I'll need you to guard me, and to wake me at the first sign of trouble. Iata will remain to be me if needed."

Iata smiled sourly.

"Actually—Iata, you should go out to the sitting room and carry on the conversation as if you are me. It's another layer of diversion."

And it put Iata at risk—but Iata knew that. He'd known that before he attempted to Change himself into Homaj.

Iata made a waving shrug. "I can do that."

"I can't," Jalava said. "I'm not Truthspoken, I don't have training in these games."

Iata pinned them with a flat stare. "You've been doing it
with me the last two hours. You can certainly do it some more."

"Yes, but I thought you were the Truthspoken."

"Then think it again." Iata had let some of his control slip
when they'd entered the prep room, but he brought it all back
now, speaking in Homaj's crisp tones. He sounded more like
Homaj than Homaj just now, who was still using the city accent,
still carrying more common mannerisms.

Jalava's gaze darted between them, at a loss again.

Homaj sighed, pushed off from his own vanity chair, which
he'd been leaning against. "I'll be in my bedroom. Zhang, with
me. Jalava, guard the rest of the apartment as you see fit. Work
with Iata, please. Be natural about it. We must get through this
next hour—then we can go from there."

He hesitated, almost asking Iata to send for more food from
the kitchens, because he'd need it, but he decided against it. A
smart observer would know that more food sent to the Truthspoken's apartment would mean there was Change involved.
He didn't want to give any more clues to his actions than he
already had. Than *Aduwel* had.

Homaj brushed a stray strand of blonde hair out of his eyes,
then nodded to Zhang and headed for the bedroom.

"Do you want me to bow to you?" he heard Jalava asking
Iata.

"No, because as a guard you wouldn't bow anyway. At least,
not how a courtier bows."

Homaj shut the door, and without hesitation, he locked
it, too.

"Same drill, as before. Guard me."

Zhang rubbed the back of her neck, looking around at the
pieces of broken vase still scattered on the floor. "Do you want
me to clean up?"

"No. I need you alert." He undid his hair, stripped out of the
guard's jacket and shirt, then trousers. He wore his undershirt

and shorts, and she didn't look away, but he didn't feel any discomfort at that. Her look wasn't invasive, only attentive.

Zhang checked her pistol and took up a position where she could see both the door to the prep room and the open door to Iata's bedroom.

But that really wasn't the door she should be guarding.

Homaj hesitated, then moved beside his bed and gently touched the satin-smooth wall beneath the white chair rail. There was no discernible place to show where to touch, it was pure spatial memory. But if Zhang knew the general vicinity, she could at least know where to direct him if he was prematurely awakened and they needed to exit fast. Or where to aim if someone did come through.

"It won't open for anyone but Iata or me. Or Commander Tavven. Vatrin and their bloodservant, Eyras, could still use it, too." He held up his hand. "We can shift the DNA in our hands." He let that sink in. "But if we need the door, it's there. It's the only access point to the back corridors from this apartment."

Zhang gave a solemn nod. She knew what level of trust that bit of information required. She glanced between the dual entry points to the bedroom and shifted to better cover the panel door beside his bed.

He pulled back the bedcovers. "A half hour," he said as he lay down. He scratched his beard—Adeius, at least that would be gone.

That was his last coherent thought as he drifted quickly into a Change trance.

16

ABSOLUTE CONTROL

Change isn't just switching from one set of attributes and features to another. Change is the responsibility of another life, and the intersections of that life with the people around you.

— HOMAJ RHIALDEN, SERITARCHUS IX IN A
PRIVATE LETTER, NEVER SENT; AS QUOTED IN
THE CHANGE DIALOGUES

Homaj woke and knew the comfort of his usual body, its boundaries he knew better than any others. Sitting up, he touched his face, and grimaced at the loose beard hair that had come off during the Change. He brushed his face off, brushed his undershirt as best he could.

"Are you well?" Zhang asked, stepping toward the bed.

"Yeah." His voice came out a croak, and he coughed to clear it. "Yes. How long?"

She glanced at her ring comm. "Twenty-eight minutes."

He didn't ask her how things were going out in the rest of the apartment—she wouldn't know. Unless there'd been trouble and Iata had come back, but her ready posture showed no indication of that.

"Okay," he said, getting up and stretching. He waved to the adjoining bathroom. "I need a shower and to dress, then we'll go out." He hadn't bothered with a shower the last time he'd Changed, but then, the last time he hadn't been going to make his bid to rule the kingdom.

Her nod was tight. "I'll keep watch, Ser Truthspoken."

He wished he could make the water as hot as possible and just...not come out for a long time. But he needed speed just now, not steam to drown his sorrows.

Homaj was out of the shower in two minutes, spent the barest minute under the drying light for his hair, then wrapped himself in a robe and headed for the prep room closet, Zhang trailing him. He frowned at the racks of his own clothes, what he would typically wear daily in the court. These clothes were, in many ways, as much calculated to project the persona of Homaj Rhialden as the clothes on other racks were meant to service other personas and identities. Everything meant to project different social messages and moods to those around him.

Most of what he wore as himself was flowing, in a variety of gender codings and styles, a mix of dark and subtly flashy materials and soft frilly pastels, which he was fond of at the moment. He needed continuity with that, certainly, but he also needed...something else today.

He touched a jacket he seldom wore that had a bold floral pattern. Vatrin always wore patterns. Always wore bolder colors. Should he do that?

But his father the Seritarchus always wore the more severe cuts, less adornment. Burgundies and golds and golden greens.

Which wasn't his style. But he couldn't just wear his own style—he'd invested too much into associating his style with his snarky, artfully apathetic personality at court, and that wasn't what he needed people to see right now. He needed their trust—if that was even possible at this point.

Homaj chose a pale lavender silk shirt and a jacket in his usual frilled cut but a bolder royal blue. A calf-length, pleated skirt hemmed with diamonds, which shifted between blue, violet, and green hues—that stolen from a different rack. Much more formal than he'd normally wear.

He hooked three gold rings in his left ear, and a single sapphire in his right.

He combed his still damp hair out and pulled it up deftly into a twist, pinning the edges with practiced ease.

He rolled his shoulders once, and he was fully back to being himself.

But he needed more than that, didn't he? More than the subtle difference in clothes, too. He needed to project more of his father the Seritarchus today, show anyone who dared to approach him that he would not, in fact, bend with the tides, but would stand like stone against anyone who tried to tear his kingdom down.

Homaj stared at himself in his closet mirror, dismay too plain on his features. Because he was not that person. He wasn't his father, or his older sibling, and he'd been trying his hardest the last few years to be *anything* but them.

He could simulate it for a time, though. He knew that. He'd been trained to inhabit any personality he needed.

And he told himself this was temporary. He'd find Vatrin, and then Vatrin could resume their place as the Heir. Vatrin could make their own bid to rule.

Homaj looked askance at Zhang, raising a brow.

Zhang shifted. "Are you asking for my opinion? I don't have an opinion, Truthspoken. I don't know fashion." She did nod to his hand, though. "You still have the Guard ring comm on."

He glanced down at the ring comm. A plain brushed steel band with a moveable darker center band, two tiny white indicator lights on the rim, and an engraved sigil of the Royal Guard phoenix along the edge. At a touch, the band would display a tiny holo of basic output.

He hadn't taken it off in the shower, or the earpiece, not wanting to lose that connection, even for a moment. He didn't have the comm on active now, though, not knowing Tavven's new preferred frequency.

Should he remove the ring? Most people would know it was a ring comm, not a piece of jewelry. It was on the same finger that he'd wear a ruler's signet ring. And the Truthspeaker had called him out in the Adeium when he was dressed as a Palace Guard. What would wearing this Palace Guard's ring comm on his signet finger say to everyone around him?

He curled his hand around it, then pulled a simple ring from his tray of rings, a gold band with a single, small sapphire, to go on the opposite hand and balance things out.

Everything, absolutely everything, had meaning.

Homaj decided against any scent but what he'd used in his shampoo. He wanted a more sober and austere showing today.

Then he surveyed himself again in the mirror. He was a visual blend of his fathers, Rhialden and Xiao, dressed but without cosmetics yet, still beautiful. Still...still too much the court rake, but that was who he was, was who he'd been. He couldn't just erase that in an instant as himself.

Could this person in the mirror be the next ruler of the kingdom?

He looked away, swallowed hard, and swept into the prep room.

At his vanity, he lined his eyes in the same blue he'd used on Iata's, shadowed his eyes with gold and indigo, gave his lips a pale rose sheen.

He was genderfluid, usually within the general vicinity of male, and feeling a more femme presentation just now.

He squinted at himself, then went back to the liner and added a flourish beside his left eye.

As Truthspoken, his skin was flawless unless he wished it not to be, and today he wanted it flawless. It set him apart. He was unnaturally beautiful. He had to assume he was, right now, the Truthspoken Heir, soon to be the next ruler of the Kingdom of Valoris.

As he worked, he made small adjustments to his body language and posture. Not so far from himself that it was implausible, but it was an opening of self, an inhabiting of space that he normally tried to slip through, not linger in on his own.

Yes, in fact, his appearance could say, "I'm your next ruler."

He took a moment to calm his racing heart, steady his breaths.

This was a performance. Just another performance, but—it wasn't a performance. It couldn't be, not fully. This might be the person he'd need to become. For the rest of his life. A person that billions of lives depended on. A person who the nobility feared.

He knew Zhang saw the shift, the last hardening of that royal armor, because her demeanor took on more deference.

And he hated that, too. Yes, he'd been trained for the possibility that he might have to rule someday. As the second Truthspoken heir and the palace being what it was, he'd always known it was a possibility.

What he needed now was both to center the attention of the kingdom on himself, give them a center to look to, and keep his enemies off balance. In the Kingdom of Valoris, there were three legal styles of rule, all associated with different personality types and likely actions. The court and general public had speculated on his personality type for years, and had generally settled on an Ialorius type, which he generally agreed with. An

Ialorius would rule with movement and change, and that was him. He was fluidly moving into this new phase of himself.

But he was certain that as an Ialorius he wouldn't be nearly as effective against the powers arrayed against him. Not when he might have to stand against a rotten Truthspeaker. Not as effective as a Seritarchus like his father would be, a pillar of absolute control. And there was more than one way to demonstrate absolute control.

Homaj stood and waved Zhang toward the door. "Go out and get Iata and Jalava. I'm ready."

17

PUBLIC FACE

It's the nature and duty of Truthspoken to never show who they really are except to those they intimately trust. And those they trust are vanishingly few.

— HOMAJ RHIALDEN, SERITARCHUS IX IN A PRIVATE LETTER, NEVER SENT; AS QUOTED IN *THE CHANGE DIALOGUES*

Zhang opened the door and stepped out while Homaj hung back, out of view of any cameras he knew about. Their fiction that Iata was Homaj was in shambles at this point, but they still had to try to maintain the illusion that Iata, as a bloodservant, couldn't Change nearly as well as a Truthspoken.

From across the hall, he heard Iata in the middle of a droning account of all the trees he enjoyed in the terrace gardens—oh Adeius, he must have run out of things to talk about as Homaj a while ago.

Iata stopped, presumably when Zhang stepped into the sitting room. Hm, and Homaj would have to remember to add a few details about the garden to those he talked to in the next few days for continuity, for the sake of anyone who might have been listening. Which could be anyone, at this point, depending on where the breech in loyalty was, but especially any among the Palace Guard.

Homaj stepped back as Iata and Jalava came back into the prep room with Zhang. Iata's face was pinched, Jalava's tense—with maybe a hint of relief.

Jalava opened their mouth, but Homaj held up a hand, only lowering it once he'd made sure the door was secure.

"Iata, please give Jalava back their uniform. I do want you in uniform, too—we don't have time to Change you back to yourself, but I think we can shift the cosmetics, and anyone who saw you before will assume it's all a well-executed disguise and not an actual Change. You have enough recognizably Rhialden features on your own." He paused for breath, painfully aware that he was close to babbling. That was a habit he'd trained out of himself in childhood, but it came back sometimes, particularly during great stress.

"Get another uniform from the closet," he said, his voice slower, words more measured. "Get different rank pins."

Iata headed for the closet, while Jalava looked about with equal parts discomfort and curiosity. Jalava would have had the last hour to come to terms with now being an integral part of the Truthspoken world.

Zhang, near the door, seemed to have already accepted this, but he could tell she was nervous. None of what was happening right now was ordinary.

Homaj, feeling everyone centering on himself, and knowing that he had to be that center, found himself off balance. Yes, it was necessary. It was the effect, the charisma he was trying to project. But he was used to people centering around his father or older sibling. He had crowds that followed him, yes, but his purpose and persona at court was to be the foil to Vatrin. Was to be...not anything like his father or sibling in any way.

Where Vatrin was friendly and always inviting discourse on ideas, Homaj was the airy socialite who let ideas slip around him. He was artful, he was approachable, but always out of reach. He was an insufferable flirt. He'd never played down his intelligence, though—he'd weaponized it. His wit was cutting and his insults legendary.

He knew how to get from that persona to an Ialorius—he'd rehearsed that before in his head. He'd hoped he'd never have to do that, oh Adeius, he had hoped.

But how did he get from there to being a Seritarchus? How did he go from deliberately fickle to steady as steel? He couldn't just be a different person—continuity was everything. And he was building a life he'd have to live in, and he'd never been anything other than fluid in everything he did.

He looked between Zhang and Jalava. What did they think of him? Zhang had a different perspective of the Truthspoken by now, certainly, and Jalava would have seen different sides of him through the whole tangle with Iata.

Would they understand that Iata's impersonation of him earlier, before they'd been to the Adeium, had been spot on to Homaj's own original personality? Not the public image he projected, not Homaj Rhialden, but Maja, the person he could only be in private among family, among those he trusted.

He took a breath. "I need you both to understand that the public face of a Truthspoken is not the private face."

Zhang and Jalava exchanged a look.

Jalava shifted their weight, watching Homaj warily. "I came up from the ranks, and I've been around long enough to see you're not what you first seem. You haven't insulted me once today."

"I never insult beneath my station," Homaj said. "Well, or beneath the general bubble of nobility."

Zhang coughed. "Ser Truthspoken. If it's not too forward, and because Jalava brought it up, and it's a good point, are you going to keep doing that? Insulting people, I mean. Because you'll make a lot of enemies really quickly if you're insulting from the position of a ruler, not a second Truthspoken."

Homaj sucked in a breath. Yes, that was very much too forward of her. But not untrue.

Her face flushed. "Sorry, I—" She waved a hand vaguely around her. "I don't know how you want me to act around you. You asked my opinions earlier. Do you still want them?"

"Very much so. In private. You too, Jalava."

Jalava's slim brows rose. "Is this a promotion? Ser Truthspoken?"

Homaj flailed in his thoughts—could he make that decision? He'd never before been in control of his own guards, he wasn't sure how to handle this. "I-I can't adjust actual rank until I'm the ruler—and I might still not be—but, yes. Consider it part of your Guard duty. Your opinions right now will help keep me alive."

Jalava gave a tight nod. Then grimaced, and gave a "fuck it" sort of wave.

"I, uh...if you really want to know what I think, Ser Truthspoken...I think Zhang's right. Your reputation is as a court player, but I don't think that's who you are, is it?" They waved a hand at the entirety of Homaj, though he hadn't been projecting that air now, he was sure. "I don't think you can do that anymore. But—you weren't like that earlier. As the lieutenant."

Homaj tilted his head. "I agree with you, on the whole, and it's not quite as simple as turning it off, but I'd like to know your reasoning."

Jalava rubbed the back of their neck, slanting a look at Zhang. "People know you're smart, but—forgive me, but you come across like you don't care. They'll underestimate you and think you can be used. My brother is like that. He likes to play down his strengths, so people won't give him as much responsibility. It backfires, though. People try to manipulate him all the time, and he usually lets them. It's caused a lot of drama."

Jalava blinked and focused on him again. "Sorry, Ser Truthspoken. I didn't mean—"

Homaj's smile twisted. "You're not going to insult me. And —that is all a part of my personality, yes, but no, it's not fully me. I very much lean on those attributes in my public persona. It's what I'm trained to do, and it's highly effective."

He paused, took a breath. He was still too off balance— these people he was confiding in, they might be who he trusted the most right now, but what about when the crisis passed? They couldn't just walk away knowing all of this about the Truthspoken. Especially if he was about to become the ruler.

Adeius save him from that, but...but this was quickly becoming more reality than he knew how to handle.

Homaj spread his hands. "Point of no return: I've already told you too much, but I don't believe it's fair to tell you more without warning that you'll be attached to me personally from here on out, even if Vatrin's found and can rule. Yes, this is a promotion, a big promotion. You're under oath as Palace Guard to not share anything you've learned from us and about us as Truthspoken outside of the Guard or below you in the chain of command. But I need another oath now, to me, personally. Under the eyes and will of Adeius. I'll be letting you into information that only Tavven and a very few others in the Guard know, those who guarded the Seritarchus personally."

He didn't say, "And look how that turned out. He didn't point out at all that the Truthspeaker almost certainly wasn't the only one who was rotten.

And he really needed to get out there. He needed to go make his bid, give the kingdom back that little bit of stability.

But he had to know the ground he stood on, first.

"You won't be able to leave my service after this. And the consequences for letting information slip will be...dire."

Zhang looked unfazed. She'd already worked this part out. Jalava inhaled slowly, nodding.

Homaj had them raise both hands and repeat the oath his father had taught him for swearing in oath-bound guards. He'd never had to use it before, his own guards being part of an ever-changing rotation. And that was part of the point—sometimes Truthspoken heirs got too ambitious. Loyalty was a thing reserved for rulers, not heirs.

The next rotation of his guards would have been that morning—and was that convenient timing that he would have had all new guards today anyway? Were Jalava and their squad supposed to be among his new guards, or had they happened along in the crisis?

But Jalava repeated the oath along with Zhang. If Vatrin was found...Homaj would just have to work it out with them that he would keep his own permanent guards. Somehow.

Homaj felt the weight of their lives, now tied to him. He'd better not screw this all up and get them killed.

"Thank you," he said, his mouth too dry, and cleared his throat.

He looked up to see Iata in a Palace Guard uniform of his own, much better fitting this time, leaning against the open door to the closet. He gave Homaj an unreadable look. Which was something, because Homaj could almost always read Iata.

But the look passed, and Iata approached Jalava, holding out their neatly folded uniform.

"Thank you for the loan, ser, I'm sorry it picked up the scent of my perfume."

Jalava glanced at Iata's new, crisp uniform, and the closet Iata had emerged from. They didn't say that the use of their own uniform hadn't actually been necessary—but it had been. The less anyone knew of exactly how Truthspoken slipped in and out of personas, the better. Especially that they had a stash of Guard uniforms and insignias at the ready.

Jalava sniffed their returned uniform, but shrugged. With the unselfconsciousness of a guard, they stripped down right there and quickly dressed again, picking the tactical street wear back up with distaste.

So now, for the moment, he had two guards he could trust —well, and nominally Iata, if Iata would be functioning for the next hour or so as a guard.

He was fairly sure about Zhang. Unless she was a master of evaku herself, and he hadn't seen any signs, she was easy to read.

Mostly sure about Iata—who had been trained in the use of weapons along with everything else. A bloodservant doubled as a bodyguard when their Truthspoken went on Change missions.

And Jalava...Homaj had been reading them all afternoon and hadn't yet detected a note of insincerity. He wasn't sure he liked Jalava, but he did think he could afford to trust them to protect him, for the moment. Jalava, at least, hadn't made any moves to ingratiate themself with him, either now or when they'd thought Iata was the Truthspoken. Jalava had been honest, often caustically so. That could be an act, true. But Homaj hadn't yet found any signs of evaku training in Jalava, either, beyond some of the basic adapted things the Palace Guard taught their own.

Zhang and Jalava were now sworn to him. Iata had been sworn to him by a different, deeper oath since Homaj was eight and Iata nine. He couldn't fully trust anyone, he knew that— but he couldn't get through the next few days alone. He might not survive the next few days alone.

"Okay," he said, and nodded. "Okay. I should tell you all, when my ten days are up, I'll be announcing myself as Seritarchus."

18

HAPPY

The three different styles of rule, Seritarchus, Ialorius, and Melesorie, focus on basic personality archetypes throughout the history of leaders. There is a broad range within each style, however. A Truthspoken doesn't necessarily have to be a natural in a style to employ that style, though an unnaturally styled ruler will have a much more difficult path.

— DR. NDARI HADI ESYN IN "A SOCIETAL
MORPHOLOGY: TRUTHSPOKEN IN THE
MODERN AGE"

Iata rocked back. "You're not suited to a Seritarchus rule, Homaj."

Adeius, he didn't want that much honesty.

Iata didn't shrink from his glare, though. "You're Ialorius, through and through."

"That's not what's needed right now."

"Yes, but you can't change your base personality, no matter what you layer over it."

"No," he agreed. "But there's more than one kind of control. The kingdom needs that kind of control, and that kind of continuity. If I decide to change my style of rule later, I can give my notice and announce that then."

Any ruler could change among the three legal styles and their corresponding titles when it best suited their needs and the needs of the kingdom, but it required three months' notice, unless the circumstances were dire, and it was a legal hassle. It almost always wasn't the best move. People tended not to trust a fickle ruler, and it would take time to regain that trust.

Homaj scowled. "I won't have a rulership to worry about if I can't hold on to it now. Or if Vatrin comes back. But this doesn't leave the room. Not even a hint. I'll carry on outwardly as if I'm aiming for Ialorius. Some people might see past that and that some of my next actions won't completely match, but I'm counting on most of them being surprised when I announce the title I'm taking and my style of rule."

"And by people, you mean the Truthspeaker," Iata said, a muscle in his neck twitching.

Nervous shifts all around. Yes, Jalava had said that they weren't willing to follow a sour Truthspeaker, but they hadn't been happy about it. Zhang had been livid in the Adeium when the Truthspeaker had outed him.

Homaj himself was religious enough, in the most secular sense of the word, and Iata was much the same. They believed in the structure of the Adeium in relation to the Truthspoken, they believed in the nature of Adeius among the stars, sure, but not in all the superstitions more devout sects took as truth. He didn't truly believe that he, as a Truthspoken, was the *actual* will of Adeius in the kingdom.

He met Iata's gaze. Iata's dark eyes were bright and burning, his jaw tight. Iata had never liked the Truthspeaker, even more than Homaj, but that was beside the point. You didn't have to like the Truthspeaker to respect his position and guidance. You didn't have to like the person to trust the office.

Truthspeaker Aduwel broke that trust when he outed a Truthspoken, maybe the only Truthspoken left, in a public place, without permission, without any obvious need—and with a much more obvious need, truly, for continued cover.

If that was all he had done, even that would be enough grounds for Homaj to set his path on taking him down for working against the best interests of the kingdom. Maybe Truthspeaker Aduwel had never liked Homaj as much as Vatrin, had considered him a degenerate—an impression which Homaj had worked to stoke—but Aduwel knew the game, too. Aduwel had helped train him in crafting personas that could sway perceptions, creating a public reality around himself that was only partial truths.

The Truthspeaker had absolutely known what he'd been doing. He was one of the most skilled—maybe the most skilled now—practitioners of the evaku arts of subtle manipulation in the kingdom. Not even the death of the Seritarchus would have rocked him that far from his own training.

So what message, what threat, was he trying to convey?

Homaj pushed off from the vanity chair he'd been leaning against. They were all watching him, waiting. How much of his thoughts had betrayed themselves in his expression, in the tightness of his shoulders—and they were tight. You didn't casually contemplate forcing out the second most powerful person in the kingdom.

Oh, disturbing thought. The *first* most powerful person in the kingdom, until Homaj fully stepped into his rule, even if the Truthspeaker's power was more religious than political. Religion *was* politics in the Kingdom of Valoris.

He would need his facts straight. He would need evidence. He would need a good share of the nobility on his side, and he was starting from the public perceptions of a rake.

"A Truthspeaker never, ever outs a Truthspoken in public," he said. "Not without setting themself up in contention to the Truthspoken's authority. If Truthspeaker Aduwel has broken faith with the Truthspoken, I can legally remove him from the Adeium. As an Adeium-sanctified Truthspoken, I have that power and that right—it's part of the checks in the system."

His throat was tight, too dry, and he couldn't find the focus to ease it with a light Change trance.

"Some believe the Truthspeaker literally speaks with the voice of Adeius." Those people, though they knew about the checks in the system—that Truthspeaker and Truthspoken both could unseat the other, given enough reason within the law— those people would always stand on the side of the Truthspeaker.

"Yes," Iata said, "and some believe the Truthspoken act with the direct will and see with the eyes of Adeius. But—you're right. Those people would still count the Truthspeaker as the highest authority. Those people won't be on our side."

Jalava slowly kneaded their hands together, something Homaj suspected they never did unless deeply distressed. Did they believe either of those things?

"We're with you," Zhang said quietly, eyeing Jalava.

Jalava nodded. "Yes. Yes, we're with you. We will protect you, from *any* enemy."

A portion of the knot in Homaj's stomach eased. They'd both sworn to him, yes. But he'd witnessed conflicts of loyalty before, and they never ended well.

He was about to witness a lot more conflicts of loyalty over the next few hours and days, wasn't he? As the kingdom shook itself out into a new rule, whatever shape that took. And, very possibly, a new Truthspeaker as well.

Adeius, Homaj wished the Truthspeaker hadn't played that card. And he wished he suspected anyone, absolutely anyone other than the Truthspeaker who'd trained him. How could he think Aduwel had anything to do with the death of his father, and whatever had happened to his sibling—and now the death, as well, of Lord Birka?

Aduwel had told him of Lord Birka's death, and that thought now was ice in his gut.

Had that also been a threat?

Stone. Homaj had to be stone. He couldn't bend around this wind.

He straightened, pulling more of his father's bearing as the ruler into his own. One more step on the path to a rulership that would be as far—farther—from his own personality than the public persona he had now.

And whether Vatrin was found or not, came back or not, was compromised or not—Homaj had to sell this. And he had to sell it to himself.

"Okay. We've taken more time than we have. Iata—"

Iata sat down at his vanity and quickly pulled out what he'd need to push his makeup as much as he could in as short a time possible.

"Right. We'll have to move quickly from here. Follow my lead, always. And—" He spread his hands, looked back at the two guards. "Trust me. I have been trained for this. Whatever I do, it has a purpose."

Did he trust himself? If he was in their place, would he trust himself?

His mouth felt stuffed with wool. His stomach growled, a hollow gurgle.

"Zhang?" Iata said, slashing over one brow with quick strokes. "There should be some energy bars in the cabinet beside the bed. Bottled water. Can you get those, please?"

Zhang looked to Homaj, and he waved toward the bedroom. He hadn't wanted—he hadn't wanted to show vulnerability just now. Because a Seritarchus never would.

Iata gave him a troubled frown in the mirror. "You still must take care of yourself. This all falls apart if you do."

Homaj wet his dry lips, shifted his weight as Zhang came back and handed him two water bottles and two bars. He glanced at her, then took a drink.

Iata was right. There was no room for mistakes now. His training was good and truly over.

"What about the others, Ehj and Bozde and Chadrikour?" Jalava asked. "Will you swear them to you, too? You brought them in here before."

Homaj paused. Yes, he had brought them in before, and yes, they would know more about him than any others of the Palace Guard besides Tavven themself. They'd have to, if they were to guard him effectively. And maybe he'd bring them further into his confidence later, or maybe not. They were, all three of them, ranked lower than Zhang, so he wouldn't have any problems with the chain of command. He'd already decided to keep his inner circle of confidence very, very small right now.

"I'll swear them to me personally, yes. You will all be my personal guards, as I said in the Adeium. We'll go do that now. But you two—you have the higher clearance. Jalava, you're in command of my personal guard, under me, with Zhang as your second. You have my personal confidence. You'll treat the information I give you directly with care."

Jalava gave a tight nod. They didn't look happy, but then, none of them were happy just now.

"Okay, then," Homaj said quietly. "Let's go make a bid to rule the kingdom."

19

THE QUESTION

There are seldom formal invites to a new prospective ruler's bid to rule, as so often the bids are made after tragedy, or political necessity, not planning.

— LEVVI KOMANDAR IN "THE TROUBLED PATH
FROM ONE RULER TO THE NEXT"

The official ceremony would be held in the Reception Hall, where all the highest court functions were held. Because the palace was still on lockdown, Homaj didn't bother with formal invitations. After he'd sworn the rest of his guards to himself, he sent a brief message on his comm to both Guard Commander Tavven and Yaliran, the Master of Ceremonies. They were to gather what nobility and notables were still in the palace and escort them to the Reception Hall with a healthy contingent of guards.

Sending a message was risky—his enemies would know where he would be. But he didn't see any other way around it, this ceremony had to be as public as possible at the moment.

And now, Homaj stood on the dais at the front of the Reception Hall, playing with a wire mesh ball he often used to divert attention in one hand, waiting. The hall, only slightly smaller than the palace ballroom, was chilly, making him wish he'd worn a thicker jacket. The gauzy skirt had seemed like a good idea twenty minutes ago.

He boosted his body temperature the slightest amount, not enough to cloud his mind, just enough to take the edge off the cold.

Iata was on his left, still Changed away from himself, every bit the alert guard. Zhang stood on his right. At floor level in front of Homaj, Jalava and Ehj watched the tall double doors at the back with their pistols holstered but hands ready. Chadrikour and Bozde were at the end of the dais to his right, covering the doors that led to the royal antechamber and the staff antechambers.

On the way down from his apartment, they'd all crowded around him, alert and twitchy. And now?

"Steady," he said softly. "I don't want anyone shooting the first noble that walks in."

Jalava made a noise but didn't take their eyes off the doors.

Then the tall light gray doors with their inlaid silver patterns opened and Commander Tavven stepped through, along with several higher-ranking guards and a group of gawking courtiers. Homaj watched the first moment that Tavven registered he'd already picked his own personal guard and Tavven hadn't been a part of that selection. Sarin Tavven had always been an ambitious person, and at forty was young to hold the post of Commander of the Palace Guard. They would of course have wanted to put their own people into Homaj's immediate confidence.

One of the wannabe puppet masters who'd wish to attach strings to him? He'd like to see them try.

But Tavven was also a professional, and they reoriented their priorities quickly. They strode toward Homaj and bowed deeply, their long gold braid dipping over their shoulder. "Ser Truthspoken Heir."

Which wasn't yet confirmed, but a necessary leap under the circumstances.

Tavven straightened and brushed back their braid, their dark eyes scanning everything. They acknowledged the nods—not salutes while they had their weapons out—of Jalava and Ehj. But their gaze landed back on Homaj. "I'll swear to you now. This kingdom needs a ruler. Though we are, still, searching for Truthspoken Vatrin and will continue to do so. You and I must talk after."

Which sounded more like a command than Homaj would have liked.

He held his poise, though, as Tavven swore the oath of a guard commander to a ruler—even an interim ruler—which reassigned the entirety of the Palace Guard under Tavven's command to Homaj's singular authority.

That oath made his insides quake, though he'd never let it show.

Homaj nodded in return. A sour smile tugged at the corners of his lips, and he let it.

"Thank you, Commander." He glanced up at the gathering influx of nobles, some of whom looked like they wanted to approach, but were being directed to stand near the back by the rest of Tavven's guards. And more onlookers were arriving now, too. Everyone, he suspected, who was still holed up in the palace and had been released to witness.

Tavven's cheek twitched, and Homaj read the brief flurry of signals they sent to their people around the room. *Be alert, only him, top priority.*

Homaj clamped down on the nervous twist in his gut and looked back to Tavven. "Do you have a dampener?"

"I do," Tavven said, pulling a small, oval device from their pocket and tapping it on.

The Reception Hall was acoustically tuned to amplify what was said on the dais. And, dammit, he couldn't step down to floor level or he'd lose his careful positioning, and Tavven couldn't come up to him without causing too much fuss in a direction he didn't want. Tavven was not yet a trusted advisor. But he needed to know what Tavven knew before he did this.

Homaj waited until he felt the slight pressure from the dampener, saw the light blur in the air which would prevent reading lips. Tavven was close enough—he knew Tavven's dampener would clear the minimum three-meter radius around them. But he still asked in a low voice, "Were you there?"

Tavven drew in a slow breath, glanced again at Jalava and Ehj, who were less than a meter away from them and within the dampener's bubble. "Respectfully, Truthspoken, this is not the time—" Tavven glanced back out at the gathering crowd.

And they were right. It wasn't. But Homaj needed to have this conversation, at least this part of it, right now.

He stepped closer to the edge of the dais, glaring down at Commander Tavven. Dampener or not, body language could still be read. "Were you there? At the hospital? Did you see—"

His voice broke, and he let his emotions, everything he'd been shoving down since that morning, well up for one agonizing moment.

Tavven's eyes widened. They took a step back. Just that one step back. And what did that mean? He'd wanted to provoke a reaction, but he wasn't sure of his answer.

Carefully, oh so carefully, Homaj shoved the bulk of his emotions back down again. But he kept them plain on his face. He kept them as a mirror—because his parents had died on Tavven's watch.

"Yes," Tavven said. "I was at the hospital, but not when it happened. I was meeting with the Commander of the Municipal Guard. Respectfully, Truthspoken—this is a conversation best saved for later. Please make your bid, this is a highly insecure location. I want you off this stage."

Homaj gave a tight nod, flipping the mesh ball in his hand. Tavven's eyes flicked to it, back to him, narrowed.

"I'm going to turn off the dampener," Tavven said. "The Truthspeaker will be here shortly."

"And Vatrin?" Homaj asked, suppressing a jolt of nerves at the Truthspeaker coming. Yes, Aduwel was an important part of confirming his bid to rule. His sincerity had to be witnessed. But Homaj didn't have to like it.

"We haven't found Truthspoken Vatrin yet. Or their blood-servant."

But they had found Vatrin's lover. And it was interesting that Tavven had so completely dismissed Vatrin's title as the Truthspoken Heir like that. They'd assigned it to Homaj, yes, but they shouldn't have dismissed it from Vatrin. Tavven had said "Truthspoken Vatrin" twice now, when they should have said "The Truthspoken Heir." Vatrin hadn't abdicated. They hadn't been found, they might still be alive.

A biting taunt was on his lips, but he veered from it. Instead, he took another step closer to the edge of the dais, holding up a hand as Tavven went to click off the dampener.

Tavven stared up at him, and Homaj saw the anger slowly building in their eyes. Anger at him? That he, Homaj, the court rake, was calling the shots just now? That he was the one about to make a bid to rule this entire kingdom, one hundred and eighty-seven worlds, all under his command?

Had Tavven had any hand in getting him to this point?

Homaj shook, a tremble of emotion that he couldn't suppress. Adeius. Roll with it.

Zhang twitched forward. She was sworn to him personally now, but Tavven was still the Commander of the Palace Guard. Was she trying to protect him, or protect Tavven *from* him?

His hands were clenched at his sides, the wire mesh ball held tight in one fist.

What he wanted to do was crouch down, look straight into Tavven's eyes just inches from their face, and say, "Yes, we're going to have a long talk, you and I. And you're going to tell me why the hell *you let my parents die!*"

But he stepped back. He loosened his hands, rolled the mesh ball around his fingers. He got himself under control.

What he actually said was, "Thank you, Commander. Turn off the dampener. Keep watch."

20

THE FIRST MAGICKER

"In the first breath of the universe."
"In the breath of She Who Speaks."

— UNKNOWN, A TRADITIONAL CALL AND
RESPONSE GREETING AMONG GREEN
MAGICKERS

His rage had found a crack in his armor and he was
having a hard time reigning it back in. Commander
Tavven had seen it—maybe everyone had seen it,
and maybe he could use that. Work with that. He was known as
someone who could spar with words, but he'd rarely let his
temper run wild.

Tavven clicked off the dampener, and the world rushed
back in full enthusiastic color. Voices hushed, then swelled
again in renewed speculation.

Tavven bowed and backed away before turning to stride
toward the right end of the dais. There, they took up their own
position on floor level, the customary place for the highest

ranking guard in the room. They glanced once at Jalava, then away again.

Tavven knew their job was on the line. Their loyalty was on the line. The Seritarchus had died on their watch, no matter if it was unintentional on their part. Somewhere in there, someone had absolutely fucked up. Or more likely, been compromised.

Homaj's gaze lingered on Tavven. And could they possibly have betrayed his father? Tavven had only held the position of Guard Commander for a few years now, but Homaj had never known them to be anything other than competent and loyal. No one got to be a Guard commander with less.

But then, Homaj would never have suspected the Truthspeaker, either, until the Truthspeaker had outed him in public.

Tavven looked back up at him, meeting his gaze, mouth pulled tight.

Yes, Tavven was ambitious. And so was most of the court. Homaj was not as ready to rule a kingdom as Vatrin had been, or—to most eyes—able to do so as competently. He felt phantom strings trying to latch onto him, and absolutely everyone, whether they'd had a hand in the assassinations or not, would be vying for a piece of the power he was about to take for himself.

He blinked rapidly, shifting into a light healing trance to calm his heartbeat, to steady his jittering body as best he could.

He surveyed the crowd, who were mostly watching him, assessing.

He saw mistrust there. He saw blame, even—did they think he was behind the attack? Adeius. That was another hurdle he'd have to overcome. He wanted to shout to them all that of course he'd never wanted to rule.

But that wouldn't be completely true, would it? He'd been content to let Vatrin take the lead, yes. But when his father would have retired from rule and Vatrin took up the reigns, and when Vatrin had two Truthspoken heirs of their own and those heirs were of age, Homaj would have been forced out of Change, forced into either social or physical exile. There could only, by mandate of Adeius, ever be three Truthspoken. Three pairs of eyes and witnesses and manifestations of the will of Adeius.

He might have married by then, he might have children of his own, but once a Truthspoken was no longer a Truthspoken, a wall would form between them and the rest of the kingdom. They had all their skills and training, so they would never be ordinary. But they would vow to no longer Change, so they could never be who they had been, either. Always less than, and also still too much.

The only path for him out of that exile was to someday rule.

The hairs on his arms stood on end.

He turned the mesh ball over and over in his hand. He saw more than a few nobles watching the ball, not him.

Was the Truthspeaker here yet? He didn't see Aduwel Shin Merna's red and violet robes, or the bubble of space he always commanded around him, but the Truthspeaker would surely be here soon.

Homaj did, however, spot the deep green aura of the gray-haired First Magicker, Onya Norren, as she strode into the room, on the arm of a much younger magicker with a much paler aura.

Homaj's brows twitched. In all the chaos and maneuvering, he'd forgotten the First Magicker was in the palace just now, staying overnight in the guest wing for a contentious round of negotiations with his father.

Well, or she had been staying for that. Now, her focus was trained on Homaj.

The mesh ball in his hand stilled. No matter what persona

he showed to the court, no matter all the nuances of his current performance, she'd see through them all.

The small knot of magickers that had come in with Onya Norren fanned around her like guards. And the courtiers, for their part, backed away to let the knot of magickers have their own bubble of space.

Most of the Green Magickers' characteristic auras were a barely visible green. Most of the magickers, barring the First Magicker, who were allowed in the palace were low-ranking at best. That was all the nobility would tolerate—they had far too many secrets for the magickers to read.

But the First Magicker's aura was like a concentrated garden around her, dense and darkly green. The coin-sized holographic rank seal implanted in her cheek, mandatory for anyone who manifested the abilities of Green Magics, was densely packed with her fractal rank insignia.

Was this someone else who'd try to attach strings to him? He didn't follow his father's stance that the magickers had to be managed at all costs, whatever the cost—and he knew some of that cost. He'd seen how magickers and their families were treated while on a mission for his father several years ago, and he'd never been able to budge his father to change those policies.

Homaj had seen enough of the world while on training missions, while being other people, to know that controlling a people through the population's base fear of them was a recipe for disaster.

And it was wrong.

If he wanted to change public perceptions of himself right now and set everyone on edge for what he'd do next, he could think of no better way than to turn the tables on the relationship between the rulership of Valoris and the Green Magickers who found themselves in an uneasy truce with it.

He caught the First Magicker's eye again and motioned her forward.

Onya Norren's head tilted in surprise, but she waved for her group to stay where they were and, still on the arm of the younger magicker supporting her, moved her way through the opening crowd toward Homaj.

21

A BID TO RULE

The First Magicker is almost always one of the highest ranking magickers in the kingdom. But with the intensity of their abilities, however, comes an intensity of their empathy.

— DR. LORD PIXI VIYALOROKKA IN "THE
SOCIAL STRUCTURE OF GREEN MAGICKERS"

The First Magicker's passage through the crowd caused a ripple, an angry murmur. Several people looked like they wanted to stop her but thought better of having to touch that dense green aura.

Tavven stayed steady at the end of the dais.

The First Magicker wasn't a physical danger to Homaj—but she certainly could be politically. Green Magickers couldn't, by the nature of the powers they manifested, harm anyone, and certainly couldn't kill. That wasn't why people feared them. Green Magickers could touch someone's skin or look into their eyes and know their truths. In a room full of secrets, that was a far more potent threat.

In reality, Homaj knew the magickers had as wide an array of abilities and skills as any other group of skilled people. Some, like the First Magicker, could certainly read people with a glance—maybe only their truth in that moment, or maybe the truths in their past as well. Others might only pick up on nuances, or need specific contact or a specific set of circumstances to read someone.

Homaj, with all of his Truthspoken training in evaku, could also read people at a glance. The magickers just read with different senses.

He told himself that as the First Magicker climbed the stairs at the end of the dais, which she finally did alone, leaving her helper standing uncomfortably beside Tavven.

Zhang took a small step back, and Homaj held out his hand as the First Magicker approached. Her steps unhurried, her expression neutral.

Jalava, watching all of this from below, stiffened. "Ser Truthspoken—"

But they stopped at a look from Homaj. He'd told them to trust him.

Jalava gave a tight nod, went back to scanning the crowd.

"Ser Magicker, I hope your day has been well," Homaj said as the First Magicker bowed before straightening to grip his hand. Her touch was warm and dry. Her aura, so visible it felt like the most vivid color in the room, felt like nothing at all.

Could he feel her emotions through her touch? He felt a warmth that wasn't physical, too, and a cold like frozen steel.

"Ser Truthspoken," the First Magicker said in her steady voice. "I wasn't expecting to stand next to you just now. What are you about?"

Homaj felt his smile, for the briefest moment, go genuine. There was irony in her emotions, he felt that distinctly.

"May I?" she asked.

He thought she was asking to witness him, so he nodded.

But a calm descended on him, like a door closing out the city noise. Some of the tension that had knotted his shoulders since he'd read Tavven's note eased.

He tried to startle at that but couldn't quite. Was she calming him? She had to be. She'd been the First Magicker for as long as he'd been alive, but he'd only ever met her a few times, mostly seen her from a distance. His father had dealt with the magickers only grudgingly and they weren't usually welcome at everyday court social functions. The people were just too wary of them. Inviting a magicker to anything was considered poor taste.

He looked down into Onya Norren's blue-gray eyes. Her long, light brown face roughened with the sun. Her ears hung with two small aventurine stones. Homaj doubted even the fittings were precious metals, which was either conscious choice or affectation. As First Magicker, she could doubtless afford some luxuries.

And yet, standing here with her, mostly a stranger and hardly an ally to the rulership, he felt calm. He felt—he felt for the first time that day that things might actually work through. Maybe not all well, but they would work through, and he would get through, and this kingdom would get through.

Homaj was aware of the hush in the gathered crowd. He said softly, quickly, "Ser First Magicker, Onya Norren, would you please witness that all I say is true? Would you please witness to my sincerity?"

The First Magicker searched his face and was no doubt searching her sense of his sincerity now through their shared touch.

"I'd be honored," she said, giving Homaj's hand the lightest squeeze. Had that been meant for reassurance?

That small gesture, kindness or not, rattled Homaj more than anything else in this room. It was the sort of gesture a parent might make. Someone who knew him completely.

His free hand still held the mesh ball, and he slipped it into a skirt pocket. He firmly set his thoughts back into place, his mask back into place. The mask would remain, but the mask had little whatsoever to do with his own sincerity. It was like clothing—the adornment, not the person wearing it.

His hand tucked into Onya's, he turned back to the crowd.

"Thank you for coming. I, Homaj Rhialden, am here to make my bid to rule the Kingdom of Valoris. The Seritarchus and Seritarchus Consort are—"

He choked on the words, and that hadn't been planned.

He felt a squeeze on his hand again, looked back at the First Magicker, gathered himself once again.

"They're dead," he said flatly. "The Truthspoken Heir, my older sibling, is still missing and I must presume compromised. Therefore, I, Homaj Rhialden, Truthspoken sanctified by the Adeium for service to the Kingdom of Valoris, declare myself Truthspoken Heir. I make my formal bid to rule the Kingdom of Valoris on this day of Jor the Fifth, in the rule of the Eighth Seritarchus of the Twelfth Dynasty, 2945 New Era—"

The back doors opened, and Truthspeaker Aduwel Shin Merna, resplendent in his red and violet robes, hair still neatly braided and beard meticulously combed, stepped inside.

Homaj's nerves jolted. Yes—yes, by asking the First Magicker up to the dais to be his witness, he'd intended to give the Truthspeaker a snub. But he'd thought Aduwel would be here already. Had Aduwel been held up, had Aduwel taken the time it would typically take to get to the Reception Hall, or had Aduwel been attempting a snub, too? Aduwel certainly wouldn't have thought that Homaj would ask the First Magicker to witness his bid to rule, not the Truthspeaker. Both, legally, could be witness. But the Truthspeaker should have been the only real choice.

And the crowd was taking notice and readying for the drama.

Aduwel inclined his head, his expression showing nothing, and he and his retinue of gray-robed speakers, Ceorre among them, took up court at the back of the room.

Now people's attention was dividing between Homaj at the front, and Aduwel at the back. The new and unproven—and known to be apathetic—ruler, and the known and trusted spiritual leader.

Homaj had followed his gut with asking up the First Magicker. Or maybe, he'd just been trying to be petty.

Another squeeze from Onya Norren, another wave of calm.

She knew what he was feeling, which was less unsettling just now than a much-needed solidarity. Her witness might lead to questions of legality and his true sincerity later, even if the witness of a Green Magicker was binding by law.

But Aduwel hadn't been here. Aduwel had, maybe, been trying to make him wait. Had been playing petty power games *now,* when the kingdom was in need. He didn't want Aduwel anywhere near him just now, even if the price was the divided attention—and maybe divided loyalty—of the room.

Aduwel Shin Merna smiled beatifically from the back and subtly raised his chin.

This was the price now, and there would be a price later. It would not be a small price.

Homaj steadied himself again. He very carefully did not let his own emotions show now in his posture, his face, his voice. The moves of this game would be intricate, and not won with quick emotions.

He looked away from the Truthspeaker. Very carefully did not look at anyone as he said, "I have made my formal bid to rule. First Magicker Onya Norren, do you witness?"

"I witness the truth of Homaj Rhialden," Onya said, "Interim Ruler of the Kingdom of Valoris."

Don't think about it. He could not think about it.

And was that something that she knew the correct forms? Had she come here with a purpose, too?

But he felt her steadiness above all else. Her anger, yes, and maybe she had a right to it.

Would killing a ruler by proxy still be violence to a Green Magicker? If that ruler was known to be against her people, and...and the second Truthspoken heir was possibly rumored to be sympathetic?

She squeezed his hand hard, and he felt...Adeius, he felt revulsion? Loathing of the thought?

He cleared his throat, used Change to steady it. "Thank you, First Magicker."

He turned back to the now silent crowd, raised his chin. "As is my right under the laws of Valoris, I also give formal notice to those who have thus ascended me to this position; I will spare no one who had a hand in the deaths of my parents—or my sibling, if they are dead, or my sibling's lover, Lord Xavi Birka, who is dead, or my father's and my sibling's bloodservants. Whoever is guilty, I'm telling you right now that your life is already over."

22

TEN DAYS

The right of vengeance is an essential part of many heirs' coming of age.

— PRINCE BLAEN XIAO IN A LEAKED MESSAGE
TO THEIR WIFE

The crowd rustled. And were they reacting to his threat, or to the news about Lord Birka's death? Lord Xavi Birka, like his sibling Vatrin, had been well loved in the court. Homaj saw shock, saw tears welling—and why hadn't those same tears been welling for the death of the Seritarchus?

He paused, half-expecting the court hysterics that would normally follow the news of a death. But it didn't come. No one was daring to do that here.

"I will hold court again in ten days," Homaj went on, following the form he'd been taught. That he'd never wanted to use. And—and he couldn't say he'd never thought of how this day would feel. That he hadn't thought about it, played it through, even knowing what it would mean. Knowing that also, with all he had, he'd never wanted it to happen, for every reason. He really hadn't.

He'd wanted to watch his sibling's children inherit, and their children, no matter what that would ultimately mean for him. No matter that it would strip his own life and right to Change away from him. Maybe he had toyed with the idea of ruling someday, of not being forced to give up the one thing he was truly good at. But not at the cost of his fathers. Adeius. Not at the cost of his sibling.

The sacrifice he'd been born to make was part of his duty as Truthspoken, it all was, and he knew that. He told himself that. As much as he'd tried to make people think he didn't care about duty, he had never not cared.

He'd wanted children of his own, he'd wanted to grow old and maybe not be at the absolute center of it all. He'd wanted his children to be...not like this. Not have this turbulent palace life with all its teeth and all its diamonds. He couldn't have that and also still be Truthspoken.

Or maybe he'd just been resigned to not think about any of it. To live out his public apathy in private, too.

But there was an awful part of himself that liked holding the center, even if it was a small center. That liked that all eyes were on him just now, and not his sanctimonious older sibling. That people were waiting for him. Waiting for *his* decisions, and that those decisions mattered.

He breathed for two heartbeats. Why was he having such a hard time controlling his emotions? He looked down at his hand still clasping the First Magicker's. When he was touching the magicker...was he unable to lie? Even to himself?

"Ten days," he said again, heart now pounding. How would this come across to the courtiers? Scared and chaotic. Everyone would think him weak. They would most certainly peg him as an Ialorius style of rule, because right now he had no control and he had no momentum, but he wasn't flowing with this moment now, either.

But was seeing him scattered like this to his advantage? Could he turn it to his advantage? He didn't know. He couldn't think that through just now, he wanted this to be over with so he could get out of everyone's intense scrutiny. He felt far, far too exposed. Bringing up the First Magicker to witness for him had been a horrible idea.

He should let go of her hand. The most crucial witness was over—but he'd wanted a witness for his declaration of intent, too. He was deadly, absolutely serious about that.

But that calm from Onya Norren was still there, too. That sense that everything would be okay.

He wanted to fucking cry, because his parents had just been murdered.

"And—and I promise you. I'm not my father, and I'm not my sibling. *So don't fucking mess with me!*"

He shivered and let go of the magicker's hand and stepped back, panting.

What had just happened? Why had he so thoroughly lost control? This wasn't in any persona, not in his previous public persona, not the new one he was trying to craft.

He caught Iata staring at him, brow furrowed. He wanted to snap that he was fine, but that was obviously not the case.

Adeius, what a way to start his rule.

He waved at the First Magicker. "Witness my sincerity."

Onya Norren turned to him, eyes shining with, what, pity?

No. Adeius. Grief. How much of what he was feeling had the magicker felt?

All of it. He knew that, because he'd felt her own rising empathetic grief, hadn't he? Echoing and amplifying his own, while she'd been trying to lend him her calm. She might be the most powerful—or at least, most politically powerful—of the Green Magickers, but that didn't exempt her from feeling pain.

"I witness," she said. Her voice was tight, full of everything he was feeling. "Homaj Rhialden is sincere. The words he's spoken are his truth. I witness in the eyes of She Who Wakes. So it is."

Homaj, gaining control again, could almost feel the Truthspeaker's rage from where he stood. To snub the witness of the head of the Adeium, the dominant religion of Valoris, in favor of the Green Magickers, who followed a religion most considered a cult at worst, a mystery at best, was an intense insult to the Adeium. Homaj could see, with widening clarity, that he'd be dealing with the fallout of that move for a *very* long time. Maybe even past the unseating of a Truthspeaker.

He glanced at Speaker Ceorre beside the Truthspeaker, but her face showed nothing. Was she still with him?

Well, he would deal with it. He couldn't have let the Truthspeaker onto the dais, not knowing what he suspected. He couldn't, absolutely couldn't, have let that man publicly witness for his truth.

"Thank you, First Magicker Norren," Homaj said, his words coming out calmer than he felt. Training. Pure training. "The Kingdom of Valoris thanks you."

The First Magicker nodded solemnly, bowed more deeply than he'd ever seen her bow to his father, and made her way off the dais. She'd stood tall beside him, but she leaned again now on the arm of her attendant, more heavily, he thought, than before. Slowly, they made their way back off the dais, back to the group of magickers who'd all drawn closer together in the First Magicker's absence.

Homaj's eyes found Commander Tavven, then, whose posture and expression were tight. Tavven gave him a nod, then a small nod toward the royal antechamber—Tavven wanted him out from this exposed position.

Homaj looked away. Not yet. Not quite yet.

But this part, at least, was over. He'd made his bid to rule.

He was, at this moment, the interim ruler of Valoris. And, without any information to contradict it, fully the Truthspoken Heir. He had a kingdom on his back, and only finding Vatrin and proving they were able to rule would shake it off.

That was absolutely his highest priority. He'd had enough time in this rare light.

Tavven frowned at him, but held up their hands to the crowd. "Please, move to the doors in an orderly fashion. The Truthspoken is not receiving any words today as a security measure. Please return to the rooms where you have been staying today. If you would like to offer sympathies or well-wishes, write them down, and staff will see they are delivered to the Truthspoken."

There was a sparse murmur of complaint for the ongoing lockdown, but not much. Many backward glances at him.

Oh he'd thoroughly fucked his reputation for inaction, for apathy. There was nothing of the witty, decadent socialite about him today.

He glanced back to Iata, then Zhang. Jalava caught the drift and made quick hand signals to Chadrikour and Bozde at the far end of the dais, drawing them back in.

"Where now?" Zhang asked, stepping closer.

"I need to speak to Commander Tavven."

And then...and then he might need to become someone else. He'd made his formal bid to rule. He had his ten days. And while he did need to speak to Tavven first, he wouldn't get far in sorting out any truths until he could go out and see everything for himself, with eyes that were trained to see things most people could not.

"Have Tavven come to you," Iata said, on Homaj's other side.

Homaj weighed that against showing a measure of goodwill toward Tavven and getting better information in return.

He shouldn't have to be questioning the loyalty of his own

guards, dammit, least of all their commander. He shouldn't need to go an extra measure to secure good information. He was about to rule this kingdom.

Homaj was already ruling this kingdom.

But he wasn't fully the ruler yet. He held those powers in interim, but not in permanence—yet.

He would need to meet, in the next day or so, with the heads of the Army and the Navy. He'd need to meet again with the Green Magickers, he'd need to meet—Adeius—with the Truthspeaker. With the heads of the high houses, with the General Assembly—who would meet this afternoon to confirm his bid to rule. Not that their decision actually mattered. The Assembly could do little to touch the affairs of Truthspoken.

But he had ten days, and a time window for finding his sibling that was quickly shrinking. He eyed Iata and leaned close, lowered his voice further, wishing for Tavven's dampener, or that he'd thought to bring his own.

"Can you go all the way?"

Iata was halfway to being him already, buried under both of their quick fixes of makeup and a solid projection of a guard's bearing. Iata had certainly shown he could reliably impersonate him.

Homaj swallowed on a tight throat. If there was any chance at all that Iata had ambitions he didn't know about, this would be the time for them to surface. If someone wanted a puppet, there was no more perfect puppet than an imposter. If the Truthspeaker witnessed that Iata was, in fact, Homaj—well.

Well, then Homaj might have the witness of the First Magicker. And how would that stand up, the word of the second most powerful person in the kingdom against the word of a magicker, even the First Magicker?

Iata, still retaining the bearing of a guard, leaned toward Homaj's ear, his face professionally blank. "Are you sure, Ser Truthspoken?"

Homaj hid a grimace. He hadn't hidden his thoughts well enough and knew his doubting Iata would hurt. He also knew that Iata understood it. Iata might not be fully Truthspoken, but he was absolutely aware of the necessities of trust.

The question alone decided it for Homaj. He might not have a Green Magicker's abilities to sense a person's truths from within, but he knew Iata. He could read him well, even through all of Iata's own evaku training.

"Yes."

He had to trust. Because he had to do what he could. And he only had ten days in which to do it.

Or maybe, he only had one.

Or maybe, with his sibling's life, he'd already failed.

23

TAVVEN

> *The position of the Commander of the Palace Guard is as much a political appointment as it is a tactical one. The commander has unprecedented access to and power over the palace—such a position can't go to just anyone.*

— FREYA OUMA, VID COMMENTATOR, IN THE
VID ESSAY "THE RESPONSIBILITIES OF THE
PALACE GUARD TO THE PEOPLE"

Homaj signaled to Tavven, and Tavven nodded, calling the rest of their guards in around Homaj as he finally descended the far end of the dais. Could Homaj read relief on their face? He couldn't tell. No one got to be the Commander of the Palace Guard without some evaku of their own.

Tavven waved toward the door to the royal antechamber. "Ser Truthspoken."

Should Tavven be calling him the ruler instead? But he

hadn't announced his style of rule yet—that would come in ten days. No, he didn't think that was a slight.

Homaj glanced toward the main doors leading out of the Reception Hall, saw the Truthspeaker still waiting near the back, pointedly not watching him. He definitely didn't want to go out that way.

"Yes," Homaj said to Tavven, "but we're going to your office."

"Ser Truthspoken, it would be safer to return to your apartment—"

"Your office."

Tavven nodded, but they didn't seem particularly happy about that. Would they suspect that one of Homaj's reasons in going there was to look into the eyes of every guard he saw there, to try and read guilt in any of their postures?

They took the services corridors down, an overcrowded parade of his own and Tavven's guards, down to the basement headquarters of the Palace Guard.

Now, Homaj tried not to fidget in the chair he'd pulled in front of Tavven's broad, utilitarian desk, the mesh ball back in his hand. Zhang stood just behind him, rigidly alert, Jalava and Iata—still acting as his guard—near the door. The rest of his guards he'd stationed outside Tavven's office, guarding the way in.

Tavven hadn't begrudged him that need. And while Homaj had searched every face he saw, searched every nuance of every posture on the way in, the depth of the bows, looking for the presence of guilt, he hadn't yet seen anything conclusive. Guilt was there, yes, but on too many faces. They the Palace Guard had failed this kingdom today. All of them had.

Tavven's office had no windows, and that, at least, was good. Palace Guard H.Q. sat below the residence wing, a subterranean sprawl of offices and a second sub-basement with a block of holding cells.

Homaj had spent the night in one of those cells on one of

his Truthspoken missions. He'd been a drunk noble who'd had far too much at a palace party and started a fight. He'd also set a particular noble house on a path to self-destruction that was long overdue, which was the point of that mission. He'd been thrown in the cell to cool his heels and had spent a good part of the night screaming obscenities at the ceiling before he'd slept it off.

He hadn't actually been drunk—or at least, he'd already smoothed away the effects of the alcohol. That had been four years ago, one of his first missions that hadn't been for training. Did Commander Tavven know about that? They hadn't yet been the Commander of the Palace Guard, but they were still a palpable presence in its structure then, working their way up.

Tavven settled with a sigh behind their desk, tucking back stray hairs that had come loose from their tight braid.

They looked up. Said as if in afterthought, "You can take my chair if you wish. It's more comfortable."

Homaj eyed their frazzled state. "You look like you need it more."

Tavven shrugged to concede the point and sat back heavily.

It was late afternoon. The assassinations had happened that morning. A lifetime ago.

Tavven smoothed their hair back, then seemed to gather themself. "All right, then. I assume you want to go off on your own after that speech, which I am going to advise you right now is unwise. You should stay in the palace under guard, and let the Palace Guard handle this investigation. But—I am sure—you are going to argue me down, so I'll save time right now and ask what you need from me, and if there's anything I can say at all to convince you to stay here, or to let my guards go with you." They hesitated. "And I can't even say you won't be safer out there, as someone else, if you're careful."

That admission, and the defeat in Tavven's posture, rattled

him. But the condescension in Tavven's tone tightened his shoulders.

Homaj paused to think. He'd been planning, at the end of this conversation, to tell Tavven that he was sending Iata out, and that he himself would stay. And to anyone's knowledge but a very few, that would be true.

Could he trust Commander Tavven to be one of those few?

He wasn't sure he could trust Tavven at all. But he absolutely knew he couldn't trust the Truthspeaker, and he didn't like the idea of leaving Iata here with only Jalava for protection —he'd already decided to take Zhang with him into the city. Iata needed another ally, risky though that alliance might be.

So he nodded.

"Yes, I'm going out. I'll take my own guard. And I want everything you know about my sibling's disappearance. I want all the details on how Lord Birka was found and where. I want every single detail you have on who killed my parents—or who allowed them to be killed."

Tavven opened their hands. "I'll give you what I can, Homaj, but it's not much, it's shamefully not much. We're working on more."

Should he press the matter?

"What happened today?" he asked. "Exactly what happened?"

Tavven stilled, lines forming on their face that hadn't been there moments before. They met his eyes, looked away.

"A successful assassination attempt," they said. "Carried out with explosives, though we don't yet know the source of them —whether they were carried in or planted. The Seritarchus, Seritarchus Consort, the Seritarchus's bloodservant, and all of his guards on duty with him, including the captain—as well as a good handful of civilians near him—were killed. More civilians were injured. Three more of the Palace Guard were killed as well, two injured. You have my word, Homaj, my absolute word that I am with you in finding out who did this and bringing them down."

Tavven's eyes glittered as they stared at him, waiting for him to accept that statement.

He kept his face calm, nodded. He saw signs of guilt in Tavven now, but was it like the rest of the guards outside, all knowing that they had failed?

Tavven looked down and opened a desk drawer, pulling out a secure tablet. It was the kind that would only connect to a very few high security consoles and not the palace or planetary networks. Tavven waved a holo display up on their desk, swiped through a series of commands, then checked the tablet before handing it to Homaj.

"Here's everything we have so far. Again, it's not much. And I'm keeping the details on this very tight."

He took the tablet and waited while it scanned his genetics, then input his weekly palace security code. The screen showed a bare-bones menu and several folders—he touched the one marked Anatharie Rhialden, Seritarchus, deceased.

The information was indeed sparse. Not anything like a report yet, only barest facts, random evidence yet to be collated into facts, and possibilities. All echoed what Tavven had just said.

He hesitated over a sub-folder with images of the assassination scene, fingers hovering, before he closed the folder again. Later. He would look at them later.

Homaj cleared his suddenly tight throat and clicked the tablet off. He looked back up at Tavven, who was now eyeing Homaj's guards.

"You've sworn in your personal guard compliment?" Tavven asked.

"Yes, though I might yet add a few more." Let Tavven think they still had the opportunity to get more on Homaj's personal team.

Tavven studied Zhang and Jalava, then Iata near the door. Their brows twitched. They'd know Iata wasn't actually Palace Guard—they'd know every guard on sight in the palace. They'd also draw the necessary conclusion. Tavven was one of the few who knew a bloodservant's capacity for Change.

"Vatrin," Homaj said. "Do you have anything yet on where they might be? Any leads at all?"

Tavven grimaced. "Lord Birka turning up—that's it. That is in the tablet as well. Lord Birka had been with Vatrin at some point, Vatrin's DNA was all over the man. I can only assume they'd slept together shortly before they fled, or at very least before he had time to change his clothes."

Zhang had had a slightly different version of when Vatrin had last been seen, and so had Ceorre—was anyone talking to each other just now? Was rumor ruling this day? He'd thought Tavven, at least, would have the most solid answer.

"Ceorre Gatri told me Vatrin came to the Truthspeaker right before the assassinations, with concerns for their safety."

"The speaker? Yes, Truthspeaker Aduwel told me that. He said that Vatrin didn't state their source of unease, and left shortly thereafter to go into the city, presumably after swapping identities. I don't know how much they'd have been able to Change—as I recall, they aren't as quick as you are or your father."

Homaj was uncomfortable that Tavven knew that detail, but he nodded. This was, at least, more than he'd been able to glean from Ceorre before, and most of what Tavven said was still matching the details he knew. So Vatrin had gone to the city. Or at least, they'd wanted everyone to think they'd gone to the city, but Tavven seemed to believe it. And maybe that was why the palace hadn't been as crawling with guards earlier as it should have been. Were all those guards out in the city searching for Vatrin?

His hand clenched around the mesh ball before he forced it

to relax again. None of this had been handled as it should have been.

"And Eyras, Vatrin's bloodservant?"

"We haven't found Eyras, no. We presume she is still with Vatrin. We hope, at least."

Was that suspicion in Tavven's voice? Homaj didn't know Eyras as well as Vatrin would, of course, but he had almost as much trouble believing Eyras would betray Vatrin as he did believing Iata would betray himself. Then again, Vatrin and Eyras had never been as close as Homaj and Iata.

And his father's bloodservant, Omari, was dead, already confirmed by Tavven.

Here, in Tavven's office, with his bid already made, in this temporary lull, the emotions were trying to claw back up his throat.

He didn't know what Tavven read in his face, but Tavven's mouth pulled tight. "I am truly sorry for your loss, Homaj. And we will find and punish who did this. They will absolutely not be spared."

The words, after everything that had happened, and flattened by Tavven's obvious exhaustion, didn't have the weight they should. They rang hollow in the room, and Homaj felt Zhang's tiny nervous shift behind him, and felt the hollowness in his own gut.

Tavven seemed to realize the sour note in the conversation and straightened, mouth a grim line.

Homaj took a breath, shoving his thoughts back on the course he needed them to go. "And Lord Birka—was he as himself, or in disguise?"

Tavven shook their head. "He was himself, though dressed in working class attire. He was shot down in the Financial District. He had nothing on him that would tell us his purpose there or where he was going, and he paid for the autocab with a prepaid credit chit. He was the only passenger. The autocab was higher quality but not weapon-proof—one of the side windows was shot out, and one of those shots hit Birka in the chest, the other in the neck. Heavy bolt-slinger, military-grade rounds."

Homaj suppressed a shudder. "Coming from or going to the Financial District?" Homaj wasn't so sure that would be the obvious refuge for a scared noble—yes, that was where a lot of the nobility in the city held court, but it was a hornet's nest of seething politics.

"Going to. The cab was shot down near the edge of the district, heading out of Gold District, though it might also have come from Blue District, as the trajectory was near that edge as well." Gold was a poorer, working class area that was a mix of business and residential, and Blue was much the same, if a little more commercial.

How was he supposed to find Vatrin in any of that? There were hundreds of thousands of people in each of those districts alone. Tens of millions in the capital city. And, if he thought of it, dozens of large cities on the planet. And was Vatrin even still on Valon?

Was Vatrin still alive at all, if Lord Birka had been found and taken out? There were any number of murders in the city every day. Vatrin could be any of them, anonymous, completely Changed. Not even Homaj would be able to tell if they weren't alive to show their tells.

"May I ask you a question?" Tavven asked.

24

TRUST

> *Can you trust a Truthspoken? I don't know. I don't know if you are one.*

— UNKNOWN (BLURRED IMAGE), AS QUOTED
BY KIR MTALOR, SOCIAL COMMENTATOR, IN A
VID ON THEIR PERSONAL FEED

"**M**ay I ask you a question?"

Homaj refocused on Tavven, waving assent.

"What was the business with the Green Magicker? Shouldn't the Truthspeaker have witnessed that part of the ceremony? Is there something there that I should know about?"

Homaj's senses sharpened. "The Truthspeaker publicly outed me earlier today." Had Tavven not known that? He'd have thought that was public knowledge by now. But then, Tavven was tracking a lot of moving pieces.

Tavven blinked slowly. They'd know the weight of exposing a Truthspoken's identity when he was not publicly himself.

And that reaction wasn't quite surprise. So maybe they had known, and were testing Homaj's response to it.

"Was it a mistake," they asked. "Or if not, surely it served a purpose."

"Not a purpose that served me, or that couldn't have been accomplished without outing me."

And he was distinctly aware that he himself might be a suspect in Tavven's eyes. That Tavven's responses to him now might all be testing him just as much as he was testing them.

"The Truthspeaker is as distraught as any of us," Tavven said. "He lost a Seritarchus today as well, and was the last here to see Vatrin before they fled—that must weigh on him. And he is still Human, Homaj, despite what most of the kingdom thinks. As are you and I."

There was a tone there, a defensiveness that was a little bit off. A little more strain in Tavven's posture than there should have been. Tavven wasn't, to Homaj's knowledge, one of the people who saw the Truthspeaker as a direct extension of the will of Adeius, so this was something else. Was Tavven trying to cover for the Truthspeaker?

Homaj was regretting his decision to trust Tavven with his and Iata's identities, but there was no going back on that now.

"Human or not, there are protocols," Homaj said. "He broke—"

"You broke protocol by letting a Green Magicker touch you during your bid to rule—Homaj, I watched you lose composure. Did the Magicker do something to you?"

Tavven leaned forward, as if they were eager for a yes. Eager for an excuse to, what, arrest the First Magicker? Pin all of this on the magickers? Oh that would be a disaster right now—especially since it almost certainly wasn't true.

Adeius, but that had been a bad choice in the moment. He shouldn't have dragged the Green Magickers into the center of all this, too.

"No," Homaj said. "Though it was my intent that it would seem that way. Thank you for confirming that it worked." He gave a self-deprecating smile and settled more of his usual air of unconcern around himself again. He watched Tavven's tight posture ease at the more familiar behavior. People truly did expect him to be his public persona, even if they knew better.

"Is there anything else I should know before I go?"

And why wasn't Tavven putting up more of a fight about that?

Tavven pursed their lips. "Do take your sworn guards with you. Will you let me send some of mine—"

"No. My guards. Less will be better."

Tavven nodded. "And don't do anything obvious that would draw fire. Be *discreet,* Homaj. Stay away from the attack sites if possible. I truly wish you wouldn't go at all, at least not until we know more. I understand it's your duty, and now your oath, but you might be the only Truthspoken left in this kingdom. Without you—" They spread their hands.

Without him, the genetic samples from his parents would be used to conceive and birth another two Truthspoken. Who would then be trained by the Truthspeaker until they were old enough to assume the duties of Truthspoken. The eldest would then assume as well the duties of the ruler. Until then...the Truthspeaker would control the kingdom. As was the will of Adeius, as decreed in the Holy Mandates. If the Truthspeaker could hold it against a coup from the high houses. Javieri, maybe, or more likely Delor would move in. Maybe had already planned the attack in the first place, colluded with— someone. Someone in the palace, in or close to the guards, in or close to the Seritarchus.

Homaj felt sick. Tavven was either resigned to Homaj's stubbornness and more observant of the right to vengeance than was prudent, or pushing him out into imminent danger. And he didn't know which it was. Tavven could want their own vengeance and was unleashing a trained Truthspoken on an unsuspecting city. Or Tavven could want him to quietly disappear.

Homaj stood, and so did Tavven.

"You do your part to catch those responsible, Commander. I'll do mine."

He had more information, yes, but he still wasn't sure what to do with it. He had the secure tablet Tavven had given him, but could he trust all of the information?

Homaj had to see for himself. He had to look and search for himself. He could trust nothing but his own senses.

The way Tavven was acting just now—not quite off, but not how Homaj thought they should be—made him not want to give them any more of his own information than necessary.

But he did have one more thing he needed to say. He'd already committed to this particular course. And maybe this... maybe this would give some interesting insights either way.

"Commander, while I'm away, Iata will carry out my duties as Truthspoken in my place. If—if you don't hear from me within ten days, that will be up to Iata, you, and the Truthspeaker to determine whether he should continue to be me."

Zhang sucked in a quick breath, and he didn't look back to see Jalava's reaction. He was fairly certain he knew what Iata's reaction would be.

What he'd just suggested wasn't legal, but then, the legal option—starting children who would eventually grow up to become Truthspoken—left an intense power vacuum. Not even the Truthspeaker could fully fill that, not with the high houses vying for their positions in the hierarchy of power. If it were up to the high houses, they might do away with the Truthspoken entirely, or find a way to place one of themselves in a position of guardianship, not the Truthspeaker. Easier, in some ways, to live the lie that Iata was Homaj Rhialden, get him married, and then start the children. Let the children of the late Seritarchus be raised as the children of Iata-as-Homaj to carry on the direct line.

Homaj did glance at Iata now, who was keeping composure, but his eyes were a little too wide around the edges. Panicked.

Adeius, Homaj wished he didn't have to place Iata in that position.

"Noted," Tavven said tightly. They didn't like that idea at all, but they also weren't denying it might be necessary.

They braced their hands on the desk as they studied Iata. "You'll be acting as Homaj? Then call on me as he would, as needed. I'll treat you exactly as I would him. I'll send guards to round out your compliment."

Iata gave a sharp nod. "Thank you, Commander."

"I'm telling you," Homaj said, gripping the mesh ball tightly in one hand, "because you need to know I'll be in the city. But you will not tell anyone else. Absolutely no one, not even the Truthspeaker. That's my order."

Tavven's brows rose. "Understood, Ser Truthspoken."

"Then, Commander, I will see you within ten days, or you will hear from me at very least. Let's hope all of this is resolved quickly."

"Ten days," Tavven agreed. "Best of luck to you, Truthspoken. And be safe."

25

VULNERABLE

Truthspoken grieve, of course. This manifests itself in different ways than the rest of humanity, however. Truthspoken seldom show their true emotions in public.

— DR. IGNI CHANG IN "FURTHER DISCOURSE
ON THE HUMANITY OF OUR RULERS"

Back in his apartment, Homaj gathered Iata, Zhang, and Jalava into his prep room. Iata, who hadn't broken his guard persona all the way back, and hadn't met Homaj's eyes, either, now headed straight for the closet and began rooting through the racks of clothing from all walks of life, all sizes.

Homaj followed to hover at the closet door.

"You'll need street wear, certainly," Iata said. "Working class, if you're going to go into the Gold District. And something suitable enough for the Financial District."

He'd already gathered an armful and set it down on a stand before rushing back out to the prep room. "Your cosmetic kit should be good. Just a few more things—uh, are you planning any particular gender presentation? Or just the usual?"

"The usual," Homaj said. "Just pack it all." He hardly knew where his sense of gender would end up on a good day, and this was definitely not a good day. He might use a more rigid gender presentation to a persona's advantage in calmer times, and though it might be a good idea just now to put that extra distance between himself and his known fluidity, he had no illusions he could deal with that today, or in any kind of long run.

He glanced at Zhang, who was watching Iata with a slight frown. Well, yes, and Iata was acting unreasonable. Iata was absolutely not talking about what they all needed to talk about.

Jalava hung back, hands awkwardly at their sides, looking supremely uncomfortable.

Truthspoken were, by nature and training, chameleons, and while most people understood that intellectually, it was different when you watched it actually play out. These were Truthspoken matters, and until today, Jalava and Zhang had never had to be faced with this particular messy reality.

All of this—having two people he'd only met today now so far in his confidences that they were watching the logistics of a Truthspoken life play out—felt far too personal. Only Iata had ever had access to this part of his life, or his father, or Vatrin. Only ever other Truthspoken and bloodservants.

And the Truthspeaker.

But how had his father dealt with this shift in privacy when he'd become Seritarchus? His own guards had certainly been in his confidence—they had to be, to guard him as closely as they did.

But not enough.

His father hadn't become Seritarchus peacefully, either. His father had to make a statement of intent, too, as had most of the rulers before him. There were more ten days of vengeance on ascension than not, and really, it was part of the test. Deal with your shit, then you can rule the kingdom and deal with ours.

"You okay?" Zhang asked.

His breathing was too fast, too heavy.

Iata paused on his way into the closet again, looking back.

Homaj closed his eyes on Iata, on Zhang, on the growing panic in Jalava's posture. Jalava had never seen a Truthspoken freak out before today, either. And Homaj had freaked out very publicly in the Reception Hall.

Adeius. How did he remotely think he'd be able to project the personality of a Seritarchus, the stability of control, if he couldn't even control his own emotions?

He felt a hand on his shoulder and looked up, startled, expecting Iata, or Zhang.

But Jalava was there, still nervous, almost flinching when Homaj saw their hand.

"Breathe with me," Jalava said, and took a large breath in, held it, let it out again.

Homaj knew how to regulate his breathing. Breath control was one of the first things any Truthspoken child was taught. It was necessary for a successful Change trance.

And he could slow his breath with a thought, too, he could move oxygen around his body, into his blood, into his brain. He didn't have to breathe with anyone.

He did it anyway. Eyes locked on Jalava's gray ones, breathing in tandem. The weight of Jalava's hand, in that moment, an anchor.

"It's okay to lose it here," Jalava said. Not in soothing tones —he didn't think Jalava had soothing tones—but in a gruff, no-nonsense manner. "You just lost your parents. You haven't been allowed to grieve. I know you don't have time for that now, either. But it's okay to take a minute and breathe. Okay? Are you okay?"

Was he?

He set aside the question of his overall state as too chaotic to quantify and focused on the momentary.

Homaj nodded. And his breathing was better.

His eyes flooded, and he sniffed hard, brushing at them with his sleeve. It just felt like too much effort to try and smooth the tears away through his Change abilities when the dam was already cracked. But it couldn't break. Not yet. Not yet.

His eyes found Iata's. "What—what should I be? To go into the city? To have access to the Gold District—I think that's the key."

He should be thinking this through on his own, as he'd been taught. But his mind was stretched too thin, far too thin.

"A building contractor," Iata said, "like a water technician, or maybe a hub technician. You're decent at tech, I'd go that way."

He could reliably repair moderate electronics if it came to it, yes. He couldn't rebuild a network hub, but he could at least diagnose it.

"Police," Zhang said. "It will give you access."

"Not without warrants." Jalava looked thoughtful. "Do you actually have police training? Do you have familiarity with the Municipal Guard?"

"A few weeks," Homaj said. "I could pass as a guard—" He gave a tight-lipped smile as Jalava made an acknowledging wave that he'd already done so. "—but I'm not sure that won't make people more wary. I need to find answers quickly. I need to be able to talk to people. Not everyone trusts the Municipal Guard."

Jalava's sour expression said they had good reason. And that was interesting.

Iata brought out another stack of clothing into the prep room and hung it on a long rack beside the door. He set the cosmetic case on a table beside the rack and opened the lid to show the array of everyday makeup, packs of colored lenses, quick hair dyes and de-coloring agents, silicone putty—the works.

Homaj wouldn't need that case until after he'd Changed, but he didn't stop Iata's bustling. Iata had his own things he didn't want to think about just now.

26

CLOAK AND DAGGER

> *I've helped others through roles and disguises, too, people who have no Truthspoken training, and it always surprises me how many people have the innate ability to become someone else.*
>
> — HOMAJ RHIALDEN, SERITARCHUS IX IN A PRIVATE LETTER, NEVER SENT; AS QUOTED IN *THE CHANGE DIALOGUES*

"Is there a chance anyone will recognize you, even after you've Changed?" Zhang asked. "I've seen you studying people—you can tell if someone is Truthspoken, right? Like how the Truthspeaker would have read your sincerity and verified you were you, with that sort of training. I've heard some of the nobility have that training, too."

"Not to our degree," Iata said, "and, well, to Homaj's. He's good. Really, really good. Sometimes I struggle to spot his tells. It's called evaku, by the way." He rooted through the cosmetic case, identifying anything missing with a scowl. Homaj sometimes pulled from the mission case and not his own vanity supplies, if the mission case had a color he wanted.

Iata strode for the vanities.

And what he'd said wasn't entirely true—Iata hadn't struggled with identifying Homaj's tells for a long time, though Homaj had gradually widened the gap for how long it took Iata to pick him out in a crowd. But Iata did always guess correctly. He also suspected Iata had let that gap widen on purpose. Iata was also very good at what he'd been trained to do.

Iata deposited three liner pencils in the case, went back in the closet, and came out with yet more clothing, this pile more cohesive than the first.

He'd picked a size that was a bit taller and stockier than Homaj's own body now.

Homaj eyed the new clothes on the rack. "I'll need more food for that."

He'd need to stop the Change halfway through to eat, maybe several times if his body needed it, especially if he was packing on muscle. Which seemed to be Iata's intent, and it wasn't a bad idea. Right now, he had the build of a dancer—athletic and wiry, if only average height. But he needed the build of a lifter. He had physical speed just now, but he might need strength in the city.

The Change wouldn't take that much longer if he left other aspects of his appearance untouched. Changing his body type would do a lot for changing his overall appearance.

"I'll need to cut your hair," Iata said. "Everything we can do to put distance. You gave your notice—people will know there might be a Truthspoken out there searching for them. They'll know you could be anyone. The more distance—"

"I know."

"Can you go female femme? Be fluid in that range for a while?"

Homaj pulled his hair from its knot, shook it out, and began combing his fingers through. He did Change to a body that was estrogen-dominant sometimes, if a mission would best be served by it, and if his sense of gender at that time was compatible, and if he was just feeling it. But those shifts were rarer for him, and that wasn't what he was feeling now. And he usually couldn't hold that for more than a few hours or a day at most before his sense of gender shifted away again, and he chafed to Change back. He didn't know how long he would be in the city.

"Not this time. We'll have to rely on my different build, the cut hair, all of it. I'll make a few more drastic Changes to my face shape. Deepen my voice. Change skin tone, change eye color. All of it."

Even cutting what corners he could, the Change would still take over an hour, but that wasn't avoidable. He couldn't go into this with anything approaching recognizability. People would be watching, and in the city, he'd be vulnerable.

"Who's going with you?" Iata asked, eyeing Zhang and Jalava.

"I am," Zhang said.

"I—" Jalava held up their hands. "I'm not good at cloak and dagger stuff."

"Then you picked the wrong ship to dock to," Iata said breezily, pulling Zhang toward the vanities.

She was eyeing them with dread.

"Zhang," Homaj said, and Iata slowed, looked back. "What are you comfortable with? People have seen you as my guard. You were with me on the dais. We'll have to change your appearance, push it as far as we can with cosmetics and prosthetics if possible. What are you okay with? Tell Iata if you're not okay with something. The makeup will wash off every night, but I can redo it in the morning. If we're away that long."

She grimaced, but nodded.

"I'll take care of her, Homaj. We've got the plan—go Change. I'll order up food. We'll cut your hair when it's over."

Homaj looked at Iata, just looked, and after a moment, Iata said, "Zhang, excuse me. I'll be back. Get comfortable. There's a tablet in the side drawer if you want to look at the feeds."

Iata herded Homaj back toward the bedroom and shut the door behind them.

Iata was keeping a bit of femme about him, too. It wasn't his natural expression at all, but Homaj understood the necessity —Iata was going to slide into his own life, and Homaj had presented very femme at the ceremony. He was still in that mode now. Continuity was everything—Iata would have to do what Homaj did, which was mostly cycle through various expressions of femme and masc masculinity.

Homaj's lips pressed tight, and his throat burned. "I can't make you do this."

"I want to," Iata said. "I need to. I already made up my mind this morning."

Homaj looked between Iata's eyes. His bloodservant. His cousin. His most loyal friend since they were children.

Iata's gaze was intent, entirely earnest.

Homaj hesitated only a moment, then pulled Iata into a tight embrace. "I might not come back."

"You will."

"But I might not. And if I don't, you'll have to—"

"I'll be fine, Homaj."

He pulled back. "Iata, if I don't come back and you continue to be me, the Truthspeaker will have you. He'll never let go, because he'll have that over your head, that you aren't me. He'll use that to make you do whatever he says. You won't be the ruler, not in truth."

Iata swallowed but didn't look away. "I'm not easily pushed, Maja. You know that."

He did. Yes, he did.

Iata braced both of his shoulders. "Go find Vatrin. Find whatever assvoid took out our family. And you make them pay,

Homaj. You must make them pay." He swallowed again. "And find Eyras, too." Vatrin's bloodservant. Who was still, also, missing. And mostly still not being talked about. Homaj had never been close to Eyras like he was to Iata, but Eyras was a distant cousin, a Rhialden, too. Still part of their Truthspoken family. And Iata and Eyras had been close by nature of their roles in the palace.

"Adeius, Iata, I'm so sorry. I'm sorry I've set Eyras aside in all of this. Yes, I'll find her, too."

Iata nodded, chin crinkled with holding back his own tide. But he, like he'd been trained, smoothed back any moisture in his eyes. Made a rolling shrug to let it go.

"Change, Homaj. Knock on the door when you need food. I'll come in. No one has to see you in the interim."

"Be gentle with Zhang," Homaj said. "She's new to all this."

"She's doing fine. Jalava, too. I assume Jalava will stay with me? Are you sure you don't want to take them? Three is better than two."

"Smaller group, stealthier group, is better," Homaj countered. "And I need someone with you I can trust. Now, go. We need every minute we have."

27

THE BACK CORRIDORS

It's speculated that there's an extensive network of tunnels and passages woven throughout Palace Rhialden. The floor below is not quite high enough to justify the windows of the floor above.

— DINESH SHARIPOV IN *INSIDE PALACE RHIALDEN: AN UNOFFICIAL GUIDE*

Zhang eyed Homaj with frank assessment. "Well you didn't skimp on the looks, did you? I thought the aim was to blend in?"

"No, the aim is to not be recognized. Sometimes that's served by standing out in a different way."

He touched at his newly cropped hair—Iata had side-cropped it in an undercut and dyed it teal. He had faintly iridescent holo-tattoos running along his jawline, also courtesy of Iata, as well as butterfly wings beside each eye. They'd hurt like hell when Iata had applied the premades, but he'd swiftly healed them. With all of these adjustments, he wouldn't need many cosmetics and could spend that time focused on Zhang, if needed.

And...Zhang. She was dressed in rack trousers and a knee-length, tan jacket that was faded around the edges. Iata had cut her hair short and dyed it a pale blue, which was in style at the moment, much more than his teal. Her makeup was contoured to alter the structure of her face, make it sharper, narrower. She had natural blue lenses, not the kind of lenses that people wore to make their eyes stand out. But though Homaj knew the artistry of her makeup, like Iata's earlier, it was deliberately non-professional. Good and solid, but not Truthspoken good.

"I look ridiculous," Zhang stated. "I never wear makeup. And I've made fun of people with powder blue hair."

Homaj smirked.

She pointed at him. "I like your hair color better." He looked in one of the mirrors. The teal worked well with his tan coloring, the softer lines of his face, his newly green eyes. He'd shaped himself to pack more muscle, yes, but hadn't fully let go of the dancer's musculature. He'd shaped his face and body, too, with a little more softness, a little more ambiguous androgyny. He was feeling that—it fit. If he slipped more masculine in the meantime, he had plenty to work with here. He could easily drop his voice, he'd already shifted it a little deeper, given himself more timbre.

"Iata went to go make the documents," Zhang said. "He said you have a printer in your med closet?" Her look was a little dubious.

"The chemicals used in the anti-forgery stamps are a little toxic," Homaj said with a grimace. "The med closet has a good ventilation system."

Iata would have been in again while he was still in Change —he had a vague hazy awareness of Iata capturing his image near the end of his trance. The software would extrapolate a waking face and one of those cheesy ID smiles.

There was a knock on the door, and Homaj pulled Zhang out of the line of sight. After a few seconds, Iata looked in, saw they were safely out of sight, and waved two slim folders of documents.

Iata shut the door.

"You locked the machine?" Homaj asked. "You should bring it back in here, no chances."

There was another knock on the door, and Iata opened it just wide enough to admit a cart with said machine on the top.

"Are they ready?" Jalava asked from the hallway.

"Nearly. You should come in now."

Jalava slipped inside, glanced around, and did a double take. They swore softly as Iata shut the door, a self-satisfied smile on his face.

"Well, that's different," Jalava said, settling on scrutinizing Zhang. They cleared their throat, shrugged. "Uh, I told the others that it will be Iata and Zhang going out there, with Homaj coordinating from here. I discussed it with Iata, and we thought that best. Then, he'll have an easy continuity into... well, you."

Homaj nodded. "Good." He turned to Iata, took the offered documents and peered at them. Iata had printed names on them—Homaj hadn't bothered to name himself, because he'd known there wouldn't be time to make the documents after.

Tanarin Grier. And Zhang was Irisa Mardav. Well.

He handed Zhang's to her—she didn't look surprised, so she already knew the name. Maybe had picked it.

She did hold her document back up and point to the emergency contact info, which read:

Spouse: Tanarin Grier

Well, and that was another layer of difference. A couple wasn't always read as individuals, but a whole. And most people knew he usually preferred men and masc-presenting people. Zhang was not that.

He held up his own ID again and read that his birth world was Tiymal, not Valon. He squinted at the tiny printed province and city—okay, yes, he knew that accent. He shifted his thoughts and the cadence in his head accordingly. Rolled his shoulders to settle himself into this different person.

"I will not get used to this," Jalava said. They glanced at Iata. "Are you ready for—for your Change? What do I need to do?"

"Just watch me. I'll be out for a while. My breathing will be shallow, but it's not dangerous."

"If he overexerts again," Homaj said, "which is a possibility because it's not been enough time, and we don't have enough time, do what we did before. Use a quick heal patch. Iata—go slowly. Please. I know there's people who are going to want to meet with you, but we're still under lockdown, and it's your job right now to stay safe. My task is a rush, yours isn't as much. Just be safe."

Iata made a disaffected wave, one of Homaj's gestures, and smiled Homaj's sardonic smile.

Homaj rolled his eyes, much more in character with this new persona, and waved Iata toward the bedroom. He knew Iata wouldn't use his own bed but Homaj's, which was as well. It would be his for the next—however long.

"I'm changing the sheets," Iata called back. "You've Changed twice. Three times? They'll definitely smell." He didn't quite shut the bedroom door—Homaj and Zhang would still have to go out that way through the back corridors.

Zhang handed Homaj a lightweight pistol. "Strap it to your back."

She reached for her shoulder pack and pulled out another, much smaller energy pistol, which wouldn't hold more than a medium stun charge. This Homaj took and strapped to his wrist under his shirt and jacket. And finally, they both tucked slim knives into a thin sheath on the other arm, handle down for quick extraction. It wasn't nearly enough of an arsenal for what they might face, but their greatest weapon was that they might not need them at all, as no one would know who they were.

Jalava still hovered by the bedroom door. Homaj grabbed the large duffel and cosmetic mission case Iata had packed, and Zhang shouldered her own duffel on the opposite shoulder from her day pack, which Homaj was suspecting held more tactical gear. He waved Jalava into the bedroom.

"We enter the back corridors through here," he said. "And you need to see the entrance anyway. Wake Iata and get him inside if there's any sign of trouble. It's a genetic lock, but Iata's touch will be able to open it, even if he's in the middle of Change. We keep certain markers while Changing that it looks for. Otherwise, we can Change the DNA in our hand to trigger acceptance. The only person who can't Change for the locks is Tavven—they do have access here, and their genome must match entirely." Not even the Truthspeaker had access to the back corridors on his own. Which right now was a more comforting thought than Homaj would have liked.

Iata eyed him while bundling off the bedsheets, but didn't say anything. Homaj saw Iata's posture and movements already shifting toward his own.

Homaj touched the innocuous spot on the wall beside his bed and the panel slid aside. Bare light flicked on in the narrow corridor beyond.

Jalava leaned forward, peering in. "If Iata's unconscious, will I be able to get out? Is there an extra passcode or voice code?"

"No, not here. And yes, if you can lever up his hand and take him with you. All of the entrances in the residence are locked on either side. It's a bit of a maze and there are no maps, but going right from here will take you further into the residence and the other apartments, and going left will take you around to the stairs and the corridors that branch throughout the rest of the palace. If you go down far enough, there are tunnels that go out into the grounds, to the Adeium, beyond the grounds, and under the river into the city. That's how we're going."

It was a risk, telling Jalava this much, but Jalava had to know there was an escape route if no other options presented themselves. They were sworn to him now.

Homaj pointed to Iata, who was now refitting a sheet on the large bed. "You're sworn to me, Jalava, and when he's me, you're sworn to him."

Jalava nodded. They pressed their hand to their heart and briefly bowed their head. "Yes, Truthspoken." They glanced at the open panel doorway. "Thank you. Hope we won't need this."

"Go, Homaj," Iata said, pausing to let down his hair. "I'll be fine."

"I'll make sure," Jalava said, resting their hand on their holstered pistol. "Iata—let me go speak with the rest of my team, I'll be back in a minute. Don't go under or whatever you do until then. Um, Please."

Iata raised his brows at that last addition, but waved toward the bedroom door.

Homaj squeezed into the back corridor, Zhang behind him, and quietly shut the door. He waited until he heard the lock click back into place.

And then it was quiet. He might hear muffled voices from within if Iata was talking loudly, but just now he wasn't.

Homaj blinked several times. He was doing this. They were all doing this.

Zhang looked around, shoulders tense. As if she was just now realizing she was with a Truthspoken, too, and they were carrying out an intensely dangerous mission.

She looked up at him, and he was taller now than he'd been. She had to look up farther. "Truthspoken...?"

He held up a hand. "Tanarin."

She nodded, some of the purpose coming back into her posture. "Right. And I'm Irisa."

"You'll do fine," Homaj said in a low voice. "Just follow my lead. We'll be fine."

But it was by no means a promise. He couldn't promise that.

"We'll have to be quiet most of the walk down. The back corridors are sound-dampened, but bugs can pick up a lot, and we'll be going far from the relative safety of the residence wing."

She nodded again. "Okay. Lead the way."

28

RIVEREDGE

Riveredge is an excellent destination if you are new to Valon City. You will find many small shops, restaurants, and pubs along the river, as well as street performers and live music, and can rent hoverboats and other small craft to cruise along the waterfront.

— TRAVEL BROCHURE FOR THE RIVEREDGE
DISTRICT OF VALON CITY

I t took half an hour for them to wend their way down into the bowels of the palace, where more doors unlocked into a series of tunnels. Homaj led them to an underground garage with electric bikes—they each grabbed one, and then headed into another, wider tunnel that descended to run under the river and into the city. In another ten minutes, the tunnel ascended again, evened out, and ended in another tiny garage.

Zhang looked around her, and to the stairs on their left that went up into the dark. "Where are we? What district?"

"Under Riveredge. There's a pub up top, very busy place.

We come out in the bathroom." He grinned at her appalled look. "It's very effective camouflage."

"Does the pub owner know?"

"I am the pub owner."

"Oh, well." She held up her hands. "This is all out of my league." She lifted her duffel off the bike's rear rack and shouldered it again. "And no one will question the duffels?"

"It's a boating pub. People come here to and from day trips all the time. We'll drop them at a safe house in Gold before we start our search."

Homaj swept the hair out of his eyes. He wished Iata had picked a style that would let him keep it out of his face, but, no, this particularly impractical cut was popular in the city just now.

He swept back his hair again and just decided to incorporate the gesture. He waved toward the stairs, and they ascended.

They'd only climbed up one flight of stairs before they started to hear the thump of the pub's music. Another flight, and the thump grew louder and added the muted sounds of people. Homaj wished, for a fleeting moment, that he could join them. Just blend in and not have to think at all for a solid hour.

They reached another locked door, which he opened, up another short flight of stairs and then a hallway that looked like a service access. Homaj led them to another door, unlocked that as well, and pulled Zhang with him into a closet-sized room. Here, the noise was almost too loud to talk over.

He motioned to a narrow door in the wall. "The pub's on the other side."

"I didn't guess that."

Homaj snorted and leaned toward the door to press an access panel next to it. He checked the tiny indicator screen— there was no camera in the bathroom stall on the other side, but the motion sensors said the stall was empty, thank Adeius.

He pulled the door quietly toward him, but he hardly needed the stealth—the music was roaring, even in the bathroom. He heard voices—other stalls were occupied, people washing their hands in the sonics, people taking a drink or a breath away from the chaos. He darted through and locked the stall door, then ducked back into the closet and pulled the closet door to almost closed.

He said near Zhang's ear, "We need to make it look like we're lovers coming out of the stall, or else it will look weird with two people coming out with their duffels. Are you okay with that?"

In the dim overhead lights of the tiny room, she made a face. "Lovers how? Like do you want me to..." She motioned to her mouth, and then dubiously toward his.

"No, we don't have to. Muss up your hair." He scrubbed his hands through his hair, wincing as the styling went all to hell.

She did the same, trying to look up and see how bad it was.

He reached out. "May I?"

She nodded, and he carefully smoothed a few spots, teased up some others. The result was artfully mussed, enough that on the street they could easily tame it down.

"Me?" he asked, and after a moment's hesitation, she did the same.

"Is that enough?" she asked.

"We only need to be plausible. Breathe heavily coming out. Smile. Are you okay to hold my hand?"

"It's only a hand," she said, and took the hand he offered.

She took a breath, looking nervous. "Okay. Okay, they definitely didn't teach this in Guard training. And—dare I even ask how you know all this? Is it normal for Truthspoken to know all this?"

"If you're nervous—actually, do this anyway—self-narrate. In your mind, narrate as if you are Irisa. This is Irisa's story, not yours."

Zhang pulled a face. "I'll...try. It's weird. You do that?"

He smiled, a little crooked, a little sour. "Always." He pulled the door open again and slipped backward, pulling her with him, crashing deliberately into the stall door to rattle it.

He moaned, raking his shirt with his own hand, banging his elbow.

Zhang bit her lip, looking embarrassed, trying not to laugh. She let out a little, "Ohhh," which might not have been loud enough to matter, but he appreciated the effort all the same. Homaj grinned at her and banged his back into the door again.

"The hell, people!" someone shouted, banging on the stall next to theirs. "This isn't a hotel!"

Homaj motioned to the door into the closet, which was still open, and Zhang pulled it shut by the coat hook on the wall. Homaj strained to hear the soft click of the latch catching. A tiny light in the coat hook gave a small flash, little more than an errant reflection. Locked.

"Ready?" he mouthed.

She nodded.

29

EVENING AIR

Can you imagine a life without Change? Can you even imagine how dull that life would be?

— VENORAM RHIALDEN, IALORIUS IV
(FICTIONALIZED) IN THE BIOPIC *VENORAM IV:
THE LIFE OF AN IALORIUS*

Homaj pulled the stall door open, forcing a flush into his cheeks, baring his teeth in a grin, and drew Zhang out after.

Someone in the busy bathroom gave a loud hoot.

Homaj made a diva pose and wave and pulled Zhang out into the pub's noise before anyone could hear her trying to suppress her snorting laugh.

No one in the pub, absolutely no one, gave them more than a passing glance. They were through, duffels and all, and out in the street in minutes.

The evening air was cool but not cold—their jackets were enough, though later in the night they'd need to dig into their bags for warmer gear. The sunset peaked through the mix of high-rises and ground level buildings, casting golden light on the walls of windows.

Homaj went to let go of Zhang's hand, but she held tight. She was still grinning, too wide. Her pulse too fast beneath his touch.

Ah. He knew that state. Feeling entirely too giddy on a mission—nervous but knowing he could not fail. Trying not to laugh at the ridiculousness of acting in real life.

So he held her hand while he pulled out a throwaway comm he used for city trips and called an aircab.

Zhang shivered, and he wrapped an arm around her, pulling her close. She leaned against him, her arm tight around his back.

The cab descended, and the door folded up with a soft whine. They piled into the single row of seats—he'd ordered a cab for two—and sat close as the cab lifted and banked toward Gold District.

Zhang opened her mouth. Did she understand it wasn't safe to talk here? He squeezed her hand.

But she gave him an admonishing look. Yes, yes she did.

"Sorry," she said. "I'm cold. We packed—we packed warmer coats, right?"

He wasn't entirely sure what was in the bags, but of course Iata wouldn't have neglected that.

"Car, temperature up three degrees," he said.

The aircab's heaters kicked on and Zhang sat back, breathing deliberately. She slowly shifted away from him. She still didn't let go of his hand, though, and she didn't have to. They were, technically, married.

Homaj sat back, stretching out his legs. He'd gained six centimeters in his Change, along with the added muscle. He didn't change his height that often—he found the shift in perspective disorienting enough to trip him up. But he'd felt that was needed here.

Zhang sat back, too.

"So, do you like the city?" he asked, because lovers in an aircab were expected to talk. Because anomalies were always recorded and reported both to the palace and those who'd pay for such information, including the Municipal Guard. Including anyone else.

"It's...it's..."

She was nervous. She was thinking too hard.

He smiled down at her. "Hey, Risa, it's fine."

Her eyes widened at the shortened form of "Irisa," or maybe the warmth in his tone, in his eyes. She gave a feeble smile.

"I'm just...I'm just tired." She pushed her hair back to cover the silence, looked out the window. "Oh, hey, there's the Nahman Building."

A little forced, but better.

"Yeah?" He leaned to look out. He'd seen the tower in its kilometer-high spiral, checkered with aerial gardens, a hundred times up close. He still looked at it in wonder now. "Oh, wow. I mean, do those plants have enough oxygen up there?" A ludicrous question. A touristy question.

"I...don't know? Maybe?"

He needed another tactic, this wasn't working.

But then Zhang seemed to relax. She settled back, looking around out the front and to his side. A faint smile on her lips, a real smile.

She squeezed his hand this time, and the look she gave him was open and fond, the kind of look you give a friend.

His breath caught. He knew what she was doing—she wasn't acting, exactly. She was incorporating him, this version of him, into her reality. As a friend.

He smiled back—not the lover's smile this time, but with his own warmth.

"I'm glad you're here," he said.

She didn't say it back, but her smile turned a few shades brighter.

30

THE SAFE HOUSE

Safety is carved between trees
Where the sky is open
But boughs still protect from
Rain.

— ARJUN NGUYEN, EXCERPT FROM HIS
POEM "RAIN"

The safe house was on a residential street in Gold District, a seventh-floor apartment in a nondescript building. Not well-off, not run-down. Exactly and appropriately ordinary.

Homaj glanced at his clothes, which were worn-in, but by no means rough, the style and cut just that bit above average. Was it too much for this neighborhood? They might need to hit a thrift shop and stock up if they were here for any length of time.

As they exited the cab, a person smoking a brill twig one door over from their building whistled in appreciation. Homaj didn't know if for him or for Zhang, but he felt Zhang stiffen beside him.

He turned and waved good-naturedly. "She's taken!"

"Are you?" the person called back. "What're your pronouns, hun?"

"He or they, and yeah, taken. But you know, I've got more love than I can give to just one person!"

The person cackled, drawing on their twig. "Okay, hun, come see me if you've got extra!"

Homaj didn't look back but waved again as they went inside. He might talk to the person later—someone who made a habit of sitting on the street would likely know what happened around here, or might be able to point him to people who would know.

Zhang was giving him an odd look, but she didn't say anything until they'd gone up the lift and he'd unlocked the door into their apartment.

Zhang looked around. The cleaning bots kept everything tidy, but though there was a sprawl of personal items and a few pieces of clothing on the couch and floor, the place had an air of abandonment.

Homaj ran his hands through his hair, grimacing as they came back greasy with hair product, then rooted in his duffel until he came out with the tube of lip gloss he always packed when on a mission. Zhang watched him, still not saying anything, aware that it wasn't yet safe.

Homaj uncapped the gloss, eased the actual gloss tube out of its shell, and squeezed the flexible shell to activate the mechanism inside. The shell gave the tiniest beep, and he slowly moved around the room with its ordinary, slightly worn furnishings, waving it at the walls, around any object that could hold a bug.

Zhang followed him to the kitchen, the bathroom, the one cramped bedroom.

He replaced the gloss, capped the tube. The apartment was wired to give off false habitation signals for the cleaning bots and utility monitors—he went to the control panel near the door and made sure they were working. They were, but the screen was a few dead pixels short of needing replaced.

As the last precaution, he checked the apartment's logs for any activity that wasn't the pre-approved motion of the bots. There had been two flies that had made their way in last week. A spider. Nothing beyond that.

It wasn't a hundred percent safe, but it was as safe as they were going to get outside his bedroom at the palace. Still, he motioned Zhang to the bathroom, which had no windows, and twisted the tube of gloss, setting it upright on the sink. It would give them a very small bubble of sound dampening and signal jamming.

He pulled Zhang close to the sink and toed the bathroom door shut.

Then, for a moment, they just stood there, staring at each other.

And it was surreal, wasn't it? He'd never been on a mission before with someone that wasn't Truthspoken or a blood-servant.

"Can we...talk?" she asked.

"Yes. But quietly, and only here, and only when this is on. And no names. We use the names we've been using. No specifics."

Her gaze flicked between his eyes, her brows knit. But she nodded.

"Are you okay?" he asked. "I know this can be a strain."

She shrugged. "I'm fine. I'm—nervous. I'm not used to this."

"You're doing fine."

She tilted her head. "Why banter with that person outside? Are you actually going to sleep with them?"

He raised a brow. "I'm not opposed to that, if that's what you're asking."

"No, I—"

"I've been everyone, of every class. You don't have to protect me from ordinary people."

Her cheeks flushed. "That's not what I mean."

Shit. His emotions were all knotted up inside of him, and he wasn't reading her as well as he might.

He leaned against the sink. "No, I don't intend to sleep with them, but flirting is useful. They know I don't mean it. Doesn't mean they won't think the banter is fun. We need informants on the ground."

Zhang held up her hands. "Okay. I just—"

"If you're worried, I won't ask you to do that—flirt, I mean. With other people. Not more than what we had to do in the pub, and I'm sorry for that."

Some of the tension left her shoulders. And there, that was what she'd been asking.

"Okay, good. Because I'm ace, that's just not what I'm good at."

He exhaled slowly, nodded. "Tell me if you're ever moving past your limits, or if I'm pushing you too far. Signal me—we didn't set a signal before, but we should now." He rubbed beside his mouth. "Like this. I haven't seen you make that gesture naturally. I'll watch for it." She repeated it, nodded. She was still watching him.

"Are *you* okay?" she asked, an echo of his own question.

"I—"

Why would she think that? Yes, he was a little off, but not enough to not do what he needed to do. He was sure. He had no choice.

"I—" He looked at himself in the splotchy bathroom mirror. He looked fine. His teal hair was a little mussed, but that only added to the appeal.

"I—" So why was his throat tightening, the words catching? Why did he suddenly need to grab for the edge of the sink, his balance gone, why did the room seem like it was tilting off-axis? He sent his awareness through his body, looking for what needed healed. But his pounding heart jangled his sense of himself.

Zhang caught his arm before he stumbled. "Hey. I'm here."

31

RELEASE

It all takes a toll. You don't realize how much until it's all there, bending you over so far that you're a breath from breaking. And yet you must go on.

— HOMAJ RHIALDEN, SERITARCHUS IX IN A
PRIVATE LETTER, NEVER SENT; AS QUOTED IN
THE CHANGE DIALOGUES

Zhang helped him sit on the edge of the tub. Panicked, Homaj reached up and snatched the lip gloss tube off the counter and set it next to him on the lip of the tub. They were still within its small bubble of safety.

He raked a hand through his hair again, and that was an annoying gesture to have incorporated into this persona. He felt a wobbly sense of ungroundedness that he hadn't felt on a Change mission in a long time. He didn't want to be this person right now, he didn't want to be Tanarin Griel. He wanted to be back at the palace, he wanted to grab the Truthspeaker's lapels and scream into his face until he spoke the actual truth. *What did you do to my sibling? Did you kill my parents?*

He was shaking and he couldn't stop. Why couldn't he stop? He'd been fine a minute ago.

Zhang sat on the cold edge of the tub beside him. "May I?" she asked, and stretched her arm behind his back, but didn't touch.

He shrugged, and she wrapped her arm around him.

He felt her presence solidify his own, and the shaking got worse. And now he was gasping for breath.

"I lost one of my parents a few years ago," Zhang said. "I went for two days without it hitting me hard enough to knock me down. I was in the middle of tests to get into the Palace Guard, and I knew I had to keep my shit together, so I did. I know how bright my eyes looked. I know how big my smile was. I know it was absolute hell. And I know we have to go back out there and find out what happened, find your sibling, but you have to let yourself feel what happened this morning right now, even if a little bit, okay? I don't know how Truthspoken normally handle stress or grief, but you're not handling it."

"I was...f-fine," he said through chattering teeth. "T-till you said s-something."

"You convinced yourself you were fine, and that's different. But it's okay. I'm here. It's healthy. It's okay."

He slanted her a glance. Was she being condescending?

No, he decided. And her sincerity, her earnest wish to help him, only made her words hit deeper.

He wanted to scream. Instead, he closed his eyes and just let his body tremble. He might be able to wrestle his muscles back under control, but his mind was glitching so badly that he wasn't sure he could reach a trance right now. He just—

His parents were gone. They were gone. And—and —everyone.

Vatrin might be gone. And Eyras, their bloodservant. His father's bloodservant, Omari, was gone. His father's guards. All people who'd been part of his life on a daily basis. All people who'd always just been there. Just—everyone.

And the Truthspeaker, who should be his ally, who should be helping him and keeping him safe, might be working against him.

And he couldn't think past all that lack. He couldn't see anything past that lack.

He gasped, and then came the sobs, convulsions he tried to shove down but that ripped through his body.

Zhang held him. She rubbed his back, she held his face as he sobbed into her shoulder.

He didn't know how long it was before he sat up again, gasping for breath. His whole body felt wrung out. He'd soaked through his clothes. But his mind wasn't glitching as hard. He was able to think past...past all of that.

Homaj sniffed hard, feeling heat rush to his face. He didn't have the energy or will to stop it.

Zhang only gave a tired smile. She got it. He sensed she really did get it—and that was a new feeling, anyone getting anything in his life.

"Food or nap?" she asked.

"I—"

Oh Adeius, his mind wasn't going to get stuck again, was it?

But he sniffed himself and wrinkled his nose. "Shower. Then food. Then—out."

He didn't want to go back out there tonight. He wanted to sleep. His body was drained—he'd made three Changes today, and that took its toll. A Change trance might look like sleep, but it used energy, and it didn't give much back.

Zhang was studying him, looking like she wanted to say something but was weighing the wisdom of it.

"Spit it out," he said.

"Will going back out tonight really make the difference?" she asked. "You're exhausted. I'm exhausted. We can push ourselves, but this doesn't feel like the sort of thing that you want to do without having your whole mind, right? Or your whole strength. We don't know who we're up against."

But they probably did. And a Truthspeaker's mind and resources definitely weren't something to be matched at half-capacity.

"A nap, then," Homaj said. "Shower, food, then a nap—no more than an hour."

"Two."

"One and a half. No more. Va—my sibling is still out there."

She gave him a troubled look, but nodded. "Then we'll find them. We know at least they're not here, right? Not in this safe house."

"Right."

He stood, wincing as his spine cracked. "Shower. Then food, then a very short nap, then out again. I want to find my sibling yet tonight."

Because there was a lot he could do, even at half strength. And he couldn't lose any more family that night, not if he had a chance of stopping it.

32

WAKING UP

> *Bloodservants are still royalty, and I think a lot of the nobility often forgets that. It surely makes a bloodservant's movements much more convenient.*
>
> — JABARI MORAEN, AS QUOTED IN *THE TRUTHSPOKEN SYSTEM: A VARIED ANALYSIS*

Iata sat up slowly, his whole body aching, his throat tight and far too dry.

Jalava, near the bedroom door, started and came over. "I, uh...are you..." They fumbled a wave with their hands. "How should I address..."

"Truthspoken," Iata said quietly, in Homaj's voice. Which was...jarring. He'd been playing Homaj earlier but hadn't managed to nail the genetic likeness then. He'd been Homaj playing someone else. "Truthspoken, as you always do."

Jalava blinked, but caught the game. Nodded.

"I need water," Iata said, and turned toward the cabinet beside the bed.

"I—I have water—" Jalava held up a steel bottle.

"No, there's bottled water here, and energy bars—" His words were too raspy, and his mouth felt like it had been stuffed with rags. Iata fumbled the top drawer open, grabbed a bar in an unsteady hand. He reached down to open the lower cabinet.

"Let me, Truthspoken." Jalava came around the bed, crouching down to pull out two water bottles. They handed both up.

Iata opened one and drank slowly at first, then when it didn't threaten to come back up, drank the rest.

He held the empty bottle out to Jalava. Which was absolutely a thing Homaj would do, but he felt deeply galled doing it himself.

Iata slowly pushed back the sheets and levered himself out of bed. He hadn't been trained for this kind of drastic Change. He knew how to get to certain attributes, and he was certain he'd gotten most of it right, but he'd need to see a mirror and make any extra tweaks needed—after he ate. His legs felt wobbly, and he sat back down on the bed.

Jalava hovered with the empty bottle. Then set that on the nightstand cabinet and headed for the door. "You need food."

They brought a cooler in from the prep room, a spicy smell leaking even through the seals.

"Didn't want to wake you up with the smell," Jalava said as they opened it. They pulled out containers and utensils, setting them on the bed.

Iata reached for one—he didn't care what it was—and tore open the chef's seal, grabbing a spoon to dig in.

He finished two containers before he could think again and headed for a third.

Jalava still stood by the bed, watching him like an anxious parent.

Iata looked up and smiled. "Thank you."

"I—" Jalava stretched their hands.

And Iata had to make a quick decision. Play out this entire

time—however long it would be—completely as Homaj, or be Iata here, away from listening ears?

Homaj was the one with all the training. What Iata knew was enough to protect and work with the Truthspoken, but not all the nuances. He could read people and adapt himself as needed. He was excellent at acting within specific scenarios, but not in the long term. And certainly not impersonating someone else for any length of time.

He wouldn't have tried for this Change earlier if he didn't think he could do it, though, if he didn't think he could pull off the role. But here in this familiar room which wasn't his, in this body, panic coiled in his gut. He was a bloodservant. He wasn't supposed to *ever* be Truthspoken.

"Can you spot any difference?" he asked Jalava.

His voice was much better now, fortified with water and food. He ran his diction and inflections through his mind to try to find any differences from Homaj's but found none.

Jalava seemed to come to their own decision, too, because they pushed aside some of the food cartons and sat on the bed beside him. They studied Iata with a careful thoroughness that made his throat tighten at the kindness of it.

"There's something around the eyebrows, I think," Jalava said. "I don't know what it is, just a little bit different. Other than that—I don't know if I've known him this closely long enough to tell."

Iata nodded. He'd check that first in the mirror. "Thank you. Here—in this room and the prep room—please talk to me as I am. I'm Iata. But out there—" He nodded at the door.

"Right," Jalava said. They tapped at one of the food containers. "May I, while you're eating? I didn't eat much earlier."

Iata stuffed another bite, nodded as Jalava pried open the container and pulled another to themself as well.

"Can I ask you something?" they asked around a large bite. "And I don't mean to pry here, but I think, if I need to make decisions in all of this to protect you and the Heir, I need to know. How exactly do you, as a bloodservant, fit with the Truthspoken? You're not Truthspoken, but you can still Change. And I get that it's not as easy for you, but...well, you can."

Iata took his time opening a fourth container. Would Homaj begrudge him this truth? But Homaj had Zhang, for the moment, who seemed to have suctioned herself to his cause— Iata needed an ally in this as well.

"My line is a lesser branch of the Rhialden line. A service branch. We are distant cousins, if you will."

"Yes, so you're technically royal, and also a servant?"

Iata's shoulders tightened. "The term 'bloodservant' is meant to make people overlook us. I serve Homaj, but I'm not a servant. I'm a silent partner. I'm family." He closed his mouth on more. Jalava might have sworn to Homaj and technically that would include Iata in the general swearing, as an extension of Homaj's household, but this was intensely private business, and intensely secret.

But Jalava was also right that they needed to know how this worked so they didn't trip over it. Homaj had literally placed his kingdom in Iata's hands. Tavven would know he wasn't Homaj, but Tavven would have little power to stop any direct decisions or commands he made, not without giving him up, and he didn't think Tavven would do that. The Truthspeaker was a different matter, and Iata intended to stay the hell away from him. But in the day-to-day right now...he had the power of the Truthspoken Heir and interim ruler in his hands, and Homaj trusted him to use it wisely.

Adeius, that was terrifying. And also sent a jolt up his spine.

He couldn't say he'd never wondered. Being around so much power, knowing he had the capacity for it, but knowing that this life was always out of reach. Never his place. Always and only his cousin's.

"What you need to know," Iata said, "and what I think

you're after, is that yes, when I'm Homaj, I am absolutely Homaj. I know him well enough to be reasonably sure what he would decide—it's been a long time since he's seriously surprised me with anything."

"So you're like a shadow brother," Jalava said.

Iata's brows flicked up. Jalava did see more than they let on. "Something like that, yes."

33

SHADOW BROTHER

> *Bloodservants are raised alongside the Truthspoken they will serve in the future. They grow up as foster siblings—one always destined to serve, one to rule. But the bond, the loyalty, is supposed to be unshakable.*
>
> — IATA RHIALDEN, AS QUOTED IN *THE CHANGE DIALOGUES*

Iata and Homaj had been children together, Iata just shy of two years older. They'd grown up as near to like as unequal siblings. They'd trained together. Homaj was the only brother Iata was likely to know.

Iata's jaw clenched, and it took effort to relax it again. Why should Adeius have mandated that the Truthspoken have all the responsibility, and the bloodservants none of the glory? Either way you looked, the system wasn't fair.

His part, as bloodservant, was vital. His role was to steady Homaj, to help keep him safe, to manage his affairs so Homaj could fulfill his duties as a Truthspoken. To not let him self-isolate or lose himself to a role. To help him prepare. To help him, if it ever came to that, to rule. His whole life was wrapped around Homaj's. Every life he lived in his limited capacity for Change was still centered around Homaj and Homaj's missions and goals, not his own.

So where was Iata? What was his life? It certainly wasn't his at this moment.

"Sorry," Jalava said, "I didn't mean to upset you."

Iata shrugged, making the thoughts roll off again. "It's fine. It's—everything is how it should be. This will all be fine."

But would it? What if Homaj didn't find Vatrin, or what if—what if, Adeius forbid, Homaj didn't come back? Iata would be alone. He'd have no one, no one at all in this palace, wearing Homaj's face, with vipers all around him. With the Truthspeaker, who he was fairly certain would do his utmost to make Iata a puppet, as Homaj had said.

Iata had to let the thoughts roll off again. He had to stay focused—absolutely had to. This was the hardest role he'd ever attempted, and he couldn't pull it off less than flawlessly.

He pulled himself back to his center. Said around a mouthful of sweet roll, "I'm going to call a meeting with the heads of military. I need to know what they know, and we need more eyes on this than just you and the Palace Guard."

Jalava hesitated before asking, "Do you have authority—"

Iata shifted fully into Homaj's bearing, raising his brow in that distinctly indifferent sneer.

Jalava sat back, nodded. "Of course you do."

They hesitated again, watching him. Watching much more openly than they would have if he was actually Homaj.

"Is it...weird? I mean, you don't do this often, right? You're not Truthspoken. What's it feel like to be someone else?"

Iata rolled his eyes. "It feels like being me. It's just a different narrative. If it weirds you out, think of me like—like his identical twin."

That, he decided, was a framing he needed as well. Despite

what he wanted Jalava to think, it wasn't quite like being himself. He'd just given Homaj's thoughts, not his own. Iata the bloodservant didn't have all the training to rule a kingdom, not on his own.

But he had to act like he did. He had to convince himself that he did, or none of this would work.

He finished his last container, got off the bed. "I'm going to the prep room—I have to make sure my appearance is perfect. Please—"

Homaj wouldn't say please. Well, or at least not often.

He tried again. "Call General Abret and Admiral Laguaya. Meet in my sitting room in one hour. Oh—have the extra guards that Tavven promised arrived?"

Jalava looked a bit bewildered at his swift shift from his own personality to Homaj's. But though he'd said the bedroom was a safe space, he was about to publicly be Homaj. He needed to think like Homaj. He needed that narrative to be dominant.

He had to look the Truthspeaker in the eyes, when he did see him, because he knew he couldn't avoid him forever, or even long. He had to do his best to show with absolute certainty that he was, in fact, Homaj Rhialden, not Iata byr Rhialden.

Iata turned back to Jalava. "My callback. Truthspoken have this thing we can do—being a person in truth. It will legally make me Homaj, not just in appearance or mannerisms. If I do that, I will assume his personality completely, not just from the outside, but for a short time, believing I am him. Whatever I say or do in that state is as binding as when it's him, and I might need to do that at times here."

He wasn't so much worried about the legality of things—if anyone realized a bloodservant was masquerading as the Heir he'd be screwed anyway—as much as what he'd do around the Truthspeaker. Aduwel Shin Merna was one of the few people who could know he wasn't Homaj on sight. But if he was Homaj in truth around the Truthspeaker, would that be enough to shift that perception? Would it be enough to hold whatever he did as unassailable even by the Truthspeaker?

"That sounds...terrifying," Jalava said, and Iata didn't think they meant for him.

He shrugged it off.

"So, my callback, if I submerge too deeply and you need to pull me out, is this." He rattled off a phrase from a military history text, and Jalava, frowning in concentration, repeated it back until they got it exactly.

Iata hesitated, then shrugged. All in. "And if that doesn't work—it should, but if it doesn't, or you're in a situation where you can't speak to me, do this. May I?" He reached for Jalava's wrist, and Jalava held it out.

He gripped Jalava's wrist with a particular series of light pressures. That one took a bit longer for Jalava to learn and be able to repeat back correctly. And then another few minutes as Jalava tried the first sequence again and got a few words wrong. They couldn't afford mistakes here, not even a little.

Jalava was looking dyspeptic but determined by the time they both headed back into the prep room. They met Iata's eyes as he headed for the closet.

Jalava gave the smallest nod.

Iata felt a swell inside his chest, something he wasn't at all used to. Jalava wasn't nodding to him for Homaj's sake, but his own. That reaching out just now, that sharing of such an intensely secure state secret as a bloodservant's personal callback, had forged something between them that Iata wasn't sure Homaj would like.

Well. Homaj wasn't here—Iata was. And for the moment, he was Homaj.

Iata ducked into the closet and began sifting through clothes, looking for what would best suit a Truthspoken Heir as the interim ruler of the kingdom.

34

THE CRASH SITE

> *Jewelry, ident cards, and other small personal items are typically sorted out of street debris, genetically matched, and returned to their owners. However, non-standard items that may be mistaken for street debris, such as rocks, non-worked glass, and other items, may be sorted into waste processing. Please be sure to secure your belongings as you walk the streets of Valon City, as we are not responsible for their safe return if dropped.*

> — PUBLIC ANNOUNCEMENT FROM THE VALON
> CITY MAINTENANCE COMMISSION

Homaj stood on the street corner and ran his hands through his short undercut hair. He hadn't put in any more product after his rest, and his hair wasn't as slick, but that was fine. That wasn't the look he was going for here.

Zhang stood nearby, watching everything in the dimming evening light. There wasn't much to see. A slight darkening of the pavement in one spot. A few pieces of glass and plastic still scattered around the edges of the crash site.

And it had rained while he'd been resting. Dammit. Adeius, but he should have just powered through. There might have been...something. Something more to go on than a few tiny shards of breakage from a shot-down cab with a murdered high-profile occupant.

But the Municipal Guard had cleared out the area, because this was the Financial District and no one who made enough money to have a say in police matters wanted the wreckage of a murder on the street. This intersection was just inside Financial District, and while it wasn't the most affluent center of the district, the streets were clean, the cars that passed on the more expensive side, the pedestrians mostly well-dressed.

All that was left of the wreckage of Lord Xavi Birka's aircar, all that told any murder had happened here at all, was that dark-ish spot and glass fragments stuck in various crevices that would be picked up by the detail bots at the end of the day.

Zhang came back to him, smiled briefly, and entwined her hand with his. She leaned toward his ear.

"Better get moving. There's someone watching across the street."

He nodded, returning her smile as he squeezed her hand, and didn't look across the street.

They'd known this site would be watched. They'd been here less than five minutes and had worn matching gawking tourist expressions. There were a few other people milling about doing the same. The crash, of course, would have been on all the various feeds, and some people had their comms out, recording the site.

Nothing about him said anything but curious bystander, and Zhang—well, at least she'd relaxed a bit more into her role.

He met her eyes, calculated if he should kiss her cheek to

try to sell the couple angle, and then decided on giving their joined hands a light swing instead.

"I think I've seen enough, not really worth the coming out. Are you ready? What was the next thing you wanted to see?"

"Mm. Uh—" She pulled out her comm, a temporary model they'd grabbed from the safe house, and peered at the screen. "I'd like to go see the lobby of Threefold Tour, the antigrav waterfall."

He nodded. "Well, can we get something to eat first?" Threefold wasn't on their way back to Gold District but on the other side of Financial. "I saw a small café this way, looked like it was good food, and it's still in walking distance."

He didn't want to hail a cab back from Financial. A cab going from Financial to Gold District could trigger alerts just now. Much better to walk back a ways into Gold and then call a cab.

"All right," she said. And added, "Sweetie."

Oh, Adeius. No. No, she was not selling that at all.

He grinned like the name was a joke, and she grinned back uncertainly.

It was getting weird. Zhang was getting better at this playacting, yes, but...but. He wasn't really attracted to her, she wasn't his type at all. He knew she wasn't attracted to him. They didn't have that kind of chemistry to sell the story.

But they'd shared an intimacy in the bathroom of the safe house, when she'd held him as he'd bawled his eyes out, and he couldn't think about that too closely now without tears threatening to well again.

He was still more fragile than he'd like.

Some barrier between them had shifted, though, and he didn't know where the lines were with her just now.

And his thoughts were straying too far from center. He was still tired from his nap which hadn't been enough, on this street thick with drowsy, post-rain humidity. At a sight where his sibling's lover had been shot down, not even a day ago.

Outside of the palace, his fears felt like they were unraveling into something he couldn't control.

But he didn't wish for a moment he was back there just now. Maybe things felt more real out here, more raw, but in a far different way than they had there.

Zhang shifted closer to him, their shoulders brushing. He didn't know if she needed that extra security right now, if she was trying a different way to sell their role as a tourist couple, or if she'd seen his escalating spiral. Was it showing on his face, in his posture?

Another panicked moment had him checking every detail of his persona and adjusting a few.

They strolled back toward Gold District, the buildings still upper-scale enough that they weren't yet out of Financial. He angled them toward the café he'd spotted earlier when they'd walked in. And maybe they should stop and eat. They'd grabbed nutrition bars on their way out earlier, galled at how long they'd both slept, and his stomach was growling now.

But he didn't have time to eat. He'd already wasted so much time, and with nothing to be found at the aircar crash, no clue that would lead him to the next clue and the next, he'd have to start checking every safe house in the city by rote, and then go from there. Maybe try to get some information from the underground, but that might require another Change. Another identity.

He had no idea what he was doing. How would his sibling have handled this? How would...how would his father?

His throat swelled again, his eyes burned, and he was having trouble smoothing it away. He should be able to just will this emotion away.

They should just call a cab now, before he made a spectacle

of himself and became even more suspicious than Zhang's awkward performance.

He was just pulling out his comm to call the cab when ahead of them, across the street, a person drew his eye. He'd seen them before, two streets back. Femme, petite, thick brown hair in a loose bun. And...there was something off about the way they were moving, almost like—

Homaj stopped abruptly, which was something he absolutely knew not to do, not when he was trying to blend in, but he couldn't help it. The person had been *flickering*. And he was sure they weren't a holo—it wasn't that kind of flickering. More like an awareness of them in his mind that brightened and dimmed.

A Green Magicker.

35

THE RISK

I know this seal is for my protection. But it also marks me as a target.

— ANONYMOUS MAGICKER, AS QUOTED IN
THE POPULAR ZINE *STAND HERE*

When Homaj stopped, Zhang stiffened and stopped, too, looking around. Being absolutely too obvious about it.

Homaj cursed under his breath, taking her arm again and walking on, which was a far less suspicious thing to do than gawk all around them. Except in this instance, he realized a beat too late, he should have just played it up. Pointed out some random detail they could both gawk at. Adeius, he wasn't an amateur. He should know better.

Not that any of that would have mattered—if that magicker was high enough ranking to be able to turn themself just barely invisible like that, the magicker could certainly know he was Truthspoken on sight. Maybe not which Truthspoken, but, well. Just now, there was an extremely limited number of Truthspoken.

It took a monumental effort not to run—his first thought was to run away. And then the rest of his thoughts caught up, and he had to restrain himself from not running across the street right there to track this magicker down. Ask them why they were here, what they wanted, why they'd so obviously wanted him to see them.

The magicker turned down a side street on the next block and walked out of sight.

"Shit," he said.

"What?" Zhang hissed as he found an opening between ground cars and they darted across the street. So much for not drawing attention to themselves.

"Not here."

He held her hand loosely as they quick-walked toward the end of the block after the magicker. Then rounded the corner.

He looked for the person—

There. Just about to go around the building at the end of the short street. Well, they'd wanted his attention, so they weren't about to let him just pass them by, were they?

The Green Magickers were no friends of the Municipal Guard, or friends of the Truthspeaker, for that matter. It had been an immense gamble to let the First Magicker hold his hand and affirm his sincerity, but was that about to pay off?

What did this magicker know, that they were willing to risk flagging him down? Him specifically—so of course they knew who he was. Or at least suspected either a Truthspoken or a bloodservant. Someone who could Change.

On the other side of the building, an aircar sat waiting. Not a cab, but a slick, private affair. The person, the magicker, waited until he approached to wave open the door.

Zhang slipped her hand from his, reaching for the small of her back where one of her pistols was holstered. "That's the person I saw at the crash site," she said in a low voice. "They were watching us. We're not getting in that car."

"We are," Homaj said calmly. He didn't think Zhang had seen this person was a magicker. He certainly wouldn't have without the magicker deliberately flickering. Even still, it would have been a detail easily overlooked in the bustle of the street —it hadn't even been that much of a flicker, but his eyes were trained to pick out any parts of the pattern that weren't what they should be.

He eyed the magicker—they didn't have the typical visible green aura that all magickers had, though he did know that some could dim their auras on command. Still, he saw no aura at all. The person didn't have a mandatory rank seal on their cheek, or a scar from its removal, either, though it was supposed to be difficult to survive its removal without the First Magicker's deactivation keys. Which she almost never used, because a magicker not having a seal was a capital offense. This was certainly not an untrained magicker who'd just manifested their abilities, not if they could flicker that deliberately. Not if they could pick him out in a crowd, Changed as he was.

So had this magicker had their rank seal removed somehow, or had they never had it implanted?

He gathered to step into the car, but froze again, his heart kicking up.

Had he read the situation wrong? Had that been a holographic illusion after all, meant to mimic a magicker's abilities and catch his eye? Was this an assassination attempt on him?

But then how, by Adeius, had the person known who he was? No, that hadn't been a hologram. He was sure of that. Mostly sure.

And why were the magickers risking everything by showing him an unsealed Green Magicker? He was the interim ruler, and an unsealed magicker was a breach of treaty between the magickers and the Kingdom of Valoris. With this knowledge, he could end them. The former Seritarchus certainly would have —but what the First Magicker had read in him must have told her that Homaj wouldn't do that.

So they both had risk here. There was mutual danger and mutual distrust.

He stared into the magicker's eyes, and they stared back. They could be reading his emotions, maybe even his thoughts, from that look. But he knew how to read people, too. He saw determination, self-possession, and yes, fear. The magicker's expression was guarded, but not insincere.

And this magicker had no gestural markers he could detect that would indicate them being another Truthspoken or blood-servant—whether someone he knew, or someone with the genetic capacity who was illicitly trained in Change, as some nobles had tried across the long Rhialden dynasties. Usually to the utter ruin of their families when the ruler called them out. Or just quietly destroyed them.

He was jittering. The magicker ducked into the car first, fully in sight, their hands in sight. Well, so they were going to do this the right way.

Zhang was so tense beside him he thought she might snap.

"Tanarin," she said, using his persona's name. "Do you know this person?"

"Of course I do," he said, and she relaxed a fraction before tensing up again, shooting him a look that spoke volumes about what she thought about that lie.

He was in no fit state for any of this. She was right, he shouldn't get in that car.

But he also knew he was going to anyway. Answers, some kind of answers, were in that car. And when he had so very few answers at all, he judged it worth the risk.

36

TRUTH

Sometimes risk analysis is as simple and as complicated as taking years or decades of training and distilling them to a feeling in the moment.

— HOMAJ RHIALDEN, SERITARCHUS IX IN A
PRIVATE LETTER, NEVER SENT; AS QUOTED IN
THE CHANGE DIALOGUES

Zhang's lips were drawn tight as she watched him climb into the plush interior of the car, and she quickly got in after. Would she feel differently about the risk if she knew this person was a magicker? Magickers couldn't do violence. But Green Magickers weren't friends of the Palace Guard, either, and the anti-magicker sentiment ran deep within the palace.

The front seats had been turned to face the back, and they all sat there, staring at each other in tense silence.

The magicker pressed a control on the door beside them and the aircar lifted with near-silent grace.

"I'm Lodri," they said, "she/her." She took in Zhang, but then settled on Homaj. She held out her hand.

He reached to take it, but Zhang clamped her hand on his wrist.

"What are you doing?" she hissed.

"She's a magicker. Magickers tell truth best through touch. They share truth by touch, too. I'll know if she means us any harm." Zhang's gaze flicked to Lodri's bare cheek. "She's—"

"Under my protection," Homaj said quietly, slipping into his own accent.

Zhang reared back. "It's not safe to talk about—"

"This is a private car, occupied by an unsealed magicker. There's going to be some identity verification going on here. It's safe, or we're all at risk."

"But—"

He didn't truly know it was safe. But it was another gamble he had to take. If the Green Magickers were possibly offering help, he needed that help.

He clasped Lodri's hand.

"I like the butterflies," Lodri said, smiling a little as she nodded at the wing tattoos beside his eyes.

He blew out his breath. That wasn't the opening salvo he'd expected. "Thanks."

"I'm Lodri ver Aminatra," she said. "Green Magicker, sixth rank."

Homaj didn't react more than raising his brows but Zhang wasn't as well-trained.

"Sixth?" she blurted. "That's almost as high as the First—"

"True," Homaj said softly, feeling that same feeling he'd felt from the First Magicker earlier. The sense of safety, of surety. It was, he was coming to realize, the sense of the truth.

"And you are?" Lodri asked.

He didn't hesitate. He couldn't afford to. "Homaj Rhialden."

Was he just condemning Iata at the palace? Adeius. Adeius, he hoped his gut feel with this was correct. If she was sixth rank, unsealed as she was but obviously not untrained, she'd have to be close enough to the First Magicker to be trusted.

Or else, working for his family's enemies.

He still didn't think so. He was betting his life it wasn't so.

"That absolutely goes no further than this car," he said.

Lodri shifted. "I am only the second magicker who knows."

At his start of surprise, she went on, "The First Magicker read your intent at your bid to rule. It goes no farther than she and I. You have both our words that it won't."

True. He felt that ringing sense of truth, as she must have felt when he'd said his name.

So then she had been sent by the First Magicker. Check. Could he trust that? Could he afford not to? What had he gotten himself into enlisting the First Magicker's help earlier?

Dawning hope spread through his chest, and though he tried to quash it, it broke through all the same.

He hadn't thought to ask the magickers for help with finding Vatrin. Magickers and Truthspoken rarely intermingled their causes—magickers rarely worked with anyone who wasn't one of their own, with good cause.

Lodri eyed Zhang, whose face was pinched with concentration. Then she held out her other hand to Zhang.

Zhang stared down at it as if it was diseased.

Homaj felt something else creep into his touch with Lodri. Unease? Annoyance?

"I need to verify your sincerity," Lodri said.

"You don't have to," Homaj said to Zhang. But everyone in that car knew that was a lie, magicker or not. There was too much at stake.

Zhang took Lodri's hand, bracing herself. "I'm absolutely loyal to Homaj Rhialden. He has my oath."

Lodri searched Zhang's expression. And, with her magicker senses, Zhang's truth. She nodded.

"True," she said, and he felt the truth of Lodri's statement through her hand.

Something inside him that had been coiled too tightly eased. Homaj knew Zhang was with him, he trusted her as much as he could trust anyone right now. But that further verification eased the parts of him that didn't dare to trust, not all the way. He knew Human nature too well to trust anyone all the way.

Still holding Lodri's hand, he asked, "How did you find us? And why did you come after us?"

"We thought you might go to the crash site. You know some magickers can see Truthspoken? To me, your souls always have a sense of overlapping personalities. An added density, if you will."

He nodded. The ability was mostly among the higher-ranking magickers, and even then, Truthspoken could sometimes minimize exposure by going deep enough that the soul layering wasn't readily visible. But he hadn't been that deep.

"Will you be the Ialorius?" Lodri asked.

"That's not a question you get to ask," Zhang said. They both still held onto Lodri's hands—Zhang could feel what Homaj also felt—Lodri's sense of needing that answer from him.

"No, Seritarchus."

Zhang almost flinched—and he got it, he really did, this information was not easily given. But trust went both ways, and the magickers had a lot of reasons not to trust the Truthspoken.

Lodri weighed his answer and nodded. The magickers needed to know that he, with his ideas of Green Magickers, which were different than the former Seritarchus's, would carry that difference into the new rule. Having the same style of rule wasn't good there, but he thought she'd be able to read his intent behind choosing it, too. He didn't intend to use the same policies toward magickers that his father had. His having the First Magicker witness him was in many ways the start of that, though that hadn't been first on his mind when he'd done it, true.

He saw her hesitation as he churned through these thoughts, felt her mistrust of Truthspoken in general rising again. He needed to give more.

"When I was eighteen," he said, "my father sent me on a mission to Medrin IV, to see why a mining colony was on strike and holding their employers captive. We found out that many of the miners were the families of magickers who couldn't find work elsewhere, because they'd been cast out by their towns and neighborhoods. They were known to have harbored their family members, magickers who didn't go in to be sealed voluntarily. A few also had undocumented magics themselves, and they used those magics to strengthen the walls of the mines and a wall that the miners built to hold their employers inside. With air and food, of course, they were civilized. And they couldn't do harm."

He and Iata had both gone on that mission, Truthspoken and bloodservant. His role had been as a Navy lieutenant sent to investigate and given full executive powers to act. Iata's role had been as a petty officer who'd also had a family member who'd manifested Green Magics, and it was Iata who had borne the brunt of that mission. The conversations Iata had with the desperate miners, to understand what was going on—the details Iata himself had to make up about his own fictional family—had torn Iata apart. Homaj had been more than a little rattled, too, and furious that this had happened at all. That it had all gotten bad enough that the miners felt it necessary.

And the most infuriating thing was, after Homaj had ended the stalemate by making promises to improve conditions for magickers and their families, and to try to mitigate the prejudice against magickers or anyone related to them—when he'd taken the situation back to his father, it had been...nothing. Waved off as, "Oh, people will do what they do. We can't control the opinions of society."

Which absolutely wasn't true. How the Seritarcracy viewed magickers had a lot to do with how everyone else did, too.

Lodri nodded. "That incident is well known to us. As are the promises made. Will those promises be kept?"

He swallowed. Yes, he'd wanted to handle the magickers in a different way than his father, but he hadn't thought much farther than that. At that time, he hadn't had the power to do so.

Now, he hadn't yet had the time.

"Yes. They will absolutely be kept."

37

THE LONG TERM

Families of Green Magickers rioted today in Nimon Square, Blue District, Valon City, for the rights of magicker children to attend the same classes as non-magicker children. This riot followed a political protest of non-magicker parents saying magicker children can cheat by mind-reading the answers off their teachers and other students.

— NEWS REPORT IN THE POPULAR VID ZINE
VALON CITY SUNSHINE

Lodri let go of their hands. "This city is a big place. If you hadn't been at the crash site, I still might have found you. I can sense Truthspoken in around a thirty-meter radius around me—and no, that's not a normal ability. That also, please, does not leave this car."

Homaj swallowed. He hadn't known it was possible for magickers to sense a Truthspoken without a direct line of sight. That could be the entire reason she was unsealed, a measure of protection and maneuverability around the Truthspoken. And she'd just handed that deeply guarded secret to him.

They were no longer touching, but he could read her well enough through the subtle body language cues everyone gave off. And at her rank, she was almost certainly still reading him through their eye contact, or even just their proximity.

"I can help you find your sibling if they're still in the city," she said, "but we have to know where to start or there's no way we'll find anyone here. Do you know if they're still here? Do you know at all where they might be?"

Her whole bearing now was tense, her gaze intent on his. She was helping him look for Vatrin because he needed answers. And he needed, if there was a chance to save his sibling, to take it. She was offering this, with the First Magicker's blessing, not because she wanted Vatrin to rule, but because she didn't.

Vatrin had many plans for social reform in the kingdom and on the capital world of Valon. They wanted to lessen the immensity of the gap between the impoverished and those stranded onworld by debt or circumstances and the wealthy. They'd been working to ease some of the religious tensions between various sects of the Adeium and other minority religions among the people, both ancient to Valon and imported from various immigrant populations. They wanted to improve the schools and the hospitals and establish better education for the masses.

All of which were excellent goals. All of which their father the Seritarchus had been slow to move on. But Vatrin had never showed any particular interest in helping the Green Magickers. Vatrin had been known to publicly shy away from and criticize the magickers, in fact.

Lodri's aura, which until then had been absent, flared and crept brighter until the air around her was luminescent with emerald green.

"You made your bid to rule," she said. "And we have to make that clear—we are supporting *you* to rule. If Vatrin Rhialden is found, if they make a counterbid, we will still support you. You may call on our services to verify that Vatrin has been compromised and therefore unfit to rule. The Truthspeaker—and to lesser degree, I believe, the high houses and the General Assembly?—ultimately decide if there are two bids, but magicker testimony is upheld as law."

"You'd lie?" Zhang asked, aghast. And rightly so. Magickers were often called on to give the final deciding testimony in disputes.

"No," Lodri said shortly. "Vatrin is unfit. They will continue to make our people suffer. We will never verify them as fit to rule this kingdom."

"The Truthspeaker doesn't have to accept your testimony," Homaj said. "Neither do the high houses, most of whom are not partial to magickers who can read their motives. Yes, you're right that it's a mix of high house and General Assembly opinions that choose between bids, and that the Truthspeaker has the final say, but the Truthspeaker won't choose against the broadly general opinion of the high houses. Vatrin might still become the ruler if we find them."

Lodri sat back, squeezing her hands tightly together. He'd thought her younger, maybe in her early thirties, when they'd first stepped into the car. But her aura deepened the haunted look in her eyes, showing the lines around them. "We're asking you, in exchange for our help, to make sure that you become the ruler, Homaj Rhialden. I do want your word on that. You will not, under any circumstances, let Vatrin Rhialden become the ruler."

He couldn't promise that. He absolutely couldn't promise that. If Vatrin was alive—if his sibling was alive—they could make a counterbid, full stop. It was their right, their duty, even.

And they had the popular opinion of the people. He, the layabout court rake, did not.

He still didn't know where the Truthspeaker's place was in all this—Aduwel Shin Merna was sour, yes, but on what vector? Did he want to keep Vatrin alive, did he want to control Vatrin? Had he already killed them?

Could Homaj argue, successfully, that Vatrin's messed up place in all of this was cause enough for them not to rule, no matter if they were a victim? Homaj was certainly not the court favorite, not in his persona until now, not certainly in his public show of rage today. The people liked Vatrin and their social policies. They like the idea of change.

And Homaj—Homaj was aiming to be a new Seritarchus. Had he been wrong in that? Did the people need that Melesorie momentum of change, or the fluidity of an Ialorius?

Adeius, he wished he could comm Iata at the palace and know what was going on there. What was Iata uncovering, if anything? What the hell should he do, and how could they know what they were each doing wasn't contradicting the other?

He still didn't know who'd killed the Seritarchus, who had motive or means. He still didn't even know the Green Magickers hadn't been involved, though that was highly unlikely—the very nature of their magics made them deeply averse to violence. They didn't kill.

"I can't promise," he said. "I don't know enough yet. I don't know what's best, I don't know if Vatrin's hidden on their own" —what Speaker Ceorre had said earlier might still suggest that —"or if they're being held against their will. I don't, truly, know they're still alive."

That Lord Xavi Birka was dead was a good indicator of Vatrin not having gone into hiding willingly. But it wasn't the only factor in play, not even remotely.

Lodri considered him.

"I do promise," Homaj said, "that I will do everything I can to help the cause of the magickers. Everything in my power to do so. Whether that's as ruler or not."

"That will be significantly less if you're not," she said. But, she sighed. "I can't in good conscience keep you from finding lost family. Regardless of who that family is. I'm not as cold as that. Neither of us are."

He blinked at that "us." She and the First Magicker? Were they close? Mentor and student? Lovers? No—no.

He realized with dawning horror just what First Magicker Onya Norran had trusted him with. It was there, in subtle body language cues, there in her features, if also subtle.

Lodri was Onya's daughter, wasn't she?

38

WHAT I CAN

> *My magics are a part of who I am, though certainly not the most important part. I experience the world in a drastically different way than non-magickers, and I think that is beautiful.*

> — FIRST MAGICKER ONYA NORREN,
> INTERVIEWED IN THE POPULAR VID ZINE
> *VALON CITY SUNSHINE*

So the First Magicker had a hidden daughter, who'd manifested out of the public eye, and who was genetically predisposed to her mother's strength in magics. Green Magics might manifest randomly among the population, but once they did, they often continued to run in families.

Homaj considered Lodri's last words with this new context. "I'm not as cold as that. Neither of us are." Unspoken was the coda, "unlike the Truthspoken."

He let his breath out slowly.

That sentiment wasn't wrong. He'd been trained to make impossible decisions. To set the good of Valoris always, always above the good of any one person or group. The good of Valoris had always meant the good of the Seritarcracy.

What had that good of Valoris done to Lodri and her family? Did she even exist in documents? Was she a legal person at all? He hadn't known Onya had a daughter, much less had trained her. And he would have known that if it was in any way official.

Had his father known? He doubted it. They had managed to hide Lodri from the Truthspoken for all of her life—not in any way a small or easy feat.

And now here she was. Showing herself to him, telling him her name.

She'd come here offering to help him find Vatrin, the one person who could derail Homaj from ruling the kingdom. Homaj being the one Truthspoken who actually cared about helping the magickers have better lives, never mind that he didn't actually want to rule. That the thought of ruling this kingdom froze him to his core.

So what was the best course of action here? Find Vatrin, save that one person who might do a lot of good, but might ultimately harm the magickers? The one person who could get him off the hook of having to rule the kingdom. Homaj didn't like Vatrin, but that didn't mean he thought Vatrin would be a bad ruler. Well, mostly. He was certain, at least, that he might do worse.

Or, should he prioritize the magickers and possibly do harm by not letting Vatrin carry out their social reforms? Vatrin's plans had more hope for the masses. But it wasn't as if he couldn't carry out some of those reforms, too. More slowly, and in a different way if he was the Seritarchus. But did he have to be Seritarchus? Maybe he could be Melesorie, be what the people wanted right now. It wasn't his personality, either, but he could make it work, if it was what the kingdom needed.

He realized somewhere in there that he'd been assuming

this was his choice. That if he found Vatrin alive and well, he wouldn't just give everything back to his sibling by default. His sibling who really was the most qualified to rule, who was the Heir, who was trained for all of this, not him.

This was his choice.

And was he, truly, that confident that Vatrin could do better?

He let his breath out slowly. "I will do what I can. Everything I can."

He met Lodri's gaze again. And she nodded.

He sat back and looked away. He hadn't done everything he could before.

How many times had he, second Truthspoken and court rake, been at a party among "friends," who were just court hangers-on, and everyone was talking about the magickers as if they were the bane of society? He didn't participate in those insults, but he didn't stop the conversations, either. He would drink instead of laugh, but he wouldn't stop the laughter. He didn't want to take that stance, because Homaj Rhialden didn't take any stance but indifference.

Homaj could argue that he was still young, that he thought he'd have years before the Seritarchus was gone, that he'd never been the first Heir and had never thought he'd rule the kingdom. He could argue he was subtle and was planning to make social changes in the long term, but that would be a lie. He'd been bored. He'd been insufferable and defiant. Vatrin didn't like him either, not even in private, and he'd been pushing his parents away the last few years as well.

He could argue that wasn't him, that was just the persona he'd built for himself, and yes, that was true. But that personality hadn't come out of nowhere. And you didn't bury yourself in a personality for so long without taking on more and more aspects of it for your own.

Whatever else, he absolutely promised himself he'd do better. He had to do better, and be better.

And Adeius help him, he did have to find a way to rule, didn't he? He wasn't sure he trusted anyone else with this kingdom. Even Vatrin.

Maybe especially Vatrin. He didn't know his sibling as well now as he had when he was younger, but he'd never gotten along with Vatrin then, either. Vatrin was outwardly the kingdom's social savior. But Homaj knew better than anyone that the outside of a person could so easily be a lie.

Lodri pulled out a small tablet, fingers hovering over the screen. "Where to? We've been in a holding pattern over Gold District, but we can join the second or third tier traffic. If you don't know where to start, I can't guarantee I'll be able to find them, but I'll do what I can. I can sense through the buildings we pass, at least their street-facing areas, if they're large. We won't be able to take a standard search pattern without notice to the Municipal Guard, though."

Financial District or Gold District had been his first guesses. Still probably his best guesses. If they were going to be searching the city by brute force, best to get those districts done first.

"Gold first," he said. "Lord Birka was fleeing from Gold. Can you set a random line that covers all areas within your range? Doubling back on some, with logical pause points? And then we'll dip down for food or shopping or something along those lines. A pattern that won't trip the Guard. Does this car have those kinds of functions?"

She narrowed her eyes at the tablet, typing in commands. "Yes, and done." She looked out the tinted side window at the now night-lit city as they banked down into the streets again. Her aura flared an even deeper green, almost painful to look at.

"I'll search," she said. "You two decide what you're going to do if I find something."

39

CALCULATION

> *All is quiet on the border this year. The Kidaa haven't had any major movements, they haven't tried to overlap or speak with us in the yes/no maneuvering code. Is that, then, the hand of Adeius? Can we safely ignore our neighbors and get back to the business of shoring up our borders with other Human nations, which I fear are the much more pressing concern? Of course, the decision is up to Laguaya, and they'll always choose to hold every border as a potential battle stage.*

> — HIGH GENERAL BANAMAR ABRET IN A
> LETTER TO TRUTHSPEAKER ADUWEL SHIN
> MERNA

Iata strode with Jalava into Homaj's—well, for the moment, his—sitting room, where two of the most powerful people in the kingdom were already sitting in the wingbacks, waiting for him to come out. Their aides hovered nearby, attentive and nervous, though they hid it well.

Homaj as cynical court lounge-about was well known; Homaj as the future ruler of this kingdom was an unknown quantity. And Homaj had almost lost it at his bid to rule.

High General Banamar Abret in eir brown and green Army uniform and Admiral of the Fleet Dassan Laguaya in their blue and silver Navy uniform stood as he entered. They both bowed with the precise, no-nonsense form of the military.

For the briefest moment, Iata panicked, his neck prickling with sweat. He couldn't do this. He could not do this.

He glanced aside and met Jalava's gaze.

It was enough. He looked back and inclined his head, rapidly calculating how Homaj would handle this situation— and not just that, but how Homaj would handle it *now*. Which was...an interesting calculation, because Iata didn't even think Homaj had thought that far ahead, not enough to fully cement his role as the future ruler and current Truthspoken Heir. Let alone the Seritarchus. Would Homaj have to adapt to whatever Iata did here? And what if Iata did it wrong?

He could not think about that, either.

He hadn't meant to keep the military commanders waiting, and they hadn't been waiting long, but at the last minute Iata had changed clothes from formal and femme, something Homaj might normally wear when he was more femme, to a dark blue jacket and trousers with more sedate flair, sliding into neutral. Homaj often made abrupt gender presentation changes throughout the day, and while he'd been more femme earlier in public, it was wise to continue his fluidity in this role.

And at the extra last moment, Iata had run back and secured the tight knot of his hair with only two razor-tipped spikes. He didn't think the general and admiral would try to assassinate him, but just now, he felt better with weapons at hand.

"Truthspoken," General Abret said. "I've had watch on those searching the city and have had my intelligence crawling the entirety of Valon's network, any lead followed. We have not yet found evidence of Truthspoken Vatrin's presence, any proof of travel, or evidence they might have gone offworld."

General Abret was older, much older, than Laguaya. Dark brown skin, fully gray hair bound up in a neat bun, face deep with furrows, weathered in all the ways a general should be. Laguaya, by contrast, was young for the position of Admiral of the Fleet in their fifties, pale brown face nearly unlined, black hair cropped short, uniform crisp and back ramrod straight.

Iata doubted Laguaya's sharp eyes missed much. He mentally checked his mannerisms—but he didn't find anything to adjust.

Admiral Laguaya gave their own terse nod. "I'm doing the same, in our fleet in orbit, Valon Orbital Stations One and Two, and any civilian traffic in or outbound. All ships docked are temporarily locked down, and there's a system travel ban in place, under my emergency order. I can't impound the foreign ships without your order, but I have been stalling them, and they're making noise. But we're not yet certain this wasn't orchestrated by foreign powers."

Iata's brows went up. It could be foreign, or have foreign agents involved, yes. But the Kingdom of Valoris—Valon in particular—was too mired in its own internal politics to make him think this was anything but betrayal by those who should have been loyal to the Seritarcracy.

"Have you searched any ships?" Iata asked. "Physically, I mean."

"Not foreign ships, no—they're territory of their sovereign nations."

"Ask them to remain in-system, under my express wishes. I don't want to risk an incident just now."

Laguaya grimaced, but nodded. "Yes, Ser. Most, I fear, will leave."

Was that the right move? He knew the current political

landscape, likely better than Homaj did, and tensions were elevated with several other kingdoms and nations just now. The Onabrii-Kast Dynasty was certainly on the list of suspects, and the most likely if this assassination had foreign backing.

No, no he should have asked for more information before giving an order. He didn't know enough. He didn't know enough of anything.

Adeius, an order. One of Homaj's first.

"Do we have official statements from any of the diplomats?" he asked, keeping tight control over his vocal chords so his voice didn't quaver. "I assume no one is claiming guilt, but has anyone been overly decrying it? Has anyone offered any information?"

"Statements, yes," Laguaya said, and they shared a look with Abret. "I've compiled a list, from those sent from orbit and those sent from diplomats on the ground, with the general's help. Out-system responses, of course, will not have arrived yet." They motioned to their aide, who held out a small secured tablet.

They spoke as if they'd planned this meeting and hadn't been summoned, that they'd been planning to present him with this list he likely could have gathered on his own—should have gathered.

He should already have this information. The ruler was always steps ahead, and while the Admiral of the Fleet and the High General could take control of local and system comms in an emergency, he should have taken it right back.

He knew Homaj's palace system passcodes and had access to his inboxes—he usually handled Homaj's communications. But would he have access to top level information yet? He would have to ask Jalava to look into it, which likely meant going through Tavven as well. Would Tavven give him that access if he didn't already have it, knowing who he really was?

Had he and Homaj spent too much time and effort on

Change? They were both used to Change as a solution, when they should have been taking back control of palace and kingdom functions from wherever they'd fallen in the temporary vacuum of power.

He was not prepared for this. He was so utterly unprepared for what he was doing right now.

Iata took the tablet, scrolling through text-only messages in a bare-bones data dump format.

Laguaya hesitated. "We had expected the Truthspeaker to be at this meeting also."

Meaning, they thought he was too young, or too canonically apathetic to the greater goings on of the kingdom. Anger rose in Iata, and it was, at least, more welcome than the doubt. Far more useful.

Neither of these heads of military had been at the ceremony earlier. And what did that mean, other than that they were busy in this time of crisis, trying to avert more crises?

Iata waved the statement off. "The Truthspeaker is otherwise occupied."

Should he use their assumptions of his own incompetence against them? No, he didn't yet know if they weren't allies. He couldn't assume they weren't and alienate those who were on his side. He needed every ally he could find.

He gestured with the tablet. "What do the messages say? Any threats?"

"Not any more than the usual rhetoric," Laguaya said. "The ambassador for the Farani Protectorate is offering their utmost help—in the form of lots of their warships, conveniently—and Oulion is sending for their head Rakoni priest to say a blessing for our dead. The Dynasty is full of flowery sympathies, and offered to send some of their Green Magickers to help search the city—I truly don't know what they were trying to accomplish with that offer, especially since the magickers would take weeks to arrive."

Most likely confusion and low-level panic over if the message was a threat or not, which was a very Dynastic thing to do. Iata made a mental note, though—*could* Green Magickers help with all of this? With sorting out the truth, certainly, but they had to have enough proof of guilt to legally read someone. Could they even begin to find a single person in an overpopulated city? Could they read the Palace Guard to find the traitors among them, if there were in fact traitors among the Guard?

Homaj had already overstepped protocol by letting the First Magicker witness his bid earlier. Iata wasn't sure he should involve the magickers any more than that, not yet, though the idea had his mind racing ahead to ways he could justify it.

They needed answers. They needed them fast.

> *The Valoran Navy isn't just a conduit for discipline and order, as the nobility likes to say. It's our pride, our heritage among the stars. We came to the worlds we inhabit on ships, and we protect those worlds with ships.*

> — ADMIRAL OF THE FLEET DASSAN LAGUAYA
> IN A PUBLIC ADDRESS AT THE
> COMMISSIONING OF THE *V.N.S. MORIN LI*

Admiral Laguaya waved at the tablet Iata held. "Most statements from diplomats beyond the performative ones are formulaic sympathies." They paused. "Which, forgive me—my sympathies, Truthspoken."

"And mine," Abret echoed. "And I've heard much the same. The First Magicker sent a beautifully calligraphed letter which I saw in Tavven's office—I just came from there—but they're checking it over before they send it up." E shifted, pulling out and handing over a tablet of eir own. Iata was fairly certain it didn't just contain sympathy mail.

He took it without a word, thumbed it on, flicked through the highest document in the tier. It was a plan for martial law, to systematically interrogate every organization that had even the most remote contact with the Seritarchus, from the Palace Guard all the way down to the cooks. There was even a plan to enlist the help of the Green Magickers in those interrogations, and a form for the ruler's permission.

Ah. Abret was ahead of Iata.

He shouldn't have felt embarrassed at that—Adeius, this was his first time doing anything like this, let alone ruling an entire kingdom. General Abret had the better part of a century of command experience.

And...and he had to be careful not to let himself be intimidated by that. The general's plan was stuffed full of unnecessary things, in the general's own agenda.

And at the moment, Iata did have the authority to shut that down.

"This is thorough," Iata said slowly. He opened another document and found a proposal to give dual military police and civilian police status to three companies of Abret's spec ops troops for the duration of this martial law—oh, Iata was definitely not doing that.

"E gave you eir martial law proposal, did e?" Laguaya drawled. "I told you he wouldn't like it, Banamar."

Iata clicked the tablet off. A gesture in itself.

"I appreciate the thoroughness of this report and your recommendations, High General, but just now, I don't intend to terrorize the populace. We need to proceed with caution."

But did they? Did they truly? The Seritarchus had been assassinated. Surely if Vatrin could be found, they'd be found sooner if civilians were ordered inside, if military order was temporarily higher than civilian.

"There's already panic on the streets," Abret said. "The Municipal Guard broke up an impromptu anti-Truthspoken rally on the edge of Blue District an hour ago, which itself is alarming. Those people usually stay underground. Gold District is running uneasy, with the news spreading about Lord Birka's crash on the edge of Financial District—condolences for that as well, Truthspoken."

"I didn't know him," Iata said coolly.

Abret hesitated only a moment before smoothly moving on. "We need more order in the streets. People know the Seritarchus was assassinated. And while a city will carry on as it does, unease can lead swiftly to fear and riots if it's not handled well. We need to—"

"I agree," Iata said. "So we will leave the Municipal Guard to handle it for now. I'll authorize them to temporarily increase their rank quotas, pull in their reserves. General, please do have troops on alert if needed, but do not move them anywhere on non-military soil without my permission. Clear?"

Abret rocked back, narrowing eir eyes. "Clear. But, Truthspoken—"

Iata turned to Laguaya, shutting Abret out. "I don't want any system space traffic—civilian or otherwise—impounded longer than it takes to search. If civilian ships refuse to be searched— ask them to stay in-system or in dock, with incentives. Don't force them."

Laguaya shook their head. "Truthspoken. Vatrin is Truth-spoken—they could be anyone on any of those crews. They could be locked up or unconscious. Coerced. I don't want anyone leaving the system but the designated courier ships, which no one has boarded or left in the time we've been watching."

Iata glanced aside, and this time didn't catch Jalava's eye. And maybe that was a good thing. He shouldn't be seen defer-ring to one of his guards, of all people.

Neither the general nor the admiral were anything but capable—but that was also the problem. Both were trying to push him in their own directions, not just with what was best for the kingdom.

Maybe he should declare martial law, let Abret set the force of his troops onto this problem. But then, where would that weight end, if he gave that concession right now, in the beginning? And Iata truly didn't think that martial law was the way to solve this problem. The people needed reassurance that their leaders were in control, not a show that they weren't yet. And Laguaya's locking down everything in system space was a good security step, he thought, but bad for business, bad for an economy that would surely already be crashing with this upheaval. He had to show that he trusted the people enough for the economy to continue, or risk greater loss of control overall. Even—even if meant losing a lead to Vatrin. Or even Vatrin themself.

Iata's chest tightened. Would Homaj make this call? No, Homaj couldn't. He thought with his heart, he always had, and it was why he'd set himself apart from the daily happenings of the kingdom.

But Homaj had already made his bid to rule. That part of the machinery of the kingdom was already moving forward. If Vatrin was found, that would be the best outcome, but at this point, it might not change Homaj becoming the ruler. The people were moving now toward any chance at stability, and currently, Homaj was that stability just by being Truthspoken. If Iata started that stability off by letting Laguaya terrorize citizens and allies in orbit, the stability would soon crumble.

But—Vatrin. He'd grown up with Vatrin and Vatrin's bloodservant, Eyras. He wasn't close to either with Homaj's distance of late, but he didn't want them to die. Adeius. He didn't want to just give up on finding them, or that they'd both still be alive. They were family.

"Be polite," he relented. "Be absolutely polite. Ask, don't force. If they resist a search, remind them of the current situation. Ask them, in my name, to consent to a search in this time of crisis, and guarantee that all contraband will not be confiscated or examined at this time. On my order. If they resist after that—then impound their ships. Without injury as far as possible to their ships or crews. And don't, as you said, try to search any foreign ships if they refuse."

Laguaya looked like they wanted to argue, but they must have seen something in his face, because they just nodded. They seemed relieved, even.

That he wasn't going to completely write off his sibling? That he'd just shown that he cared?

Adeius, had they been taking his hesitance to exert control in orbit as proof that he'd helped orchestrate all of this?

He sharpened his focus, looked between both of them. "This kingdom," he said, "is stronger than the death of its ruler. We will do everything we can to recover my sibling and their bloodservant, and to find out who did this and punish them to the fullest extent. But we cannot do this at the expense of the greater stability of the kingdom."

Abret nodded. "Agreed, but—"

"You have my orders. Have plans in place if we need to escalate, but do not escalate unless and until I say so."

If Homaj was determined to be a Seritarchus, ruling with control, it was best Iata lay those lines down now.

Both Abret and Laguaya seemed unsure of what to do with his sudden assertiveness. It wasn't how an Ialorius would rule. An Ialorius would wind the conversation around so that the military commanders came to these conclusions on their own. Or maybe would present their own solutions—but Iata didn't have better solutions just now.

He had control, for the moment. He had the weight of hundreds of years of Rhialden Truthspoken rule.

Adeius, he wished he could take Abret's spec ops and comb through the city. Take the Green Magickers, even, and do...

something. It wasn't that he didn't care—he cared so much. But he couldn't, absolutely couldn't, let that caring shatter the kingdom.

Homaj was searching the city, and Homaj was incredibly resourceful. He had to hope Homaj would come up with something, because otherwise, it was no good to start a Seritarchus rule already giving up essential control.

Abret sighed and wasn't subtle about it. "Truthspoken— with all due respect—you don't yet have the experience of your father, to know—"

"Oh," Iata said, stepping closer. Homaj was average height, but Abret was not and had to look up at him. And Iata had not yet invited any of them to sit. "Bad move for you. You do remember who I am? You seriously think I haven't driven your tanks, or flown in your fleet, admiral?"

He stepped back again, deliberately calming his posture.

"Find me a trail, any trail, that leads to my sibling. Find who assassinated my fathers—coordinate with the Municipal Guard, but do not overstep them! Don't cause panic. Work with orderly caution. You can do that, right? You're both *experienced* enough at your jobs to do that, right?"

He was breathing heavily, and he dropped himself into the top layer of a trance to smooth his rapid pulse, to ease more air into his lungs. That...that had been too far. But it was one hundred percent Homaj.

He didn't apologize—he'd never do that, and the gall of them to even condescend, using his *father*—well, Homaj's father. He, as himself, would never be allowed to publicly mourn for the Seritarchus like Homaj could. But Iata had always been a part of the royal household, and the Seritarchus had been a constant in his life. Had helped to train him, as had his bloodservant, Omari, too.

Iata had never known his own parents. As a bloodservant, his only family was supposed to be the Truthspoken.

Iata was a shadow. No one acknowledged the bloodservants as capable of having emotions or ambitions of their own.

He knew his eyes were shining, felt the sting of tears. Abret and Laguaya were looking at him now with some alarm.

He couldn't afford to lose control like that, either.

Iata held up a hand. "Send any further information to me directly. You have my priority comm codes. If it's too sensitive, send it by courier. If it's so sensitive it might burn the city down —then you may come back. But I am done with you tonight."

41

PRIVACY

> *People think that Truthspoken have it easy at the pinnacle, that everything has been given to us. The truth is, we must fight to maintain. It's never not a struggle, with everyone working to tear us down.*

— HOMAJ RHIALDEN, SERITARCHUS IX IN A
PRIVATE LETTER, NEVER SENT; AS QUOTED IN
THE CHANGE DIALOGUES

Iata didn't storm out of the sitting room—which Homaj might have done. He simply walked out, leaving his guests to find their own way out. And yes, he'd called them here, because he'd known he'd have to and wanted to get a better bearing on the overall picture—but would everyone treat him this way? Was everyone expecting Homaj to be so easy to push around?

Homaj had never downplayed his intelligence, only his willingness to do work within the system of the Seritarcracy—and yes, people did equate that with less intelligence. Why would a Truthspoken be so deeply cynical, so apathetic to what was happening, unless they didn't understand it? The high houses, after all, would kill for such privileges as Homaj seemed unmoved by. Homaj hardly even seemed interested in his lovers. How could a person like that be trusted with a kingdom in turmoil?

They didn't know how much he cared about everything. They didn't know that his apathetic armor was in large part survival.

And what was Homaj going to do now that he had to let that armor go?

Iata shut the door to the prep room too fast, and Jalava caught it behind him, easing it shut.

"Lock it," Iata snapped, then drew a breath, shut his eyes. Homaj had shown Zhang how to lock the prep room door, but had anyone shown Jalava? The palace lockdown had eased, and the door would no longer lock automatically.

"Your Guard code of the day will work," he said, and tapped in his own bloodservant's code to demonstrate. "But it won't unlock it from the other side. Someone with Truthspoken or bloodservant DNA can override the lock, though. Or Commander Tavven."

Jalava nodded, attentive, but kept looking up at him.

"I'm fine," Iata said, and it came out too much like a snap again. He hit the sound dampening controls for good measure and waited for that slight tightening of the air to know they were working.

And—

Now what? He wasn't trained for this. Homaj wasn't even properly trained for this—everyone had just assumed it would be Vatrin ruling, everyone had just assumed that none of the assassination attempts would ever get through.

He had assumed, anyway. He hadn't truly thought his life would change. He'd never seen himself, certainly, giving orders like he had any right to, which he didn't.

Iata caught his reflection in the mirror above Homaj's vanity table and slowly drew closer, unable to stop himself.

Yes, he'd seen himself as Homaj earlier. He'd dressed and applied his own cosmetics. And he'd known it wasn't a game before, certainly. He knew these were the highest stakes, and he knew what he was doing now was immensely dangerous.

But all of that was different than standing in a room with both the High General of the Army and Admiral of the Fleet of the Navy and telling them, basically, to fuck off.

Had he actually just done that?

Adeius, what had made him think he *should* do that?

He still felt, in his bones, that had been the right move. They were trying to move on Homaj's power in a time when the kingdom was unstable, trying to take advantage—and yes, that's the way politics were played, but just now it made him sick.

He sat and carefully removed the razor-tipped spikes holding up his hair. It fell loose, and he combed his fingers through before winding it back up again in a more elaborate style, reaching for smaller pins in a jar on the vanity. It was a style he'd given to Homaj several weeks ago, but his fingers fumbled now. It was much, much different trying to do this style on himself.

He breathed through the process, though, and kept his movements, the pattern of his surface thoughts, Homaj's.

Jalava tentatively stepped closer, hands out.

"Ser Truthspoken," they said, and good, they'd caught that nuance. He was still very much being Homaj right now. "How can I help?"

He didn't know. He hadn't expected that last meeting to go so poorly—should he even try to meet with anyone else? Should he try to be seen and start weaving a new perception of Homaj to the court? But the palace was still under a lighter lockdown, and there would be no social functions. Him even trying to attend one if there was would only cement Homaj's reputation as uncaring right now, when his parents had just been killed. So, not that.

And anywhere he went, he'd be surrounded by guards. Tavven wouldn't let the newly minted Truthspoken Heir, the future ruler of the kingdom, go out about on social calls just now. Even if it was Iata in that role, not the Heir himself.

But—Homaj hadn't just put him in this role as a place-holder. Homaj had, by nature of the request, asked him to live his life as if he himself was living it.

Iata couldn't just do nothing. At the moment, he had very real power and the very real chance to screw things up.

"Did I just mess up?" he asked.

Jalava seemed to brace themself, as if warding against the question. Or maybe warding against having to answer it.

Iata waved it away. "I shouldn't have asked. You're my—right now, you're my guard, and you shouldn't have to—"

"No, no," Jalava said, hands up. "I think those bast—well. I think the military is trying to take power from the Seritarcracy that they shouldn't. If you want my opinion, I saw them treat you not like a future ruler, which they should have, but like... like a bad commander might treat a raw recruit who doesn't want to be there. Dismissive, assuming that—no, that analogy doesn't really work. Forgive me, Truthspoken, I am not good at this."

Iata smiled at them, his own smile. "You're here. That's good enough."

Jalava's cheeks flushed, but they nodded, and kept nodding until words came back again. "I think you did well. You're defending the rulership. That's what you were assigned to do, so, no. You didn't mess up, but I think it might still cause problems."

Iata sighed and resumed poking at the arrangement of his

hair, selecting several more elaborate jeweled and enameled pins.

He should meet with the palace chamberlain—except he wanted his role as Homaj more solidified before he did that. The chamberlain had been around all of them growing up, Truthspoken and bloodservants alike, and Iata was sure the chamberlain had more evaku than he should.

He should meet with the leaders of the General Assembly —but, he was on shakier ground politically there, too. The General Assembly was made up of lesser nobility and the wealthier among the merchant class, and Homaj's circles and the Assembly's circles had seldom intertwined. Iata hadn't had to keep up with the Assembly's doings as often as he should have in Homaj's everyday dealings.

He should also meet with the leaders or representatives of the high houses, but he had to at very least be able to get past the chamberlain before he attempted that, unless they first came to him, which was entirely possible. There was no organized structure of high houses—they were all too fractious for that—but he wouldn't put it past them to form impromptu alliances to try to push him into something they wanted, too.

He needed access to the Seritarchus's personal inboxes, or at least, get the messages that should go there dumped into Homaj's inboxes. And what access did Homaj currently have?

Homaj had given Iata his comm and taken a generic one into the city, so there was that.

Iata, finally settling his hair with one last pin and only mostly satisfied with the results, pulled Homaj's comm out of his jacket pocket and unlocked it. Which he could do, now that he was genetically and biometrically Homaj, within that very small tolerance of error. Then he flicked up the messaging apps —both palace internal comms and broad news feeds—into an array of holo windows in front of him. He thumbed off the privacy controls that would let only his eyes at his exact viewing angle see them.

"Come look at this," Iata said, and Jalava moved closer. Warily, now that they realized what they were looking at—and it *was* all access. A pulsing window to the right held the Seritarchus's personal inbox. Tavven must have released the controls in the palace system that transferred power and access from one ruler to another—the only other person who could do that was the Truthspeaker, and Iata didn't think he would have.

He pulled up the internal security logs—and, well. Control had been released by Truthspeaker Aduwel. But okay, Homaj had made his bid to rule and had been witnessed in his sincerity—albeit, by a Green Magicker. Legally, this access had to be released to him.

"I shouldn't be looking at this," Jalava said.

And they were right—there were access windows and leads to various palace surveillance at Iata's command now, along with...everything. In the palace, the city, the world, and beyond it.

"You have my permission," Iata said. "And...right now, that matters."

42

THE SUMMONS

> *As Humans under the will of Adeius, we much always strive, therefore, to be better than we have been. In our personal lives, and in the greater picture of the kingdom.*

— TRUTHSPEAKER ADUWEL SHIN MERNA IN
"STRIVING FOR PROSPERITY"

Iata just barely kept his hands from shaking as he waved away some of the more terrifying access levels in his comm to focus on the Seritarchus's grossly overcrowded public-facing inbox. Which itself was heavily filtered by the palace staff, and still dumped hundreds of messages into his hands. Not, after a certain time that day, addressed to the Seritarchus, but to his heir. To Homaj.

Entreaties, petitions, plans. Most not even relevant to the situation at hand. Every one of the senders an opportunist, most looking for some edge in the chaos, for more power.

But was that fair? He saw a few petitions from Green Magickers to improve their rights within the capital and the kingdom. While the time might not be right, they weren't wrong to send them now. Not when everyone else was sending and if they didn't, their voices might be drowned out.

But after the tenth or the twentieth message, Iata waved them away as something he couldn't focus on right now and pulled up Homaj's more private, internal palace inbox. He managed it often enough for Homaj through his own comm, so he was familiar with its contents.

A message near the top immediately stood out. It was from the office of the Truthspeaker.

Iata stabbed at the message, and it expanded.

From: Aduwel Shin Merna, Truthspeaker
To: Homaj Rhialden, Truthspoken Heir

I request your presence in my office at your earliest convenience so that we may discuss strategy for your rule, if Truthspoken Vatrin is not found when ten days are up, as well as how best to fulfill your obligation of the oath you made today. I look forward to your response.

—Aduwel

Iata stared at the message. There was so much, so much packed into those few lines. One paragraph. So much that could be read in so many ways. Could he trust that he had the training to read all the nuances?

His heart pounded in his throat, and he managed a light trance to calm it down.

"You can't see the Truthspeaker," Jalava said, still looking over his shoulder. Iata had wanted their help, but now, their input suddenly felt like an intrusion. These were Truthspoken matters.

But he couldn't do this alone. Especially couldn't deal with Aduwel alone, Adeius, no.

Jalava's face was pale, their brows drawn down.

"I can't refuse him," Iata said.

"But he saw through you before, or at least through, uh," they waved, at a loss for what to call Homaj when they were staring at Iata, who was visibly Homaj.

"Maja," Iata supplied. "It's his private name."

Jalava pulled back. "Should I know that?"

"Yes, you're one of his personal guards now. You'll know a whole lot more before all of this is done. If I say it, or if he says it, you really should know."

Jalava made a sort of grimace, an aborted attempt to rub at the bridge of their nose, and straightened. "Right. But he— Maja—is fully Truthspoken. And the Truthspeaker saw through him at the Adeium. You really think you can convince the Truthspeaker that you're—*him*?"

Iata shrugged, caught the movement in the mirror, and adjusted it to match Homaj's more fluid movements.

"I have to go. I don't have a choice in that. If the Truthspeaker summons—the Truthspoken must listen. So. I'll have to be Homaj in truth."

He had, of course, been trained to be someone in truth. It was a useful skill for a bloodservant to have—he could be sent to play minor roles that would have major impact, and testify after that he had no role in them whatsoever. Technically, he wouldn't have, being someone else entirely. Or he could do a task as someone else and disappear, with no one able to call a witness, and no magicker able to fully verify that Iata would know anything about it. He would, of course, but at that remove holding a different personhood in himself gave.

When Homaj and he had been sent to deal with revolting miners several years ago, Iata had settled shortly into being one of them in truth for an evening, and that insight had led them both to make the decisions that resolved the situation.

He had even, in training years ago, been Homaj in truth before, and Homaj had been Iata, though Iata had never Changed to Homaj's likeness before. But that was years ago, before they'd both reached adulthood. That was training, and it had, in many ways, still been a game. Homaj had been trending toward apathy toward Iata until then, and he'd treated Iata a little better after that. Homaj had, over the years, molded himself into his apathetic and rakish role at court, but he'd never been cruel to Iata. Not more than the typical leak-through of a long-term role.

"So," Jalava said, watching him with a certain wariness. "You're going to do what you described before? Where I'll have to use a callback to get you back?"

Iata considered. "I'll be going as deep as I can. You'll need to treat me exactly as you would Homaj—because I will be. Fully and truly."

Jalava nodded. "Should I practice the callback again?"

"Do you think you need to?"

Jalava considered, then shook their head. "No, I have it." Their shoulders jerked in an involuntary twitch of tension, but Iata watched them wrestle their body back under their own rigid discipline. A guard through and through.

"So what now?" Jalava asked.

Iata considered the question, looking at it from every angle.

The problem for him with being Homaj in truth wasn't that he couldn't—it was that, right now, he wasn't sure which Homaj he should be. The Homaj of this last day had been drastically different than the Homaj he'd grown used to every day before then. But the difference was jarring—today, he'd seen the Homaj of years ago, before Homaj had molded himself into the court rake. He'd seen his friend again, his brother in spirit, if never in blood. It had taken this—Adeius, it had taken *this* for him to fully see that person again.

But who would the Truthspeaker be expecting? Homaj had shown temper at the ceremony earlier and had shown that he was trying to unsettle expectations. But that wasn't a fully cemented personality. And the Truthspeaker would know that Homaj's court personality wasn't fully his own.

The truth was, too, that Iata *didn't* have all of Homaj's training. He had enough to carry out his duties as a bloodservant and no more. It had taken every bit of skill he'd had and then some to Change into Homaj earlier. It would stretch everything he had—and he'd still probably ultimately fail—to be Homaj in truth, at least true enough to fool the Truthspeaker.

But he didn't think there was anyone left alive who knew Homaj as well as he did. There was no one else alive who could do this but him. Not even Vatrin knew Homaj that well.

"Now..." Iata said, "now, I'm going to shift my cosmetics, I think, and layer on the personality I'll assume. I'll have to compensate for some things I'm more naturally inclined to do, direct myself to do others. Once I have this reality built, I'll be able to shift back to it more quickly, but I have to build it now first."

"Can you stall?" Jalava asked. "There is so much here that looks urgent. Could you set up more meetings—"

Iata exhaled in a rush, feeling a little dizzy as that possibility broke his gathering concentration.

Could he?

"It's a summons," he said. And, unlike the general and admiral earlier, the Truthspeaker was someone who could wreck him if he wanted to, Homaj or Iata both. "And there's a read receipt on all messages from the Truthspeaker to Truthspoken, and the same the other way around. It's checks and balances."

Jalava was looking pale again, but nodded.

Iata waved off the comm windows and turned back to himself in the mirror. Stay neutral? Go more masc like his own sense of gender? Or go more femme?

Femme, Iata decided. The shift again in cosmetics would give him something to layer his personality to. And slowly, he began the process of building the personality he'd need to submerge within.

43

A FRIENDLY CHAT

Most acolytes come to the Adeium knowing that they'll leave again within a year or a few months. And that is well, that is part of what the system of the Adeium is for, to be a refuge to those who need it. But those who stay and become speakers are a gift, a treasure for the worlds.

— DR. SPEAKER AVA HAYAT IN *EVOLUTION OF A SYSTEM: SPEAKERS THROUGHOUT HISTORY*

Homaj Rhialden strode across the courtyard to the Adeium with his retinue of guards around him— Chadrikour and Bozde in front, Jalava and Ehj just behind him. This late in the evening, the sky was nearly dark. Aesthetically planned but strategically placed floodlights shone down across the palace courtyard, leaving no real blind spots.

There were no courtiers milling about, as there usually were. Sometimes, he'd be among them. But with everything that had happened, social access was still locked down.

The Adeium guards parted at the iron gates as he

approached but still demanded his guards' weapons. But his guards knew the drill and silently handed them over. If anything happened to him within the Adeium itself, the kingdom would truly be in trouble.

Homaj continued inside, his disarmed but still useful guards with him. They stayed close to him through the entry and the sanctum—he only paused briefly to nod at the curious petitioners kneeling on the floor. Had they known he'd come? Had they been waiting? The Adeium was nearly full, and it was never full.

Or maybe they were all just scared.

His party passed through the door at the front of the sanctum into the office suite, passed the secretarial desks, no one looking surprised to see him there, either.

Speaker Ceorre Gatri waited at the end of the rich wood-paneled hall, hands clasped in front of her, posture open but lips tight.

"Truthspoken. The Truthspeaker will see you now."

Homaj made no visible sign of his annoyance, but he wanted to comment on that nuance. Desperately wanted to snap that the Truthspeaker shouldn't condescend to him, that wasn't how checks and balances worked—they were equal.

But he kept his mouth shut. Kept his body still and his own expression no more than agitated, which was to be expected.

The Truthspeaker's office was small for his station, with a large wooden desk taking up most of the room to Homaj's left as he entered, three chairs neatly arranged in front of it.

"Wait outside," Homaj said to Jalava, who nodded and waved the others to their stations outside the office door, and two farther down the hall near the doors into the sanctum.

Ceorre stepped into the Truthspeaker's office as well and closed the door behind her. Closing Homaj off from his protection. And his easy way out, though he was still certain his DNA would open the Truthspeaker's door if it locked.

The room was heavy with the smell of freshly brewed coffee.

Behind his desk, Truthspeaker Aduwel Shin Merna smiled at Homaj. He'd never been handsome so much as distinguished, broad features a little asymmetrical in his tan face, his brown hair pulled up in a tight masc-style knot. His smile would seem, to anyone not trained in evaku, to be generous. Beatific, even. But Aduwel's eyes were ever-calculating. Homaj had never mistaken Aduwel's smiles for compassion.

"Truthspeaker," he said, and resisted the urge to dip that small bow he'd always been required to make when he was in training. This wasn't training, he was a full Truthspoken, and he was, at the moment, the interim ruler of the kingdom. Yes, he could be summoned. But he would not give any more ground than he had to.

Aduwel tilted his head, studying him. Then drew his brows closer together, sitting back. "You plan to be a Seritarchus."

Homaj sat in the middle chair across from him, not waiting for an invitation.

He had decided to slowly start projecting along Seritarchus personality lines, shifting some of his body language, his gestural language to that of stability and control.

That Aduwel had picked up on it was to be expected. What he would do with it, though? That Homaj was less sure of.

"Yes. It's what the kingdom needs."

Aduwel nodded, "Yes, and also, it's not your natural style. You're Ialorius, Homaj. It might be possible to hold a Seritarchus positioning in the short-term, but we are talking about an entire reign. Yes, you can change it later, but not without losing ground and popular assurance."

He knew all of that. And he knew, too, that he wasn't wrong about the kingdom needing stability just now, not fluidity or momentum.

"I have no intention of changing it later," Homaj said, and

sat back. That act of asserting his space was also a very Seritarchus move.

Aduwel's smile flashed again, sharper this time. "Well, if Vatrin is found, we may not need to find out how well the people will receive you like this."

Homaj kept his expression tightly controlled, easing back a little into some of his usual laconic persona. "I've already made my bid to rule, Aduwel. I'm not convinced, at this point, that Vatrin wouldn't be compromised. Or that the kingdom would be best served by them stepping in when it's already aligning now to me."

"Admiral of the Fleet Laguaya and High General Abret expressed concerns that you were overwrought," Aduwel said.

"Did they?" Homaj asked, his words sharp as knives. The two had tried to control him and failed, and so had gone past him to the Truthspeaker?

Ceorre, who'd been standing near the door, now moved further into the room, deliberately breaking the tension. She took the seat to Homaj's right.

He broke his glare with the Truthspeaker to follow her, and her smile at him, fleeting though it was, was truly genuine.

She studied him now, too, and it was an entirely different sort of assessment than the Truthspeaker had given. Aduwel's look had been judging and coming up with him distinctly lacking, as it always did. Aduwel had never liked him.

Ceorre's look was probing for his strengths and finding them. She didn't have as much training or experience in the art of evaku as Aduwel, but being in training to be the next Truthspeaker when Aduwel retired, she was still one of the most expert evaku wielders in the kingdom. As expert, likely, as himself.

"In any case," Aduwel said, pressing a control on his desk to bring up his holo displays, "that isn't why I asked you here. As you are the interim ruler and have access now to the ruler's files and inboxes, I thought it best to brief you on one matter personally. This also might have bearing on who was behind these tragedies in the Seritarcracy."

"Assassinations, you mean."

"Yes." Aduwel's face didn't so much as flicker at that less than subtle probe.

He brought up a series of windows, then waved them around to the front of his desk for Homaj to see. "Ceorre, you had best see this, too."

Homaj leaned forward. The text was just short of easily readable from where he sat. Was Aduwel going to make him scoot his chair closer?

But Aduwel saw and dialed the text larger.

The center and most prominent window was...what? A medical lab report? There was no name attached to it.

His chest tightened. Adeius, was Aduwel showing him coroner's reports for his parents—

No, wait—upper corner. "Infant Rhialden" was all the report said. And then a tight list of attributes: blood type, various levels and factors, and a key that would lead to raw genetic data. There was a date, but it wasn't the right date, surely. The date was seven months before Vatrin's birthday.

Unease coiled in Homaj's gut.

"Is this report from Vatrin's birth? And what am I supposed to be seeing?"

Aduwel pointed at a second window. Also a lab report, with the same sort of notation. Same blood type, similar attributes. This one with the name Vatrin Rhialden. This one was on Vatrin's birthday.

Homaj looked between them. Then the first had to be Eyras's? Vatrin's bloodservant was older than them, though Homaj had thought it was by more than a year.

"What am I supposed to be seeing?" he asked again.

Aduwel waved two more windows to center. A third report

like the first, listing only Infant Rhialden, with a birthdate around eight months before his own. And then another with Homaj Rhialden, on his own birthdate.

He looked up. "So...Iata and Eyras are closer in age to us than we'd thought. What does that have to do with—"

Aduwel brought up four more windows in quick succession. Each looked to be raw genetic data in Truthspoken syntax. A fifth window popped up in front of them all, showing a genetic analysis in progress. The loading bar moved swiftly, and then a report appeared: the analysis between four samples showed genetic variances typical of siblings sharing the same parents.

Which, yes, Vatrin's and his own should show that, as they were full siblings.

Aduwel scrolled down the analysis report and circled a section with his finger. Parents' names for these four samples were Anatharie Rhialden, his father the Seritarchus, and Jamir ne Xiao Rhialden, his father the Seritarchus Consort. All four samples.

He heard the very slightest hitch in Ceorre's breath. He glanced at her, while his own thoughts were racing to catch up.

All four samples.

44

SAMPLES

We have commercial gene scanners, and have perfected ways to create children from any combination of sex and genders among parents. But what the Truthspoken do in their labs is still a mystery to us. It might be the same—the greatest secret might be that they are no different than any of us. Their zygotes look like our zygotes.

— DR. ESABEL DIOP IN A POST ON HER
PERSONAL FEED

"Are you saying that Eyras and Iata are—are also my siblings? My actual blood siblings?" Homaj shifted in his seat, fighting the urge to stand and pace. There was no room in the Truthspeaker's small office. "But the bloodservants are a service branch of the Rhialden line, we're distant cousins—"

Aduwel pulled the windows back to himself and sent up two more. A lab report for, again, Infant Rhialden, and another for Anatharie Rhialden. That would be his father and his father's bloodservant, Omari. The date on the first was also off of what he thought it should be.

"You're saying that my father and Omari were also blood siblings?"

He gripped the arms of the chair. "But...but—"

His head stabbed with a vicious headache, and he broke off to do his best to smooth it over. He didn't know what the Truthspeaker was trying to do here, whether this information was true or not, or why he felt the need to share it right now, when Homaj was already off balance. It absolutely was a malicious move, though, he did know that.

"It's motive," Aduwel said, and sounded pleased with himself. "Omari knew and has known for years. But if Eyras or Iata found out that they are full Rhialden siblings, and also actually the elders of their two sibling pairings, that would certainly be motive to make their own bids to rule. Would it not?"

Aduwel's eyes speared him, and he stared back. Emotions hovered outside of him while he still fought to make sense of this.

"You think Eyras killed my—our—parents? But she's also missing, and I've already made my bid, that doesn't make sense—"

"Or Iata." Aduwel shrugged. "Does it make sense with how everything has played out so far? Maybe, maybe not. But it's information you, as the interim ruler, need to have."

"But—" Homaj stopped, steadied himself. He looked at the air where the reports had just hovered. "Why are we siblings? Why aren't they of the Rhialden service branch?"

"There is no Rhialden service branch," Aduwel said, sighing. "Maybe there was at some point. Those records have either been lost or destroyed. But what records I have for the last three rulers show as these did here." He shrugged, picked up his large coffee mug, and tapped the edge on his desk. "Bloodser-

vants have to come from somewhere. And they have to be able
to Change. Bloodservant children are trained away from so
closely resembling the royal Rhialden line, given images and
genetic traits of their theoretical parents as ideals to strive for."

That was...he itched badly to move, but he stayed so, so still.

That was monstrous. And it would have had to be the
Truthspeaker and his own father doing that training. And
Omari—who'd had it done to himself. Homaj's own father,
purposely setting two of his children in the roles of servants? Of
never calling them his own? Did his Xiao father know about
this? No, Homaj wasn't sure he wanted to know just now. And
how could he be angry, how could he be heading toward
furious when both of his fathers were now—

He stood. Managed a "Thank you, Truthspeaker," and the
Truthspeaker didn't try to stop his way toward the door.

Ceorre rose, too, hip banging the back of a chair as she
followed him out.

She touched his arm just outside the office, just when the
door had closed, leaning close to his ear.

"Pull yourself together."

Her words were stern, her look fierce.

He focused on her eyes and saw sincerity there, and it did
steady him. Not much, but enough.

Jalava hovered closer as well, looking like they didn't know
how they should react.

"Truthspoken. Are you well?"

Homaj glanced aside at them, was aware his eyes were
glassy again, watering, and made an effort to smooth the tears
away. To calm his heart rate, to calm his breath.

Damn Aduwel. That he'd drop this on Homaj right now,
rock him off his center. But—but was this information he
needed? What if Eyras—or Iata—

Adeius, no, Iata had nothing to do with what had
happened. He knew that. He absolutely *knew* that.

Iata gasped and swayed, gripping Ceorre's arm to steady himself.

He was going to be sick. He swallowed hard, swallowed again, and again.

"Look at me," Ceorre hissed.

His eyes locked on hers.

"Homaj," she said, and he heard her subtle emphasis on the name. She knew who he was. "You're going to pull yourself together. You're going to walk out of here. Go back to your apartment. I'll come later, when I can, if I can. But I can't come with you right now."

Did he want her to? Was it possible that she truly hadn't known this, too, and was only learning it now?

Of course she hadn't. These were the kinds of secrets that could set the kingdom on fire. Maybe already had.

Aduwel had known what he was doing, telling him right now. Aduwel had to have seen through his being Homaj in truth. But why give him this information right now, and was it possibly true? Could it be a fabrication, to knock him off his course, to knock Homaj off when he came back, too?

This information was purely poison. A finely aimed weapon.

Ceorre let go of him, and he straightened as best he could. Drew in on himself, pushed Iata back down until there was only a little of himself in his center, and mostly, again, Homaj. But not in truth.

"Thank you, Speaker Ceorre."

All of his guards were watching. This corridor would be under Adeium Guard surveillance. Office staff here might have seen this little scene as well.

And yes, everyone knew that he'd just—oh fucking hell, he *had* just lost his parents. He had to get out of here before he caused any more of a scene.

Ceorre dipped her head in a bow and stepped back. Jalava

hovered like they wanted to support him, but weren't sure that they should.

Iata rolled his shoulders, rolling off everything he'd just learned until he was in a safe space to process it. He smoothed down his tunic, smoothed down his flowing skirt.

"Back to my apartment," he snapped, and his guards fell in line to get him out safely.

45

THE SEARCH

> *For all the Truthspoken see, can they not, for a time, put themselves into the life of a magicker? Not manifesting magics themselves, of course, no one has control over that, but understanding. Knowing what it is like to live in a world that sees an aura around you and a seal on your cheek and sets you firmly apart.*

— FIRST MAGICKER ONYA NORREN,
INTERVIEWED IN THE POPULAR VID ZINE
VALON CITY SUNSHINE

They'd been flying for over two hours now, and maybe Homaj knew that realistically it was a large city, one they likely couldn't cover in one night, let alone two hours. He found himself bobbing a knee in frustration.

He wasn't doing any good here. It was Lodri who was sitting, eyes half-lidded, listening or sensing or however she could feel the presence of Truthspoken. *When* she felt them, because that hadn't happened yet, beyond an earlier false alarm that Lodri had said a few moments later wasn't a Truth-spoken. There hadn't been enough density of soul.

He'd taken over the driver's seat and had been flying them in what he hoped was a random enough pattern, but with enough purpose not to trigger a flag in the city's abnormality systems. He had codes to make the car invisible to those systems, but, well. Those codes would always ping the palace after their use.

"We should get another car," Zhang said. She had the seat beside him and was watching the night-lit streets as they passed by below. "If we go much longer flying around, it will probably trigger the city systems to watch us."

Homaj smiled tightly. When this was all through, he was absolutely keeping Zhang.

"All right," he said. "Find me a good place to set down and swap."

"This is my private aircar," Lodri protested, though her voice had a distant quality, like most of her attention was else-where. "It's a customized model. For security."

"Well, then, find me a place to park. A more affluent area, I think, for this car."

They flew another few minutes in silence.

"We're still in Gold," Zhang said, manipulating the map holo over the dash. "We need to get to the other side of Gold, then we can head to the more gentrified areas of Blue."

He gave a snort, and she threw him a look.

"Gentrified?" he asked. "Did you grow up around here?"

"No. I'm from Dimera, on Gavri Continent." The largest of Valon's two continents, an ocean away to the southwest. Dimera was an inland city famous for its elaborate rock opera shows. Not a large city, but well-cultured, certainly.

"And we have gentrified areas in Dimera, too," she said.

Could he hear a Dimeri accent in her words? Maybe. But it was subtle enough he hadn't marked it before.

That was common enough among the Palace Guard, with the training school for potential guards just outside Valon City. The intensity of Guard training tended to have a cultural flattening effect, which was deliberate—loyalties had to be turned fully to Palace Rhialden, not home cities or worlds.

He opened his mouth, about to ask more, when he heard a soft intake of breath from Lodri.

"What?" he asked, nearly swerving the aircar into another lane. The autopilot took over and got him back in the right sky lane, giving him a stern warning to pay attention or manual driving privileges would be revoked.

"Fuck you," he mouthed at the dash, before asking, "Did you sense something?"

"Go down. Turn around, circle back. It might be a street away—but I felt something, yes. I'll see if I can catch more."

Lodri had cautioned them that her ability to sense Truthspoken wasn't always accurate, like her false alarm earlier. Sometimes, she'd find nobility who'd been heavily trained in the nobility's version of evaku, though that didn't quite feel the same as Truthspoken training. Sometimes, she'd sense stage or vid actors if they were near. Or people who had trained themselves into living double lives for whatever reason. But again, she'd said, those all felt different than actual Truthspoken, and if she sensed deeply for a few moments, she could tell.

"Truthspoken souls are multi-layered and heavily dense," she'd said. "You're not just one person, you're many, and I can see you shift around and between those people in realtime. That's what I'm looking for."

That explanation had been...less than comfortable. But Homaj was grateful for it now, grateful for any lead, as he dropped them down to just above street level. He followed Lodri's directions, and they ended up another street down.

He drove more slowly this time, letting the car's auto-systems smooth out his flight as he surveyed the buildings around them, turning up the night filters in the windows to see better. It was a mixed industrial and residential area, with rows of well-lit apartment buildings interspersed with office buildings and smaller warehouses. He checked his internal map—did he have a safe house nearby? Maybe, five or so blocks away, but it was more a bolthole than anything. A few supplies, a single room he could stay in if he needed to. He was sure Vatrin would know about that safe house, too.

"Slower," Lodri said, holding up her hand. She leaned forward, her eyes closed, head craned as if straining to listen.

"Yes," she said. "Truthspoken. Or a bloodservant."

He hadn't had to tell her that bloodservants could also Change—being who she was, she already knew that, saying that bloodservants didn't look much different to her than Truthspoken. Maybe a little less soul-dense. Maybe not.

Homaj waited for a break in traffic, then set the car down on street level, feeling the soft rumble as the hover engines reconfigured for ground travel before smoothing out again.

Lodri's eyes opened, and she looked around alertly.

The street wasn't busy, but there was traffic. Not a lot of cars as fancy as the car they were in now, though. And yes, they definitely would need to ditch this car, or park it farther down if they needed to circle back on foot.

Homaj glanced down at himself. His clothes weren't too fancy for this neighborhood, but he wasn't dressed to blend in, either. Neither was Zhang. But it was night, and maybe their brightly colored hair wouldn't be so out of place even if this area didn't look to have a vivid night life.

"There," Lodri said, pointing to a smaller, three-story brick building that might be a house or hold offices. The front windows on the first floor had a soft golden glow. "In there, that house."

Homaj continued on past the house. The car's windows were opaqued from the outside—Lodri still had her aura visible—so no one could see inside. But what sort of surveillance systems would the building have? It wasn't a safe house he knew of.

"What floor?"

"Ground floor. Toward the center of the building."

Adrenaline washed through him, but he kept driving, looking for a place to park.

"This car has auto-retrieval," Lodri said. "We can get out and set it to circle and pick us up when we call."

Homaj nodded. He glanced at Zhang.

"All right. We need a plan."

Zhang was looking back through the rear window. "There's no one around the house. No guards. No other parked cars that I can see."

"Lodri," he asked, "did you sense anyone else in the house?"

"Two, maybe three others. Not Truthspoken. I'm not close enough to tell again now."

He nodded. And what covers could they use for such an unknown situation? It wasn't too late for business yet, though getting close. What excuse could they have for approaching that wouldn't scare the occupants away?

Or get them shot?

"Zhang. We'll be Municipal Guard, plain clothes."

"We don't have badges to prove that," she said.

Which he should have thought of somewhere in there, but too late for that now.

"Private investigators, then. Bounty hunters, even."

Around a corner onto the next street, he pulled the car into a small lot beside a storage building, the lot in a gap between streetlights. He didn't see anyone nearby. And he was making the call just now not to set down too far from where they had to go. They'd be visible on approach, and he didn't want them in the line of fire for more time than was necessary.

The car hummed into idle mode.

Lodri's aura went dim, then invisible as she arched her back in a stretch. "Bounty hunters might be a little dramatic. You have been on these fabled 'Truthspoken missions' before, haven't you? You've done things like this before?"

Homaj gripped the yoke before letting it go. Of course he'd been on missions—but, not so much lately. And he'd never been trained specifically to retrieve hostages, he'd usually been sent on missions that played to his strengths, which were getting people to do what he wanted or sabotaging relationships in any given circle. Iata had more practical guard training than he did.

But he was here. And Iata wasn't.

"You're coming with us?" Homaj asked, as he pulled out each of the weapons he'd strapped on earlier under his clothes and checked them in the car's overhead lights. An energy pistol in the small of his back. Another tiny pistol with limited charge on his left forearm, a thin blade strapped to his right. The cuffs of his jacket were a little tighter than he'd like for easy use of the weapons, but he checked his extraction flow several times, as he'd done earlier, too. He'd be okay with that.

Lodri watched him, her lips pressed tight. "I can't fight if it comes to that. But you might need me. To identify the Truthspoken or where they are in the building, or tell you who's ahead. I won't show I'm a magicker, though."

Homaj nodded. "But if there's violence—"

"I'm not a stranger to violence. It sickens me if I see it, yes. I might vomit. But I won't pass out."

She held his gaze, her own set and determined.

This wasn't just his fight. This was her fight for her people, too, to keep him safe, to see him safely to the rulership.

He set aside the tightness that made in his throat and nodded again, decisively. He drew up the car's control holos, looking for the circle and wait for recall function.

"There," Lodri said, pointing to an unobvious icon. "I have the recall on my comm."

He set the car to lift when there was no activity within it for two minutes, then got out into the balmy, post-rain air.

"Private investigators?" Zhang asked softly as she came back around. "Same identities as we had before, then?"

"They're the identities we have," he said, and sighed. They would need to scrap those identities when they left—he'd need to Change again. Redo Zhang's careful cosmetics. Maybe even help Lodri, though she was already a ghost in the system.

But the safe house had machinery for the identities, at least, though the use of that, too, would ping the ruler's inbox. Nothing he could do about that, or their identities, now. But their identities would be safe with Iata.

He started walking toward the brick building. The smart thing to do, if he had all the time he needed, would be to set up surveillance around the building, find out who was inside, their numbers, their weapons, their intent. But he didn't know that he had that time. It was dark now, providing at least some cover, even if that was mostly superficial. And they had Lodri, who could not only sense people, but he was fairly sure would be able to feel intent as they drew closer.

"Tell me everything you can sense about that building and its occupants," he said in a low voice as they walked.

46

LAYERS

When a Truthspoken is tired or distressed is when they're at their most vulnerable. Like anyone else, except the stakes are always the kingdom.

— HOMAJ RHIALDEN, SERITARCHUS IX IN A
PRIVATE LETTER, NEVER SENT; AS QUOTED IN
THE CHANGE DIALOGUES

They had the barest outline of a plan, sketched out in hushed arguments as they walked. They weren't the only pedestrians on the street, at least, so there was that.

Lodri had done what Homaj hadn't wanted to in the car—pulled out her comm and looked up the building to see what kind of offices or residences were inside. Whoever was in that building could have alerts set on any hard pull of regional data. That wasn't standard practice for most businesses, no, but they weren't dealing with standard circumstances, were they?

Well, it was done now.

"A law office, a commerce agency, and...a small artist's

studio. Huh. Law office is on the first floor. That's where our person is."

"Are there any lookouts?" Homaj asked. "I'm counting on standard business surveillance, at very least."

And so was she, or more than that—he hadn't missed her quick substitution of "person" for "Truthspoken," or her acting like she was reading data off her comm, not directly pulling it from the world around her with her magics.

Lodri's face pinched. "Not that I can tell." Which was as much as she could say, right.

None of which stopped him from scanning the street ahead, from each island of light beneath each streetlight, for anyone who might be hostile.

Homaj ran a hand through his short hair, looking more broadly around. A few people ahead laughed as they piled into a car. A couple walked on the opposite side of the street, picking at handheld takeout and chatting while they ate.

Their side of the street, though, was mostly deserted. Mostly storehouses on this side, he thought, or businesses that had already closed for the night.

"We should be clients, then," Homaj said. "I don't want to come in with guns out anyway. We don't know—we don't know the situation there. But the lights were on."

He didn't know if it was Vatrin inside, didn't know if Vatrin was hiding on their own initiative, or if that's where they were being held against their will. He didn't know how to determine that quickly, either, other than going in.

"Still only three?" he asked Lodri.

"Yes." She looked toward the target building. "All close together, still on the first floor, still near the center, or maybe toward the back."

Homaj almost hesitated. Almost called it off then, because how should they play this? They had a plan—

No. They didn't have a plan. They were going on almost

nothing here, and the relief of having something to follow, any kind of step at all toward finding Vatrin, had flooded his mind with a potent mix of adrenaline and invincibility and that was not how he'd been trained.

But he didn't have the training for this. He'd been trained in dozens of professions, had a true polymath's worth of skills, both useful and otherwise, but among all of them, dammit, hadn't been any kind of clear direction on how to approach a building when your sibling was inside, maybe your only close family left, not knowing whether to storm it or approach with caution lest they get spooked and flee. Didn't know if the people inside would get spooked and hurt his sibling, either.

He didn't have enough information. He just didn't have enough information, and if they'd been seen, they couldn't walk away from this and come back later. There was no time to call in reinforcements—time was precious now. He had this Truthspoken here, in this building. They might not be here an hour from now. They might leave minutes from now.

Homaj didn't trust the Municipal Guard, anyway. He didn't trust the Palace Guard. He did trust Zhang and, for the moment, Lodri.

Zhang was straining her own skill sets, too, he knew. Her face was pinched, her eyes looking everywhere for threats, and if they were trying to approach this building in the guise of clients, if they were being watched—and surely they had to be—

His breath caught. They were being watched. What they did on the way to the building was as important if not more than what they did when entering. This was a performance. *Oh.*

And now he was on more steady ground.

His thoughts flicked, discarded scenarios, landed on something solid enough.

He'd been holding the mannerisms and outward persona of Tanarin—letting it slip maybe more than he would have liked in the stress of the last few minutes—but he pulled it back around him again. Made it all absolutely solid. He was Tanarin, if not quite in truth.

And then he layered a different person entirely beneath that.

Homaj Rhialden was at the palace—whoever was in this building would likely know that, or at least assume. He had been trying to decide if he would reveal himself or not if he confirmed it was Vatrin inside, or present himself as Homaj's agent. He had no idea how compromised Vatrin was, and if Vatrin had captors, he couldn't assume they didn't have enough evaku to spot a Truthspoken if they already had one in their custody.

So—so, he would misdirect.

He leaned toward Zhang's ear. "I'm Iata," he whispered.

47

THE APPROACH

The obvious approach is rarely the best approach.

— HOMAJ RHIALDEN, SERITARCHUS IX IN A
PRIVATE LETTER, NEVER SENT; AS QUOTED IN
THE CHANGE DIALOGUES

Zhang started, gave a quick glance back.

Homaj had, for the moment, set his own mannerisms—what little showed through Tanarin's mannerisms—aside entirely. He'd set his own personality aside and had assumed Iata's, not a layering but more a temporary replacement. He wasn't quite Iata in truth, just as he wasn't Tanarin in truth. He still knew who he was. But he'd have to play this deep if it was going to work at all.

Iata, though trained well, wasn't fully Truthspoken. That Iata could pull off a full impersonation on his own wasn't something Vatrin knew, and Vatrin had always had a bad habit of underestimating and dismissing the bloodservants as more servants than blood. Vatrin would see the hints of Iata showing through Tanarin as something to be expected for Iata. Would Vatrin look deeper than that?

Zhang surveyed him, and she wouldn't see all the subtleties of what he was doing, but she nodded. She understood he thought this was necessary, at least.

Lodri eyed him as they walked, too, her brow slightly creased. And what would she see with her magicker senses? Could she see that he had just drastically shifted personalities?

They were approaching the front of the building. He felt the indent of the pistol against his back. The subtle weight of the slim pistol in his sleeve. No, he didn't want to go in there with weapons out, but he was ready to use them if needed.

He glanced to Lodri as they neared the steps leading up to a small porch. Her expression hadn't changed, no signal that anything in the situation had changed. Would she be able to tell if the emotions of the people inside spiked? If they had violent intent?

Zhang climbed the stairs ahead of him, and he didn't protest—that would have turned into an argument just now, he suspected, and the time for those had passed.

The building had the standard buds of surveillance cameras above the door. The lights inside gave a soft glow through the frosted glass.

Zhang reached for the door handle—locked.

Well, okay, it probably was a little late for clients to be visiting their lawyers. Or their commerce agents. Whatever. But circumventing a locked door would force them into a different situation entirely—or maybe not. Everything depended on who was inside that building and if they were watching just now. And what they were seeing in him.

There was a keypad beside the door. Homaj could enter his Truthspoken override—the security system of this building was almost certainly in the city's network. But that would ping the palace that it had been used. Was there any chance that more than Iata at the palace would know he was here? Tavven, or the Truthspeaker? Did he want the people inside to know he had an override? Iata did know the overrides, but he wasn't officially supposed to know.

Lodri leaned past him, gripping the handle, and gave it a turn.

It *did* turn, and the door opened, a soft scrape as the seal on the bottom brushed the rug inside.

He met her cool gaze. That hadn't outwardly looked like magics, but that had been a dangerous show all the same. More dangerous when someone discovered the lock mechanisms would have been crumbled inside. This was that important to her to risk exposing herself like that?

Important that he get through this alive, yes.

Lodri waved at the door, and he took that as a sign that they shouldn't draw weapons yet. She'd said the occupants had been toward the back of the house—if she wasn't alarmed and alert to their presence just inside, they should still be near the back.

Zhang stepped inside, and he followed.

The entry was old-fashioned, chrome fixtures highlighting wallpaper designed to look hand-painted, the holo swirls shifting through pastel colors. There was a slight must in the air, a smell of cooking, or maybe takeout. There had to be some restaurants nearby.

A lamp shone golden in the reception area, but no one was at the cluttered desk. The scattering of tasteful but older-style chairs in the waiting room were empty. From somewhere deeper in the building, the murmur of voices came, though it was a murmur only. He couldn't hear words.

Homaj paused, still listening, tensed to reach for his weapons. But there was no sign that whoever was in the other room knew they were here. Or were they just waiting for him to come to them?

He rubbed the back of his neck, one of Iata's gestures, bleeding through Tanarin's.

They couldn't act like they were clients—unless they were prepared to try and bluff through the door having been unlocked. He was fairly certain the occupants wouldn't be that gullible—especially not Vatrin, if it was Vatrin here. But he still wasn't ready to pull weapons. He didn't hear shouts, or signs of pain. He heard what sounded like an ongoing conversation. Maybe an argument, but not particularly heated.

His heart kept trying to speed up, and he was having trouble slowing it back down again.

Zhang moved toward a door ahead, leading further into the building. She tried the handle—unlocked—and carefully turned it.

He glanced at Lodri again. Her face was tight with concentration, but she still gave no sign that they should draw weapons. Adeius, he wished he could openly ask her now what she sensed.

Zhang slowly pushed open the door.

The door creaked and gave a soft whine on its hinges.

Shit.

The talking in the other room paused.

Lodri held up a hand, two fingers pointed like a gun.

Shit.

He drew the pistol behind his back, fumbling in the rush of adrenaline to get it out of the holster, out from under his jacket. So did that mean they were dealing with Vatrin's kidnappers, or just people who were startled and wary?

He'd checked before that the pistol was on stun rounds. He wouldn't shoot to kill unless he knew what was happening here.

And what had he expected? That he could just walk into that back room and say, "Hey, Vatrin, it's Iata, want to come back to the palace with me?" Had he thought no one would challenge him?

He heard footsteps and scrambled back from the door, back toward the reception desk. When whoever was coming came through that door, he'd have to assess them in a glance and talk fast.

He holstered his pistol and glared at Zhang until she did the same. Her eyes were flashing, lips drawn tight. She looked like she wanted to snarl.

He knew he was off balance. He knew he was playing this wrong, knew everything about this was off, but he was in it now. He couldn't stop. He was so close to—to something more than he had. To Vatrin, he hoped so much to Vatrin.

Putting his weapon away was a gamble, but the person coming hadn't bothered to hide their heavy steps. They hadn't come stealthily. Maybe they'd have a weapon, but he wasn't intending to present himself as a target. Just a prospective client who had found the door open and come inside.

He glanced at Lodri one last time. Her shoulders were tight, arms folded against her stomach. He showed her his weaponless hands, and she glanced at the door, nodded.

He had a chance, then.

Then something changed. Lodri's eyes widened, and she pointed toward the back of the building. Pointed *emphatically*.

Oh, no. Whoever was back there was running, weren't they? This person coming toward them wasn't a sentry, but a distraction.

Homaj pulled his pistol again, and Zhang swiped hers, too, having it up and trained on the door before he did.

The door swung open.

48

COMPETENCE

It all comes down to the moment. No matter how much you're trained or how much you prepare, it's whatever you do in the moment that ultimately matters.

— LIEUTENANT FANRIYA SANN OF THE VALON CITY MUNICIPAL GUARD, INTERVIEWED IN THE ZINE *THE COMMON VOICE*

Homaj barely had time to see the person coming through the door before Zhang fired, two shots in quick succession.

He jerked and ran forward, dizzy with panic, oh god, please let the sentry not be Vatrin—

He peered down at a stocky person, short black hair, weathered face with a scar on one cheek.

"Stunned," Zhang hissed, then ran through the open doorway, pistol out.

He looked at the stunned person again, but there was no time to try and figure out if it could be Vatrin. He didn't think so.

He caught enough breath to follow and charged after Zhang.

Behind him, he heard a gagging sound from Lodri—was she sick even with the person just stunned?—but he couldn't think about that now.

He caught up with Zhang through the center hallway, then she threw open a door to the left, in the direction he thought the voices had come from. She swept her pistol in an arc through the open doorway, but he charged past her, ignoring her shout, and barked his shin on a low couch, heading toward a half-open door to the back.

A door slammed further beyond that, shaking the building.

No!

He sprinted.

Vatrin! Adeius, he couldn't lose his sibling if he was this close. He had no idea where Vatrin would go from here.

Or be taken from here, he reminded himself. He still didn't know. He *still* didn't have enough information.

Tears stung his eyes, absolutely inconvenient.

"Trin!" he yelled. "Trin, it's Iata!"

Which was a horrible risk to admit even that, but he had to try. Had to do something.

He charged through what looked like a maintenance room, the lights off, only the light from the door showing piled boxes and cleaning supplies. He rushed past them and threw open the back door.

An engine whined, and an aircar lifted fast and unsteady from a narrow parking lot, making him squint from the glare of its lights, blowing dust into his eyes.

He quickly shoved his pistol into its holster behind his back and waved up at the car, broadcasting as many of Iata's tells as he could manage.

"Trin! Trin, it's—"

But the car was up and over the building, engines protesting the abuse.

Zhang grabbed his arm, trying to pull him back inside.

"What are you doing? Get inside!" she shouted, and she sounded furious. "Fucking get *inside*—"

He was still struggling with her, but he didn't know why. It was something to do. Something, when any sort of momentum was crumbling through his hands.

And the exhaustion of the day—had it only been a day?—made his movements slower, made his breaths seem tight, the world in various shades of sparks around him.

He was sobbing. And he couldn't seem to make it stop.

He needed to go after that aircar. Recall Lodri's car, chase it down. He couldn't let his only lead get away.

But he could barely see through the tears to stumble back inside, letting Zhang pull him.

How was he supposed to rule a kingdom if he couldn't even do this? Just this one thing, find his sibling, bring them home.

He knew it was more complicated than that. So, so much more complicated. He also knew he'd failed. Failed in so many little ways he couldn't count them all. He was much more courtier than guard. His weapons were words, personas, and he hadn't even gotten to wield them. He didn't think his whole subtle performance as Iata being Tanarin had been noticed at all, or else why would Vatrin have fled?

And that in itself was assuming more than he should.

There was another distant slam, and he started, jarred from his inner spiral.

He was shaking off Zhang and running toward the front of the house before his thoughts fully caught up with him again.

Had the person Zhang shot woken up? He couldn't let them go. They were his only link to Vatrin, the one thing that might salvage anything from all of this.

He tore back through the building, vaguely hearing Zhang

cursing behind him as she sprinted after him. He passed Lodri, a blur in the large well-lit sitting room, but didn't stop. He didn't stop, even, when he reached the entry and saw no sign of the person Zhang had shot. He threw the front door open.

The aircar had landed in front of the house and its side door was just closing. Had the person woken up, or been retrieved?

Before he could call out, Zhang seized the collar of his jacket and yanked him back inside again. Lodri slammed the door shut behind them.

He fought to free himself from Zhang's grip. "I have to—"

"You can't! Let them go!"

"I have to—"

She hauled him back away from the door before he could reach for it again. He staggered, trying to regain his balance. Then she was right there, in his face, gripping the front of his jacket tight in both hands.

"You're not okay. We shouldn't have come here. We should have rested for the night. You're not thinking straight, I know you aren't. So stop. We'll get out of here, we'll be safe, we'll try again tomorrow."

He shoved her back. "There is no trying tomorrow! They might flee the city—"

She staggered, regained her own balance. "You don't even know it's—it's who you're looking for."

"It has to be! Why else would they have—"

"Listen!" Zhang hissed. "I followed you in this because I know it's important, I don't want to see you killed, but *I don't want to see you killed!*" She drew back, looking rattled that she'd just shouted at him. She ran a shaking hand through her blue hair. "So—weapons down, okay?"

He stood, shuddering, trying to make his thoughts come back into any kind of cohesion.

Finally, he closed his eyes, let as much of everything else

drop away as he could, and focused on finding the state of a Change trance. Just enough to calm his heart, smooth away some of the adrenaline spiking every nerve.

It wasn't an easy Change. Exhaustion etched every line of his body, much more than he'd thought.

Adeius. Adeius, he knew she was right. Had he had any business at all even leaving the palace after his bid? He was Truthspoken. He was a damned good Truthspoken, even if he tried not to show it, but how could he defeat this unseen enemy, whoever had taken down his parents, mostly alone, with so few resources and less information? He had no solid vector to aim at, no clear enemy to fight.

Homaj had needed to do something. He'd pushed for this direction, and everyone had followed, assuming he knew what he was doing.

He had assumed he knew what he was doing. Or at least, he hadn't let himself pause long enough to consider anything else.

But what other way was there? He had ten days. He'd been hoping Vatrin would take over the rulership from him so he wouldn't have to have this responsibility, but that wasn't what he wanted now. Or maybe it still was what he wanted, but he knew it wasn't what he was planning to do.

Or maybe he'd just needed to get out of the palace. To not be himself. Adeius. He'd run and left Iata to handle all of that, and Iata was less prepared to rule a kingdom than he was.

He saw a movement on the other side of him and jerked around. Lodri had her comm out, holding up her hands when he spun.

"I recalled the car—I just recalled the car. It'll land in thirty seconds—out front. We should go." She hesitated, her face more lined than he remembered it being before. "I'm sorry."

Sorry that he'd lost his lead and their target? Sorry that she'd offered to help? Sorry that he'd made a disaster of all of this?

Was she second-guessing her decision to get behind him as a ruler? Because he certainly was.

She took a breath, looked like she would say more, but paused. She looked past him, toward the back of the building. "Someone's coming. I think—Truthspoken. But not who was here before."

49

THE STRANGER

You're telling me you did your best today? I saw the report, you botched that extraction all to hell. But I'm going to let it pass because everyone got out alive, and I won't lose a good officer to one bad day.

— COMMANDER MEVI MOHAMUT IN THE VID DRAMA *VALON CITY BLAZE*, SEASON 3, EPISODE 5, "THE STANDOFF"

He started moving before Zhang could stop him, heading again for the back of the house, the direction Lodri had been looking. He knew it was stupid. He was past caring if it was stupid—he just wanted something, anything, to salvage all of this.

Zhang gripped his arm and vaulted past him.

"Stay behind me," she barked, glaring back at him.

His mouth pulled tight, but he nodded.

"I'm behind you," Lodri said. As if she didn't want to let him out of her sight this time, either.

"You're sure they're Truthspoken?" he asked Lodri. Was this

Eyras coming to see what had happened to Vatrin? Or the other way around?

"Yes." She tilted her head. "Maybe. The sense of them is... less dense than a Truthspoken should be. Be careful—I don't know if they are a Rhialden Truthspoken."

Zhang held up a hand before they reached the large back room again, though Homaj could see through the doorway. Whoever had been in there had left a scattering of restaurant wrappers near the couch nearest the door where he stood. Had that been where they'd been speaking before? Could he see any signs at all that it had been Vatrin here?

Vatrin had always been messy in their own persona, more precise in others. But that messiness was a true habit that their father had never been able to train out of them.

The back door to the building opened inside the maintenance room, out of sight, the hinges making the softest creak.

Damn those hinges.

He heard steps on the rug inside, then on the wooden floor.

Homaj's heart hammered in his throat. He checked his layers of personality—they had slipped again, and he pulled them back as much as he could. Iata beneath, Tanarin fully showing.

"Back," Zhang hissed. "Back, go back into the hall."

He let her herd him backward, because yes, it was smart. Lodri reached for his shoulder, squeezed it, her touch lingering. He felt warmth from her, an attempt at soothing his nerves. He didn't quite shake her off, but she withdrew her hand all the same.

Homaj drew his pistol again from where he'd hastily re-holstered it behind his back. He wasn't about to make that mistake a second time. He didn't raise it, though, just waited, hand feeling slick on the grip. He watched, past Zhang, what he could see of the mostly closed door to the back room.

The inner door slowly opened. A hand with a pistol came

through first.

Homaj swallowed, shifting his grip on his own pistol, twitching his finger toward the trigger, though he still didn't raise it.

Zhang had no such reservations. Her pistol was up and trained steadily on the person as they stepped inside.

Tall, masc. Light brown skin, dark narrow eyes. Long hair braided back in a no-nonsense style. Handsome but in an ordinary way, not vid star handsome like the nobility usually tried to be. Mid-forties, maybe.

He searched frantically for tells.

The person stopped when they saw Zhang, her pistol aimed at them. Theirs wasn't quite pointed yet at her.

There was…something about how the person carried themself that was familiar. He tried to match it to Vatrin's tells, but couldn't come up with anything solid. To Eyras, but not there, either.

"Identify yourself," Zhang snapped, but that would get nowhere. Not if this person was Truthspoken. They could literally be anyone, and they didn't have to say who. Though Lodri, at least, would know if they were lying—as long as they weren't being someone in truth.

Homaj made one more likely stupid decision and stepped around Zhang into the room. She gave a soft huff of breath, but didn't try to stop him this time. That would have been an argument, too, and this *definitely* wasn't the time for arguments.

The person's eyes trained on him. He sensed more than saw them reading him, taking in his own tells. Which were, at the moment, solidly Iata's, and very deliberately showing through.

They lowered their pistol and held up their free hand. "We have to talk. Not here. I have a car." The words were terse, with an accent he couldn't quite pin. He'd need to hear more.

"So do we," Homaj said. The car should be waiting now out front.

He still wasn't reading Vatrin or Eyras in this person. He *was* still getting that weird sense of familiarity, though. Could it possibly be Omari, his father's bloodservant? Had he, after all, escaped the attack? A traitorous flutter of hope—but no, those cues weren't there, either.

He had the prickling feeling, though, the person had recognized him. As Iata, at least, and there was a very, *very* short list of people who'd be able to recognize a bloodservant's tells.

"Will you come with us?" Homaj asked this maybe-stranger.

They considered, still watching him, then taking in Zhang again and Lodri. They slowly re-holstered their pistol on their hip, then nodded.

Okay. Okay, so here was someone—Truthspoken-trained in some capacity—here was still a lead, however tenuous.

The sharpness of that relief made his throat burn. But he absolutely would *not* let his eyes start tearing again.

He gathered what energy he had left and locked his emotions down. He would have to deal with them later. Truly, later.

He'd made a lot of mistakes today. He'd rushed far too quickly into all of this and without doing the preparation he should have—but he still felt he hadn't been wrong to assume that whoever had been here would have been gone before long. The place just hadn't been set up as a fortress. And he truly didn't have much time where life and death were concerned. That whoever was here had run so quickly meant they knew people were after them.

The hairs on his arms rose. Had Vatrin been moving from location to location, chased by their father's enemies, while Homaj had been busy Changing and napping and generally not being productive?

He was right to not have taken the time to sleep longer. Whatever other mistakes he'd made—he was sure he was right to have kept pursuing his sibling.

But would those same enemies after Vatrin start chasing him now, too?

He was increasingly convinced that Vatrin had been here of their own free will—seeing the empty takeout containers near the couch, knowing Lodri's demeanor before they'd alerted the occupants, and just not having the sense that this had been a place of unwilling violence.

And yes—yes, he had royally screwed that up.

Or could Vatrin possibly be afraid of *him?* Even of Iata, if Vatrin had seen him coming in? If he didn't know who to trust just now, who did Vatrin think *they* could trust?

He was mostly sure Vatrin hadn't seen him coming in, though. There was no surveillance equipment here. And there'd been no sign that the people here had known anyone was coming until Zhang had creaked the hallway door.

So Vatrin wouldn't be with professionals. Wasn't even with their assigned guards, maybe. Vatrin themself had much less training and proficiency with Municipal and Palace Guard practices than he did.

Adeius, he hoped whoever was with Vatrin would keep them safe. They'd bundled Vatrin out of here quickly enough. Which also made him more certain than before that it had in fact been Vatrin here.

Silently, with tension crackling around them, they all filed back through the building and out the front door.

Homaj did his best to maintain some appearance of the ordinary, not that anyone watching outside wouldn't have noted an unconscious person being hauled out the front door, or an expensive aircar idling. People would draw their conclusions. The Municipal Guard might already have been called.

All weapons were away again, at least.

He glanced again at the stranger, then waved them into the waiting car.

50

DYNASTIC CITIZEN

The Onabrii-Kast Dynasty successfully broke away from the Kingdom of Valoris over two hundred years ago, but they don't let their people forget it. Animosities between citizens of the Dynasty and citizens of Valoris have been cooling in recent years, however, with the last war falling out of immediate public memory. One would think it's almost time to start a new one.

— DR. AMI TIERNEY IN THE OPINION PIECE, "DYNASTIC FOLLIES: WHAT THE ONABRII-KAST DYNASTY CAN DO TO GIVE THEIR CITIZENS PEACE"

Lodri lifted the car. "I'm not keen to use autopilot just now. Do we have a destination?"

Homaj considered the stranger sitting beside him in the backseat. Across from him, facing back, Zhang sat tensely, pistol in her lap. Very much not hiding the fact that she was a guard, not a civilian.

The stranger's eyes flicked to Zhang, back to him. Their lips drew tighter, and they turned in their seat to more fully face Homaj.

Their familiarity was itching at Homaj's mind. Their bearing was self-assured, aware of themself and those around them. That, in itself, wasn't the mark of a Truthspoken, but it certainly was in that direction. Were they someone among the nobility? Who happened to have an uncanny knowledge of Iata's own tells? Could he possibly have missed someone Truth-spoken trained at court?

Just because they had Truthspoken training hardly meant they were a friend, too.

"All right," Lodri said, "I'll just fly a pattern around the usual nighttime tourist traps. For the record, again, it's safe to talk in here. I just changed the chameleon systems, too—we have a different ident and color now than we had on the ground. But I don't want to keep flying a holding pattern if anyone's flagged us and it stuck—please make this quick."

The stranger nodded, as if that was all very reasonable. They didn't, however, take their eyes off Homaj.

Homaj studied them more closely. They wore plain clothes, a little casual for this district, a black jacket and denim pants. They wore no cosmetics that he could see. No jewelry, either, except for a dark blue ring on the ring finger of their left hand, which looked like some kind of tech rather than ornamenta-tion. They gave off firm masc gender cues, but that didn't mean they were male.

Their look back at him was bemused. They took a breath, the intensity of their gaze finally breaking. "It's safe to talk? What level of security?"

"Military," Lodri said. "Flag equivalent."

Homaj only had her word on that, and he'd trusted her before, but if she was a high-ranking, unsealed magicker, it was something he was willing to trust. He nodded.

The stranger paused, as if deciding whether to trust that

themself, and he wondered if they had their own dampener or scrambler on them. But military-grade scramblers weren't small or light, so he doubted anything the stranger had would equal Lodri's tech.

"Good," the stranger finally said. "My name is Weyan Odeya. He and him pronouns."

His accent—his accent, here in the car, was turning more Dynastic, from the Onabrii-Kast Dynasty. That was the hint Homaj had picked up on before, and that was unusual. With tensions as they were between Valoris and the Dynasty, Dynastic citizens on Valon who weren't also ambassadorial were rare.

Wait, but was that how Homaj knew him? Was he part of the Dynastic ambassadorial staff?

He hadn't paid that much attention. And it would make sense, a horrible sort of sense, if the Dynasty trained Truthspoken of their own. It wasn't as if that had never been speculated, or watched for. They had, after all, used to be a part of the united Kingdom of Valoris, before they'd broken off into their own kingdom. They had a Seritarchus, too, if not quite the same as Valoris. No, not even remotely the same.

His father usually saw to ambassadorial things, though. Adeius, why had he been so set on *not* paying attention to anything political these last few years?

"You're Dynastic," Homaj said. Keeping his own persona and accent as Tanarin tight. That's what Iata would do, and he kept Iata's personality centered, too.

Weyan smiled tightly, glanced at Zhang again, then at Lodri. For a long moment, he seemed to be weighing his options for trusting there, too. Then he straightened—which was odd. The move felt spontaneous, not calculated. If he was Truthspoken-trained, he should be more tightly controlled than that.

"I was also once known as Keressorian Rhialden."

Homaj choked and had to smooth out his breath. His aunt

—his *uncle*. The familiarity—it wasn't his appearance, though now that Homaj knew, he could see the barest hints of Rhialden in the sharp cheekbones, the particular shape of his face. But more like a very distant cousin than...than...his uncle?

But his uncle had left court when he was young, had gone into exile. His uncle had foresworn Change. Truthspoken trained, yes, but no longer Truthspoken.

"You've—you've been living in the Dynasty? Does the Seritarchus—"

He bit off his words, bile rising. Did. *Did* the Seritarchus know.

New suspicion rose up with the bile. Was it coincidence—no, of course it wasn't coincidence that his uncle was already here, onworld, when his parents were assassinated. Could he have done it? Was he trying to take out all of the Truthspoken so only he would remain, reclaim his status as Truthspoken and claim the throne?

Weyan held up his hands. "I have absolutely no desire to rule Valoris. I gave up that claim years ago. I have a family in the Dynasty—I have two lovely husbands and five children, and I would very much like to get back to them."

What? Homaj's already sluggish mind was struggling to keep up with this new information. He had...Dynastic cousins?

He wasn't a magicker, and he wasn't going to ask Lodri to verify all of this and expose her as a magicker. But he was Truthspoken trained, and Truthspoken could verify the truth, too. He could read enough signals to know with reasonable certainty that Weyan was telling the truth. But then, his uncle was Truthspoken trained, too.

"Why are you here?" he asked, spreading his hands with, he feared, more than a little exasperation. His head felt stuffed, too full of things he was struggling to understand. Not full enough of the things he needed to know.

Weyan's eyes flicked again to Zhang. Apparently he had

things even more sensitive to discuss than his identity, which was a political bomb all on its own.

"She's sworn to me," Homaj said—and realized his mistake. Adeius. Sworn to *Homaj*. He was broadcasting himself as Iata.

Weyan's brows went up, a gesture so like his father's that it made his throat tighten.

Weyan's look sharpened, re-calculating. So his layering Iata beneath Tanarin had been working, until he'd made a child's mistake and blown it.

"Does everyone in this car know who you are but me?" Weyan demanded.

It was a probing question, without giving everything away. Homaj could still say he was Iata, and Weyan would know otherwise, but it would tell Weyan that the others in the car still thought he was Iata, too.

"They know," he said quietly.

He saw the flash in his uncle's eyes, something he had a vivid flashback to from childhood. His uncle's temper had been legendary, and he'd been on the receiving end of it more than once. He absolutely remembered that.

"Why are *you* here—and why by all the gods were you storming into that house without backup?" He didn't address Homaj by name, or mention his true position—and maybe that was wise, even with Lodri's security. If it got out that there was a bloodservant impersonating him in the palace...Adeius.

Homaj gave a tight shrug. "I'm trying to find Vatrin."

"Yes, I've been tracking them, too. And I would have made contact, I think, if you hadn't flushed them out just before I got to them."

Homaj sat up straighter. "Then that was Vatrin? I thought, but I didn't know—"

"You need to get back to the palace."

Weyan leaned forward, tapping the side of Lodri's seat.

"Take us to the river district." He frowned at Homaj. "I still remember the ways in. You'll have to open the doors, I'll have been keyed out, and I can't Change. But I'll see you back in safely. And stay there, please, Iata. This kingdom needs you to be alive right now."

51

THE ARGUMENT

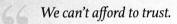 *We can't afford to trust.*

— HOMAJ RHIALDEN, SERITARCHUS IX IN A
PRIVATE LETTER, NEVER SENT; AS QUOTED IN
THE CHANGE DIALOGUES

Homaj felt his face heat, his world narrow. This was the first time he'd spoken to his uncle in years—he did remember the last time, but he'd been a child. But his uncle had just shown up again and was now trying to give him orders? His uncle, who wasn't even Truthspoken anymore?

If he had been more centered in his own personality, he knew he'd have already bitten out a sharp retort. Iata's personality, too, was trying to meet that indignity with...something.

He closed his eyes briefly, looked out the window at city lights moving past below them. They weren't near the river, but into Blue District, heading back toward Financial. As far as he could tell, Lodri hadn't veered from her current course, though he saw her increased tension.

And uncle or not, he still couldn't trust this person beside him. He didn't know why Weyan was here.

He also didn't know exactly why his uncle had left all those years ago, why he'd done something so drastic as to swear off Change and renounce his title, position, and holy mandate. Years before he'd had to. Homaj didn't know what that epic fight between his father and his uncle had been about, and that was suddenly vastly important.

"What did you fight about?" he asked quietly. Moderating the volume of his voice being the only thing he knew would work to moderate the tone.

Weyan grunted, sighed, sat back. His mannerisms were far too casual, too spontaneous for someone Truthspoken trained, and that was weirding Homaj out. It wasn't feigned or controlled, he was sure of that. Weyan had been living a life that wasn't...Truthspoken. Did his husbands know his origins? Did they know his position before he'd left Valoris?

Did it matter?

It mattered here, but this was Valon, where every political apostrophe and period mattered.

"The Seritarchus..." Weyan stopped. He grimaced, and then just looked grim. "I am sorry. He sent for me because...well." He glanced again at Zhang, then Lodri.

Homaj bridled. He'd already said Zhang was sworn to him. If both Zhang and Lodri knew who he was, that should imply he trusted them. He trusted both of them a lot more than he trusted Weyan Odeya.

"You can speak here," he snapped. And that ire was completely in line with Iata's values of loyalty.

Lodri set the autopilot, turned her seat around, and flared her aura.

Homaj drew in a breath. He hadn't been expecting that. Why would she risk that?

Weyan twitched in surprise, but didn't recoil. He definitely noted the lack of seal on Lodri's cheek.

She extended a hand. "Weyan Odeya. I am honored to meet you."

Weyan took her hand, watching her closely. "And you are?"

"Lodri," she said. "I stand with this person and will give him what aid I can."

Holding her hand, Weyan would sense the truth of that statement. Not exactly an ironclad statement, but for the moment, enough.

Weyan pulled back. "Well." He looked back to Homaj. "Well, I guess you should know. Not that it's entirely relevant anymore—"

"It is," Lodri said decisively.

Lodri knew why his uncle had left?

Weyan's smile twisted. "Well, then, maybe it is. In short, I left because the duke I'd been in betrothal talks with suddenly withdrew. Or, his family did, in any case. He himself was forcibly secluded after manifesting Green Magics."

Homaj glanced at Lodri—she was not surprised by this information. He hadn't known, though. Not even that his uncle might have been betrothed. But, Adeius, his uncle's duke had manifested Green Magics? Homaj had never heard of a duke manifesting Green Magics.

"I thought that was a ridiculous reason to break an agreement that might end in love," Weyan continued. "It had been going that way. And the marriage certainly had political benefits. The Rhialdens sorely needed that alliance with the Eprallis. But my brother, the Seritarchus—he was adamant. And he said things that I could not forgive."

He shrugged. "Could not forgive then, when I was a lot younger and infinitely more foolish. Or, maybe not so foolish. One of my husbands is a magicker. Consequently, he used to be a duke."

Homaj swallowed hard. His uncle's words were light, but the old, simmering anger in his eyes was not.

Okay—okay. So that was history, maybe relevant to what was happening now, maybe not. The fall of the Epralli family from the high houses made more sense now, but he couldn't immediately see a motive why they might attack the Seritarchus now. They had comfortably settled into industrial innovation as lesser nobility and hadn't made any significant social ripples in years.

"But—why are you here? Why now? Did you know that something might happen to the Seritarchus?"

Weyan's brows drew together. He might have just shown his anger, but this now was very real sadness. "The Seritarchus knew that someone he trusted was going to betray him. He was gathering evidence against this person, preparing to make it public—no, I don't know who. He didn't say. He wanted me here because he didn't know who he should trust."

"And he trusted you? After you fought and left like you did—"

"Of course he trusted me. I have nothing to do with Rhialden politics. I have nothing to do with Dynastic politics, for that matter. I'm a manager of a large shoe distributor." He smiled, the corners of his eyes crinkling, but it quickly faded. "I am not—was not—friends with my older brother, but I do love him. Did. Love him. Gods."

Weyan pinched the bridge of his nose, sat back. After a minute, he said, "I trust that you were not the one he was talking about."

52

REASONABLE QUESTIONS

> *Decreed this day of Nurun the Eighth, in the rule of the Eighth Seritarchus of the Twelfth Dynasty, 2930 New Era, that Keressorian Rhialden has abdicated as Truth-spoken and foresworn Change.*

— OFFICIAL ANNOUNCEMENT FROM PALACE RHIALDEN

Homaj's world flashed, his ears ringing. Had his uncle just accused him of—

"No," he said, sitting forward. "I would not—Adeius, don't say that." He closed his eyes, trying desperately to smooth away the sting.

"All right," Weyan said, not entirely gently. "It was a reasonable question. Especially with Vatrin on the run. And you barging into their safe house. And me finding you there."

Homaj reached for Lodri's hand, and she took it. She didn't have to be asked to hold out a hand to Weyan again, who took it as well.

"I had nothing to do with the deaths of Anatherie Rhialden,

or Jamir ne—" His voice broke. He swallowed and forged on. "Jamir ne Xiao Rhialden."

Lodri flinched, letting go of his hand. Weyan swallowed, ran a shaky hand over his head, leaving his neat braid mussed. "All right. That, I can't refute. All right. So."

"It was the Truthspeaker," Homaj said. "That—that I am almost certain of. Somehow. He—uh, outed Homaj this morning, publicly, in the Adeium." He had almost slipped again there. He didn't even know if it mattered here, but he had to get a grip on himself.

"Is that why Homaj had the First Magicker witness for him, not Aduwel?"

"Yes. Partly. Mostly." He glanced at Lodri, who gave a small shrug.

"And Ceorre—she's his Truthspeaker in training—does not trust him, either. Vatrin was last seen with him. Well, until now, if that really was Vatrin. Do you know for sure it was? How did you track them there?"

Weyan rubbed the side of his neck. "I spent all today since I arrived trying to scrape what information I could out of the city's underground. The crime bosses, those with connections to the nobility—you would not believe how many connections to the nobility. I was trying to find what I could, any clue about who had done this, and where Vatrin and Eyras might be. All word said they were still missing. Tavven said that—"

"You spoke to Commander Tavven? They know you're here?"

"Yes. The Seritarchus directed me to speak to Tavven when I arrived if—well. If I arrived too late." He closed his eyes. "I spoke to Tavven right in the middle of the chaos earlier, before you made your bid. That's what I walked out to, in the spaceport—utter chaos. My shuttle was the last down from the station, and no one wanted to let me out, but I still have my emergency I.D. that marks me as a person of confidence with the Seritarchus. I had Tavven's comm code and used it. I was not...at that point, I was not surprised by what they told me. And they told me precious little. Enough to guess."

He shifted. "There's a rumor that Homaj gave a monumental dressing down to Abret and Laguaya, and that wouldn't have been long ago. Word is traveling fast from the palace, with all the focus on what's happening there."

Iata had dressed down the joint commanders? Adeius. Could that possibly be true?

Weyan shifted again, and his voice held a tight edge. "Were you at the palace when that happened?"

Homaj took a breath. He knew what Weyan was asking, and he hadn't at all wanted to get into this. He still wasn't sure how much he trusted his uncle—and he was eyeing Lodri again, wanting to verify his uncle's truth as Weyan had done to Homaj. Would that offend him? Did Homaj have the luxury of offense here, if his uncle could be an ally and had information he needed? He had so very few allies.

Weyan made a noise, waved at Lodri. "Please, if you can verify again?"

She held out her hands again, and Homaj and Weyan took them.

"I also had nothing to do with the death of Anatharie Rhialden or Jamir ne Xiao Rhialden. I had nothing to do with Vatrin's disappearance. I am here because Anatherie asked me to come. I have no intent to harm you, or Homaj, or take the rulership myself."

All of it, as far as Homaj could tell from Lodri's sense of the truth, was true.

He nodded. Let go again.

"I have been searching for Vatrin since"—he didn't even know the time—"for most of the day. I've been in the city."

Weyan's face went gray, his expression openly horrified.

Homaj recoiled. The situation wasn't that bad, surely. He

trusted Iata. He trusted Iata with his life, *actually* with his life, and wasn't that what a bloodservant was for?

He knew he'd pushed beyond what he should have done. And yet. It was what he had done.

"Were you there when Homaj made his bid to rule?" Weyan asked.

"Yes."

Weyan took a breath. Eyed him, and Homaj could almost see him thinking.

"Iata," he said slowly. "Do you know who you are?"

Homaj tensed. Well, yes, he knew he wasn't Iata. He wasn't Iata in truth, even though he was still carrying a lot of Iata's personality and mannerisms over his own. But that had slipped quite a bit. Blended in weird ways with his Tanarin persona. This—all of this—was just so much to track, and he was tired, and way too keyed up.

"Yes."

He didn't know where his uncle was going with this.

Weyan read his expression, read everything about him. Then sighed. "No. I fear you don't. Iata—bloodservants are full Truthspoken siblings. You might not have as much training as Homaj, but you have as much bloodright claim to the rulership as he does. More, even. You're older."

Iata was...what?

His ears began to ring.

His body understood the implications before his mind did and kicked his heart into high gear.

53

GO BACK

As a bloodservant, I learned to walk quietly in the palace halls, being everywhere and also invisible.

— IATA RHIALDEN, AS QUOTED IN *THE CHANGE DIALOGUES*

Homaj stared out the aircar window, his thoughts on fire. Holding Iata's personality as center to his own just now was...was...suffocating.

He'd known Iata since they were children—they'd grown up together. They'd trained together, though Iata hadn't been a part of all of his training, certainly. Iata managed his daily life. Iata had always tried to temper him from being too...well. Too caustic. He knew he was caustic. Iata had been, in many ways, like his brother, though he'd known they were distant cousins, not brothers.

But they *were* brothers? Actually and truly full siblings?

His stomach tightened. Iata had been trying to Change into him at the beginning of all of this, that had been Iata's first instinct when everything had gone wrong. Iata had played it off as loyalty, but...was it?

It would be so easy. So immensely easy, from the position Iata stood in now, to take over his life.

"How?" he asked, his voice coming out rougher than he wanted. "How are we actually brothers?"

Weyan waved a hand. "There is no service branch of the Rhialdens. I found out when my brother was planning to start his heirs—he told me, actually. He'd been horrified and wanted to know if he should also tell Omari." He sighed. "He did, and Omari was livid. Loyal, but livid that he'd never been told. That he'd never known his father had been his father. But when Anatharie started his children, there was little else to do but repeat the cycle. Bloodservants are required."

Adeius. Adeius, he did not *need* this complication right now. Did Vatrin know about this? Did Eyras?

Did Iata?

He closed his eyes, fighting back that claustrophobia of personalities and pulling Iata's closer. Wrapping it fully around himself. Almost—*almost*—in truth. He had to know what Iata would be thinking.

It hadn't been Iata's idea to take over his life earlier. It had been Homaj's. Hadn't it? Or had there been little signals, had Iata been trying to push him in that direction?

No. No, that wasn't it.

Yes, Iata had tried to Change into him earlier. It had made sense, the only kind of sense—protect Homaj at all costs. At significant costs to himself. He'd never accomplished a full like-ness Change before, certainly not that quickly, though he'd done plenty of smaller Changes, some of them approaching likeness Changes. He did have the training for that, mostly, if not all the exact combined experience. He was observant and attentive to all of Homaj's needs as a Truthspoken. Iata had always felt a bit stifled by the residence wing environment and his place in it. But he would never, Adeius he would *never* do anything to deliberately harm Homaj or his position. It wasn't who he was. It didn't align at all with his personal beliefs.

And would that change if Iata knew that he was Homaj's full sibling? Was his *older* sibling?

No.

Homaj let out a breath, still letting it all unpack in his thoughts, feeling what Iata's emotional responses might be. If Iata knew he was a full sibling, that might change some of his immediate responses, give voice to some of his ambitions, but it still wouldn't make him disloyal. It wouldn't change his loyalty. Not right away, at least.

Homaj was also almost certain Iata didn't know.

He opened his eyes, letting some of his tight grasp on Iata's personality go.

Did Eyras know? Vatrin and Eyras had never had as close a relationship as he had with Iata. They were distant to each other, cold. He'd seen resentment before in Eyras, though he'd thought it understandable—Vatrin had never had much regard for the bloodservants around them, seeing them as less than equal. They'd even tried to oust Iata and Eyras from their training sessions, once. Which notion their father had shot down.

All of that—all of that gained more nuance. Maybe. So much depended on if Vatrin and Eyras knew about this.

But he hadn't just left Iata with his appearance, with a role. He had left Iata with the actual ruling of a kingdom while he'd run off to try and find Vatrin—

Adeius.

He hadn't truly understood that. He'd run off because he'd thought it was what he had to do. Maybe he wasn't wrong about that. But he had left Iata in a horrible position. A lot worse than he'd thought—did the Truthspeaker know Iata was a full sibling? Who else in the palace knew? The lab tech who'd started their incubators would have. But that was almost thirty years ago, starting with Eyras—were they still there now? Did Tavven know?

"You need to get back to the palace," Weyan said again.

And what would Weyan gain if he did? Weyan was pushing him hard in this direction, and Weyan had said he intended to help, that he had no intention to harm, but there were too many ways to get around solid statements, even statements witnessed by magickers.

Weyan had said he hadn't been involved in what happened to Homaj's fathers, but what was his involvement now? He'd been trying to get to Vatrin. Had that truly been out of the goodness of his heart? Homaj wasn't sure such a thing existed. There was always a motive. Everyone had their reasons for everything they did. Even Iata's loyalty had motive—his continued place and balance in the social web of the palace.

If going back to the palace got Homaj off the streets, it would give Weyan more room to act, to do whatever he was already doing.

"You still don't trust me," Weyan said, sounding offended. Or maybe even hurt. But, he sighed. "Of course you don't trust me. You're—well. You're you. Whatever you do—Change again. You were seen going in and out of that building, and I don't know who had access to the surveillance. Wherever you were staying, if you were in a safe house, might not be safe, either. You could have been traced back through the city. Can you accept that logic, at least?"

"You just told me that the Seritarchus said someone close to him was plotting against him. So I'm not convinced that going back to the palace is any safer."

"And it might not be. Adeius, I do not miss these games. Listen. If you don't want to go back to the palace yet—and I still think you should—I can go back with you, if you want me to, I'll do my best to protect you. I can't Change, but I don't think

I'll be identified by most people there as I Changed after I left, and I haven't forgotten my evaku training. There is a chance the Truthspeaker could know me, though. Tavven will as well.

"Otherwise—" he rapped a knuckle on the window beside him. "I'll keep searching in the city. Vatrin might have fled again, but I have a few more ideas on where they might be. Or at least, I can tap into where others are tracking them to and pray I get there before their enemies do."

Should Homaj go back to the palace just now? His instincts were running in multiple and opposing directions. He needed to think. And not here, where his uncle was trying to push him. And Zhang was eyeing all of this with rigid alarm.

He met Lodri's eyes, and she stared back at him, face tight.

54

A WALK NOT HIS OWN

> *Truthspoken Change all aspects of themselves, absolutely anything that can identify them to anyone but those trained to see who they are—and sometimes not even then.*

> — HOMAJ RHIALDEN, SERITARCHUS IX IN A
> PRIVATE LETTER, NEVER SENT; AS QUOTED IN
> *THE CHANGE DIALOGUES*

Lodri banked the aircar back toward the double ribbon of lights that lined the river, set it on auto. She turned her seat back around and popped open a compartment on the dash, pulling out two compact gray bags.

"Anti-surveillance kits," she said, handing them back. "They're not unobtrusive, but it will take you off system tracking long enough to get somewhere safe."

Right. Right, she was no stranger to needing to hide from the city's surveillance system, either.

She pulled out another bag and set it in her own lap.

Was she planning to come with them? He hadn't counted

on her help past finding Vatrin—and, well, they hadn't quite done that yet.

He opened his bag, and Zhang opened hers. There were anti-pattern masks inside, various expandable foam wedges that might quickly alter body shape or gait when triggered, throat stickers that would crudely warp voices. All of this to be done mid-walk.

These were crude tools and not usually needed for a Truthspoken. Should he try to force a quick Change right now? But Lodri was right, and his uncle was right. If they were being tracked, and tracked at the highest levels, they'd be identified again as soon as they got out of this car, even if the car itself had managed to evade the systems. Best to get out and stagger their use of these props. Disappear on the go.

It wasn't impossible for a Truthspoken to accomplish quick, feature-obscuring Changes on the go, but it was dangerous and draining, and he didn't think he had that capacity just now. Lodri might be able to disappear with her magics, but Zhang couldn't, and she couldn't Change, either.

He quickly ran through the available safe houses and glanced at the dash map. They were nearing Riveredge, which was at least close to the pub where he'd entered the city.

There was still the chance of leading someone to a new safe house, but it would be less of a chance with Lodri's props. And when they got there, he could Change, he could switch up Zhang's cosmetics, and Lodri's if she would let him. They could make new idents, though the machines would ping the Seritarchus's inbox at the palace. Which he was certain Iata would by now control. Was that a risk?

Maybe, but not the sort of risk Weyan thought.

Outside the window, the river below gleamed in the glow of lights, and beyond it, the soft, warm glow of the palace.

"Lodri—set us down...there." He pointed at a place on the map. Near enough one of his lesser known safe houses, not so close as to fully point to it. The bloodservants wouldn't know about that safe house, but Vatrin might.

"Weyan—" He stopped. How would his uncle contact him, when he'd burn his temporary comm as soon as he got out of this car? He'd get another at the safe house, but Homaj wasn't keen to lead his uncle there.

"Uncle," he finally said, ironically, because it was now true for both the Homaj and Iata instances of himself. "If you need to contact me, send it to this code." He said the string of his private comm code, which Iata would have now. He repeated it twice, and his uncle said it back.

That was a risk. Homaj's code might be known to their enemies. But it was a smaller risk in a sea of larger ones that night.

"Lodri, are you coming with me?" he asked.

Her brows knit, but she said, "Yes. I can set the car to drop us off and park somewhere else. Somewhere not close."

That—yes, that was a good idea.

"Do you have another anti-surveillance kit?" Weyan asked.

"I don't. Sorry."

Homaj debated handing over his own—he really only needed the mask, he could drastically shift his walk and posture. But could he afford to not use every tool at hand? He might need the added protection of a different silhouette. And he was tired enough he didn't want to rely on his Truthspoken skills alone. Not when so much was at stake.

Weyan shrugged, as if to say he'd gotten this far on his own. He pinned Homaj with a level look as Lodri dipped the car down.

"Be careful. Be so very careful, Iata. And get back to the palace as soon as you can. Homaj will need your help."

Homaj gave a tight nod. "Be careful yourself. And if you find Vatrin—keep them safe."

Weyan smiled. Reached to squeeze his forearm. Just one brief touch of acknowledgement, affection.

The touch flooded his eyes, burned in his throat, and for a moment, his breath caught and he couldn't move. He couldn't think past the roaring in his ears.

The car reached ground level, the engines whining faintly as they switched to hover.

Weyan got out and left without a glance back, blending into the night.

Homaj took a ragged breath, gathered himself, looked out the window. He knew where they were. "We'll walk two blocks west, meet up again at the tackle shop. I'll go right, Zhang center, Lodri left. Don't acknowledge each other. I'll put on my mask at the count of thirty. Zhang, sixty. Lodri, ninety."

He shoved one of the foam wedges into his right shoe.

Clipped another two of the expandable ones on either side of his hips inside his pants, to be expanded on the way, and watched as Lodri did the same. Zhang hesitated, unsure—he pointed at what she needed.

"These, the shoulder pads. Doesn't need to be pretty, just different."

"We should go," Lodri said, looking up from where she'd been programming the car with her comm.

Homaj nodded and pushed out into the cooler, dank air, shifting his walk as he went. The foam wedge was an annoyance, but it kept him from falling into any usual patterns.

He didn't look back to see if the others followed, or when the aircar lifted, though he did hear the engines change as it lifted.

Then he was alone. Walking by himself on the rain-slicked side street of Riveredge. The air heavy with humidity, thick with the smells of fried and spicy things coming from a nearby pub. Drifting with the sounds of laughter, of music. Of people walking, and the soft whirring of cars both on the ground and overhead.

He tapped at his hips to trigger the foam expansions and shifted to a more swaying gait. He pulled the mask over his face, weaving around a group of people talking, drinks in hand. The medium brown of the mask would have warps and waves to its coloring, making surveillance have a hard time tracking his features. It would look weird to passersby, though, so he avoided gazes and kept his walk steady and measured. A walk not his own.

55

PROOF

I didn't always know
And I always wish I had

— CHIKE USMAN IN FAER POPULAR SONG,
"WHO IS MY BROTHER"

I ata heard little beyond the ringing in his ears. It couldn't be true. It could *not* be true. The Truthspeaker was trying to get inside his head. Trying to manipulate him, blackmail him, even.

Back in Homaj's apartment, he headed straight for the prep room, waving Jalava after him. Jalava, looking flustered, told the rest of the guards to take up their positions before hurrying after Iata.

Iata didn't stop there, though, heading straight for the bedroom.

"Ser Truthspoken," Jalava said, following. "What happened? Were you threatened?"

Yes, Iata thought. He had been. Threatened that this whole thing could plausibly be pinned on him now if he didn't fall into line. If he didn't allow himself to be controlled. Adeius, what Homaj had feared was already happening. He wished he had a way to contact him—Adeius, maybe his *brother*—but Homaj had taken a generic comm that had no connections to the palace and a rotating address number.

Iata touched the Palace Guard comm ring on his finger, the one Homaj had been wearing earlier—but, well. It was on his finger. Not Homaj's.

Should he contact Commander Tavven? And say what? That the Truthspeaker had threatened him? It had been one of those insidious threats that wasn't a threat without context. And Iata wasn't sure that Tavven, given what the Truthspeaker had threatened him with, wouldn't start suspecting him, too. Because he was, just now, absolutely perfectly placed to carry out his own coup. To have carried it out from the beginning.

Iata shut the door to the bedroom—too sharply, but Jalava caught it, eased it shut. That was becoming a thing.

"What is going on?" Jalava asked. "Please, talk to me. I can't protect you without knowing what—"

Iata held up a hand. One of Homaj's gestures, and just now, he couldn't ease back into himself. Not without knowing who and what he really was. Not without knowing for sure. He'd snapped out of being Homaj in truth in pure shock at the Adeium, but his mind was still reorienting itself back to his own, too.

"I need to confirm something," he said, and rummaged in a large cabinet across from the bed before coming out with one of the genetic scanners they used in training and sometimes complex Changes. It could sample objects for DNA left behind, sample fluids, sample anything that could even conceivably hold a small amount of genetic material. And it could project a holo, extrapolate a genetic sequence from traits input into it, generally help any newer, younger Truthspoken or bloodservant with Change tasks and persona building until their innate sense of genetics and traits took over. He and Homaj still used it occasionally to help build variation into what roles were required of them, but it had been months since either of them had last touched it.

Iata turned it to scan himself—but no, that would only show Homaj's genetic code, or as close to like. That wasn't going to help him just now.

Toothbrushes. He headed into his own bedroom, which suddenly felt smaller, tighter than he'd ever thought it was before. Into his own small bathroom, plucking up his toothbrush.

But—no. The Truthspeaker had said that bloodservants were trained into distancing their appearance from the royal Rhialden line. Did he remember doing that?

He remembered being shown holos of the Seritarchus, and of a handful of people who had been bloodservants in the past. He remembered hoping that one of the bloodservants, maybe, had been one of his parents, though his questions about that had always been deflected. He remembered the Seritarchus's bloodservant, Omari, gently saying that when Iata made a Change, come back to *this* ideal. Cheekbones a little sharper. Brow a little more prominent, jaw a little wider. *This* was the mark of the service branch, and he couldn't now remember a time when that hadn't felt natural to him.

How could Omari have done that to him if he'd known? But —had he, at that point, known? But the Seritarchus would have known, surely. The Seritarchus would have ordered for Eyras and him to be made, just like...his own children.

Jalava hovered just beyond the doorway to the bathroom. "Are you...yourself?"

Iata's shoulders tightened. "A minute, Jalava." Then, "Yes." Because Jalava had stayed with him this far, and he didn't need a panicked guard on his hands.

Jalava breathed out. "I don't need to—"

Iata saw Jalava's gesture to their own forearm in the bathroom mirror. They meant recalling him from being Homaj in truth.

"No. That happened outside the Truthspeaker's office."

"Oh. *Oh,* yes, I saw that. All right."

Iata turned back to his scanner. So how was he going to prove this?

Had what had been done to him—if any of this was true—well, *why* had it been done? Why would the Seritarchus take two of his own children and mold them into rulers, and two others of his own children and mold them into servants? True, a bloodservant was far, far more than a servant. They were, in many ways, co-rulers, shadow support, if the system functioned as it should. But why had he been destined for the shadows, and Homaj for the light?

Bloodservants had to come from somewhere. If there was no service branch, then...where? They had to be able to Change, certainly. And their genetics couldn't be sourced from any of the high houses, or their loyalties would be in question.

But why not tell him?

Or—or, were bloodservants supposed to be the backups? So if something happened like what was happening now—if the ruler and the Heir, and even the second heir, were taken out, there were still people who could be shown as Rhialdens and step back up to rule? Either replace the original Truthspoken, or step up in their own right?

And how many times throughout history might that have happened?

If this was true.

Iata shivered.

"Truthspoken," Jalava said.

Iata flinched at the title. No, it hadn't been meant to describe him, Iata. But it might have been.

He had to know, and the only way he could think to know

for sure was to tap deep, so deep into his body's own memory of itself that he remembered his first and original DNA. He and Homaj had both drifted from their original appearances, of course, through training and preference and necessity for the roles they must play in the palace. They'd both reset their internal "home" sequences as the bodies they called their own now.

Iata stumbled back to his bed, sitting hard on the edge, making the mattress creak. He held his hand out in front of him, closed his eyes, and flowed into a semi Change trance. He sifted through his automatic home recalls to pull deeper, to try and settle into an older genetic priority. But if he'd been so young when he was trained away from that, would he even remember?

And if he was meant to be a backup to the ruling Rhialdens, had that training been as horrifying as he'd first thought, or protection? A camouflage?

No. No, it had been wrong. So utterly wrong.

He strained to find the oldest priority recall, but his strain was only muddying his thoughts. So he centered himself, willed his own calm, and submerged deeper into the trance.

A few minutes later, he blinked open his eyes and looked down at his hand.

From his wrist down, the skin was just a little lighter, but hardly noticeably so. The structure of his hand hadn't changed.

He reached for the scanner he'd dumped beside him and pressed his palm to it, waiting for the soft beep.

He looked at the results. This scanner, because of its use in high security missions, wasn't connected to the palace networks. He had to periodically update it by hand himself, and those updates only went one way. So there was no danger of what he was scanning now getting back into any palace network.

His Changed hand shook as he waved up the holos to see the results.

Iata byr Rhialden
Age: 25
Blood type: A+

He scrolled past the list of his specific traits in Truthspoken syntax to get to the bottom.

Relations: Classified

He swallowed. Same information as it had always given him, even now. But he'd Changed his hand. Had he Changed it enough? Was his body trying to re-assert his current default template? Or had the information the Truthspeaker given him just been wrong?

56

ADMINISTRATIVE MODE

> *We don't know exactly what happens during a Change. The processes behind what makes a Truth-spoken able to use their thoughts to affect their bodies is still one of the most closely guarded state secrets.*
>
> — DR. T. DOSELA IN *THE TRUTHSPOKEN*
> *SYSTEM: A VARIED ANALYSIS*

Iata mentally felt within his hand, felt the bounds and shape of it, felt the genetic instructions he'd given it—they were still intact. His current genetic recall template hadn't reasserted itself, though he was straining for it not to. And it hadn't gone back to Homaj's DNA, either, which it would need to when he was finished here.

Jalava seemed to have given up trying to get him to talk and now stood across the room, their arms crossed and expression tight.

This scanner wasn't showing anything. Or rather, it was showing him what he'd always seen before, but that shouldn't be the case just now, not when he'd just Changed his DNA away from the profile it would recognize as him. But if the scanner had the old data still in storage, his birth data, would it still give him the same information now? Would he need to do a full Change to prove this theory?

He didn't have time for that. He needed to continue being Homaj, the interim ruler.

Was that what the Truthspeaker had been trying to accomplish, distracting him from holding control of the kingdom?

Iata scrolled through the scanner's data. At the end of the genetic report, there was the option to view the full report, the raw genetic data, or go into detail with specific attributes. And below that, in the lower right corner, was an icon he'd known was there but always ignored. A small key icon—the Seritarchus's or Truthspeaker's override icon, which would allow them to see metadata and usage data for this profile. He'd seen them both use the icon to check his and Homaj's progress toward hitting various goals in training.

Iata touched it now, with his hand that had Homaj's DNA, not his own, and was prompted for a passcode.

He flailed around for a moment, trying to think which code might possibly go to this, before he gave up and decided to enter the day's current ruler command passcode, which he'd memorized earlier from the data on Homaj's comm.

Nothing happened.

Iata felt his hopes sinking before he remembered that the scanner, not being connected to the palace system or updated recently, wouldn't know that Homaj was currently the ruler.

He stretched to grab his own comm, not Homaj's, off the bedside table, running quickly through the sequence of commands that would allow him to update the scanner's data from the palace system's current data. He synced the update, smoothed his hair back, and tried again.

And...it worked.

A new holo window popped up with extra controls. He'd

seen this window before. He'd watched his father use it, and knew how to access iterations, accuracy curves, everything a trainer might need to check and fine-tune progress. But there was also a button to put the scanner in administrative mode.

He hit that—it wanted the passcode again, both written and spoken, and had the specific icon that required a ruler's clearance, with the warning symbol that indicated an unsuccessful attempt to access would hard reset the scanner.

Adeius, he knew he'd gotten Homaj's intonation right, his voice. If he hadn't hit Homaj's genetics exactly, after that last bit of fine-tuning earlier, he was sure he was within the acceptable range of genetic variance. He'd been able to unlock the door to the prep room with a touch. He knew this would work.

And still, his voice shook a little as he spoke the passcode.

The scanner blanked, then refreshed.

Had it wiped itself?

No. The training screen was still there.

He went back to the first data and...it was different.

Infant Rhialden
Age: 24
Blood type: A+

And then the list of his specific traits in Truthspoken syntax.

And at the bottom of the list:

Relations:
Anatharie Rhialden, parent
Jamir ne Xiao Rhialden, parent
Infant Rhialden, sibling
Vatrin Rhialden, sibling
Homaj Rhialden, sibling

Iata closed his eyes, his breaths out of his control. He knew he was hyperventilating, and that he absolutely had cause to do so.

He felt his hand, even now, trying to resolve itself with the greater whole of himself—patched Changes without Changing the whole body always took effort to maintain. He let his hand reharmonize with the rest of him, back to Homaj's DNA.

The bed shifted beside him, and he looked to see Jalava sitting down.

"Iata," Jalava said. "Please tell me what's going on. You're upset. I need to know how to help you." They were doing a good job of trying to hide it, but Adeius, they looked scared.

And they had every reason to be. They were here in a situation far outside their previous experience, moving in the highest realms of power. With someone who should not be holding that power.

That outside perspective, for the moment, grounded him. He did have to tell Jalava. He couldn't navigate this himself, alone.

Iata, still holding the scanner, turned it so Jalava could see. He didn't give it to Jalava—he didn't think it would work outside of Homaj's touch. Not in administrative mode, anyway.

"This," Iata said. "The Truthspeaker told me, and I think I just confirmed it." He stabbed a finger at the list of relations. "This...these are the relations under my DNA. My full siblings. Eyras, Vatrin, and Homaj."

Jalava stiffened. They were quiet a long moment. And they hadn't always been the quickest on the uptake before when it came to the twistiness of Truthspoken matters, but every officer in the Palace Guard had at least some understanding of the nature of Truthspoken.

They finally looked up. "You still think the Truthspeaker is rotten? Could he have fabricated the data on this scanner?"

Iata thought that through.

Went back into the scanner's settings and pulled up a log of every update to the scanner's system—before today, it hadn't been updated in months, like he'd thought.

Not yet satisfied with that, he pulled up exactly what had been updated this time, the raw data. It was the designation of the ruler, and the usual batch update to the genetic data it typically stored—that of the courtiers, the palace staff, the guards, important officials in and around the city. A fair sampling of random citizens' DNA as well, to aid in composite personas. He ran a search—there were no updates whatsoever to the profiles of Iata byr Rhialden, Homaj Rhialden, Anatharie Rhialden, or Infant Rhialden. The only update to Homaj was his new allowed access as the interim ruler.

Iata stared so hard at the screen his eyes were blurring.

He didn't see how the information in this scanner wasn't true. And maybe the most cutting weapon the Truthspeaker could possibly use right now *was* the truth. Because true secrets could be revealed and proven, not just used as threats.

"I know he's rotten," Iata said. "I absolutely know he is. I don't know if he killed the—the Seritarchus"—he couldn't say "my parents" out loud, not yet, maybe not ever—"but he is holding this over me now. And I swear, Jalava, I didn't know until just now."

Jalava looked at him. They knew what he was saying. Did they believe it? Because yes, Adeius, yes, the evidence was now damning.

But Jalava nodded. "What now?"

That trust—Iata's chest burned at the intense relief of it. Jalava barely knew him but had already formed their own opinions and were holding to them.

He clicked the scanner off. So the Truthspeaker could, if he wished, use this against him. He didn't think the Truthspeaker would use this information publicly unless he absolutely had to, but the threat of it was enough. If the Truthspeaker decided to level murder charges against Iata, charges of treason, of—of patricide, he certainly could. Iata would not survive those charges, not without Homaj to defend him.

Would Homaj believe he hadn't known?

Yes. Iata was still close enough to centered in Homaj's personality to know that. He knew his Truthspoken. He knew his...brother.

Homaj trusted him with his life, and Iata had no intentions of betraying that trust.

But Homaj was in the city, in who knew what danger. Or maybe he was safer than Iata was in the palace?

At that moment, though, Iata could only wish for him to come back swiftly. Because right now, if the Truthspeaker told him to jump, he'd have to.

Iata needed evidence of his own. He needed proof that the Truthspeaker was, in part, behind all of this. Or barring that, to find out who was. There had been accomplices among the Palace Guard, certainly. So no, he couldn't go to Tavven with any of this, either—if Tavven themself didn't already know.

"Come with me," he said, pushing up from the bed. And added, "please," because no, he was not Homaj, and no, no matter who his parents were, he was still not an Adeium-sanctioned or even fully trained Truthspoken. He was still not, himself, the Heir or the ruler.

Jalava nodded and followed him back into Homaj's bedroom. "Where are we going?"

"Vatrin's apartment. They're not in there. But—" But it was a place to start. And it would be off surveillance if they went in through the back corridors. He didn't know what they'd be looking for, didn't know what he was hoping to find. But... something. Anything. More than he knew now.

Iata touched the hidden panel door beside Homaj's bed, and the panel slid aside.

57

THE NINTH UNIT

*A walk in the evening along the river after the rain is
an experience not to be missed.*

— TRAVEL BROCHURE FOR THE RIVEREDGE
DISTRICT OF VALON CITY

It was full night now, and the normal crowds that would
haunt a Riveredge street at this hour weren't as thick,
were more subdued. Some people carried on as usual—
there were still laughs, there was still loud conversation drifting
from various bars and restaurants and arcades along the street.
But less than there should have been.

The city, the world, the kingdom had just lost its
Seritarchus. Solemnity should have been required.

Still, some crowds were useful to blend into. Homaj
neared the tackle shop—closed now, but with its neon sign
still flickering as always—and spotted Zhang heading toward
him, too. She met his gaze through her obscuring mask, and
he didn't stop, so she didn't, either. Then he glanced back and
saw Lodri crossing the street—she would be able to follow if

she could track Truthspoken from a distance, so he kept walking.

One thing that had been bothering Homaj since leaving the building where Vatrin had been, since talking to his uncle, was why Vatrin hadn't left the city, or even the world? It would almost certainly be safer than being chased from location to location within the city. He understood why Vatrin hadn't come back to the palace—they had to know something more about what was going on than he did, maybe that the Truthspeaker was behind all of this, too.

But his uncle had said someone close to the Seritarchus had betrayed him. Could that be Aduwel Shin Merna, or was there someone else?

Could it have even been Vatrin? Was he in fact chasing his fathers' killer?

The thought seized him up, forced him to focus on smoothing out his walk for several steps.

Or could it have been Eyras, Vatrin's bloodservant? Now that he knew who Eyras was as well. Adeius. His oldest sister. The oldest of all of them.

He knew he hadn't betrayed his father, and he would bet his life—he had bet his life—that Iata hadn't, either. It very obviously hadn't been the Seritarchus Consort, his father Jamir, and almost certainly not Omari, his father's bloodservant, if Omari had been killed, too.

Who else was close to his father? The Truthspeaker, yes, by necessity, but Anatharie Rhialden and Aduwel Shin Merna had never particularly been friends. The relationship between a Truthspoken and a Truthspeaker was by necessity, though, one of closest trust. It had to be, or the kingdom would be significantly weakened by the rift. So what had Aduwel been trying to pull by outing him in public? That had forged an immediate rift of mistrust.

And what about Commander Tavven? Could they themself

have been behind the attack? Guards had certainly been involved. But Tavven themself?

Less close to his father was the captain of his father's personal guard—but he was also counted among the dead, along with, Homaj assumed, most of his father's personal guards. The rest would likely have gone underground as under suspicion, whether they actually were guilty or not. That was the traditional response when a ruler was assassinated. Homaj doubted any of them would resurface, and most wouldn't be looked for too hard. That, too, was tradition.

And then there was the palace chamberlain, and the palace physicians. Possibly even his Xiao father's family, though they weren't close, and Homaj didn't know more than a few cousins. That didn't make sense, though, because the High House Xiao would now lose their greatest point of influence in Jamir— they'd never made much effort to get to know Homaj or Vatrin.

Homaj couldn't bring enough reasonable threads together to make a plausible case for any of them on what he currently knew, but Palace Rhialden politics could move in many layers and currents. There could have been blackmail involved, or bribery by the high houses. Any of that was possible. He would have to dig deeper there.

Still. Aduwel. He was certain the Truthspeaker was a part of what had happened in some capacity. And if Vatrin knew that, and their lover, Lord Birka, had also been killed—

Homaj broke into a cold sweat. Being here in Riveredge, passing people who were drunk and, if not happy, then at least for a time happily oblivious, had made him want to slip sound-lessly into that anonymity. This was the point of intensity, in his normal flow of life, where he would find some willing, anony-mous person and lose himself in the oblivion of an epic night of sex. In someone not knowing who he was, in the safety and danger of two strangers passing through. He, as an expert in body language, could keep his partners entertained for hours.

The longer, the better. It prolonged his having to return to his own reality.

The temptation to slip away into the night was so strong that for a moment, it stole his breath.

And then he turned down a side street that would lead to the apartment block where the new safe house was. Because as hard as he'd tried to convince everyone else otherwise, he wasn't someone who walked out on what needed to be done in a crisis. Or walked out on his family.

He glanced toward Zhang—she was still moving on a parallel course to his own. That might start to be suspicious to anyone watching, a pattern where there shouldn't be one. But he wasn't willing just now to separate himself from her, to fall back, circle around. Not when he was feeling this vulnerable. And she needed his direction on where to go in any case. Lodri, he left to her own skills.

The apartment block with the safe house had faded fairy lanterns hanging in the trees. He'd only been here once before, a few years ago, but he remembered that. The lanterns were still there.

And it was the ninth unit in the building? Correct? His tired mind, a mind that was *truly* done for the night, couldn't quite remember, but he did know visually which unit it was. He climbed up the flight of metal stairs to the second floor, glanced at the door number—yes, nine—and pressed his hand to the door plate. He'd Changed his palm on the way over to not his own, he'd decided, but Iata's, which would still open all safe house doors. That, and holding the genetics of his hand apart from the rest of his body, had further drained his reserves.

Inside, the air was stale, though the apartment itself was clean from the cleaning bots. Lights flickered on, and soft music began to play, a welcoming routine. He squinted in the brighter lights and didn't take off his mask yet, not until Zhang stepped inside, and she waved him to keep it on even then.

"Stay here," she said, and moved quickly to each room to clear it. Two bedrooms, two bathrooms, the open kitchen and living area.

"Clear," she said.

A soft knock came at the door, and Zhang raised her pistol.

"Lodri," Homaj said, and moved to the door, but Zhang held up a hand. She leaned to the window, peered out through the blinds, then pushed him back as she opened the door.

Lodri slipped inside, flickering into full view.

She shut the door and locked it behind her.

58

TIRED

" We're safe. Thank Adeius, we're safe.

— SERGEANT ARTHIT SHEY IN THE VID
DRAMA *VALON CITY BLAZE*, SEASON 5, EPISODE
8, "OFFWORLD BLUES"

In the safe house apartment, Homaj glanced at the closed and opaqued blinds and finally pulled off his mask.

"No," Zhang said, "we should clear it of bugs first—"

"You already cleared each room."

"Yes, and we know no one's here, but we don't know if anyone's watching."

"I'm tired. And this one is known only to Truthspoken, not bloodservants or any of the Palace Guard."

He knew she was right. He should do a full sweep for bugs, for anything dangerous. But he was just so damned *tired*.

He sank into the nearest comfortable looking chair, dropping his head into his shaking hands. He needed—he probably needed to eat, certainly needed to sleep. The nap earlier hadn't been enough. And all the emotions he'd allowed to go numb again were now vying with a host of new emotions, new information, everything conflicting.

He really should just Change, do everyone's cosmetics, and they all go again, maybe do several more Change and leave routines to confuse anyone who might yet be watching. He knew he wasn't out of danger, that their anti-surveillance masks and measures on the way in weren't nearly as effective as he'd like. But he was just so...tired.

"Here," he said, pulling his bug-sniffer lip gloss out of his jacket pocket. He tossed it to Zhang. She'd watched him use it earlier and opened it now, repeating the steps he'd used in the other safe house, beginning her sweep again.

Lodri settled on a couch nearby.

"Air system," Homaj said, "circulate."

Deeper into the apartment, he heard the air system kick on, and a moment later, a cool breeze swept through the room, pushing back some of the staleness.

"Is it working?" he said, as Zhang came back through the living room on her way to check the kitchen. She gave a curt nod. She looked exhausted, too, and he wanted to get up to help her, but his legs wouldn't move. He could not make himself move from this place.

His uncle. Why, by Adeius, had his uncle shown up?

His uncle had told him why. He'd verified his uncle's sincerity. But it was still too much, in a chain of too much.

Zhang took her bug-sniffer back into the bedrooms, maybe for a more thorough check this time.

Lodri got up and went to the kitchen, opening cabinets. She opened the cooler and brought out three silver-foiled packaged meals. Pressing the heat controls on all of them, she leaned back against the counter, waiting.

"Decent place," she said.

It was inane. It was nonsense. She knew they couldn't talk.

After a span of minutes, long enough to heat their meals, Zhang came back from the bedrooms, handing the lip gloss back to him. "I think it was working right, but I didn't find anything."

She pushed her pale blue hair out of her eyes. Looked like she wanted to sit on the couch, too, but instead she angled toward the kitchen table as Lodri brought the steaming meals over.

Homaj grunted and levered himself up, and managed to get to the small table and its four metal chairs. Tasteful decor, but two decades old, at least.

They all sat. Homaj didn't see and didn't care which meal he got, he only grabbed the fork provided and dove in. He barely tasted anything.

They ate in silence. Which would have been suspicious to any listening ears, but then, if anyone knew to listen here and why, they would already have a good guess as to the apartment's occupants.

"So," Zhang finally said. "Are we going to go back?" She was watching him closely. Trying to gauge his reaction? She'd been there through everything that had happened between him and Iata today. Did his uncle's warning seem credible to her? Seem vital? Was he not seeing a threat because he didn't want to?

"I need...to sleep." He should Change and then sleep. And no, maybe it wasn't fully safe here. But it wasn't safe at all to go back to the palace in his current state, either. It wasn't safe to keep crawling around the city. He knew his body fully as a Truthspoken, knew its limits and its bounds. He truly needed rest.

But his uncle wasn't wrong that he should be at the palace. He almost certainly never should have left—he should have sent Iata out here to track down Vatrin, not gone himself.

Homaj had thought he'd have the harder, more vital task with tracking down Vatrin, but that logic had resulted in Iata chewing out two military commanders—two allies he might sorely need—and who knew what else was happening at the palace just now. He didn't know, and that was the point. He should know. It was about to become his palace, his kingdom, his life.

He looked up to Zhang, then Lodri. "Will one of you stay up? While I sleep?"

And keep watch while he Changed, too. He was going to do it quickly, he didn't want to be vulnerable for more time than necessary. Though he could technically be awakened from a Change trance while in the middle of it, if the need was high and situation dire, it wasn't good for his health, and might be intensely painful to try and function in that state. He'd need someone to protect him, if—well. They still weren't safe.

"I will," Zhang said, though she punctuated that statement with a yawn.

He wished she could sleep, too, he would need her tomorrow, but someone had to keep watch. "There will be stimulants in the bathroom cabinet."

She nodded.

Lodri yawned, too, and stood. "I'll take the couch."

There was a guest bedroom, but, well, the outside door needed watched, too. Not that Lodri could do much if anyone did try to get inside, but she could at least warn them about it.

She was still suppressing her aura. She would continue to do so, he thought, until she knew they absolutely weren't being watched. And maybe even then—she was a high-ranking, unsealed magicker. And he was determined to leave her that way.

Homaj levered himself up, his meal sitting heavy in his stomach, but he'd need it for the Change.

The sleep that would come after Change was a high motivator to get to the bedroom, strip out of these sweat-grimed clothes, do what he needed to do.

He stretched, finally starting to let his thoughts unspool, and headed for the bedroom.

A knock came on the door.

59

THE DOOR

It's on the third knock that the illusion ends.

— WILLOW VER PURALA IN THEIR NOVEL *A ROAD APART*

Homaj froze. Lodri, who'd been plumping pillows on the couch, squinted toward the door. She looked back at him and mouthed, "Truthspoken."

His uncle? Would his uncle know about this safe house? Had his uncle tracked him from the aircar?

Or, Vatrin? Or Eyras?

Adeius. Why hadn't Lodri picked whoever it was up before, or had she not been trying? Or were they all just that tired?

Zhang pulled out her pistol, and he didn't stop her this time. He wasn't going to be stupid about this again.

Homaj quietly pushed back his chair and moved deeper into the kitchen, to where he could just see the door but wasn't in easy line of sight. Or line of fire. The kitchen, at least, had no windows.

Zhang opened the door only as far as the security chain. "Yes?"

"I need—please, let me in."

Alto voice. Not his uncle, then. Was it Vatrin? Their voice was alto, but that didn't necessarily mean anything with Truthspoken.

He wouldn't know until whoever it was came in. Until he could see them, gauge their tells.

Zhang stiffened, but to her credit, didn't look back at him to give away where he was standing. She opened the door, and a single person entered, a single set of footsteps.

The door closed behind them. Homaj heard the lock click and chime that it was engaged.

"Who are you?" the person asked—and that tone, *that* tone, was all Vatrin.

Homaj edged from the kitchen, wary, and the person turned.

Medium height, light brown skin, curly dark gold hair. Wide-set eyes, freckles. Light makeup. Casual but expensive clothing. All the appearance of a stranger, but there were Vatrin's tells beneath the layer of a new persona. And Vatrin had never been the best at the acting necessities around Change. Not as good as he was, anyway.

He felt his sibling surveying him with as much scrutiny, and he set himself firmly in Tanarin's gestures, which he was still using, then Iata's tells underneath. And then—he didn't have time to judge the decision, or the gut feel, the sense of danger that propelled it, but he was too tired to truly fool Vatrin into believing that he was Iata, not Homaj. So from one heartbeat to the next, he submerged. He became Iata in truth.

He saw recognition flicker in Vatrin's gray eyes. Vatrin pulled something from their pocket, and Zhang reacted by raising her pistol, but Iata held up his hands.

"No—Zhang, no. It's all right."

Vatrin frowned at Zhang, but set something on the table—a sound dampener. They turned it on, set the perimeter dial to three meters, and Iata's ears popped with the pressure.

Lodri had come back from the couch and stood nearest the door, just inside the kitchen and the dampener's sound bubble. Did she think she'd have to flee?

Iata watched Vatrin warily. He'd been sent to the city to find them, and so now, apparently, he had. But Vatrin had found him, and he had the uneasy sense that might not be healthy for him.

"Iata," Vatrin said sharply, "sit down."

He went back to his chair and dropped into it. He didn't *have* to obey Vatrin's commands, Vatrin not being his Truthspoken, but he didn't want to antagonize Vatrin just now, either.

Vatrin pulled out a chair and sat, too, looking haggard but intent. "That was you who found me earlier."

"Yes," he said. Then, "Vatrin, are you well? Have you been injured? Who is after you, do you know who did this to the Seritarchus—"

Vatrin waved a hand, and Iata sat back. Vatrin, for all their want of social reforms, had always been imperious with him and Eyras. He let his gaze drop to the table, which he never would have done, or felt the need to do, with Homaj.

"Forgive me. Truthspoken. I am only concerned for your wellbeing."

"And you should be," Vatrin said. Their eyes darkened. "My brother." Iata stopped his flinch at that, knowing what he did now, but Vatrin continued. "My lounge-about brother has decided to make his bid to rule."

Iata let out a slow breath. "Truthspoken, you were not there. He had to make his bid. Please, do you know who did this? And how did you track us here?"

"Who's with you?" Vatrin asked, looking at Zhang, then at Lodri. "What level of trust do you place in them?" But implying, by the tone, that the trust Iata placed in anyone wasn't the highest factor Vatrin would use here.

"Vi Zhang of the Palace Guard," Iata said. "Sworn to Homaj. And Lodri. One of Homaj's informants. She is also sworn to him."

"My brother has seen fit to swear in his own guard?" There was danger in that mild tone.

Iata hit a fist on the table, his anger rising. "You were *not there*. Truthspoken. Homaj would gladly have deferred, but you were not there."

"That's because someone has been trying to kill me," Vatrin spat. "They—they did kill Lord Birka." Their voice cracked, and Iata saw the anguish, the terror behind the previously calm facade. Their gaze pinned back on him. "And I'm trying to decide if it was my brother. Who is now making his bid to rule."

Iata blanched. "I was with Homaj this morning, and he was in his quarters when he got the word. There were witnesses—"

"Are you that naïve, Iata? We don't deal in death ourselves, we have proxies. We hire people. We use, we coerce. So who has Homaj manipulated—"

"He is the very last person who wanted the kingdom! Don't you see he's spent the last few years trying to push that duty away from himself?"

"And made many enemies while he's at it."

"Not—not enemies as such. Just, not friends." Iata clasped his hands together to keep them from shaking. "Truly, Vatrin. Maja had nothing to do with this. And I'm supposed to find you —I did find you earlier—"

"To assassinate me, too?"

He pushed back his chair, but stopped himself from standing. "For Adeius's sake, Vatrin. I would not do that! I'm a blood-servant—"

Vatrin stared at him, gray eyes cold and steady. "I know what you are."

Oh, Adeius. Did they? Did they know the whole of it, that he, Iata, was also their sibling?

Vatrin sat back, breaking eye contact. "I need your help."

Iata leaned forward again, gripping the edge of the table. "Of course! Of course I will help, that's why I'm in the city, when I should be helping my Truthspoken—"

Vatrin gave him a tight-lipped smile. "My parents are dead. My lover is dead. I would very much like to save this kingdom from my brother driving it into the ground, and I hear he's made a spectacular start of it, Adeius, being witnessed by a *magicker*. You'll help me do this. I know you have your loyalty to him, but you have a higher loyalty to the Kingdom of Valoris. Will you allow that loyalty to take precedence? Will you help me take my kingdom?"

60

THE REQUEST

Homaj and Vatrin were always evenly matched but with different skill sets, and their personalities were diametrically opposed. While Vatrin Rhialden as the Truthspoken Heir sought to win the hearts of the people, Homaj sought to wreck them.

— EMIL LÓPEZ IN "AN ANALYSIS AND COMPARISON OF TRUTHSPOKEN VATRIN RHIALDEN'S AND HOMAJ RHIALDEN'S SOCIAL APPROACHES"

Iata blinked. He didn't like this barrage of questions and threats and information without giving much in return. But Vatrin was right, it was his duty as a Rhialden bloodservant to uphold the kingdom above all, but—but his duty would always, first and foremost, be to Homaj.

He held up his palms. "I want to help. But I need to know what's going on. I need to know who I can trust—Homaj will welcome you taking the kingdom from him, I know that, and he won't ask, I also know that, but—I'm asking. How do I trust you if you won't tell me what you know? I will help you, but you have to let me know what we're up against."

Vatrin stared hard at him, mouth tugging to one side, considering. "Iata, you have always thought far too much for a bloodservant. But, unfortunately, Homaj wanted you trained that way, didn't he? And I am asking you to give your loyalties— temporarily—to me. I do value that loyalty."

Iata sat still, not letting his face, his body betray what he felt about that pretentious, condescending statement. Adeius, he had to completely set aside for the moment that Vatrin could be such an ass.

"Yes, Truthspoken," he said, though he was fairly sure the statement had been rhetorical.

"It's the Truthspeaker," Vatrin said, and looked grim. "He called me to his office this morning and tried to blackmail me."

"Adeius, with what?"

Vatrin flashed a humorless smile. "I've been trying to maneuver a way to marry Lord Birka. I may have...considered some unsavory options on how to make that come about."

"Like what?" Iata asked, unmoored in this new angle he hadn't known he should consider.

"Oh, nothing major. But major enough to put a stain on an eventual wedding." Pain flashed in their eyes. "But that won't matter now." This said lower, much lower, almost a whisper.

Iata swallowed. "But—that doesn't follow that the Truthspeaker would kill the Seritarchus. And we were there at the Adeium, Homaj and I—Ceorre said you came forty minutes before the assassination happened."

"Did she?" Vatrin asked softly.

"Vatrin, we were trying to find you! The whole palace was searching for you."

"Yes—yes. I went to the city to decide what to do, if I should tell Father about what the Truthspeaker tried to do."

"And you think that threat was enough to kill the Seritarchus?"

Not that Iata disagreed that the Truthspeaker was rotten. But did Vatrin think him so gullible as to believe that the most logical course for the Truthspeaker to take, in that instance, would be to kill the Seritarchus, and not Vatrin? Or had Vatrin meant the Truthspeaker had tried to do both? Was maybe still trying?

He was watching Vatrin closely, and Vatrin, as Truthspoken, could lie better than almost anyone alive. But the best lies were smothered in truths.

Whatever Vatrin wasn't saying, it was surely damning for... something. They'd admitted to using less than ideal means to try to arrange a marriage for themself. But that was almost certainly the misdirection. Something else was going on here. Why not return to the palace, enlist Commander Tavven's help, and arrest the Truthspeaker pending an investigation? It would be a drastic step, yes, but within the realm of possibility. Taking that action might have saved the lives of the Seritarchus and Seritarchus Consort, by Vatrin's logic.

There was absolutely more going on here.

Vatrin tapped the table, regaining his attention. "Iata. Listen. I know you're a bloodservant and not trained fully in Change. But—do you think you could Change to someone specific? Could you Change to me, enter the palace as me? I need to go back to the palace, but I need to know what will happen when I do."

Iata coughed, reaching for a drink that wasn't there. Instead, he smoothed away the sudden tightness in his throat. "What? I can't—Truthspoken, I'm not trained for that. I can make small Changes, I can create personas and Change to play them out, within boundaries, but—"

Vatrin tapped the table again. "You look absolutely nothing like yourself right now. You can Change."

"But—"

Adeius, Vatrin wanted him to be bait? It wasn't that Vatrin trusted him to play the role of Vatrin the Truthspoken—it was that Vatrin wanted him to draw the fire meant for themself.

Which—which, was his job as a bloodservant, yes.

"Where is Eyras?" he asked. "Can't she do this? Surely she'd know how to be you better than I would—"

"She's indisposed."

Which meant...he didn't know what that meant.

Zhang stepped closer, watching him with an intensity he wasn't sure what to do with. Trying to tell him something?

Vatrin was trying to bully him into this, but—they weren't wrong that if they entered the palace, it might be their death sentence. Especially if the Truthspeaker was rotten, and whatever Vatrin had spoken to him about had triggered all this. And also, especially, if someone in the Palace Guard had been in on the assassination. Well, and how could they not have been? That should never have happened.

"Okay," he said. "Okay, I'll try. But you'll have to help me, I'm not used to trying to hit a specific genetic target. I don't have that training."

Zhang's lips twitched, and he looked up, Vatrin's eyes following his this time.

"I'll stand guard," she said. Though he was certain that's not what she'd wanted to say.

"Good," Vatrin said, and stood. "Iata, I want this done quickly. What's happening in the palace has to stop—we must restore order to this kingdom."

61

LOOKING FOR ANSWERS

> *Bloodservants are almost certainly more than they appear, or what the Rhialdens wish us to believe. Scholars have speculated, but never definitively proven, that their place in the palace hierarchy is much more than trusted valets to their Truthspoken.*

> — DR. T. DOSELA IN *THE TRUTHSPOKEN SYSTEM: A VARIED ANALYSIS*

Iata could tell Jalava was deeply uncomfortable moving through the back corridors—they kept looking around everywhere, hand resting on their holstered pistol, though not drawing it. Neither of them spoke. Though the back corridors were sound-dampened to muffle steps, they were built to amplify conversations in the rooms around them that weren't also dampened. Words spoken here could be amplified back as well.

Or was Jalava just nervous about Iata's discovery about his parentage? *Iata* was nervous about that. He was trying hard not to let it overtake his thoughts just now, to keep him from being as aware as he must be. But the thought that he had both gained actual parents and lost them in the same day kept threatening to boil his emotions over.

He stopped at the panel entrance into Vatrin's bedroom. Held up a hand for Jalava to be completely still—and Jalava tried to motion in the dim overhead lights for him to step back, let them enter first, but Iata shook his head. He had to be the one to get them inside. And anyone other than him coming into that room was more likely to be shot than he was—if anyone was inside. Which he deeply doubted.

Iata pressed his palm to the lock and input the ruler's access code. That—that was becoming a power he should be careful with, use only when strictly necessary. But every time he'd used it so far, it had been necessary.

He hadn't come armed, hadn't re-armed since going to the Adeium—and a ruler shouldn't go armed anyway, it was showing a lack of control—but he reached back now, and Jalava pressed the cool metal of a pistol into his hand. Iata checked the charges—they were set to stun rounds. Okay.

He slowly pushed the panel door open. Waited, listening. Vatrin's bedroom was dim, only the strips of the dim ceiling night lights outlining the large, four-poster bed.

He stepped further into the room, arcing the pistol around, taking in the rumpled bed, the sequined heap of something on the floor—a jacket? That had to be Lord Birka's, because Vatrin dressed loudly but never that ostentatiously.

The door to the prep room was slightly ajar. The door to the bathroom was closed, and the door to Eyras's small bedroom suite, like his own, was also ajar.

Iata paused, listening. He heard nothing but his own and Jalava's breathing.

He lowered the pistol, handing it back to Jalava, who did not re-holster it, but held it pointed toward the floor.

"What are we looking for?" Jalava asked softly.

"I don't know. There shouldn't be surveillance here, though."

Jalava nodded. "Should I clear the prep room? The other room—that's the bloodservant's bedroom? The layout is similar to yours."

"Not yet. I want you with me. And I want to look through this room first."

He was holding very tightly to his persona as Homaj just now—alone or not, surveillance or not, this was not a safe place. Jalava, at least, was following him as if he was Homaj. For saying that they weren't good at these games, Jalava was doing just fine.

He walked around the bed, feeling...lost. Feeling like an intruder, because he had no idea what he was doing here. The bedroom as a whole was disordered, though, and that was certainly like Vatrin. There was no clue in that.

He checked the bathroom. The toothbrush was dry. Which...didn't tell him more than that the last time Vatrin had brushed their teeth was more than a handful of hours ago.

Frustrated and feeling like this was a waste of time, he moved swiftly into Eyras's room. The contents here were neater, at least, the bed made. Did that mean anything? Had Vatrin left before Eyras, or Eyras before Vatrin? Or had they all left in a hurry? Would Lord Birka have been with them, if they'd all been seen together at the Adeium?

Eyras's comm was still on the bedside table. And that...that was odd. He hadn't taken his own comm with him today because he wasn't himself, but Eyras had been seen at the Adeium as herself.

Iata moved toward the comm. Was this another time when using his ruler's override was justified?

Yes. Yes, it had to be. He needed answers, and he needed them now.

He picked up the comm, then froze.

Had he heard something, out in Vatrin's bedroom?

Jalava, too, was looking toward the door, tensed. They glanced at Iata, waving him back, out of line of the door.

Then Jalava dove to one side as a silenced shot coughed, pinging the back wall. *Not* a stun round.

Shit. Shit, and he didn't have a gun. Iata grabbed the comm and crouched behind the bed. He reached to twist his guard's comm ring, call for help, when he heard a familiar voice.

"Who are you? Show yourself!"

Eyras.

"Eyras!" he called. "It's me! Don't shoot!"

"Maja?"

She stepped into the room, gun raised as he held his hands up, rose slowly.

62

EYRAS

> *If you have stun rounds and live rounds loaded into your weapon, be sure to set the toggle to stun rounds if you are in most situations. Using live rounds requires a permit on most worlds, and may not be permitted for civilian use on some, or in some areas and municipalities. Check with your local safety authority for more information.*
>
> — PUBLIC HEALTH AND SAFETY ADVISORY
> FOR THE KINGDOM OF VALORIS

Eyras slowly lowered her pistol. She glanced to the side where Jalava was still tensed, poised to shoot.

"Jalava, stand down," Iata barked, and Jalava lowered their pistol, too. A lot more slowly than Eyras had.

Iata looked back to her. She was herself, dyed blonde hair pulled back in a knot, face free of cosmetics, like she preferred. A little rumpled, her hair not as neat as it usually was, but herself.

"Maja, what are you doing in my room—"

She stiffened, then raised the pistol again. "You're not Homaj."

He held up his hands again, still holding her comm, and she saw that, too.

He let his own tells show through, cycling quickly through them.

"Iata." Though she wasn't as quick to lower the pistol this time. Her gaze was sharp, intense. "What are you doing in my room? With my comm?"

He carefully set the comm on the bed. "I haven't done more than pick up your comm. We only just got here."

Her gaze flicked to Jalava. Back to Iata.

And he knew—he saw on her face the picture that was forming. And he knew that she knew what they both were, as bloodservants. And it wasn't new information to her. She wasn't surprised. She was...calculating.

"The Truthspeaker just threatened me with the knowledge that I'm Homaj's brother. I was looking for answers."

Eyras swore, then stepped fully into the room, closing the door.

"How long have you known?" he challenged.

"Four years. Four bloody years, and he did not let me ever forget it."

"Who, Aduwel?"

"Who else? Iata—why are you Homaj? Where is Homaj?"

"He's—"

"Fuck, is he in the city looking for Vatrin? Would he be that foolish—yes, yes he would, wouldn't he? Iata, he set you up to be his double?"

That question was going dangerously back toward the original suspicion.

Iata held up his hands again, a conciliatory gesture this time. "It was his plan. It...may not have been fully thought through."

Jalava shifted, unhappy with that statement, though Iata couldn't parse that response just now.

Eyras tilted her chin at Jalava. "You've sworn in guards?"

"No, Homaj has. Lt. Jalava is loyal. To Homaj. Homaj made the bid to rule, I'm only holding his place until he comes back from the city."

He was actively holding the rulership, though, and that fact hung in the air between them.

He had the ruler's codes. He had the ruler's comm in his own pocket. He had the ruler's face and voice and biometrics. He'd faced down an admiral and a general earlier, and publicly gone to see the Truthspeaker. How much of all of that did Eyras know?

"Can you contact Homaj?" Eyras finally asked.

He shook his head. "Not without going to the city myself. I have no idea where he is." He didn't add that Homaj had wanted it that way—that was a given.

"He's running out on his responsibilities again," she growled, moving restlessly around the room now, picking up and pocketing her comm.

Jalava shifted again at that last statement.

"You have something to say, guard?"

Jalava glanced at Iata, then said stolidly, "Iata has been doing all he can to maintain order while the Truthspoken is carrying out his oath."

Eyras stopped, closed her eyes. Opened them again and looked at him. Her bearing was...not quite that of a bloodservant. Neither was his, but he wasn't currently supposed to be himself—she *was* herself.

She'd known that she was the eldest of their four siblings for four years?

"Does Vatrin know?" he asked. "About...us, the bloodservants?"

She didn't answer, poking at her comm. A small array of windows popped up, blurred from this angle.

"Iata—" She looked up again, pursed her lips. "Because he's not here, you'll have to keep doing what you're doing."

He knew that. He *knew* that, and yes, as the bloodservant to Vatrin, she technically outranked him as the bloodservant to Homaj, but Homaj had given him his power to hold until he came back. So did he, at this exact moment, outrank her or not?

"Eyras," he said, stepping closer, "what happened this morning? Why did you all go to the Adeium so quickly, what did Vatrin sense, what did they know?"

She didn't answer that right away, either. Her brows drew together, and she smoothed at the seams of her form-fitting gray pants.

"Aduwel was blackmailing me for four years with the information that I was the first among four," she said. "Three days ago, I told him I wasn't going to take that anymore. I told him I was going to tell Vatrin. And I did."

Iata drew in a breath. Three days ago? That couldn't, just couldn't be a coincidence, with the assassinations today. He swallowed hard.

"Vatrin went to confront the Truthspeaker," Eyras said. "Among other things. They sent me and Xavi ahead into the tunnels while they spoke with the Truthspeaker."

All of those statements, Iata sensed, were true. But they were also carefully spoken. And could just as easily be meant to hide other truths.

He felt a burning in his gut, an unease that set his hairs on edge. What did Eyras know that she wasn't willing—or had been ordered not to?—tell him? Or tell anyone.

"Did the Truthspeaker...did Aduwel order the attacks?"

She looked down. "Aduwel is a jealous man. He's bribed or blackmailed half the palace staff by now. I was going to tell my —our—father. I did not get the chance."

That wasn't really an answer. But Iata didn't press. He was all too aware that his own position in all of this was deeply precarious. That she might not believe that he'd only just found out, that she might think him inhabiting Homaj's form and persona was something else entirely.

"Iata," she said, shifting her weight, then putting her comm away into her pocket. "I have to go. I only came back for my comm—"

"Wait," he said, following her to the door, "wait, where is Vatrin? Do you know where they are, are they safe?"

"I don't know," she said. "But I need to get back to the city. I need to find them. It's not safe for me here—or for you. Iata, I'd say you should leave, but I think if you do, Aduwel will claim the palace for himself. Eliminate the Truthspoken altogether, consolidate power. But be careful. Please, be careful. Trust no one."

"Not even you?"

She didn't smile. "Especially me."

She strode quickly to the panel door in Vatrin's bedroom that led to the back corridors and slipped out.

Iata stood still, trying to decide if he should go after her. Try to follow her. But she had been elusive, either because she didn't trust him, or because she didn't want to say more. She wouldn't lead him to Vatrin, even if she knew where they were.

He clenched his fists, slowly opened them again.

"She was shooting to kill," Jalava said, coming up beside him. "You made sure your rounds were on stun."

They shared a look. Was Jalava implying that Eyras had a shadier part in all of this?

But she was scared. They were all scared, and didn't know who their enemies were.

Had Eyras truly risked coming back to the palace just to retrieve her comm? Or did she have another purpose? And what was on that comm?

What now? He still had more questions than answers, other than knowing that Eyras was still alive. That was something—a big something—but he also didn't know what her place was in all of this. She'd given him non-answers and maybe-truths, all of which amounted to little. He did know that she knew about their parentage, though, and that Aduwel had been black-mailing her. Her ire at that absolutely rang as true.

But she was as skilled at evaku as he was—he could easily read truth and lies in ordinary courtiers, but he wasn't sure where in Eyras's web of information and half-truths to turn for actual truth.

He needed—

Well. He really needed to go to the source of all of this, didn't he?

He motioned Jalava back toward the panel door, then waited. If he was right that Eyras was going back to the city, then he wouldn't have to worry about passing her in the corridor, or her seeing where he was headed.

He opened the panel door and peered into the dim corridor, looking both ways—Eyras was gone.

He stepped back out, this time heading toward the Seritarchus's—his father's—study.

63

THE STUDY

> *My father's study was a place where I learned how to be a Truthspoken. It was also a place where I learned how much I wished I didn't have to be.*

— HOMAJ RHIALDEN, SERITARCHUS IX IN A
PRIVATE LETTER, NEVER SENT; AS QUOTED IN
THE CHANGE DIALOGUES

If stepping into Vatrin's apartment felt like an invasion, stepping into the Seritarchus's study felt like... like...sacrilege.

He swung the panel door open on silent hinges, holding his breath. Behind him, Jalava didn't make a sound.

Iata slowly stepped inside.

Lights came on. The holographic fire in the hearth flickered. No one had turned it off.

He swallowed. Stepped further inside. Jalava came in just as hesitantly, as if entering a cursed ancient tomb in the holo dramas.

Iata silently shut the door behind them.

That his palm and code had gained him access at all was just as unsettling.

He stood just inside his...father's...study. The cedar and musk scent of Anatharie Rhialden still lingered, a palpable presence. Iata had been here before, with Homaj to be briefed on missions, more often when they were younger and in active training. It had been a while. The decor hadn't changed, though. There were still the straight-backed, horribly uncomfortable pair of black leather loveseats at corners to each other in the center of the room. The enormous and imposing onyx desk at the far end of the room. The walls shimmering in a faintly metallic geometric pattern on subtle matte purple. The whole thing was meant to be inviting to those who owned this power and intimidating to those who did not. Homaj would absolutely redecorate the first chance he got.

Iata moved slowly toward the desk. And when he reached the back of it, glancing at the scattered hard copy papers and system standby holo icons, he took a shuddering breath. And touched the surface of the desk to activate its systems.

A scanning icon appeared. Verified him as Homaj Rhialden and required the ruler's access code. By now, that came easily, and he spoke it in a quiet monotone, shifting his posture firmly back to Homaj as well, if that mattered. He didn't know if it did matter, but he was terrified to be himself in this room.

The scanning signal cleared, and the windows the Seritarchus had been working in before he'd died that morning came up.

Should Iata even be looking at this without Commander Tavven to check for any clues to who'd assassinated the Seritarchus?

But Jalava hovered behind him, their eyes missing nothing.

Most of the windows were reports from various departments of the kingdom, from Admiral Laguaya for the Navy, from Prince Javieri requesting a change to the shipping schedule between Ynasi III and Valon. He flicked through all the windows, scanning the text. He didn't see anything that would have led to his father's death, nothing that indicated an assassination was even on the horizon.

Not that assassination was never *not* a possibility for a Truthspoken. Being feared had a double edge.

Iata pulled up the files in the Seritarchus's personal account, feeling his chest tighten at this further invasion, but he had to look. Had to know.

Daily ruling logs, notes, drafts of various messages. There was a draft of a message to the First Magicker, informing her that magicker students would soon be required to take extra courses in ethics. Which was appalling, but not out of character for Anatharie. And not something the magickers could have acted on to kill him—magickers couldn't do violence.

"What's that?" Jalava asked, pointing to a folder named with only a long number. They seemed to have gotten over the worst of their reticence and were now in full forensic mode, keenly focused on the data.

Iata opened the folder, scrolled through more numbered text files. He didn't see a pattern to the numbers, not dates or addresses or any other codes that he could tell. He opened one at random.

I hope this day finds you well. The children are making great progress—more than us at their age. You would be proud. I've attached the latest single from Buloran's new album "Shining from the Heights, Wailing from the Depths"—it's not released yet. They sent me a copy first. It's quite good, and I know you like them, if you still do.

Iata blinked several times. What...was he looking at? A personal letter, from Anatharie? Was it supposed to be a code?

But—"More than us at their age." Why that line, specifi-

cally, in this random file in a randomly numbered folder that
was included at the highest level of Anatharie's files?

It shouldn't have been at the highest level, though. Iata had
that strong and nagging sense.

Anatharie did nothing without purpose. Had he anticipated
this folder would be found—had he wanted it to be? And
maybe he'd moved the folder to the higher levels, maybe it was
supposed to have been buried.

Had he known, on some level, that he might be killed?

Iata swallowed hard. Was he reading too far into that?

He read the message again, trying to parse the context.

Could this have been sent to Anatharie's younger sister, the
former Truthspoken who'd sworn off Change? Could it be
exactly as it was shown, a letter? It had none of the Truthspoken inference code that he could see. And maybe that
would have come later, maybe this was the base file before
Anatharie reframed it to encode it and sent it...where?

Adeius, Iata had almost forgotten about Keressorian
Rhialden. She'd left court after a fight with the Seritarchus
when he was younger, and hadn't been a large part of his life
before then—except, on occasion, to chew him and Homaj out
for being rowdy in the halls.

He remembered vividly now her telling him that as a bloodservant, he had an obligation and a duty to keep his Truthspoken from behaving in ways that would jeopardize the
kingdom. They'd been running down the central residence
corridor—he'd hardly thought that was jeopardizing the
kingdom.

Iata swallowed.

But what was important in an inane letter to a sibling in
exile? Other than the fact, maybe, that Anatharie had still been
in communication with her?

He opened several more of the numbered files and found
similar messages. Ordinary correspondence, gentle even, and

Anatharie had never been a gentle person. There were a few dozen, charting, mostly, the growth of "the children." All leading up to the last file, whose creation date was still tagged, around a month ago.

There is much to discuss, I'm afraid, and it's close. Please come. T can help you when you arrive.

The hairs on Iata's arms stood on end. He sat forward. "This. This is significant."

No references to children this time. And the only letter among any of them to state any hint of a name.

"Who is 'T'?" Jalava asked.

"Tavven. It has to be Commander Tavven."

He tried not to look at that line, "I'm afraid." Because he knew what that meant. Anatharie had to have known something was about to happen, or at least suspected his life was in danger.

Jalava tilted their head. "I'm guessing from the context that these were to the former Truthspoken Keressorian Rhialden? Am I right on that?"

"I think so, yes. But he asked her to come. Adeius, did she? Is she here? Did she come to help him, or…"

The Seritarchus had asked his exiled sister to come home, and Iata knew he wouldn't have done that lightly. He hadn't, as far as Iata knew, talked about her once in all the years since she'd left.

What had Anatharie found out, what had he seen or heard that had made him fear for his life? Had he known the Truthspeaker was blackmailing his courtiers and staff?

"This is evidence," Iata said.

"Yes, but, is it useable evidence? There's no indication it's been sent. Can you find the actual message log?"

Iata backed out to the Seritarchus's personal inbox, but he

knew without looking that he'd find nothing there. Those files had to be drafts—the message wouldn't have been sent like that, but put into the plain inference code that Truthspoken used among themselves. That code was nearly unbreakable, because it relied entirely on context that only the senders and receivers knew.

It wouldn't have been sent from the Seritarchus's personal inbox, either, but likely from one of his personas, and Iata had no idea where to begin with unraveling all of those. He'd seen no notes—Truthspoken were taught not to keep notes on the personas they inhabited, lest those notes be found and used against them.

Okay, so, he knew that Homaj's aunt had been asked back to the city. *His* aunt, too. He didn't know if she'd come, but he could guess that she hadn't lived outside of 2-3 weeks travel time. Maybe less, if she could afford to travel on a ship that employed a magicker. Anatharie wouldn't have sent an urgent message if he hadn't thought she could arrive in good time.

Iata didn't know who she was now, because he doubted she'd been living under her Rhialden name, and he didn't know how to contact her. He'd have to do a lot more digging to find that out. But could her arrival have been one of the things that spooked the Truthspeaker to act? Or had that been Eyras's confronting him, or...something else?

Iata blanked the desk comm back to the home icon and focused on the hard copy papers. But those were mostly high-level palace reports, easily carried between departments. Working with hard copy wasn't standard practice, but the Seritarchus had preferred it to digital text for some things, saying it wasn't as easily compromised. Iata saw nothing odd in his first look.

He pulled out the desk drawers—found mostly trinkets, a few pens and styluses, a ring with a large diamond in the center. He touched it, but left it where it was.

"Tap the drawers," Jalava said. "Maybe there are false bottoms."

"You watch too many vid dramas," Iata said, but he did it anyway. And the drawer on the left did have a more hollow thunk than the others.

Iata shuffled around the drawer's knick-knacky contents, but he didn't see any obvious seems. He got down on the carpet and peered up from below—nothing obvious there, either. They were well-made, solid wooden drawers set into the onyx frame of the desk. They had rollers, tracks, and metal bottoms.

He got up again, staring at the inside of the left drawer. Was this really the thing he should be focused on just now? Really, truly, he should open the Seritarchus's public inbox and start trying to tackle the absolute mound of correspondence that had shown up in Homaj's inbox all day, relayed from Anatharie's accounts. He had to find a way to fully switch that over to Homaj's accounts—or would that be done automatically when Homaj's ten days of his bid to rule were up?

Homaj wasn't the ruler yet. Interim ruler was still quite a way from actual ruler.

Iata frowned at the drawer and placed his palm down onto the metal bottom.

Something clicked.

"That worked?" Jalava asked. "There—the left edge."

Iata saw it, and carefully tugged at the tiny gap that had opened. The drawer bottom folded upward, revealing a shallow compartment. Inside was a card with handwritten ink writing on one side: "Weyan Odeya." And then a long string of a comm address that had to be outside of the kingdom. In the Dynasty, maybe? Was that a Dynastic routing code? And then a second string of numbers that Iata didn't know what to do with.

Weyan Odeya. Was that the name Keressorian used now? Could that possibly be related to the letters?

The drawer had opened to his touch. The palace systems

might be responding to him as a ruler just now, but he didn't think Anatharie's physical desk locks would be tied to them, as extra security, like the genetic scanner.

So Anatharie would have programmed Homaj's touch to be able to open that compartment. And maybe Vatrin's, too?

Again, he'd known.

Iata stared at the card, trying to memorize the comm code, but his thoughts were too jumbled. So instead he set the card on the desk, brought the desk system back up and opened the population database, broadening parameters to the Onabrii-Kast Dynasty, and the Farani Protectorate beside it for good measure. If those didn't match, he'd go wider.

The name "Weyan Odeya" had over ten thousand hits. Iata bit his lip, then began sifting by age as best he could—not by gender, though, Weyan was looking to be a more common name among masc and male people, though not exclusively so. And age was tricky, too—Keressorian might have sworn off Change, but the same training that made a Truthspoken able to heal themselves quickly kept adult Truthspoken looking much younger than their actual ages, unless they consciously decided to show their age. He'd have to start exerting that aging in himself, soon, as a bloodservant who wasn't supposed to be able to Change—Homaj, of course, would remain looking at his prime.

Even after sorting, Iata still ended up with a list of thousands. He just could not remember enough about the Seritarchus's sibling to narrow it more.

Frowning, Iata saved the search and put the card back into its palm-locked vault. He closed the bottom of the drawer. That card had to have been precious to be stored there. But not so precious as to never be found.

Like the letters themselves.

Iata sat back, wiping at his face. He grimaced—that was one of his own gestures, and he'd smear his heavy cosmetics, which he wasn't used to wearing. Instead, he smoothed away the sheen of sweat by Change.

Everything in this room was so, so far above the realm of anything he should be looking at that he was in a low-grade panic. But he had found something. Maybe a very important something. At very least, he now knew Anatharie had known he was in danger.

"What now?" Jalava asked.

Iata swallowed, eyeing the inbox icons glowing with their constantly upticking numbers. "Now...I start attacking the inbox."

Stable ruler or not, bids to rule or not, the kingdom still had to function.

64

BOUNDARIES

Have you ever been anyone in truth, Uncle?

— HOMAJ RHIALDEN, SERITARCHUS IX IN A
PRIVATE LETTER, NEVER SENT; AS QUOTED IN
THE CHANGE DIALOGUES

He opened his eyes, his senses heightened, his adrenaline already kicking in. He was in an unfamiliar room. Unfamiliar bed with unfamiliar firmness. A slight tang to the air, like sour fruit. Or unwashed bodies.

His own?

His mouth felt flat and dry, the taste rank.

He felt the boundaries of his body—unfamiliar. And he—

Adeius.

Was he Iata? Was he Homaj? He truly did not know.

Something moved beside him—a lump he'd assumed was a pile of blankets resolving into a person in the dim light from the floor strips. He jumped, and she held up a hand.

"Lodri," he said. He did know that. Oh, Adeius, what had happened, he had to have been someone in truth before he'd Changed without being called back, but he couldn't parse out which way around it had been.

His eyes stung, a flood of panic.

Lodri gripped his hand as he reached for her. She searched his eyes, leaned close to his ear.

"Iata?"

"I—"

She was a magicker. His brain caught up to what he already knew, had already been reaching for. He felt the shape of that name, matched against his own sense of truth, which she felt through him, which he felt back through her. Not strongly with her aura tamped down, but still there.

"I am Iata," he said. And that—that was untrue.

He shuddered.

Adeius, he must have submerged as Iata before he'd lay down to Change, and he did remember that now, and why, the memories sorting into their proper places.

Memories experienced when being someone else in truth could be mushy, disconnected, like parts of a dream. But he remembered Vatrin, and remembered his half-baked reasons why he'd felt the urgent need to be Iata just then, not Homaj.

He felt Lodri's attention on him, not just external, but closely reading what he was feeling. Maybe even his thoughts.

She'd been afraid—she'd been just that little bit afraid that he'd somehow fooled her. That he hadn't been Homaj, hadn't been himself after all.

He still wasn't one hundred percent sure that he *was* Homaj.

But he did know that Vatrin could absolutely not know that he was. He was still trying to catch up on why that had felt vitally important to him, why it was still important now.

"Why are you—" he waved at the bed. At her, in the bed beside him. Adeius, was there more he didn't remember?

She let go, drawing back. "No, *that* didn't happen. And it definitely won't." She yawned. "I thought you might need some...help, when you woke up. I rested for a bit while you and the Truthspoken talked through the Change, then spelled Zhang when you were out, which took a little convincing. That woman is absolutely glued to your side, but she needs sleep, too, at least a nap. The Truthspoken took the other bedroom and locked the door. I thought they might be a shorter time, but it's nearing morning. They mentioned they have their own people watching this apartment, so we should be somewhat safe. Though how frightened they seemed of the Truthspeaker finding out where they are did not make me think we're safer with them here."

He lurched up. "Adeius. I—okay." He surveyed himself again, and remembered, through the hazy lens of his submerged memories of being Iata, the condescending session of how-to-Change he'd had with Vatrin the night before. Oh, *that* had been fun. And reminded him now of all the reasons, every single reason, he was not close with his sibling.

And now—and now he was supposed to *be* Vatrin, to walk into the palace as Vatrin, to present himself as a target for whoever was after his sibling. Had he seriously thought this was a good idea, even as Iata in truth? Would Iata not have also thought this insane?

But then, hadn't Iata just done the same thing, becoming Homaj and presenting himself as a target at the palace, too?

At least he had Iata's personality right. Hell and all the holy mandates.

He got out of bed, sniffed himself—oh yes, he definitely needed a shower—and stumbled to the small washroom attached to the bedroom. He grabbed a disposable cup from a stack on a shelf to take a drink from the tap, and that at least made his mouth feel less wooly.

He glanced in the mirror—yes, he was definitely Vatrin. More petite, finer-boned than himself as Homaj, their dark hair short and curly unlike his own long and straight. Thick manicured brows, expressive smile that could charm a crowd.

He wasn't smiling now.

They'd switched once, years and years ago, more a prank than anything else. They'd argued too much throughout the process for it to be successful and had never tried again.

But despite how he looked, despite the role he'd be playing, his body was always his body. If he was a twin to Vatrin just now, then he would think of himself as Vatrin's twin.

A few minutes later, cleaned and wrapped in a robe that had been hanging on a peg, which he hoped was clean, he came back out to—Vatrin themself.

It was only the two of them in the room. Lodri must have fled—and yes, he heard sounds coming from the kitchen.

Homaj checked all of his tells, absolutely making sure they were Iata's. He didn't want to submerge as Iata again, not yet, but he set most of himself aside, pulling Iata's personality to the fore.

Vatrin had Changed, too. Vatrin was one of their guards, a guard he'd had in his own rotation a few months ago. Taller, stockier, less handsome and less androgynous. Which was probably similar logic to what Homaj had used at the palace the day before in becoming Lt. Reyin.

Homaj dropped his gaze in deference, but Vatrin gripped his chin, pushed it back up again.

His skin crawled with the callousness of the gesture.

"It only took you enough tries last night, but I think this is good," Vatrin said, inspecting him.

"Forgive me, Truthspoken, but I'm not trained for—"

"Iata, you've always been vain. I know you've always reached for more than you should."

His lips tightened, and Vatrin smiled.

"Now. Diction. Posture. Gestures. Now."

Homaj took a breath, calculated just how much perfection he should pull off as Iata, and shifted his stance, shifted the flow of words in his head.

Vatrin. Becoming—passably almost—Vatrin.

65

NO VISIBLE FEAR

> *Half of Truthspoken performance is Change, the other half is getting people to believe the illusion.*
>
> — HOMAJ RHIALDEN, SERITARCHUS IX IN A
> PRIVATE LETTER, NEVER SENT; AS QUOTED IN
> *THE CHANGE DIALOGUES*

He met Vatrin-the-guard's eyes, didn't look away this time. Found his lips curling in that self-assured smile.

Vatrin's brows rose. "You'll need to do better than that, if people are to believe that you're me."

"I'm doing fine," he snapped back, calibrating his tone. Yes, that. "I don't know how it was with you and Eyras, but Homaj and I made games of this beyond our training. I am absolutely capable of pulling this off." He blinked. Added an out of character, "Truthspoken."

"Are you, now?" Vatrin asked, eyes narrowing.

Homaj didn't let his pulse spike at that. Didn't let himself even think that Vatrin might have seen through him.

"So will you claim, now, that you're fully Truthspoken?" Vatrin stepped closer, their voice softening dangerously. "Will you claim your family heritage?"

Homaj kept himself contained. He kept his reactions off his face, out of his body. Vatrin was good at evaku, good at Change, but Homaj—Homaj knew he was by far the master. And this game, now, this game had to be played to perfection.

"My family heritage?" he asked. Just that tiny note of fear.

Vatrin smiled, pulled back. "You can't show that kind of reaction when you're me. I don't show fear." They turned a tight circuit of the limited space beside the bed.

Homaj rolled his eyes. Iata would absolutely roll his eyes.

"All right," he said, "no fear. Even though I'm stepping into a hostile situation, with a high possibility of being assassinated, I will show no visible fear."

Vatrin turned back, frowning. "Within reason."

Homaj waved that away, one of Vatrin's own gestures, and that brought Vatrin up short.

Vatrin pointed at him. "You're me, from now on. Do not break character. I'm Lt. Seyra. When we reach the palace, you will avoid Homaj, avoid the Truthspeaker, and call a meeting in the Reception Hall to make your bid to rule—"

"You want *me* to make your bid to rule?"

That break in his voice, the surprise, was absolutely justified.

"Yes, I'm not going to put myself in that kind of danger. You'll be me in truth—I know you can do that."

He took a breath. And could he do that, being Iata in truth, being Vatrin in truth, two layers deep? He would have to be Iata in truth first, or he might accidentally give himself away on the callback.

Oh, Adeius, his callbacks. Vatrin would try to use Iata's, which wouldn't work on him, he didn't think. He hadn't taught his own to Zhang or Lodri—there hadn't been time, though surely, with Zhang, he should have thought of that.

He had to hope he'd get kicked out of it normally, though that could also pose issues with him being disoriented, or coming out at the wrong time. Or, try to set his own trigger that he was likely to encounter to kick him out, at least back to being Iata in truth, and hope he didn't cause a scene.

"What about the Truthspeaker?" he asked. "He'll have to witness my—your—bid to rule."

Vatrin's lips curved in a way Homaj was growing to hate. "You'll be witnessed by a magicker. Won't he be, Lodri?"

Kitchen sounds that had been coming from the other room stopped, and there was silence.

Adeius, had Vatrin not turned on a dampener for that whole conversation? Homaj had just assumed, and he'd been too distracted by Vatrin to realize the kitchen sounds would tell there wasn't a dampener on.

Lodri came to the half-open doorway, didn't quite enter. She watched Vatrin warily.

"Yes?" she asked.

"You will witness my bid to rule."

"I'm not a—"

"No, you're not. Your *mother* is, though. Please call her to the palace, to be ready to witness to *my* truth."

Lodri's eyes were wide, her face pinched. She glanced to Homaj, back to Vatrin.

Homaj stared at her, communicating as much as he dared. Yes, do this. Somehow, we'll find a way to work this to our favor.

Had Vatrin seriously just blackmailed her, and by proxy, the First Magicker? Implying that if she didn't do as they said, she and her mother would be exposed. And how had Vatrin known she was a magicker, or the First Magicker's daughter? How much surveillance from the city did Vatrin have access to?

Homaj had known Vatrin had their hands in many, many pots, but he hadn't known—he hadn't been paying enough attention. Not at all, for the last few years. And this was who would have been the future ruler of Valoris? Who might still be?

His stomach turned. He knew Vatrin was hiding much. What they were doing now was not to anyone's good but Vatrin's. And he still had the gnawing feeling that something was off, something between the words said and left unsaid was deeply, personally dangerous to him. And maybe...maybe had been deadly to his fathers?

Is that what had made him hesitate last night and feel the need to meet Vatrin as Iata, not himself?

His resolve there was only solidifying. Vatrin could not know he was Homaj. If they did, his life was absolutely in danger. And he was reasonably certain that Vatrin still didn't know.

Oh, Adeius. He'd been in the city trying to *rescue* Vatrin. But what if Vatrin hadn't needed rescuing at all?

He swallowed. No, he couldn't go there. And he had no real evidence beyond some gut feelings, which could mean a number of things. Vatrin themself was scared, that was still obvious. And Vatrin had said they believed the Truthspeaker was behind all of this—and Homaj did have evidence to that effect. Not enough, and that was held together by a lot of gut feel, too, but some.

Homaj wasn't ready to believe that the traitor Weyan had said his father knew about was Vatrin. Vatrin could be a slime, but Vatrin had never hated their fathers. Vatrin, throughout last night and this morning, was still showing obvious signs of distress.

Vatrin turned back to him. "The witness won't be a problem. Do you think you're competent enough for this?"

Homaj set everything he was feeling aside. All the stakes had just gotten higher.

He raised his brows, a perfect twin to Vatrin's own responses, when they were themself. He tilted up his chin. "Why would I not be?"

66

READY

Fear is a quality we usually associate with Truth-spoken in the context that the people are afraid of them—their power, their ability to be anyone and anywhere. But what do Truthspoken fear?

— DR. NDARI HADI ESYN IN "A SOCIETAL MORPHOLOGY: TRUTHSPOKEN IN THE MODERN AGE"

Because Homaj was now very visibly Vatrin, and Vatrin wanted him to survive long enough to make a bid to rule, he suffered through Vatrin's hand at cosmetics to make his identity less obvious. His appearance ended up far more femme than Vatrin would typically be. He suffered through a few lessons, too, on how to walk and present himself. Adeius, did Vatrin not understand that even as a bloodservant, Iata had been trained with the rest of them to play almost any role?

But the role he was playing now dictated that he go along with this.

Zhang, just visible through the bedroom door on the living room couch, met his bemused gaze. He knew she wanted to hover around him, but he was Iata here, not Homaj. She'd guarded him last night while he'd Changed, but that was reasonable in a situation with unknown danger and him being vulnerable in a trance. Right now, with Vatrin, it would not be reasonable for her to guard him as Iata.

Thank Adeius she understood that nuance without him having to tell her. Yes, he was definitely keeping Zhang.

Vatrin, following his gaze, raised their voice. "You, guard. You will obey me in this. For this mission at least. You can go back to Homaj and whatever he's doing after."

Zhang looked to Homaj, and he gave the smallest nod.

"Yes, Truthspoken," she said.

And then came a ten-minute test wherein Homaj should be absolutely Vatrin, with Vatrin as Lt. Seyra doing everything they could to make him break the act. But they didn't manage it, and they wound down, after a time, looking both annoyed and pleased.

Homaj barely suppressed another eye roll.

"All right," Vatrin said. "We go."

They walked in two groups back to the Riveredge bar that Homaj and Zhang had come through the day before—he and Zhang, Vatrin and Lodri, and two athletic people who'd melted in from the sidewalk when they'd come outside and now stuck close to Vatrin. Vatrin had said they were with them, but they weren't anyone Homaj recognized. Not Palace Guard, then. He didn't know if that was good or bad.

Homaj took Zhang's hand as they crossed the street and wove into the bar. Vatrin had decided that they would be lovers again. Thank Adeius Vatrin had not made them practice that.

Zhang gave him a tight smile, the neon lights over the bar reflected in her dark eyes. It was still early, but the music was blaring, a twangy beat that nudged him a little too close to a headache. He didn't have enough concentration to smooth it away in this crowd.

He squeezed Zhang's hand and led them into the bathroom. And—shit. The stall they needed was occupied.

Zhang glanced at the feet showing beneath the stall door, looked to him, raised her brows. The other stalls were empty, no one else in here. They couldn't plausibly stand around and wait for that *one* stall without having a reason to wait.

Homaj grinned, pulled her closer, wrapped his arms around her. She didn't stiffen this time. She knew the drill. She hugged him back.

Vatrin and the rest would be in the pub by now, would stagger their own entrance into the hidden passage. Lodri had tried to follow Homaj, but Vatrin had gripped her arm—and there had been no choice but for her to stay with them, Vatrin's hostage for the moment. Which made Homaj's blood boil.

The person in the stall was making settling noises. Homaj suppressed a groan and rested his forehead on Zhang's shoulder. He was shorter, just barely taller than she was now. Was she freaking out at all that he looked like Vatrin beneath the cosmetics, beneath the veneer of other personality Vatrin had wanted him to use until he was ready to make *Vatrin's* bid to rule?

He was. He was definitely freaking out, very quietly, very self-contained, about all of this.

"Are you—" he started.

"Are you all right?" she asked into his ear. Her voice was as low as she could make it and still be heard over the roar of the pub's music, just barely muffled in the bathroom.

"Is this a good idea?" she asked.

He glanced past her to the closed bathroom door. How long would Vatrin wait to come in? They'd said five minutes, but Vatrin had never been patient. Were they trying to see if Homaj was recognized and assassinated here before coming in?

A flush—*finally*—came from their target stall.

He said into Zhang's ear, "I'm fine. Listen—if things go weird, take me to—to my brother. He'll know what to do."

She did stiffen then, but she nodded.

A person pushed out of the stall, ambled toward the sinks, and Homaj pulled Zhang inside. There was enough noise and the person who'd come out seemed oblivious enough that he didn't feel the need, or have the stomach, to play up the lovers act any more than they had.

He placed his hand on the back wall, one finger tapping out the entry code. The panel softly clicked, recognizing Vatrin's DNA, and the narrow door swung into the cramped room beyond.

They slipped inside and shut the panel behind them.

"Can we talk?" Zhang asked as he unlocked the door to the corridor beyond.

"Better not to risk it. The others will be here shortly."

She nodded as they filed down the corridor then toward the stairs that led to the small staging area below.

Down there, they waited. He leaned against an electric bike, his body language that off-shade of Vatrin's they'd insisted he use. Zhang stood with her arms crossed, eyes darting around with nervous energy.

He needed—he desperately needed to teach her his callbacks. But he didn't know if Vatrin had been down here earlier, had planted surveillance. He didn't know, and couldn't risk it.

He could, though, at least warn her of the process. Had she seen what he'd done the night before, submerging as Iata? Had she understood? Lodri had. And when he submerged again as Iata, he would submerge *again* as Vatrin. His life could depend on her knowing what was going on.

"When we get there," he said quietly, "I won't be myself."

She gave him a searching look, maybe trying to parse out what lay behind that obvious statement.

Finally, she asked, "What does that mean?"

How much did he dare say? How safe was it, even talking within a subject Vatrin knew about? Could the Truthspeaker have bugged this area as well? Could one of the Palace Guard? These access tunnels were keyed to be used only by Truthspoken and their bloodservants, but that hardly felt like safety now. He couldn't step near Zhang and try to speak quietly here, either—if Vatrin had this room under surveillance and saw that, they would be suspicious.

He tried to think of a way to reframe what he needed to say but kept discarding possibilities.

Distantly, he heard footsteps on the stairs above. He had to hope—had to trust that the warning he'd given Zhang in the pub, to take him to Iata if things went wrong, would be enough.

Her eyes flickered, and he saw fear there. Maybe echoing his own.

Homaj checked every nuance of his current performance, tweaked it all in each layer to be as airtight as possible.

He'd be at Vatrin's mercy once he fully submerged. Well, he would *be* Vatrin, but he wouldn't come out of it until the actual Vatrin said he could. Or until Zhang got him to Iata—and he was growing more certain that was how that part of it would have to play out. He hoped to Adeius that Vatrin would chalk that up to his incompetence as a bloodservant and not the truth that he wasn't actually Iata. And what if Iata couldn't find a way to shake Vatrin for a few minutes to recall him? He hoped to Adeius that Iata could fool Vatrin into thinking that he was Homaj. Iata seemed to have others at the palace fooled, at least. He hoped.

Oh, this was so shaky. This was such a bad idea.

Zhang's look was turning pleading as the steps down the stairs came closer. Wanting him to call this off? Yes. And yes, he should. He really should. Somehow. Get on these bikes, ride into the palace, make their own way in.

Otherwise, what he was about to do was deeply dangerous on just about every level, and he wasn't entirely sure that he *would* be able to go two layers deep, or that it wouldn't scramble his mind in the process. He knew the warnings. He knew the risks.

But his gut was still telling him that staying with Vatrin would lead him to the answers he needed. He was not who Vatrin expected him to be, and neither was Iata. That was an edge, and he had to take it. He had to be close, and he had to protect Iata, too, if Vatrin was planning anything sour.

And what if he, as Vatrin, drew fire? Well, then maybe he'd get some more answers there, too.

The door opened, and Vatrin and their group came down the last open flight of stairs—one of the unknown guards first, then Lodri, then Vatrin and a guard bringing up the rear. Lodri flashed Homaj a look that screamed "get me out of this mess."

He would. He promised himself he would, set it as a core intention along with everything else he'd need to focus on in the next few moments.

Homaj carefully set his boundaries and intensions, built up what he'd need to know as Iata, rebuilt and reshaped all the subtle details to shift his center truth. He'd need a few minutes as Iata, at least, before attempting the second layer submersion into Vatrin. Another core imperative: give his mind time to acclimate.

Adeius. Adeius, he was doing this.

By the time Vatrin reached the bottom step, he was Iata.

"Well, Truthspoken?" Vatrin asked, a little too sneering to fully pull off their role as a guard to Iata's Truthspoken.

"I'm ready," Iata said.

67

A SECOND BID

> *Truthspoken siblings are often public rivals, sometimes friendly, sometimes bitter. One has to wonder if this is a condition of the power they hold, or an amplification of normal sibling rivalry?*

— DR. KIRAN STRIGEN IN "THOUGHTS ON THE NATURE OF TRUTHSPOKEN PSYCHOLOGY"

"Truthspoken. Truthspoken, you need to get up."

Iata blinked up at Jalava hovering over him. Truthspoken—did Jalava mean him?

He looked around and—and scrambled up, realizing where he'd fallen asleep. He'd been curled up on one of the two vastly uncomfortable loveseats in the Seritarchus's study, Adeius. *The Seritarchus's study.*

He stood in the center of the room, adrenaline on high alert, but slowly, slowly forced his body to calm.

He was Homaj. He turned a hand studded with Homaj's rings over, gems catching the light. He was *still* Homaj. He had, at the moment, a right to be here.

Okay.

He glanced around for a clock—Anatharie had never kept wall clocks or displays, calling them crass.

"It's seven in the morning," Jalava said, following him to the desk. He'd camped at that desk all night, struggling to keep up with the flow of requests and reports and information—so much information—that just kept coming in.

"Seven," he said, looking up.

He pulled Homaj's comm from his jacket pocket, then surveyed his clothes—he'd definitely need to change them, and shower, but did he have meetings already scheduled for this morning? Who would do that scheduling, the Seritarchus's office staff? Were they scheduling for him now?

He pressed his palm to his forehead, closing his eyes against the overwhelm.

"Truthspoken—"

He wanted to snap at Jalava to not call him that. But...but, well.

"I just heard over the guard channels that Truthspoken Vatrin has returned," Jalava said, shifting restlessly. "They're in the Reception Hall now, only waiting for enough witnesses to make their bid—"

"Shit," Iata said, and took off running for the back corridors and his own—Homaj's—apartment. Jalava followed close behind.

It took too long to wend the back way to Homaj's apartment, and too long to pause, let the panel scan his hand, give him entry.

"How long ago was this?" he asked Jalava once they were in Homaj's bedroom.

No time for a shower. He shed clothes as he ran to the prep room closet, sorted quickly through the racks. Nothing too elaborate, there just wasn't time.

He pulled out a green silk shirt, black trousers, a frilly white jacket. Not all the right tones, but he wasn't entirely sure what tones he *should* be setting.

Had Homaj succeeded in finding Vatrin, or had Vatrin come back on their own? And wasn't this what they'd both wanted, for Vatrin to take the rulership and let Homaj off the hook? So Homaj wouldn't have to carry on a position he wasn't suited for? At least, Homaj thought he wasn't suited for?

But meeting Eyras the night before had left Iata with the sour feeling that Vatrin might not be as apart from all of this as they should be.

And he *could not* let Vatrin make their bid to rule without him being there. That was exactly Vatrin's intention, he knew that. He had never particularly cared for the Truthspoken Heir —and they'd never bothered much to care for him, either, or Homaj.

He glanced at himself in one of the closet mirrors, made a frustrated sound as he unbound his sleep-messy hair, raked his fingers through it, and braided it as quickly as he could down his back. It was a lot harder doing this on himself than Homaj.

Two gold hoops in each ear. A gaudy emerald pendant that would have to make up for the lack of frill elsewhere. His makeup was...passable. Slept in, but well-done the day before, at least. He knew it would be remarked upon, but he wasn't willing to take even fifteen minutes to fix it. Fifteen minutes would be too late—he might already be too late.

"How can I help?" Jalava asked, hands out but not knowing what to do with them.

Iata made some quick distance calculations—if he took the back corridors to the service stairs that went down to the first floor, he could run most of the way. No, no, he could go completely by the back corridors, down to the Reception Hall antechamber. It would give some social ground coming out that way—or maybe not. That was where the ruler entered the

Reception Hall after all. And he was still, for this moment, the interim ruler. A counterbid wouldn't change that, only challenge the end result.

He swallowed, dashed out of the closet to grab a water bottle from a cabinet beside his own vanity, one he'd stocked himself three days ago—took a gulp.

"Have the rest of the guards—my, uh, guards—meet us in the Reception Hall." He shoved the water bottle at Jalava, then took off for the bedroom and the back corridors.

It took too long even to run, and he knew his running steps might be overheard, even with the corridor dampeners. No help for that.

Jalava, at least, was right behind him, talking low into their comm. Vatrin might be alerted he was coming, but Iata would rather have his guards there than not.

He ran as nimbly as he could down narrowed stairs to the first floor, wound around again through the corridor maze.

He slowed before he reached the panel door that led into the royal antechamber off the Reception Hall. Took a breath—took several. He had to be composed, entirely composed. It didn't matter that his mind was chaos just now, that he still wasn't as awake or alert as he liked—only appearances would matter on this day.

Even still in the back corridors, he could hear the muffled sound of an amplified voice in the Reception Hall.

Okay. One more deep breath. He centered himself as much as he could in Homaj before pushing into the antechamber. Which was blessedly empty.

He glanced in a mirror across from him set for *just* that purpose, fixing a few strands of hair that had come loose on the run. His hair wasn't perfect at all. His cheeks were flushed—he smoothed it away.

Perfectly calm. He fixed on a faint, sardonic smile.

If his appearance wasn't perfect, then he'd carry this with all the dignity and devil-may-care grace Homaj always did.

And then he stepped out.

68

THE CHALLENGE

A healthy palace is one where the Truthspoken and Truthspeaker are united in balance. But when the balance tips, turbulence is sure to follow.

— DR. T. DOSELA IN *THE TRUTHSPOKEN SYSTEM: A VARIED ANALYSIS*

Iata stepped into the Reception Hall, taking in the high-ceilinged space in one glance. The raised dais to his left held Vatrin, though with a heavy overlay of femme makeup, which wasn't like them. Beside them, he recognized Lt. Seyra, one of the rotation guards who'd been with Homaj a few months ago. Then Zhang—oh Adeius, Zhang—and two more guards he didn't recognize, and who looked more like street toughs than Palace Guard. At the far end of the dais, a femme person with dark brown hair in a tight bun stood, holding their hands in front of them, looking distinctly uncomfortable.

The aging First Magicker was making her way from the end of the dais closest to him toward Vatrin.

Adeius. The First Magicker.

Vatrin was copying Homaj's impulse to use the First Magicker to witness—Vatrin certainly wouldn't have engaged the First Magicker on their own. Vatrin had been outspoken before against magickers having a place in the court.

A scattering of nobles had gathered in the Reception Hall, with more coming in. Commander Tavven stood near the back with a handful of their guards, hands clasped, face drawn tight. Their gaze went to him, as did most others' in the room.

Tavven's expression shifted, something Iata didn't have time to read with everything else. Relief, maybe. Or, maybe not.

But he was Homaj. He *was* Homaj, though he still held that hair's breadth between being Homaj and being him in truth.

He didn't see the Truthspeaker.

With Jalava stiff and formal at his side, he casually made his way to the front of the gathered audience.

So, Zhang was here. That meant Homaj was involved with this move of Vatrin's somehow, but where was he? He obviously wouldn't be himself here, not with Iata still in play as Homaj, but was he in this room? Iata hadn't seen any hint of Homaj in the people he'd looked over. The anxious person at the end of the dais might be the best bet—but, no.

And there was a high danger, too, that Vatrin might recognize Iata for who he was. He wanted to play this out in his own mind, not be subject to Homaj's whims in his personality, but Vatrin, who'd pointedly ignored his entrance, was turning toward him now. Did he have a choice?

He spiraled his thoughts down quicker than he'd ever done before, rapidly reformulated his truths, and slipped fully into being Homaj.

Homaj found a place at the front of the crowd that suited him, crossed his arms, and stared up lazily at his sibling. Who was alive—oh, Adeius—but trying to outmaneuver him.

"Brother," Vatrin called from the dais. "So good of you to join us at my bid to rule."

Homaj smiled. "So good of you to make your bid."

In the frigid silence, the only sound that could be heard was the First Magicker's steps as she slowed to approach Vatrin.

She glanced over her shoulder, looked his way but not quite at him before turning back to Vatrin.

Homaj would not snark at his sibling. He would play this straight, he had to. He had much less social credit than his older sibling, and if he tried to undercut Vatrin now, that would only work against him. Homaj, as the second Truthspoken, had the weaker claim to the rulership.

He swallowed against a dizzying wave. He could sabotage his claim now, and he'd be off the hook. He'd never have to worry about this responsibility again.

Vatrin stared down at him, beatific. Absolutely condescending. Though maybe the crowd would read it as the confidence a ruler should carry.

And Homaj wasn't just the second Truthspoken anymore. He was the interim ruler.

The First Magicker bowed to Vatrin and rose, smiling. A little tightly, Homaj thought, as she clasped Vatrin's hand. "I'm here to witness your truth, Truthspoken."

And so she did. Vatrin made their bid with the authority of someone who knew it was their absolute right. Not like he had, all haphazard rage. But then, Vatrin would have had another day to process it all. So that was hardly a fair comparison.

He'd made his bid because Vatrin hadn't been there.

Homaj narrowed his eyes, watching shades of relief wash over the faces around him. Relief that he, in fact, would not remain as the ruler after his ten days were up? Nine days, now.

Vatrin's counterbid only put them in a place to prove themself, but not yet rule. The final decision, then, would be decided by a quorum of the Truthspeaker, the heads of high houses or their representatives in court, and the section leaders of the General Assembly. That was the only way to resolve a forked bid. And Homaj knew, if nothing changed in the next few days, who they would vote for.

If either he or Vatrin resolved the assassination of their parents, though, it would go a long way toward proving their competency. He *hated* that this was where the line would be drawn, that he'd have to use his parents in this way, but he didn't see another option. His sibling was alive—and for that he was glad. He really was glad.

But he was still far from proving anything against the Truthspeaker. From what he'd learned last night, he needed to track down his father's sibling and see what they knew, and he wanted to know exactly what Vatrin had been doing yesterday morning, and where they'd been since. Not that Vatrin would tell him. They would have zero incentive to make any of this easy for Homaj.

"I witness the truth of Vatrin Rhialden," the First Magicker finally said. "They are sincere. The words they've spoken are their truth. I witness in the eyes of She Who Wakes."

Almost the exact words she'd used at his own bid to rule, and he tried not to feel the betrayal of that. It wasn't personal. She was merely doing what she'd been asked to do, in her duties as a Green Magicker.

The room seemed to collectively take a breath, then their relief of the last few moments spiked back into tension. And that particular glee the court always had when watching someone about to take a fall.

They all looked to him, to see what he'd do.

He did nothing. He stared up impassively at his sibling, and for a long moment, Vatrin stared back, their eyes a hard challenge.

Nine days. He had nine days left to prove that he should hold this rulership, or else concede it.

Vatrin could try to assassinate him. The next Truthspoken ruler was expected to be able to hold their place, but direct violence was strongly discouraged. If it didn't succeed, it would drastically hurt the bid of the one who'd initiated it. But if it did succeed? Then there was only one choice left for the rulership, wasn't there?

He wasn't about to murder his sibling. But he wasn't sure Vatrin would feel the same way, especially with him currently holding the power of the kingdom.

Vatrin thanked everyone for coming, made some supercilious speech about how they would work tirelessly to find their fathers' killers and restore order and peace to the kingdom. Homaj—Homaj had ended his own bid with a threat. He didn't have to think too hard about which was the most effective strategy with this crowd. He watched people turning to Vatrin like Vatrin was the dawning sun.

And then it was over. He'd rushed to be here, but he wasn't sure his presence had done anything other than show he couldn't stop the force that was Vatrin Rhialden.

Homaj swallowed hard, smoothing away the burn in his eyes, the turning of his stomach. He hated these power games in his family. He'd given himself the position of royal rake to take himself out of that line of fire. But if he held his ground now, if he somehow, miraculously, won his bid to rule—this would be his life forever.

Vatrin stepped down from the dais and actually let the courtiers approach, invited them over. They shouldn't have, not with the palace still in crisis. Not with their fathers so newly gone. Commander Tavven would likely be tying themself in knots just now.

Homaj hung back, unsure what he'd even say. He'd made it his mission these last few years to *not* be seen how people were looking at Vatrin now.

Bile was rising, and he had to do something. He had to turn the tide, or he'd lose his rulership here, today. He hadn't wanted it, no. But—but he absolutely knew, knew to the depths of his core, that Vatrin should not be the next ruler.

"I've vowed," he said, not loudly, but pitched to carry, "to find who murdered our parents and make them pay."

The courtiers around Vatrin paused, turned toward him. A small victory.

Homaj slowly stepped closer, straining with every trick he knew to pull the charismatic center of the room back toward himself. "I've found much already. I will make my case." His eyes never left Vatrin's. Looking for a twitch, an eye flick, anything that might betray them. "And those people *will* pay."

He stopped half a meter from Vatrin, posture open, aggressive even.

Zhang, hovering beside Vatrin, tensed. She'd sworn her oath to *him,* not his sibling. She was *his.*

Vatrin's lips twitched, not quite a smile. "You do that, Brother. You make them pay." And they turned toward one of the courtiers beside them, a blatant dismissal.

Rage flared in his chest, but didn't go beyond it. His composure was exactly as it should be. Still aggressive, not backing down. He stared at Vatrin a few beats longer, then flicked a hand at Jalava and the others of his guard who'd come in during Vatrin's bid. They were now standing to one side, ready to assist him. He was, after all, the ruler.

He might have just set himself up as an antagonist to Vatrin's hero, but at least he was still in play. And if he'd planted any seeds of doubt in anyone's mind that Vatrin wasn't as blameless as they'd like to appear, that was something, too.

It wasn't enough. He was sure it wasn't enough, or even fully what he'd needed. But it was what he'd been given to work with, and he'd done what he could.

He gathered his guards and exited through the public doors at the back, broadcasting his own charisma like a damned parade. He passed Truthspeaker Aduwel, just reaching the doors and looking stormy.

"Truthspeaker," he said. "You are too late to witness Vatrin's bid."

And then he swept past the Truthspeaker, not giving a further look. That—*that* caused whispers among the courtiers coming in.

So all right, Vatrin might be winning in the court of opinion, but Homaj absolutely knew the value of a well-placed insult. He knew how to push and pull at the people around him until they saw what he wanted, were talking about what *he* wanted.

If Vatrin thought he'd fold easily, they had no idea what was ahead of them.

69

IN DEEP

I almost lost myself in a role, once. Maybe several times. If that would ever happen, I wonder, would I die and someone else live on in my mind? Or would I just become someone else, the same person with different parameters?

— HOMAJ RHIALDEN, SERITARCHUS IX IN A
PRIVATE LETTER, NEVER SENT; AS QUOTED IN
THE CHANGE DIALOGUES

"**M**y *brother*," Vatrin growled as soon as the door to the antechamber closed behind them. "Adeius, he looked so smug. What the hell does he think he's doing, challenging me like that? I'm the Heir!"

They paused to catch their breath. Their head felt too tight, their thoughts confined. They had a slight tremor to their right hand that they'd been suppressing, but it came back again now.

But it was done. They had made their bid to rule and been formally witnessed. Whatever was happening now must be nerves, because they hadn't known what Homaj would do.

They hadn't known if they'd simply be shot at, from any of the players involved. Commander Tavven had seemed both relieved and displeased to see them, though they hadn't been showing much emotion whatsoever, and Vatrin's head was *so tight*.

Zhang stepped closer, her brows drawn together. Her hair was still light blue, which felt out of place, which made them dizzy. "Are you well? Truthspoken?"

"Fine," they said.

"Good," said Lt. Seyra. Who'd been asserting themself much more than usual lately, and Vatrin didn't like that. "Ser Truthspoken. I need to check on palace security. May I have leave to do so?"

The question sounded odd, the tone off. But they didn't immediately see a reason to deny the request, they were absolutely concerned about palace security.

"Yes, go."

"Thank you, ser. I suggest you retire to your apartment until I come back with the all clear."

Another suggestion they couldn't quite refute.

"Come back quickly," Vatrin said.

Seyra saluted and turned, leaving the antechamber through the door into the administrative suite on the other side. One of Vatrin's other guards followed after Seyra, but the last stayed, along with Zhang and the unsealed magicker, Lodri.

Vatrin narrowed their eyes at the magicker. And what trouble would she cause them?

"Ser Truthspoken," Zhang said. "We should go back to your apartment."

She was agitated, that was clear. And the looks she cast the other guard weren't friendly. Was she trying to imply Vatrin was at risk from their own guards?

Vatrin made a snap decision. "You," they said, pointing to

the guard. "Go after Seyra, help them. Meet me back at my apartment."

The guard stiffened. "Ser, I have my orders—"

"From who? I'm giving you different orders. Go!"

Vatrin strode toward the panel door that led into the back corridors. Paused, taking longer than they should to recall exactly where to place their hand. But they remembered it and pressed their palm to the wood.

They hadn't heard retreating footsteps. They looked back— the guard was still there, looking frustrated.

"Go!" Vatrin said, and the guard shook themself, made a sloppy excuse for a salute, and left.

Vatrin stepped into the back corridors, breathing deeper in the familiar dimness. It was, at least, a temporary safety.

Zhang stepped after them, and they held up a hand.

"No, you're not part of my guard—"

"You can't dismiss all of your guards. Truthspoken."

"I'm here to protect you as well," Lodri said. "Let us protect you."

"A magicker is no protection to me. All right, Zhang, with me. Magicker—find your own way up."

"Ser Truthspoken—" Zhang said, but Vatrin gripped her arm, pulled her in after them, and shut the panel door. They'd had quite enough.

Zhang took in a sharp breath. In the dim overhead lights, Vatrin saw her visibly tremble.

They let go of her arm, dismissing her from their thoughts as they stepped quickly through the back corridors, finding the stairs that led up to the second level. Zhang would either keep up or she wouldn't.

But, she did. She was behind them when, finally, they stopped at the panel door to their own apartment.

"Ser Truthspoken," she said, "your brother is asking to see you."

Vatrin paused. "Homaj has disrupted me enough for today, I think—"

She held up her guard's ring comm. "He's asking as the interim ruler. Ser Truthspoken, I don't think it's really asking."

Vatrin stiffened, trying to gather the edges of their temper, but it was hard. Adeius, so hard, and why couldn't they think straight? Had someone given them something, slipped something into their drink? But surely they would have detected poison. They were trained to detect and neutralize any poison or drug they were given.

Had the magicker Lodri done something to them? The First Magicker, even? Magickers had never been friends of the Rhialden rulers. That was one of the first things Vatrin would do when they ascended—further separate and deprioritize magicker roles at court. The magickers truly had no place at this court, though maybe Vatrin couldn't do that immediately. They had, after all, just allowed the First Magicker to witness their bid.

Adeius.

Maybe they should see what their younger brother wanted. They were fairly certain Homaj was too much of a coward to actually kill them. Best get this meeting over with—however it had come about, Homaj *was* the interim ruler for the next nine days, as much as that grated.

Vatrin nodded at Zhang and continued on down the corridor to their brother's apartment instead.

70

THE MEETING

I was you. I'm so sorry, but I was you. I only did what you would do yourself.

— VENORAM RHIALDEN, IALORIUS IV
(FICTIONALIZED) IN THE BIOPIC *VENORAM IV:*
THE LIFE OF AN IALORIUS

Vatrin pushed open the panel door and stepped into Homaj's bedroom, looking around. The bed was made—it didn't look slept in.

Their headache was getting worse—they'd need to stop soon and try to pull enough of a trance around them to smoothe it away. But not here.

Zhang moved ahead, peering into Homaj's prep room. No one was there, so Vatrin followed her in.

"Where did Homaj say to meet?" Vatrin asked.

"Here," Zhang said, though there was just that note of hesitation.

Vatrin narrowed their eyes.

And here they were, with a guard who wasn't sworn to

them, in their brother's apartment. Their brother who had an opposing bid to rule to their own.

The outer prep room door opened, and Zhang drew her pistol.

Vatrin tensed.

Homaj, coming partly inside, froze before his expression closed, and he swept in as if finding Zhang in his private quarters with her pistol out was nothing special.

Another guard—the name surfaced, Jalava—came in behind him, looking wary.

Vatrin waved Zhang's pistol down—they did note her shift in loyalties there, defending Vatrin and not Homaj—and stood their ground in the center of the prep room as if they owned it. Which they would, soon enough, when the palace was theirs. "Brother. You summoned me?"

Homaj showed nothing on his face, but Vatrin saw the slightest hesitation in his step.

"Yes," he said.

So Homaj hadn't summoned them?

Zhang spread a hand to Homaj. "Help him."

Homaj looked back with incomprehension.

Vatrin shifted. "What the hell is going on here?"

The other guard, Jalava, made a stuffed sound.

"Truthspoken," Jalava said, approaching Homaj. "I have urgent, uh, news." They leaned close to Homaj's ear and spoke something softly.

Vatrin stepped closer. What was going on? Their senses were prickling, there was something very wrong here.

Homaj twitched, his eyes fluttering, looking rattled. He turned to Jalava. "Thank you. I'll see to it."

That...had looked alarmingly like a callback. A callback from what? Was this actually their brother?

"Maja?" Vatrin asked. "Why did you summon me here? It had better not be something inane, or waving about your newfound power, which will be short-lived, I assure you—"

Homaj's eyes widened, and he rattled off a nonsense phrase. No—no, that was one of Homaj's own verbal callbacks.

Vatrin paused. That made no sense.

"It didn't work," Homaj said. The look he cast Zhang was almost panicked. "That should have worked."

"Use—use whatever you'd use for yourself."

And *that* made less sense, sending prickles of danger up and down Vatrin's arms.

They reached for the comm in their pocket, but Homaj lurched forward, gripping their arms. Gripping in a specific pattern—

Iata gasped, grabbing onto Homaj's shoulders as the room spun.

He was in the prep room. Oh, Adeius, he'd been Vatrin in truth, he'd made the bid to rule, and where was Vatrin themself? They'd gone off, said they'd meet him back in their apartment, he should be there—

"Hey, hey," Homaj said, and his tone was off. His body language off. "Hey, look at me, are you okay—"

Iata focused. "Maja."

Homaj reared back. Then said, "fuck," and spoke his own callback phrase again, and—

And his head stabbed with pain, and his knees gave out. But he couldn't even think through who caught him, lowering him more slowly to sit on the floor.

He stared at the carpet, his mind blank. Trying to sort through a nested tangle of thoughts and impressions and experiences.

"I am..." he bit his lip. Looked up at—Iata. It was Iata, very much not hiding his tells, and that was a profound relief. That was something he could center on.

His voice was still Vatrin's alto. But he was not Vatrin, of that he was absolutely certain. And not Iata, if Iata was here in front of him. So then, he was Homaj.

He set that center and began the arduous task of realigning his realities back to it.

"Maja," Iata said, not bothering to hide his distress. His face was a map of confusion. "What—what did—you're being Vatrin? I don't understand."

He couldn't help the laugh at the panicked desperation in Iata's voice. At the absolute ridiculousness of the situation. It was better than crying.

He shoved a hand back through his hair, his own gesture, a grounding gesture. "Vatrin found me. Well, I found them first, but then they followed. Iata, I don't trust them, something is off. So, I submerged as you, I didn't want them to know I was me... and things got a little out of hand."

"You fucking think?" Iata said, voice rising.

Homaj grinned, baring teeth. "Yeah. Vatrin wanted me— well, Iata, then—to go back to the palace and be them, so I could draw out any fire meant for them."

Iata's face contorted before it smoothed out again, with not a small effort. Homaj absolutely understood that emotion.

"Yeah," he said. "Vatrin."

Iata opened his hands, acknowledging Vatrin's Vatrin-ness. "So, that was you? Just now? You made Vatrin's bid to rule—"

"In truth. It's still legal if it was in truth, still Vatrin. Vatrin made their bid to rule."

"I—that's—"

Iata stopped, gathered himself. "Okay. So, we switch again? You want me to be Vatrin? Because they wanted me to do it anyway? And, Maja, you went two layers deep? You were me in truth, *then* Vatrin in truth?" His voice was rising again.

Homaj rubbed at his forehead. "I have a massive headache that doesn't seem to want to smooth away. Or maybe I just can't concentrate enough. And...my memories are a little jumbled.

Having odd impressions. But I think I'm okay. I'm not planning to do that again, in any case."

Iata was shaking his head. "Then, okay, I'll Change to Vatrin, but I might need help with that, I don't know them as well as you—"

"You could do it," Homaj said, the other big surprise of yesterday coming back into focus in his thoughts. Iata was his *brother*.

He felt three separate sets of reactions to that fact, the ghosts of those other personalities trying to overlap again with his own.

He closed his eyes briefly, pushed *Iata* and *Vatrin* away.

He said softly, "You can do it, Brother."

71

CONVINCING

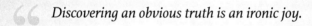 *Discovering an obvious truth is an ironic joy.*

— ANONYMOUS

Iata's breath hitched. "You know?"

"I found out yesterday. You know?"

"I was you, and the Truthspeaker summoned me. He presented me with this information, all threats implied. He knows I'm Iata." Iata's shoulders were tightening as he said this, but he noticed, deliberately relaxed.

"That...is a complication," Homaj said.

"I confirmed it with a genetic sample, administrative mode on the scanner, with your ruler's codes. It is true, Maja. Unless he tampered with that system somehow, but I don't see how he could have, I even checked the logs—"

"It's true," Homaj said. "I learned from my—our—uncle."

"Weyan," Iata said, looking up.

Homaj sat up straight. "Weyan, yes. How did you—"

"It's in the Seritarchus's desk. In a hidden compartment, in a drawer, he had Weyan Odeya's name and comm code. He wrote dozens of letters to Weyan over the years, and, Maja, the last one—he knew something was coming."

Homaj had to take a moment, get past the fact that Iata had invaded the Seritarchus's desk—because, truly, he had as much right to do so as Homaj. And he had to have been looking for answers, just like Homaj. And Homaj had left Iata the keys to the kingdom.

"Maja, Weyan's important in all of this. Was he friendly? Do you think he was behind this?"

"Not behind it, I think," Homaj said.

"Also," Iata went on, "I talked to Eyras last night. She was in the palace, in Vatrin's apartment. She said the Truthspeaker has been blackmailing her about her sibling status for four years. That he's been blackmailing a lot of the staff, the courtiers."

"Weyan told me that someone the Seritarchus trusted was working against him. That could be the Truthspeaker. That could be someone else."

"And...Vatrin?" Iata asked, waving at him. "You didn't tell them you're Homaj."

A statement, not a question.

"And if you pulled this," Iata went on, "you're sure they still don't know. You don't trust them."

"No." Homaj searched Iata's face, more open in his distress than usual. "You don't, either."

"That doesn't mean I think that they killed your fathers."

"*Our* fathers. Ours."

Iata swallowed, staring at him.

He stared back.

His brother. Iata was actually his brother. And he still didn't know what to feel about that. Hadn't yet had the chance to process it. Like everything else in the last two days. He wondered belatedly if it should have felt different talking to Iata now, knowing what he knew now, but beyond the fact that they were both not currently who they actually were, it was just...Iata.

Iata blinked, and his whole demeanor in that instant became more guarded. Had it just occurred to him, too, that Homaj might look differently at him?

Homaj opened his mouth to reassure Iata that they were fine, they were good, he did trust Iata. Adeius, one of the only people in all the worlds right now that he did actually trust.

But Iata said, "I know you're Homaj, but you also could still be Vatrin, be playing me just now—"

"He's not," Zhang cut in. "I'm absolutely sure of that."

Homaj jumped. He'd almost forgotten she and Jalava were still there. Zhang looked adamant, but Jalava's hands were behind their back, eyes locked on the floor.

Iata searched Zhang's face for a long moment before nodding. He levered himself up from the floor, turned back to Homaj.

"So, I'm guessing, if you said I'd summoned you, that Vatrin didn't send you here, and you're not here—well, weren't here—on your own volition? As Vatrin?"

"No," Homaj said, carefully pushing up, too. Zhang moved forward, steadied him. Adeius, being three people was draining. But he was feeling more himself. At least, he was sure that he *was* himself.

"So what now?" Iata asked. "Is Vatrin here in the palace? Did they stay in the city?"

"They're Seyra, one of their current guards, I guess. I have no idea where the actual Lt. Seyra is, they didn't say. The other guards are ones I'm unfamiliar with, and I don't like that at all. Not Palace Guard. Maybe the only ones Vatrin feels safe with, maybe...something else. But yes—Vatrin will be waiting for me soon in their apartment, or else looking for me now."

Iata pursed his lips, his movements flowing back into Homaj's own. Homaj wondered if that was even conscious, or if the last full day of playing that role had left it hard to shake. Iata had been him in truth at least once—and Homaj was *very* familiar with how disorienting that could be.

"I can Change fairly quickly, I think," Iata said, "but not that quickly."

"We *will* train you more," Homaj said.

Iata shrugged. "But that doesn't help me now."

"No, and—I'm already in this with Vatrin. You're already involved here. We don't have time to catch each other up on everything. And I also want to have that buffer, I want there to be that hidden reserve. The Truthspeaker knows you're not me, but he doesn't know that I'm not Vatrin. He won't."

"He saw through you yesterday morning," Iata said, shifting.

"I was in distress. I was too anxious to be at my best. That won't happen again now."

"But surely Vatrin will see it, too, and you can't keep being me in truth, not after going deep like that. Adeius, Maja, please tell me you won't do that again."

"No," he agreed. "But, I'm good. I know I'm good. I'm better at this than Vatrin. You are, too. No, I know you don't have all the training, but your acting skills are better. They won't see you. You know all of my tells. There—that cheek twitch, that looked instinctual. You have this, I trust you. I don't think you have to submerge, either, and we should both be able to think clearly. I have a feeling this is all going to come to a head soon."

Iata closed his eyes, swaying. "Homaj, I insulted the Truthspeaker in the corridor, on the way out of the Reception Hall. Publicly. I was you in truth, and with everything here, with"—he looked back at Jalava—"I didn't think about that until now—"

Huh. Well, yes, Homaj might have done that himself.

"So..." He grasped for the pieces of the patterns floating around him, all of these disparate threads that were slowly weaving together. "So, tell Aduwel you want to rule. Ask for his help in making that happen. Frame it as if from me, like you are Homaj—but let the undercurrent be that you're taking him up on whatever offer of power he's giving."

Homaj nodded, the idea growing on him. "Yes. You can be sure that offer wasn't just blackmail. I think he wants a ruler in his pocket. And he's trying to create a scenario where that will happen. Whether it's Vatrin, or Eyras, or you. I know he's pretty certain he can't control me. I've never liked him, or he me."

"Eyras told him she wasn't taking his threats anymore," Iata said. "She told him three days ago—four days ago now. I think that must have escalated things."

"So, we'll draw him out. Play into his hands. Find out what you can. *I* know you're loyal. I absolutely know that—I thought all of this through again while I was you."

Iata coughed a laugh, made a helpless gesture. And Homaj understood that feeling, too. Nothing was the right side up in any of this.

Iata's ironic smile faded. He stepped back and leaned against the vanity chair behind him, Homaj's usual chair, though he knew Iata would be using it now.

"And if my playing into his hands draws fire on you?" Iata asked. "You as Vatrin, I mean. What if the Truthspeaker decides to take Vatrin out, eliminate the counterbid? And what do I tell him about you—*Maja* you, I mean?"

Homaj blinked slowly. "Tell him that I have been dealt with. And that you're ready to take the place you should have had all along."

Iata shivered. They locked gazes, held it a long moment.

Iata could make it convincing. Homaj trusted him, but he also knew, absolutely knew that having held the power of the ruler, and faced down the military commanders, and whatever else Iata had done as Homaj, Iata wasn't going to have the easiest time going back to the role of a dutiful bloodservant. Not, especially, knowing what they both knew now.

The best deceptions were rooted in truths.

Jalava cleared their throat, breaking the silence. "Should we have heard that conversation?"

"Absolutely," Homaj said, and Iata said a tight, "Yes."

They looked back at each other. Iata waved to him, his mannerisms, his posture fully Homaj's now.

Homaj scrutinized every angle, looking for a flaw. He wasn't sure he saw one—maybe tiny, tiny details. Or maybe not. His own eyes looked back a challenge at him.

"If this goes sour," Homaj said, "find Weyan Odeya."

"I have his comm code," Iata said. "I'll retrieve it, share it with Jalava."

"And I think we can trust Ceorre Gatri," Homaj said.

"I do, too."

"And there's a magicker in the palace—Lodri ver Aminatra, daughter of the First Magicker, unsealed. She was the one at the far end of the dais. She wants me to rule, not Vatrin. She's been helping."

"An unsealed magicker?" Iata asked. But it wasn't with the suspicion or outright fear that most courtiers would have said that. Or even their father the Seritarchus. He and Iata had both experienced the angst magickers and their families faced when they'd been sent to resolve the miners' standoff.

"She knows about the miners," Homaj said. "I think that's part of why she's helping us. And also that Vatrin isn't partial to magickers."

"But the First Magicker witnessed Vatrin's bid. Was that your idea?"

"No," Homaj said, "unfortunately. Vatrin knows Lodri's a magicker, too, and they're using it against her, which I definitely don't like. I can only hope the First Magicker saw everything that's happening."

Iata's smile was small, spare. Absolutely Homaj's.

This would work. Whatever happened from here—it would work. They had a direction, at least.

Homaj rolled his shoulders, rolled them again, and when he let them relax, flowed back into Vatrin's posture and mannerisms.

He flashed Vatrin's smile, then motioned to Zhang to follow him.

One moment at a time, he told himself. One moment at a time.

"Wait," Iata said, and strode back toward him. Leaned to his ear. He spoke the ruler's passcode for the day, the code that would open any lock or any door, if Homaj also Changed his biometrics back to his own to match. Iata said it several more times until Homaj nodded. He had it.

"Good luck," Iata said. Then added a tentative, "Brother."

"Good luck as well, Brother."

Homaj smiled before he let it drop again, pulled Vatrin back around himself, and slipped with Zhang into the back corridors.

72

CODES

> *The security system that the Truthspoken use in Palace Rhialden is nearly uncrackable. Unless, possibly, you're Truthspoken.*
>
> — DINESH SHARIPOV IN *INSIDE PALACE RHIALDEN: AN UNOFFICIAL GUIDE*

Iata stood near the door to the bedroom, staring after where Homaj had gone into the back corridors.

His brother. Which Homaj now knew, and which he hadn't been inclined to distrust Iata about. He was still trusting Iata with his actual life.

"Truthspoken?" Jalava said softly.

Iata spun. "Don't call me—"

He snapped his mouth shut. He had too much of Homaj in his personality just now, that was how Homaj would have responded.

But maybe not Maja. He had seen Maja beneath the layers—Adeius so many layers—he was using just now.

Two deep. Maja had gone two deep, and that was so

dangerous that Iata didn't want to think about what might have happened if he hadn't been able to snap Maja out. If Iata's own callback hadn't worked—and that was astounding that it had. That should have been impossible. Maja had been truly *him*.

His brother. His brother knew him well enough to be called by Iata's own callback.

And Maja had been wearing Vatrin's body, Vatrin's mannerisms. Fooling Vatrin at the moment—at least, so he thought— and that was not a small thing, either. Vatrin had all the same training Homaj had, and while Homaj was right that Vatrin wasn't as good at Change and evaku as Homaj was, Vatrin wasn't someone to underestimate.

And then there was what Homaj had asked him to do.

Iata ran a hand over his hair—it was still in its braid, that loose braid he'd hastily tied earlier.

If he was going to see the Truthspeaker and say what he had to say—and Iata felt that urgency, too much was in motion to hesitate—he'd best renew his armor. He was Homaj just now, but he didn't look his best. And Homaj always, *always* looked his best.

He turned, smiled a tight apology to Jalava, and hoped they would get the context. He had to fully be Homaj now, an uninterrupted persona, but not in truth—just as close as he could get to it without going under. He had to be good enough to fool Vatrin, if not the Truthspeaker.

His stomach tightened, but he smoothed it out. Smoothed the anxiety from his face—he glanced in the mirror, and yes, all signs of anxiety were gone, but he did need a shower. And his hair and makeup were not, truly, acceptable at court.

He hadn't eaten yet, either.

"Get breakfast," he said. "I'll shower, dress, then we'll go to the Truthspeaker."

Jalava still looked unsettled, but seemed to get that no, he would not talk more about this now. Could not.

"Truthspoken," Jalava said, and that didn't feel wrong this time. Jalava gave a perfunctory salute before moving to the hallway door.

Iata thought of something—

"Wait." He pulled out his comm, bringing up the palace system controls, which he fumbled with, because he'd seen them used but never used them himself before. Then the residence controls, and the security system for this apartment specifically.

He touched the allowed list for access to the bedroom suite and entered Jalava's name, choosing their Palace Guard profile.

He entered his ruler's code when prompted—denied.

Shit, it was a new day.

Iata backtracked to his securities menu and went through the exhaustive sequence of biometric verification before the system gave him his code for the day. He stared at it, memorizing the random pass phrase, while an indicator counted down from a minute.

He had it long before the code vanished. Tavven would have a copy of the code, too, which they couldn't use on their own without actually being the ruler. And he could always go through the biometrics again if he forgot it—but he wouldn't have to.

He'd given Homaj the wrong code, though. If Homaj tried to use it, if he was in a pinch, it wouldn't work.

Well. He couldn't change that now.

Iata went back to the residence security menu and softly spoke the code.

Accepted.

"You're in the system," he said. "You can access the prep room and bedroom if needed. Now, I'm getting a shower."

He clicked his comm off and strode for the bedroom before Jalava could respond.

73

UNCONSCIOUS LIES

What you wear can be just as important in the public eye as what you say. Because it's the same thing.

— HOMAJ RHIALDEN, SERITARCHUS IX IN A
PRIVATE LETTER, NEVER SENT; AS QUOTED IN
THE CHANGE DIALOGUES

Out of the shower, dressed again in a much more deliberate choice of flowing black trousers, a silky shirt in rose with gauzy gold trim, and a knee-length rose vest-tunic, Iata felt much more armored. He coded his makeup heavily femme and carefully did his hair the same —which took two tries, because no, it definitely was not as easy on himself as Homaj.

Jalava watched, but didn't try to help. They wouldn't know what to do in any case. And was it highly ironic that Iata felt the need just now for a bloodservant?

But he accomplished everything in under an hour, which was a feat of its own. Then sat straight-backed, surveying his work in the mirror.

Yes. This was Homaj at his most magnetic, balancing his usual flair with a more sober subtlety than usual. That it was himself he was looking at just now wasn't weirding him out as much as it had the day before. This was a performance, but then, the persona of Homaj was *always* a performance, even if he thought Homaj forgot that sometimes.

He rose, grabbing one last roll from the tray he'd picked at while dressing.

Jalava had barely said a word to him while he'd been in his flurry, and he hadn't spoken, either, using all of his concentration to parse through the right styles and meanings, to craft what image he wanted to convey. He didn't always choose Homaj's specific looks for him, but he had a hand in most of them. Had crafted some of them entirely. This was a persona he absolutely knew how to play.

Iata paused to catch Jalava's full attention.

"She and her," he said. "For the moment."

Jalava blinked. Would they know he wasn't genderfluid like Homaj? But Homaj's shift to female or at least mostly female happened most often when he was stressed. This was a likely time. It fit Iata's gut sense of Homaj, and also, it would be that extra layer between himself and the role.

Jalava nodded. "She and her. Truthspoken. Shall I call the rest of your guards?"

"Yes, do. Call ahead to the Adeium as well that I am coming to see the Truthspeaker."

Jalava saluted, and went ahead into the rest of the apartment, calling for the guards.

Iata centered himself. Allowed himself to feel his nerves for one solid, heart-clenching minute. Then forcefully calmed his body's responses.

He stepped out to Ehj and Bozde and Chadrikour forming up, while Jalava with their back turned murmured into their ring comm.

He would be especially on display today, after Vatrin's performance that morning. Maja's performance—Adeius. No, he had to think of it as Vatrin's, because Maja had been Vatrin in truth.

But people would be watching him as Homaj, watching to see how he responded. Would he carry on as the ruler, or would he cave to his older sibling's challenge? Would he cower? Would he do what Homaj had been doing the last few years and do everything he possibly could to get out of any formal responsibility?

Homaj had never avoided all responsibility. He reported the relevant social details he learned to the Seritarchus. He still went on occasional Truthspoken missions, mostly smaller ones these days. He still maintained his various personas throughout the palace and occasionally the city. But Anatharie had transferred most of his attention to training Vatrin to rule, not Homaj.

Homaj had never been meant to rule this kingdom. But that didn't mean he wouldn't have a good idea how, even if he hadn't been planning to ever use that training. He might have a lot less practical experience than Vatrin, but he was by no means ignorant.

Iata had some of that training by proxy. He had a lot of training in how to run Homaj's affairs and household behind the scenes, from the Seritarchus's bloodservant, Omari. Who, he supposed, had also been his uncle. Adeius.

He knew he could fake competence, and knew he would have to.

"Stay close to me," he said to the guards. "Now that Vatrin's back, that still doesn't take the risk off of me. And I'm using she/her pronouns just now. I'll let you know when that changes."

"Yes, Ser Truthspoken," came the near-unison reply.

He smiled tightly. "Thank you. Jalava—are we clear to go?"

Jalava turned back to him, nodding. "Yes. Truthspeaker Aduwel is in his office and awaiting you."

Iata tried to parse if the Truthspeaker would be annoyed with him for requesting time with him—maybe. Or maybe it was something he'd wanted.

He would keep all senses alert.

And he would continue to test out his own inner truths, his own wants, expanding them beyond what he'd ever let himself think before. Dangerously more.

He needed those truths, the dangerous ones. That would be what carried this meeting with the Truthspeaker, not his ingrained, unconscious lies.

Iata reminded himself that Homaj had told him to do this.

He waved to the door.

"Let's go then."

74

THE FUTURE

> *A bid to rule is something all rulers must make at the start of their rule. Whether they come to their power through tragedy or through the abdication of their predecessor, it's always been a necessary signal of intent.*
>
> — DR. KIRAN STRIGEN IN "PSYCHOLOGICAL EFFECTS ON A NEW RULER AND HOW THEY AFFECT THE KINGDOM"

Iata settled himself in the chair across from the Truthspeaker's desk. He wasn't here as Homaj in truth this time, and he was having to work harder than he'd like to keep all of his stress responses tamped down. And keep his personality as close to Homaj's as possible without submerging.

Aduwel surveyed him, his expression pleasant. Iata couldn't miss the hard glint in his eyes, though. Aduwel had not liked Iata's rebuke in the corridor earlier. He could not like that

Vatrin had snubbed him, too, by using a magicker to verify their bid.

Aduwel would know, too, that Iata wasn't Homaj in truth just now. Of anyone in the palace beyond Homaj himself, the Truthspeaker would know.

"So," Aduwel said finally. "You now have competition."

Iata's smile was acid. "So do you, apparently."

Aduwel's brows didn't so much as twitch. "Have you been talking to Vatrin? To Eyras?"

"Eyras, yes. She had interesting things to say about your relationship the last few years."

Now, finally, an emotion crossed Aduwel's face. Anger, Iata thought. But it was just as quickly gone.

Aduwel tapped a ringed finger on his desk. "Eyras has an agenda of her own. Be careful around Eyras."

Iata sat forward. He might not talk to the Truthspeaker this frankly, but Homaj would. And Homaj was still coloring all of his thoughts, his movements. "What is your agenda, Aduwel? You exposed me yesterday—that wasn't an accident."

"I exposed *Homaj*," Aduwel said, and there it was. The opening threat.

Iata sat back, but didn't for a moment relax his mannerisms into his own. "Yes. That doesn't change the question."

He would not let his heart hammer in his chest. It beat steadily, a little faster than normal, but within bounds.

Aduwel's smile was slow, showing teeth. "Did you verify the information I gave you?"

"Yes."

"And what do you think about that?"

Iata shrugged. "What am I supposed to think? What purpose did you have in showing me my bloodservant's heritage?"

Aduwel ran a hand through his own black hair, a very familiar gesture. Iata didn't know in that moment if it was a deliberate provocation, or if Homaj had at some point picked up the gesture from *Aduwel*. Which made Iata's skin crawl.

But he couldn't show it. Absolutely couldn't show it.

"Ah. Well. I would think that purpose is clear," Aduwel said. Then, "Where is Homaj?"

Iata blinked. "I'm right here—"

Aduwel waved a hand. "You know my office is bug-proof, and I always have low-level scramblers and dampeners on. Such is the nature of my work."

Iata didn't know that Aduwel wouldn't make a recording for his own purposes, though.

He didn't visually drop the act, but he did say, "Homaj has been taken care of."

Aduwel's brows rose. "Ah? How, might I ask?"

"You may not ask. You wouldn't like it, I think. But...you will not see him again."

Iata carefully, so very carefully, speared each statement with its own truth. No, Aduwel wouldn't at all like that Homaj was planning to thwart him just now. And yes, Iata had taken care of him. He'd always, as best he could, taken care of Homaj. Maja was Vatrin just now. And Aduwel wouldn't see him. Maja wouldn't let him. And after all of this played out and Homaj reclaimed his life again? He would never let anyone see him, truly. He never did.

Iata let out all the ambition that had been growing this last day, and over a lifetime, all the small cruelties and the intense pain of *knowing* that he could have had more purpose than he'd been allowed, if only his fathers would have told him he was theirs.

He let all of the things he had never dared to look at before surface now, like how he was the one running Homaj's household while Homaj did his very best to avoid political responsibility. He was the one who sent gifts to Homaj's discarded lovers, hoping to quietly avoid political scandals. He was the one who carefully steered Homaj behind the scenes, hoping to Adeius that some of it would stick, because Homaj had been steadily on a path to destruction. And that would never be good for the kingdom.

It was all maddening and infuriating. And to know that he himself was the elder, that he, if he'd only been given the chance, could have made much better use of this life than Homaj, scorched him most of all.

He let it burn in his eyes and held the Truthspeaker's. *Look at me, Aduwel. Look at me and see someone who has been thoroughly screwed over, and is taking some of it back.* All of it, if he could. *He,* not Maja, was a more legitimate heir. *He* was a more capable ruler. And he would kill to keep this kingdom safe. He would.

He was killing Homaj now. Killing any chance at Maja molding this persona on his own. Whatever happened now, Iata's personality would be a part of the driving force behind Homaj Rhialden.

Aduwel's gaze lingered a long moment. He'd know Iata wasn't telling the full truth, or telling lies by omission. Aduwel had been one of the people who'd taught him how to do that. He hadn't had nearly as much time training with Aduwel as Homaj had, but it was still taking everything he had not to automatically assume that Aduwel knew everything.

Iata straightened, locking eyes with the Truthspeaker. "Yes, I have thought about what you told me. And I've thought a lot about what I'm doing right now. Who I am. What body I'm in, and the job I'm carrying out. I am a Seritarchus personality, not Homaj's Ialorius or Vatrin's Melesorie. What the kingdom needs right now is control, someone who can hold it firmly in check. Find those who killed my—my fathers—and move us into greater security."

"And you think you are that person, Iata?"

He swallowed, almost flinched at the use of his name. And carried it into a different truth.

"That's not my name. Not now."

Aduwel's lips twitched, not quite a smile. Which had to be deliberate, because little with Aduwel was not deliberate.

"I'll remain Homaj," Iata said. "I'll fully become Homaj."

His fingers dug into the fabric of the chair.

Aduwel nodded, as if this was the wise choice he'd expected all along. "Because the people would never, ever accept a bloodservant to rule them, and yes, you know that." Aduwel's words were soft, almost regretful. But his eyes never left Iata's.

Iata wanted badly to break the eye contact, but he didn't dare.

"Yes," he agreed. "This was never a job suited for my younger brother."

Homaj could do it—but suited to him, no. And Homaj wasn't a Seritarchus personality, no matter that he was determined to try to fit himself into one.

"And Vatrin?" Aduwel asked. "How do you propose to take care of Vatrin, if you, as you say, took care of Homaj?"

"By finding who killed our parents. By winning the people over. I did what I had to with Homaj, but I don't intend to kill my other siblings, if that's what you're implying. Not if there's any other way."

"Not at all."

Iata couldn't tell the truth of that statement either way.

"And in return for my support in this endeavor?" Aduwel asked. "I support you, publicly, as Homaj. What then? Will you continue to snub me as you did in the palace earlier? Will you enlist the Green Magickers to verify your truths, not me and the sacred office of the Truthspeaker?"

Oh, yes. That had made him angry, deeply angry, that Vatrin had snubbed him in their bid as well.

"No," Iata said firmly. "I will support you. You have my word on that."

And he had to give his word, fully and sincerely. He would have to trust Maja to take undermining the Truthspeaker from here, because he couldn't do this without full sincerity. Maja would know that. Maja would have to know.

"Thank you," Aduwel said. There was no smugness in his tone or his posture, but it hung in the air all the same. "Thank you, Seritarchus."

All the hairs on Iata's body stood on end, and his heart gave a clenching lurch. He couldn't stop the flush in his cheeks. He felt like he was going to throw up.

This could be his right now. This really, truly, could be his.

He got a handle on his emotions and nodded. "Thank you, Truthspeaker."

Aduwel opened a desk drawer and pulled out a small leather pouch. He stretched across the wide desk to set it right in front of Iata.

"I believe you might pull off winning the people over, but I also can't trust that you will. Take this. Use it at your discretion. This is the kingdom on the line, Homaj. Do not forget that."

Homaj. So the Truthspeaker, for now at least, was committing to the act. And if this was carried through, eventually it wouldn't be an act. He would adjust Homaj's public persona and personality over time until it aligned with his own. A perfectly blended person.

Iata carefully took the pouch and unclasped the opening, looked inside. Four glass vials, each marked with—

Fuck. This was poison. Poison, and Aduwel had labeled it? Did he think Iata was stupid enough to carry this on his person, so Aduwel could call the Palace Guard and have it discovered?

He closed the pouch and handed it back.

"This is absolutely not what's best for the kingdom," he said stiffly.

Aduwel broke out into what looked like a genuine smile, which was...confusing. Disturbing, even.

He'd been implying without actually saying it that he had killed Homaj to replace him. Did Aduwel believe that? Would he still believe it with Iata's reaction now?

Iata wasn't sure if he'd just passed that test or failed it.

"Good, good. Then we won't worry about that. Yes, Iata, you have my full support. *I* witness your bid to rule, if it ever needs to be reconfirmed. By Adeius, under the holy stars, it is done."

Iata swallowed. All of that rang as true to him, the tone, all the micro expressions, the posture, everything he could see and sense with all the training he had.

Adeius, he had done it? Had he just done that? He hadn't truly thought Aduwel would go that far. Hadn't thought the Truthspeaker would support him, and what did that mean?

Aduwel must have read his confusion, because he said in a more gentle tone, "The kingdom is in a crisis. You are doing the right thing, I assure you. I have been watching your progress for years, and you are steady. You've managed Homaj's affairs well. You will make a good ruler, and I will be here, always, to support you."

That feeling of his skin crawling was at odds with the Truthspeaker's words, with his tone, but Iata trusted it. He clung to it, even if he let his body's responses react to Aduwel's words instead.

He inclined his head, a gracious acknowledgement without irony, because it was good to hear he'd been doing well. It was.

"Thank you, Truthspeaker. Aduwel."

"Good," Aduwel said. He stood with renewed vigor. "Good, we should discuss this day's meetings, and which you would like me to attend, and which you can handle on your own. While I admire your handling of our esteemed military leaders yesterday, I don't think it would be smart to repeat that performance. Rather, we should take a more reasoned approach."

Iata's throat tightened, even as he nodded. This was Aduwel's excitement—to have a willing puppet. To have someone he could, unequivocally, own.

This was what he'd feared before. And now?

And now, if Homaj couldn't do what he needed to do, it would be a reality. It would be Iata's reality—the kingdom wouldn't be his, but Aduwel's. And there was nothing Iata would ever be able to say without losing everything himself. Without, if this went on long enough, shattering the kingdom in the process.

He was in the Adeium. He was in a sacred space. And he prayed, oh Adeius, he prayed that this would not be his future.

75

THE MAKEOVER

> *My older sister has never regarded me as her equal.*
> *But I never thought she was mine, either.*

> — INSAMMAN RHIALDEN (FICTIONALIZED) IN
> THE BIOPIC *VENORAM IV: THE LIFE OF AN*
> *IALORIUS*

"**W**here were you?" Vatrin demanded as Homaj slipped back into their bedroom. They were still Lt. Seyra, though their bearing was all Vatrin.

Homaj raised an ironic brow, one of Iata's gestures. His body language was a carefully calculated blend of Iata's and Vatrin's, his smile all Iata's.

"Homaj summoned me."

Vatrin went rigid. "And? He saw who you were—"

"He didn't. I was still you in truth. Though seeing him kicked me out of it—"

"And he saw that?"

"No. Zhang covered for me."

Vatrin glanced to Zhang. "Well?"

"Yes, Truthspoken. It is as the bloodservant says." A quick glance at him. "Truthspoken Homaj does not think he is Iata."

That was true enough. More points in a growing list of points for Zhang.

Vatrin scrutinized her a moment more before shrugging one shoulder and storming back out to the prep room.

"Iata. You're going to be making the social rounds today. You need to be seen—"

Homaj followed. "Shouldn't that be you out there? Commander Tavven has the palace under control. We saw that."

"We saw my younger brother barge into my bid to rule and Tavven did nothing about it."

He followed Vatrin into the closet, where they began loudly shuffling clothes on the racks. Vatrin's closet, like their prep room and bedroom, was messy and sprawling. But it was, at least, organized.

"Homaj had a right to be there."

Vatrin glared back at him. "Yes, I get your loyalty. But it's misplaced, I assure you. He challenged me, publicly, at my own bid to rule."

Did Vatrin think they could live their own life by proxy and then claim the insults as personal?

"Here. Wear this. And we'll need to get that makeup off, redo it. You'll need to be recognized as me."

Homaj took the stack of clothing shoved at him and quickly surveyed the choices—not what he would have chosen, certainly. Not quite sober enough. Full of Vatrin's colorful style, but too light and glittery for the day and occasion. As if their fathers had not just been killed the day before.

He said nothing, but moved back out to the prep room, eyeing Zhang hovering near the wall. He stripped and hastily pulled on the skirt, tunic, and knee-length coat he'd been given.

Zhang moved once as if to help him, and he wasn't as steady on his feet as he'd like, no. But he waved her off.

He wasn't sure how he was going to get through an entire day of being Vatrin, absolutely Vatrin, to everyone around him, especially when being Vatrin just now left a rotten taste in his mouth. But he would. He had to. He needed to give Iata time to put his end of things in motion, and he needed to find out exactly who Vatrin's allies in the palace were. He needed to see who'd come to him, and who'd stay away.

Homaj really needed to see how the Truthspeaker would react to Vatrin being back in the palace, but despite what he'd said to Iata earlier, he wanted to prolong that meeting as long as possible. He desperately needed to get his bearings again, and he wasn't at all sure he could pull this off in front of Aduwel on a good day.

He was an expert at evaku and Change, yes, but Aduwel had helped teach him. There were very few tricks he could use that Aduwel wouldn't see right through.

Zhang came up beside him now, helping to fasten the row of tiny buttons up the back of his tunic. Vatrin would have chosen something impossible to get into and out of on his own, wouldn't they? But then, that was the type of clothing they liked to wear. Fashion that required their bloodservant to serve them.

Vatrin emerged from the closet with a handful of jewelry, looked him over, then nodded to the vanity—Eyras's seat, not their own.

"Get back in character. I know you know how to do Homaj's makeup, but you don't know how to do mine, so I'll have to do it again."

As if that was a great and honoring condescension.

But he slipped obediently and fully back into Vatrin's mannerisms, and as much of Vatrin's personality as he could stomach.

He suffered through Vatrin first wiping off the cosmetics

from earlier, then rebuilding the layers. Their own cosmetic style was terse and dramatic, more flash around the eyes and mouth than he typically wore as himself. His own cosmetics tended to make statements in their subtlety with vicious little details.

Zhang watched, occasionally retrieving things when Vatrin asked for them. She was steady in her own patience when Vatrin insulted her intelligence for not immediately knowing where those things were, after only coming to this room for the first time today.

Homaj studied Vatrin in glimpses as they worked. Their brow was tight with focus, their tongue unerringly sharp exactly where it would sting the most. Were they this bad to Eyras, or was this the stress of everything that had happened and was still happening? Was this grief? Was it an act, for whatever reason Homaj had yet to tell?

Vatrin had always been impatient, but Homaj hadn't thought they were this bad when they'd all practiced together as kids.

Then again, he'd never seen his sibling through a bloodservant's eyes.

"There," Vatrin said. "That will be good enough. Smile. Make sure the angles are right."

He ran through a range of expressions, and Vatrin nodded.

Homaj rose. "Will you be nearby, as Seyra?"

He still didn't know where the actual Lt. Seyra was—not in the palace, apparently.

Was Seyra dead?

His throat tightened.

He smoothed the tightness away. He could not afford it.

"I'll be near, as I can," Vatrin said. "I won't let you die, Iata, if I can help it."

And that was a truly wonderful thing to say.

"But I don't anticipate an attack. This is only a precaution."

Homaj spread his hands, breaking character, just a little, back into Iata. "What should I say to people who ask about your policies? Or offer condolences? I can give a speech, but these people know you—"

"Condolences, I'm sure, you can figure out. And you know my policies—everyone knows my policies. And no one actually knows me. Really, Iata, this will not be that hard. I will have the harder job, looking out for any trouble."

Then why was Vatrin still insisting that he play the role of their own life? And if, as Vatrin just said, no one knew them— and Adeius what a thing to say—how could they possibly think that he could be them convincingly?

"Trin," he said. "I know you, well enough."

Vatrin shrugged. "Outside the family. No one you'll meet today will know me. Now, are you ready?"

He hesitated, but nodded. And if Vatrin thought Iata was naive enough to think that watching for trouble was the harder job today, or that Vatrin's only motive in hiding was their safety, he wasn't going to burst that bubble. If Vatrin wanted to under-estimate him, that could only work in his favor.

"Please keep Zhang nearby, too," he said, slipping back into Vatrin's tone and cadences, where the request was just short of a command. "I trust her. Out of anyone in this palace, I do trust her. You can trust her with your life."

Vatrin eyed her. "My people that I also trust are not particu-larly suited to court niceties, so she will have to do. Zhang, do you have court training?"

"Some, Truthspoken."

Did she? She'd handled herself very well so far—he had to believe that.

"Good. We have a reception in twenty minutes in the Lavender Hall. Let's go."

76

LAVENDER HALL

The nobility have a corner on saying things without meaning them.

> — ADMIRAL OF THE FLEET DASSAN LAGUAYA
> IN A CONTROVERSIAL VID INTERVIEW AT THE
> END OF THEIR CAREER

"Truthspoken Vatrin. I am so, *so* sorry to hear of your loss. Of course it is devastating to all of us. The Seritarchus was dear to our hearts."

There wasn't a true word in any of those statements, but Homaj inclined his head, taking Count Sirem Javieri's outstretched hand and giving it an acknowledging squeeze, as he'd seen Vatrin do many times before.

"I am gratified and honored, Count Sirem. This is a sad day for us all."

Sirem's smile was perfect. But Homaj's training was better. And maybe what Vatrin had said was true—no one knew them outside the family, not even their closest friends.

Was that true for himself?

He decided not to think about that just now.

"Call on me after your bid has been accepted, Truthspoken. We'll have a drink and talk the continued mutual good fortune for Javieri and Rhialden."

He didn't miss that she'd put Javieri first, either. Or that this "close friend" talked with Vatrin like they were business colleagues, not actual friends.

And he'd known that, on some level. But he'd never experienced it from Vatrin's perspective.

No, people didn't know him. But he didn't talk to them like they were damned *business associates,* either. His persona was approachable, if in a caustic way, and maybe some people knew *Homaj* and not truly Maja, but that was entirely different than whatever was happening now with him as Vatrin. Homaj's friends could make insults and tell their jokes. They knew he'd be smiling—ironically, but smiling—with them. He'd worked hard for that camaraderie. He'd worked hard to be seen as degenerate. Maybe not a friend, but a semi-reliable ally. It was a place in court he could live with.

What had Vatrin worked for with this friendly aloofness? What was the purpose?

"Of course, Sirem," he said. He let go of her hand, and she retreated. Not even a backward glance to see if he—well, Vatrin —was okay.

Would his own friends at court ask if he was okay? He didn't have access to his own inbox just now. Would there be messages?

Of course there'd be messages, but would anything in them be genuine? Or would they be after his sudden rise to power?

And yes, as Truthspoken they were taught to cultivate distance in personal relationships. Truthspoken were sacred in the eyes of Adeius, meant to carry out the god's will in the kingdom. They were meant to mingle, but not to *mingle.*

Was there anyone in the kingdom not intimately connected

to the Truthspoken who'd even care that his heart was currently trying to crush in on itself under all of these condolences? That he wanted to find a dark corner and shut out everything, for just a few minutes? For a lifetime.

The next person to pounce on him was still a few steps off.

And Adeius, he hated this. This reception, informal as it was meant to be, was exactly the kind of gathering he usually tried to avoid or crash with maximum impact and style.

He should be on the sidelines, offering cutting commentary to his circle of hangers-on. But instead he was here in the center, playing a role he despised. This was what he'd been trying all his life to avoid.

No, he was not okay. He would not ever be okay if this went on much longer.

"Truthspoken."

Admiral of the Fleet Dassan Laguaya parted the crowds toward him, cutting off another lord who'd been about to reach out. Their uniform and hair were neat and crisp as always, though just now they looked a little flushed. Had they been drinking? Adeius, that would be a first.

No, Laguaya seemed agitated. Seemed, of everyone here, to actually remember that this was only a day after the death of the Seritarchus.

Homaj rallied himself because he had to. Because he was good at what he did, and this was his life and his kingdom on the line.

He smiled, the same somber smile he'd been giving people all day. "Admiral, it's good to see you well. I trust all is well in orbit?"

"Well enough, Truthspoken. And forgive me, I am deeply sorry for your loss, and sorry for the kingdom's loss. I'm not here on social graces, unfortunately. Would you have some time—after this reception, of course—to go over some details with me?"

"Of course, Admiral. I'll call General Abret to be there as well, if you wish. You have both handled this horrific situation so well, you have my commendation."

He was going to vomit. And Laguaya's return smile was genuine, even gratified.

He wished he had been there when Iata had torn Laguaya and Abret and their scheming ways apart, because he just knew these two had been angling for power and thinking the young new acting ruler was an easy target.

But he was Vatrin. Vatrin worked well with anyone they wished to. So he made a few more minutes of small talk with the admiral before they nodded and strode off again, their immediate goal accomplished.

He wanted to sit. He looked around and saw Vatrin a few paces behind him, their posture guard-steady. Zhang stood to their right.

And how many people did he have to get through yet?

Fuck it. He was Vatrin. Vatrin, no matter who they were, had still just lost their parents—they couldn't be expected to stay here all day, listening to these ridiculous excuses for sympathy.

He broke into a cold sweat before he had a chance to smooth it over. If he succeeded in his bid to rule, would this be his life? Would this forever be his life, even as himself?

Steady. Steady.

He held up his hands, and after a moment, conversation around the room died down.

"Thank you all for coming, and for offering your support in this, my most devastating hour. You have and will always hold a place in my heart. I must attend to the business of the kingdom, however. Rest assured that you will all be with me today. And I will do my utmost to see the kingdom stable and thriving once again."

He made the barest suggestion of a bow to them and received deep bows in return. Not from everyone, but from a very significant portion of this room, which wasn't only full of Vatrin's supporters.

How was he supposed to compete with this? Vatrin gave them hollow comfort, gave them nonsense promises. Yes, Vatrin did follow through on their social reforms, at least trying to get those reforms past the Seritarchus's approval, and they were passionate about their causes. But couldn't these people see that Vatrin wasn't the hero here? Vatrin, this sparkling and compassionate leader, was a lie. It wasn't even a particularly *good* lie. But it was the lie these people wanted.

He left, hardly seeing who he passed, hardly knowing the nothing words he said to them.

He felt numb all over, and was that still the effects of going two layers of identities deep, or the effects of seeing what he was truly up against?

He couldn't win this. Not unless he could come up with absolute proof that Vatrin had been involved in the assassination of their parents, and he didn't know if that was true. He still knew something was wrong, something was definitely wrong, but he couldn't pull down someone like Vatrin on a hunch.

At least Iata would have the Truthspeaker's support, for whatever that was worth for the moment. Vatrin had made an enormous mistake when they'd chosen the First Magicker to verify their bid as well. Not that they could have done much differently, if they thought the Truthspeaker was trying to kill them.

And maybe Homaj had just sent Iata to his death. He didn't know. He just didn't know. He was moving on hunches and half-baked ideas, and moving far too fast.

He stepped into the Lavender Hall's antechamber, equally as lavender, and Vatrin approached, leaning toward his ear.

"What are you doing?"

"I need a break. And you need to talk to the Admiral of the

Fleet. *You* need to talk to them, not me. I don't know all of your plans—"

"It isn't safe to talk here," Vatrin hissed, and pulled back.

No, it wasn't. But Admiral Laguaya, maybe thinking his retreat was for their benefit, stepped into the antechamber after him.

He should have had more guards with him, and those guards should have stopped Laguaya.

"Truthspoken," the admiral said. "May we go somewhere to talk?"

"I am busy, Admiral—"

Vatrin made a small movement with their hand. A narrowing of their eyes. They wanted him to have this meeting.

"—but, yes, we will go to a secure room. There is one just down the hall. Lt. Seyra, if you will clear the way."

Vatrin led them out the back of the antechamber into an adjoining corridor, striding quickly enough that Homaj had to quicken his own steps to keep up.

He thought Laguaya might try to chat on the way, maybe to ingratiate themself with him, but they kept quiet, only their assured, steady pace sounding on the stone tile floor alongside his own.

Laguaya was still silent when they all stepped into the secure room down the corridor, and Vatrin shut the door.

The admiral glanced at Zhang and Vatrin, back to him.

"I would like to speak alone, please."

"Respectfully, sir," Vatrin said, "the palace is still on alert status. We must remain to protect the Truthspoken."

Laguaya let their annoyance show. "I have served Valoris for most of my life. I have no interest whatsoever in harming the Heir, and I can't share what I need to share with anyone but them. Respectfully. Lieutenant."

Vatrin, not nearly as cowed as they should have been as a

guard taking that line from the commander of the Navy, looked to him. "Please, Ser Truthspoken."

Everything Homaj could read on the surface of Laguaya was sincere. Every angle of their body language radiating agitated sincerity. And—they were scared. He saw that, though they were doing a very good job of hiding it. Laguaya certainly had evaku of their own.

"Very well," he said. "Seyra, Zhang, wait outside."

Vatrin's mouth pulled taut, but they saluted, as did Zhang, and retreated.

Homaj waited until the door clicked shut behind them, then stepped to the door panel and its privacy controls. He tapped the privacy filters on, watching the admiral out of the corner of his eye. They could attack him now. If he cried out, no one would hear.

But then, everyone would know Laguaya had done it. And nothing in their body language signaled that kind of tension or aggression just now.

"All right," he said, crossing his arms. "What is this about?"

77

THE BUYER

Crime is certainly present on the streets of Valon City. The Municipal Guard, however, does an excellent job of keeping our streets safe.

— LORD SAFIA TAIYEN, INTERVIEWED IN THE POPULAR VID ZINE *VALON CITY SUNSHINE*

L aguaya hesitated. They looked around them at the secure room, its elegant trimming and expensive ocean wave resin table and wooden chairs to one side.

"Your brother, the—the interim ruler—told Abret and me to inform him of any developments in this case. Please understand that I would normally do so, as I respect my orders."

"But you do not respect him," Homaj said, with perfectly tuned understanding.

Laguaya grimaced. They held up a palm, a fending-off gesture. "You'll understand why I'm coming to you with this when you hear the information."

Homaj shifted. He didn't like where this was going at all.

But he made his face and posture more attentive, made sure there was an undercurrent of anticipation in his eyes.

Laguaya spread their hands, smile tight. "We found the weapon that shot down Lord Xavi Birka's aircar. It was dumped in a trash bin in Gold District—recently fired, matched our prediction of its make and model. A heavy ground rifle equipped with havoc rounds."

They paused, watching him closely.

He waved an impatient hand for them to continue. Because Vatrin would do that. But he himself was going silent. He would have waited, would have let the silence be filled by everything they knew.

"We traced the weapon back to when and where it was purchased. Not black market—well, not the worst of the black market, in any case. A gun dealer in Gold District with a shopfront selling soft drugs, stims, aphrodisiacs, that sort of stuff. Not a legal sale, but she keeps meticulous records in case there's trouble."

Another pause.

"And the records said?" he prompted.

"The biometrics on file for the sale of that weapon were your brother's. Homaj Rhialden."

He rocked back. What?

"When was it purchased?" he snapped. No, moderate his tone. That was too much of himself.

He stopped, very carefully rebuilt first Iata's personality over himself, then Vatrin's.

Laguaya didn't seem to notice his lapse. They had gone gray around the edges.

"Yesterday morning. Shortly after the assassinations."

What?

But—

"You're sure?" he asked. "You are sure that the biometrics were Homaj's, not faked, or the system hacked—"

"I made sure," Laguaya said tightly. "I absolutely wouldn't have brought this to you if I wasn't sure." They brought their hands together. Their knuckles cracked in the tension.

So.

He stepped back, began to pace. As Vatrin would. Fingers flickering across his hands, restless, furious. But inside, Homaj's thoughts had a different kind of fire.

His biometrics. Well, they certainly weren't his. So that left the people around him who could Change. Vatrin, Eyras, Iata... Weyan. This was after the assassination, so it couldn't have been his father or his father's bloodservant, Omari. And that wouldn't make sense at all.

Did Vatrin make sense? It was Vatrin's lover who'd been killed.

Eyras? What motive would Eyras have to kill Lord Birka? But Iata said she'd been blackmailed by the Truthspeaker. Could he have ordered her to do it?

And Weyan. Weyan was still a wildcard. He'd said he was here to help, and that he didn't have anything to do with the assassinations, but they hadn't talked about Lord Birka.

But...why? What motive could Weyan have to kill Vatrin's lover? Weyan lived in the Onabrii-Kast Dynasty now, could he have switched his allegiance? Had that been a cross-borders assassination?

But...why?

No. No, that didn't fit the pattern. It was too far-flung, and what was happening now, all of what was happening now, was much closer than that. Weyan had said so himself. And Iata had found Weyan's information in their father's desk, presumably as someone to trust. That had been Iata's take, and Homaj trusted that.

And Iata? Iata had been in the kitchens that morning, hadn't been with him when he'd gotten the news. Had that been enough time to go into the city, purchase the weapon, Change and come back—

No. Of course not.

And he knew Iata's heart almost as well as he knew his own. It hadn't been Iata.

So...Eyras. Or Vatrin. It was possible this was someone else, someone Truthspoken-trained. But to get his *exact* biometrics right was implausible for someone not raised in the palace, with no access to that extremely protected bit of information. And whenever he used his own biometrics anywhere outside the palace, kingdom-wide bugs would lock down the information immediately, leaving it only accessible with top level clearance—which Laguaya had.

It was possible to get a DNA sample from hair or skin cells and run it through one of the genetic scanners they used to train, but the design of those scanners was fully within palace security. Again, it was possible. There were surely knock-off copies of the technology, though manufacturing it would be difficult and dangerous at best. Extremely expensive and illegal for all the reasons above. So, possible, yes. But plausible?

He was back to Eyras. Or Vatrin.

He stopped, aware of Laguaya tracking his movements.

"Any more information, Admiral? Any other details I need to know?"

They'd crossed their arms, a protective gesture. "The purchaser was logged on surveillance, but was not anyone I recognized. Skin pale. Medium height, weight thin of average, hair light brown and straight, shoulder-length. Masc presenting, possibly male sex."

A weight was settling inside his gut. Those specifications leaned more toward Vatrin after a rapid emergency Change, not Eyras. Could Eyras Change that quickly?

Probably. Almost certainly. She was his oldest sister.

"Exact time of purchase?"

Laguaya stated a time that—yes, was less than a half hour after the assassinations.

Vatrin. Or Eyras. One of them had intended to kill—and then killed—Lord Xavi Birka. A heavy weapon that could take down an aircar. Why had Lord Birka been in that aircar? That entire kill had been orchestrated.

His mind settled on, hovered over, the idea of Vatrin. He didn't know Eyras as well as he probably should, Vatrin did not like her to mingle with his own household more than she had to, but she'd never been the mastermind type. She'd never liked Vatrin's shadow, either, and he knew from many subtle cues that she and Vatrin did not often get along. But if she'd killed Lord Birka, he didn't think it was on her own initiative.

And Vatrin? They'd shown genuine grief when talking about their lover's death. His mind shied away from even pursuing that line of reasoning, but he pushed through. He had to.

Vatrin had wanted to marry Lord Birka. Did someone want them not to? The Truthspeaker was the obvious answer.

But, the Truthspeaker was the *obvious* answer. Homaj couldn't trust obvious answers as a given.

His parents had been assassinated less than an hour after Vatrin's, Eyras's, and Lord Birka's meeting with the Truthspeaker. And in that similar timeframe, someone who could Change had purchased a heavy weapon that could take down an aircar. And a few hours later, Lord Birka was shot down on his flight away from Gold District. Fleeing? Running to someone? Had Vatrin ordered, or asked, him to go to the Financial District?

And the fact that whoever had bought the gun had used Homaj's biometrics was...what? Meant to implicate him as it was doing now? Or the panicked decision of the purchaser, reaching for the best option in a pinch? One of the only options, and that might have been instinctual.

A quick Change. An instinctual reach to a familiar pattern of DNA that could be Changed in the hands and eyes and voice only.

It was possible Eyras had those skills. Fit that profile.

But was it probable?

He shook himself. He'd gone still, and that wasn't like Vatrin at all.

He met Laguaya's eyes.

"I will make my sibling pay for that. Rest assured. Thank you, Admiral, and tell no one else what we spoke of here today, not until and unless I ask you to. Those who found my brother's biometrics—have you locked them down?"

Laguaya nodded. "Oh, yes. First thing I did. There will be no leaks from my people." They hesitated. "You have my full support, ready to bring in any forces you need. I don't have Abret's ground support, but the Navy has a full staff in Onworld Command in the city. You need only say the word."

"Thank you, Admiral," he said softly.

78

TENSION

> *I'd like to say when everything is calm is when disaster tends to strike—but when is anything ever calm?*
>
> — AARAV ANIYAN, SOCIAL COMMENTATOR, IN
> A POST ON THEIR FEED

Homaj wanted an hour to compose himself after meeting with Laguaya, but he didn't even have a minute. Vatrin slipped back into the secure room after Laguaya left, a storm brewing in their eyes. Zhang stepped in behind them and shut the door.

"Well? What did the admiral have to say?"

And Homaj had a decision to make. Had this game gone on long enough, had he just received all the information he would get, and should he stop this now and confront Vatrin about killing, or having a hand in killing, their lover?

He still wasn't sure Vatrin had done it. But he was almost certain that the person had purchased that gun had been Vatrin.

But if Vatrin might have killed their lover, who they obviously loved, what would they do to their brother? Who warranted seriously less affection in their eyes?

He settled himself firmly back into Iata being Vatrin.

"The Admiral does not have good things to say about Homaj. Apparently he gave them a dressing down yesterday along with Abret—"

"I heard that, yes. Stupid move. Though I can't say I haven't wanted to do the same. Is that all?"

"They were afraid Homaj might try to kill you and pledged their support and aid to prevent that."

"And did you accept it?"

"No. That would hardly look good to have marines trailing you around, would it?"

Vatrin made a face, sighed. "No. That was the right call. Though if Homaj does try anything—"

"He won't. That is not Homaj."

"Then you don't know your Truthspoken," Vatrin said. "People will do anything for power. Anything. My brother is hardly exempt. I do not trust his layabout routine. Though I suppose it has been useful. It's absolutely working against his bid at the moment. You couldn't hear all the conversation around you in there, but support for me is nearly absolute. No one wants Homaj to rule."

Homaj smiled tightly. Because Iata would smile tightly. Because he wanted, at that moment, to punch his sibling's face. How could Vatrin be so knowledgeable, and so off the mark? About who he was as a person, at least.

If they weren't so entirely convinced that bloodservants were less than Truthspoken, they might have seen through his act by now. It might not have even occurred to them that Homaj might willingly hand over his life as the ruler to someone else. Someone he trusted.

Could Vatrin be putting on an act? Did they already know he wasn't Iata, and were they using him? Toying with him?

He didn't think so, with the same conviction he had about Vatrin's part in all of this. Vatrin's weakness was their vanity.

"What next, Truthspoken?" Homaj asked. Vatrin didn't seem to care that he hadn't responded to their rant.

Vatrin straightened. "I have another informal gathering with economic leaders from the city. We must assure the industrial sectors that we have the kingdom under control. Similar format to what we just did, you can carry that off. I am impressed, Iata. Homaj has trained you well—one of the only truly useful things he has done, I assure you. If you are ever tired of not having enough work to suit your talents, I can absolutely make use of you in my service."

Homaj bowed his head in acknowledgement of the compliment. "Thank you, Truthspoken. I will consider your offer."

He was so proud that none of his rage made it out of his core. Time enough for that later.

And there would be a later.

IT WAS another three hours and two more gatherings before they finally returned to Vatrin's apartment, and Homaj had had enough. He was almost vibrating out of his skin to get out of Vatrin's skin, to not have to say another word of Vatrin's particular brand of bullshit.

He wanted to talk to Iata. He needed to know how the meeting had gone with the Truthspeaker—obviously it had done something, as Iata had been on his own whirlwind tour of meetings today, he'd heard. He wanted to know how that had gone, and tell Iata what he had learned, see if they could put together the disparate pieces into a cohesive whole. He was feeling the shape of the thing, something snarled and complex and...he knew it would be devastating. He almost didn't want to know. Almost.

But it was only early afternoon, and he was certain Iata would still be busy. While he hardly had an appetite after everything that had happened today, his body needed food. He'd burned through his reserves going two deep earlier, and he knew Vatrin would put him to work again after they ate.

Vatrin, thank every god there ever was or would be, didn't eat with him, but had gone off to check on "palace security." So who was Vatrin's contact, or contacts, and what were they talking about? Or planning?

Yet more he didn't know.

Homaj sat in the prep room across from Zhang at a folding table she'd brought out from the closet. He hadn't relaxed his personality from Iata, but he wasn't currently holding any of Vatrin's, and that was an intense relief. Zhang had called up a meal for him from the kitchens, and now she set out an array of high calorie containers while she grabbed a bag of sugar snacks for herself. When she moved to pour him chilled tea, he swatted her hand away.

"I'm a bloodservant. I know how to pour tea." The look she gave him was...long.

He gave her the hint of a smile. All he could give her. There should be no surveillance here, but that didn't mean Vatrin wouldn't have their own surveillance.

"Do you want tea?" he asked.

"No, thank you. It's green, and that makes me need to use the washroom five times an hour."

He did smile then, and she smiled back, the pinch between her brow clearing for the first time that day, if only for a moment.

She held up the half full bottle of a protein shake. "I got this earlier, from the staff."

He nodded. Guards on long or intense duty shifts were always cared for.

"And I ate a few energy bars between the last few hours,"

she said. "The Truthspoken, too, though they complained that it tasted like dirt." She shrugged. "The bars aren't that bad, though, just not a hot meal."

Homaj nodded, feeling the tension of the day settle over him as he ate, a muzziness hovering around his senses. Was it just the strain? Or had going two deep earlier affected him more than he'd thought? He had sorted out his thoughts again, but they were feeling untethered now, less cohesive. And his hands were tingling.

Homaj's eyes went wide.

He dropped the spoon he was holding, and the fried protein strips that he'd been eating. His ears were buzzing, his vision growing wavery.

Poison.

79

DAMAGE

> *There are over three million known poisons, most of which are surpassingly hard to manufacture or obtain. The antidotes, I'm afraid, are often even harder to find, and for some poisons, nonexistent.*
>
> — DR. BAY KRADIOF IN THE BANNED TEXT,
> *MEDICINAL USES FOR MICRODOSING OF*
> *POISONS, THIRD EDITION*

He knew this poison.

Homaj shut his eyes, folded his arms on the table, and let his head drop as he pushed straight into a Change trance. He searched out the offending molecules and neutralized them, pushing them out. Healing the damage, reversing it mid-stream.

He came back to himself feeling shivery and queasy, Zhang crouched beside him looking panicked.

"Truthspoken?"

He coughed, and his mouth tasted vile.

He felt within himself. He'd gotten all of the poison. He was sure of it. But why was he still feeling weird? He might be tired from the Change, but he shouldn't feel ill. His training had involved neutralizing hundreds of different poisons. He knew what he should feel like after this one, even if it had been a higher dose.

Had he been wrong about which poison?

His stomach lurched, and he put a hand to his mouth, but it stayed down.

"Should I get help? Truthspoken!"

Should she? Was it someone here who had poisoned him? Vatrin, their other guards, the kitchen staff?

He still felt weird. And there was a slow coldness creeping over his limbs. He hadn't caught everything. Or, no, there was something more. A second poison, slower, more subtle. Deadly because it wasn't immediately expected.

Fuck. He dipped inward again, searching for the second substance.

It was subtle, and with his mind swimming, if he'd only suspected it a few minutes from now, it might have been too late.

Trance. Now.

He dropped his head on his arm again and vaguely heard Zhang yell before all his concentration was on finding every molecule of the second poison and pushing it out. No time for him to be subtle.

He shoved the poison out through every path his body gave him. And Adeius, it wouldn't be pretty, some distant part of his mind told him. But he might yet stay alive.

He jolted back again, Zhang holding his head so he wasn't lying in his own filth.

"Are you with me?" she asked. "Are you with me?"

She wavered in his vision, but he finally, finally focused on her.

"Zhang," he croaked.

He coughed, and already he was feeling better. He stank, and he knew he'd soiled himself. His body had a sour, metallic odor.

He sat up straight and ran a shaking hand through his hair, pushed up from the table.

"No," Zhang protested, "you need to sit. I should call for the physicians—"

"No! I can't—we don't know, Zhang, I'll be fine. I got it all out. It was—" He coughed again, and spat on the already disgusting table.

A pause, and a quick delve again into his body, thorough this time, left him further drained. But he felt no more poison. He'd have to heal the remaining nerve damage as he went.

She was shaking now, harder than he was. "How close? How close was that?"

"I'm fine. I'll be fine."

She gave him an incredulous stare. Then somehow, Adeius bless her, managed to gather herself.

"Can you shower?"

"Fuck yes."

Zhang followed him into the shower, and he didn't care as she helped him strip. As he weakly clutched the sides of the stall, she scrubbed him down in quick, efficient movements.

He felt like he should be embarrassed, but he had almost died. And that was only now sinking in.

Even in the hot stream of water, he started trembling uncontrollably.

Zhang turned off the shower, folded him in a towel, and set him down on the dressing chair inside the washroom.

She crouched in front of him.

"I thought Truthspoken could neutralize poison. I thought it didn't affect you."

"It can weaken us if it's strong enough or unexpected, and it can also kill us. Much, much less chance of that than a regular person, and I think it's only happened once in the history of Truthspoken—the other time didn't count, because poison was used to weaken the ruler so he couldn't react in time to a killing blow."

Zhang's incredulous look was back.

He laughed, a desperate giggle. "This was two poisons, a good combination. I recognized the first—a strong dose, enough to kill, so I thought that was it—and maybe the second. I was already in less than optimal condition."

There was a sound out in the prep room, a sharp bark that sounded like a curse.

"Iata!"

Vatrin barged into the bedroom, then the washroom, took in the scene.

"It smells horrible out there!"

Homaj had just enough of his wits left to wrap Iata back around himself.

"Poison does that," he said through chattering teeth. He watched Vatrin's reaction. Watched them visibly swallow.

They looked scared, truly scared, and crouched down, pushing Zhang aside.

"Are you hurt? Is it out?"

Was that actually concern? Or were they checking to see if it was still possible to finish the job?

His stomach lurched again, and he knew this time it wasn't from the poison.

"Yes," he bit out. Then, "You were right. Someone would try to kill you."

"Almost succeeded in killing him," Zhang growled.

"Two poisons," Homaj said. "One high dose. One slower. Subtle."

Vatrin's lips pulled into a thin line. "Do you know which?"

Iata had as extensive a training in poisons as he had, as Iata would sometimes test his food and had to be able to detect and neutralize poisons in himself. Homaj was so used to that he hadn't even thought to test the food himself, to be wary of poison in the first bite.

He looked to Zhang in renewed horror. If she'd eaten more than the pre-sealed snack, if she hadn't had her own drink—

By the queasy cast to her face, she'd caught up to that fact, too.

"You need to see a physician," Vatrin said.

He clutched at their arm. "No. This can't get out. It'll destabilize the kingdom even more. I'll be fine. I just need to rest."

"But we have more engagements—"

"No, we don't. Unless you want to Change and go to them yourself. And, as your current temporary bloodservant, I really advise you not to do that."

Vatrin rocked a moment on their heels, then nodded. Helped him stand, with Zhang, and get to Eyras's bed. Which apparently they thought she wouldn't be using that night. Homaj filed that fact away to examine later.

"I'll stay with him," Zhang said. "In case something goes wrong."

Vatrin frowned at her stating a fact, not asking for permission. But they nodded.

He sagged onto Eyras's bed and was already drifting.

80

DOWN

Sometimes, when the wind is right, you can smell the river from the palace grounds. You can be sure that we'll always have a clean river.

— DINESH SHARIPOV IN *INSIDE PALACE RHIALDEN: AN UNOFFICIAL GUIDE*

It was late in the evening when Iata finished with a whirlwind tour of meetings, statements, and introductions. A few of the heads of high houses, members of the General Assembly. Diplomats and billionaires. Aduwel had made it clear exactly the line he wanted toed. And it wasn't that Iata disagreed with all the positions the Truthspeaker wished him to take—which were framed as subtle suggestions only, but absolutely orders—but the fact that they were mandatory ate at him.

The Truthspeaker didn't stay with him throughout all of the meetings, but he would be watching, Iata knew. He would be reported to. And who among the palace staff was on the Truthspeaker's payroll? All of them?

He'd changed his pronouns back midday to he and him. He'd subtly shifted his presentation, he knew he'd absolutely and unequivocally been Homaj to everyone who'd seen him that day—with the exception of Aduwel. And Ceorre, who'd woven in and out of the day, her attention sharp and on him. Did she think he'd betrayed Homaj? What had the Truthspeaker told her?

Iata was still keyed up and crossing the central palace courtyard, back from the last meeting of the day with two diplomats in the guest wing. It wasn't standard for a ruler to go to those they wished to meet, but Aduwel had said that the Onabrii-Kast delegation should be treated differently. And who was Iata to say he wasn't right?

The palace had settled into an eerily quiet evening, without the usual chaos of the various social gatherings that went on most nights. True, he'd seen plenty of people coming in and out of the palace today, and there had been gatherings and receptions, but those had been mostly somber affairs.

It was still only the day after the Seritarchus had been assassinated. There would be no celebrations yet, no spaces open to anyone not generously vetted to be here. But the Rhialden Court functioned largely on its people, and the Truthspoken had little actual power without the people they moved in and around. What was evaku without people?

And so the palace had opened again to a select set of those people. Iata did not envy Commander Tavven their job just now, in any capacity.

He frowned. He had not had a chance at all today to try to parse out anything about the Palace Guard and their place in all of this. He wasn't sure he'd have that chance tomorrow, either. Or any day after that until this ended.

Movement ahead caught Iata's eye as he neared the doors back into the main palace, and he slowed, then stopped, as a person approached. He was certain—wasn't he certain?—that the person hadn't been there a moment before, but they weren't that close to the doors.

Dark brown hair, lean frame, sharp features, femme. Mid-thirties, maybe.

He'd seen them that morning—they'd been on the dais with Vatrin at Vatrin's bid to rule. And he was remembering now, just from moments ago, them approaching him now, but this was the first time he'd actually *registered* that the person was here. Like they'd only now come into his mind's focus.

His senses, overwrought and worn out from the day, went on high alert.

Homaj had said there was an unsealed magicker in the palace. That she was an ally. Was this her? Adeius, he hoped Homaj was right that she was an ally.

"Yes?" he asked curtly.

His guards had all stiffened, Jalava shifting closer to him.

"Truthspoken, we should continue to the palace," Jalava said. Had they noticed the weirdness of the person's arrival, too?

"A moment only, please," the person said in a low voice. "My name is Lodri ver Aminatra. I have helped your sibling, and wish to offer my help to you as well."

Then she was Homaj's magicker.

He studied her in the courtyard lights. She held herself tightly controlled, tightly contained. And if she was a magicker, she would have to be hiding her aura as well.

Homaj had said she was the First Magicker's daughter.

Did she know who he was? He had to assume yes, if she was working with Homaj, if she felt comfortable enough to approach him, the interim ruler.

She'd never have gotten close if not for her magics.

"Truthspoken," Jalava said again, looking around.

"Walk with me." Iata motioned toward the palace doors ahead. "We'll discuss more inside."

Lodri gave a gracious nod, dipped more deeply into a bow. Her brow furrowed as she straightened, looking uneasy.

As they started walking again, he thought her unease might be because of him, or something he'd said or hadn't said, but Lodri was casting glances to the right, in the direction of the Adeium across the wide courtyard.

He looked over as well—he only saw two Adeium guards stationed outside the Adeium gates.

He tensed. Was she waiting for something? For someone?

Or, if she was a magicker, was she sensing something he couldn't? Was she sensing Aduwel's malice coming from that direction? Was she afraid of him?

Between steps, the air hung poised. A slight breeze played at Iata's blouse, carrying with it a light scent of the river just in front of the palace. A hint of roses from the gardens behind the palace. The sound of their footsteps on the stone, the soft hum of one of the palace air systems.

Iata drew a breath—trying, Adeius, trying—to slow down even a little bit from the absolute hurricane of the day. He couldn't be paranoid in every moment, he had his guards, he had to calm down. He had to regather his thoughts.

Lodri yelled, "Down!"

Jalava didn't hesitate, even on that word from a stranger. They pushed Iata to the ground as a brace of energy rounds hit the wall behind where Iata had just stood.

Iata lay cheek to the cool, rough stone, pressed down under Jalava's weight, looking up out of the corners of his eyes at the smoking holes in the palace wall.

The moment, surreal and fragile, shattered as Ehj and Chadrikour fired back across the courtyard, Bozde calling for backup.

Jalava rolled off him, rolled to place themself in the line of fire first before hauling him to his feet.

"Get up. Run!"

His thoughts had hardly caught up. But he found his feet and didn't question, charging the remaining distance to the palace doors. Homaj had always been the better runner, and that worked for him now.

His whole body tensed for the impact of the next shots hitting his own flesh. Burning through his clothes, leaving smoking holes in his body.

Lodri caught up to him, gripped his arm, and he felt a lurch as the world went a little grayer. A mental barrage of disgust and fear and hopelessness hit him, but stopped abruptly when they passed into the palace proper and Lodri let go.

He goggled at her. She flickered for a moment, almost as if she was a hologram—but he knew she wasn't.

Then, she solidified.

What had she just done? Had she pulled him into invisibility with her?

Was she, in fact, an ally? She'd caused him to stop, had been looking in the direction of the shooter.

The guards inside the palace crowded around him, asking what had happened, was he wounded, would he please come with them to a safer location—

The guards started to separate him from Lodri, but he locked eyes with her.

The desperation in her gaze hit like a punch to his gut.

"She comes with me," he said, as the guards bundled him farther into the palace.

Jalava caught up, ashen-faced, eyes darting in every direction.

"Truthspoken. We go to your apartment."

"Agreed," Iata got out. His guards inside were already moving him in that direction, forming a wall around him as more guards joined them.

"Palace is on alert," Jalava said. "Going into lockdown."

Fuck. For the second time in two days—and he'd almost just been shot.

He'd almost just been *shot*.

If he hadn't stopped for Lodri, he might not have been a target.

Or he might have anyway, if she hadn't been there to warn him. He might have just died.

His mouth pulled tight. He shunted the panic of that thought aside and, with nowhere else to go, the fear settled down into his bones.

"I want to see Commander Tavven in—in the Seritarchus's study at their earliest convenience." With him being the interim ruler, that meant *now*.

81

THE STUDY

> *Coming into a place that wasn't previously your own but is now, a place you've never inhabited before and maybe saw from a distance, or maybe is entirely new, is a soul-expanding experience.*
>
> — IMNOTREALLYHERE999 IN THE VID FEED
> *TIPS FOR LIFE*

They moved past Homaj's apartment, down the central residence corridor, past the checkpoint where the Seritarchus's guards would stop anyone who came any closer, but no one was at the checkpoint now.

Jalava waved Ehj and Bozde to stay there, and the rest of them continued.

Iata still wasn't letting himself panic. But as he reached the apartment door, he hoped—oh Adeius, he hoped—it would actually let him inside.

He'd gained access to the Seritarchus's study last night, but coming in from the front felt vastly different than through the back corridors.

He gripped the handle, leaned close to the door's sensors and murmured the day's pass phrase.

The door clicked open.

It felt like an intrusion. It felt *intensely* wrong, coming into this apartment as if it was his own. As if he had a right.

Lights eased on, the opulent entry immaculate with its indigo walls, brushed titanium and pearl decor. The entry lead into an equally opulent sitting room in teals and copper, with a hallway to the right that led to bedrooms and, at the end, the study.

He saw Lodri looking around—saw all of his guards trying hard *not* to look around, because they certainly never would have gained access here before. He carefully ignored all of that and strode for the hallway, straight back to the study.

Another pause at the study door to unlock it, and then he was inside again.

He'd slept here the night before. And yet it still felt like he was coming in by himself for the first time. Like he shouldn't be here, oh Adeius, he shouldn't be here.

And what was making everything inside him squirm was that the Truthspeaker had just witnessed his own—Iata's—bid to rule. That had actually happened, and he knew enough of Valoran and Adeium law to know that witness had been real and legal.

Jalava caught up with him again and told Chadrikour to guard the study door—she nodded and took up position outside it.

Iata waited until Lodri was also inside, then carefully shut the door. It locked automatically. He felt the small pressure as the dampening and signal scrambling systems turned back on. This was the safest room in the palace.

So how much, just now, should he trust? How much could he? Did he dare ask for more allies, did he dare tell what he'd just done with the Truthspeaker? He didn't know this magicker.

But Homaj did, and there was certainly a way to find out her trustworthiness.

He stepped away from the door and held out his hand to her—she seemed to be expecting that and gave her own readily.

"I'm Lodri ver Aminatra," she said, though she'd given her name before. "I am a magicker, and the First Magicker is my mother. I have spoken with—your sibling."

"With Homaj," Iata said firmly.

Lodri's gaze flicked to Jalava, noting their lack of surprise at that statement. She nodded.

"Yes. With Homaj. He verified my truth as you're doing now. I want him as the ruler. We all do, the magickers. He is sympathetic to our cause, so we will lend what help we can. At the moment, that help is myself. Use me however you need me now."

Her lips tightened, not a smile. "Truthspoken Vatrin also knows I'm a magicker, though I did not tell them. They're holding that and may continue to hold that over me."

Iata grimaced, but he didn't yet let go of Lodri's hand. Everything she'd said felt true, the sense of it clear, unquestionable, and ringing with an intensity that buzzed in his bones. She wasn't just sure of her words, she was angry, alight with purpose.

Iata had been read by a magicker once before, and his own sense of them hadn't been nearly as clear, or the sense of gut-level *truth* as prominent as it was now. Lodri was unsealed, but she wasn't a low-ranking magicker. Especially not, Adeius, if she'd turned them *both* invisible just minutes ago.

He wanted to ask what that had been, the twisted, ugly emotions he'd felt from her just then. But that wasn't the most important thing here.

His instincts spiked that he shouldn't trust a stranger.

But was someone a stranger if you knew, absolutely knew, where they stood?

And now, his turn. Because he also sensed a wariness from her, a mistrust of him. How much had Homaj told her about him? What part had she played in whatever had gone on in the city?

She already knew he wasn't Homaj. Did she know that he was actually Homaj's brother, though? Yes—yes, she had used "sibling," and while that could have meant Vatrin, he was almost certain that wasn't what she'd meant for him to hear.

"I'm Iata byr Rhialden. I am Homaj's bloodservant. I am loyal to him with all I am, and will do everything in my power to see him rule. He asked me to hold his life for him while he searched for Vatrin, and I'm doing that. I will readily give it back when he asks."

Lodri's brows twitched, and he felt her echo back the less-than-true part of that statement.

He took a breath, said more quietly, "I *will* give it back."

That was true.

Even if there was a part of him—Adeius, a very large part of him—that wasn't keen on going back to his life as a blood-servant.

He'd had to unbottle too many of his own hidden truths to convince the Truthspeaker, and he didn't have the luxury yet of pushing them back down again.

He also didn't want to think about if he *could* push them back down again.

Lodri nodded. She made to let go, but he gripped her hand tighter.

"One more thing, Ser Aminatra."

Her posture went back to mistrustful. Maybe she could sense the roil of emotions rising inside him.

"On Homaj's suggestion, I presented myself today to the Truthspeaker as willing to rule in Homaj's place. As Homaj.

The Truthspeaker..." He swallowed. "He legally witnessed my own bid to rule."

Lodri stiffened, but nodded.

"I have no intention whatsoever of carrying that out," Iata said, meeting both her eyes and then Jalava's. "He's been using me as his puppet all day."

Jalava looked grim. Iata hadn't yet had time to unpack that detail to them, but Jalava had to have guessed it by the flurry of activity the Truthspeaker had put him through that day.

He turned back to Lodri. "I know someone just shot at me, and right now, they think I'm Homaj. But—do you know who Homaj is right now?"

"Yes," she said, her emotions cold as steel.

"Then he's in danger, too. Greater danger, maybe. If this gets tangled, if Homaj gets killed, and if the Truthspeaker tries to set me up fully as his puppet—"

He didn't know what he was asking. No, he did know, and it was more than one thing. The realities were catching up with him—that someone had just tried to kill *him*, that Homaj was also a visible target, that he had just made a valid bid to rule, that if Homaj was killed and Vatrin still lived...would Vatrin be a better choice for the kingdom than himself? Distrusting Vatrin as deeply as he did? As deeply as Homaj did.

Iata hoped they were both wrong. He hoped that this was all the Truthspeaker, and that they would find a way to draw the Truthspeaker out.

Could he ask Lodri to witness, if necessary, that the Truthspeaker had accepted his own bid to rule? That he was actually a full royal Rhialden? But that would blow too many secrets out into the open and further destabilize the kingdom.

If Homaj was killed—

He started to shake. Damn. Damn, he hadn't had a reaction when he'd run into the palace, he'd thought he wouldn't have one, but his body was catching up, rebelling against his own rigid control.

"You should sit," Lodri said, and looked around.

He didn't move. He didn't even look toward where he'd slept the night before, in the central sitting area.

Lodri squeezed his hand. How much of his thoughts had she picked up? Iata's arms prickled.

"If you need me to witness your truth, Ser Rhialden, I will, however it needs to be witnessed. You were with Homaj with the miners. You were the one who suggested much of the solution, even if it wasn't carried out."

He swallowed. "That—I couldn't help that. Neither could Homaj. The Seritarchus—"

Lodri nodded. "We know."

She would witness he was Homaj, too, if that's what it came down to?

She let go of his hand and unceremoniously steered him toward the couch he'd slept on.

"But let us hope it doesn't come to that," she added. "Let us all hope."

Jalava followed them over, then stiffened, twisting their ring comm, head cocked to one side. "Commander Tavven is at the apartment door."

Iata, shivering on the couch, hiss through his teeth. His posture and mannerisms hadn't drifted far, but he brought them firmly back. But his composure—he tried to dip into a light Change trance to still his body's shock reaction, but he knew that in itself was dangerous. Truthspoken might be able to make their bodies do what they wanted, but they couldn't neglect their minds as well.

Damn. He was the one who'd summoned Tavven—he couldn't not see them. And yes, he did need to see them. Someone had just *shot* at him, as the interim ruler, in the palace courtyard. The palace was on lockdown. He had a million things running through his mind, and a whole lot of reasons not to trust anyone in the Palace Guard—especially when someone had just shot at him, and wasn't it far more plausible the shooter had been a guard or had help from a guard rather than someone had managed to sneak a sniper rifle past the guards?

"Have Chadrikour escort them in."

Jalava shook their head. "Ser, you're not in any state—"

"I know, Jalava. And if I'm in danger, Homaj is also in danger. We have to talk to Tavven. Right now."

He might be trembling, but he could still watch and listen for every nuance. He was alert enough. And he wasn't alone—Jalava and Lodri would be observing, too. Even if Tavven asked, he would not dismiss them.

"Tavven knows who I am," he said to Lodri. "But I'm not sure they are a friend."

He would like to think they were. He liked them well enough. But one successful and one failed assassination attempt had now happened in the last two days on Tavven's watch.

Was Tavven one of the people at the palace being blackmailed by the Truthspeaker?

Jalava opened the study door to admit the Commander of the Palace Guard.

82

CONTEMPT

> *The Commander of the Palace Guard is always a person with the utmost integrity, they have the trust of the Seritarchus, and you'd do well to remember that.*
>
> — COMMANDER MEVI MOHAMUT IN THE VID DRAMA *VALON CITY BLAZE*, SEASON 2, EPISODE 10, "THE COMMANDER"

Iata didn't rise. He didn't make any more attempts to stop shaking, either. He sat on the uncomfortable couch, watching as Tavven stepped inside, quietly shut the door, and walked over to him.

Tavven bowed, deeply. A single small ruby in each ear caught the overhead light. Their hair was pulled into a tight tail at their nape today, secured with a no-nonsense clip.

For the second time in a handful of minutes, Iata's own hairs stood on end.

He kept himself centered as fully as he could in Homaj. He knew exactly what kind of effect one of Homaj's favorite stares had and used it now.

Tavven straightened, and their eyes flicked over his face, his posture, with uncertainty. They knew Zhang had come back into the palace—it wasn't unreasonable to think Homaj had as well.

"Ser Truthspoken," Tavven said, and Iata saw the moment they decided to err on the side of caution and believe he was Homaj. "I am sparing nothing to track down the shooter and any accomplices—"

Iata held up a hand, the rings catching the light of the holographic fire across the room. Tavven's eyes flicked to his hand, back to his face. Their own expression grew tight. There was something there. The barest hint of contempt that their own evaku training, which was not equal to his own, couldn't hide.

"Commander Tavven," Iata said. Then he shifted gears. Homaj liked to call it acting on a hunch, but for Iata, it was coming to the end of a conclusion, acting on data when a piece solidly fit into the pattern. That look of contempt—that look was danger.

"Commander Tavven, you are dismissed."

Tavven opened their mouth, closed it again. Their eyes, for a moment, flashed incredulity, then fear, then relief.

"Of course, I will come back when you are rested—"

Iata was still shaking, and decided it was a good effect just now, driving home all the points he wished to make. "No-no. You are dismissed from my service."

Tavven froze. The fear was back, mixing with an edge of horror. Then—and that was the moment Iata knew he had been right—the contempt again.

There might be a world to pay in the morning. But he didn't know if he had until morning. Or if Homaj would have until that long, either. He had to know who to trust, and Tavven wasn't it.

"With all due respect, Ser Truthspoken, we are in the middle of a crisis. I—"

"Yes, a crisis which you did not prevent. That's your job, Commander. If you can't perform your job, then you are dismissed."

Tavven's cheek twitched. Their look settled into a glare. "You don't have the authority to dismiss me. In nine days, Vatrin—"

"Don't address the Truthspoken with such familiarity," Iata hissed. "You don't have that right anymore."

But Tavven wasn't new at their post. They weren't new to the palace, or to the whims of the Truthspoken. Their posture stiffened, their jaw setting.

"If I'm not coordinating, it will be impossible to find the shooter, or your father's killer. With every respect, Ser Truthspoken, this is a bad move. If you want me to resign later, I will resign. But not now, not when the palace is in lockdown."

That argument might be sound if Tavven hadn't let three of their charges be attacked within two days. Four, counting Omari, which he would. And if he gave Tavven time, they could rally support. Maybe go to the Truthspeaker. Go to Vatrin. Tavven could stall, and Iata knew they were bargaining for the remaining nine days to be up and Homaj's bid—and his orders—to be overturned.

Iata's trembling was slowing, and exhaustion was now settling over him. He couldn't break concentration to try to smooth it away, though, and truly didn't know if he could smooth it away. He was feeling frayed in every way it was possible to be frayed.

But he leaned forward. This needed to be done.

"Commander Tavven. Do you have your comm?"

"Yes."

They knew, or at least suspected, what was coming.

"Good. Take it out. Hand it to Jalava."

Iata pulled out his own comm—well, Homaj's. He didn't know exactly where he needed to look for the palace official assignments, but he knew the menu structure, and several inputs of the ruler's code got him to a screen listing the foremost palace officials and their levels of access.

He tapped on the commander of the Palace Guard.

"This is a waste of time," Tavven said. "I could be out there right now, tracking down the shooter."

Iata opened up the menu for the command position. There was an option to reassign. He tapped it.

He grimaced as an info window popped up, informing him that the Truthspeaker would be notified of any change in Palace Guard command.

He proceeded anyway. If the Truthspeaker thought the ruler was dangerously out of line, he could countermand a royal order and freeze the decision. He couldn't do it often, or without political consequences, but he could do it.

Would he?

Iata deselected Tavven, glanced at Jalava and hoped they wouldn't hate him for this, then put Jalava's name and profile into the position instead. He locked it, then sealed with his full biometrics. If the Truthspeaker did countermand the order, it would have to be a public proceeding.

He didn't think the Truthspeaker would. Iata had presented himself as a willing puppet, and Tavven's star was already falling fast.

His comm flashed a red, "Change logged."

Iata glanced up. He knew Tavven and Jalava hadn't seen exactly what he was doing, but Tavven's eyes were bulging. And Jalava looked deathly pale.

"Commander Jalava," Iata said, and Jalava started.

They held up their hands as if to ward off the promotion. "Ser, no, there are dozens more qualified—"

"*Commander Jalava.* Please call in Bozde to escort Tavven to their quarters. They are to gather enough for the night and leave the palace. They may send an address to forward their belongings to in the morning."

Tavven jerked. "You can't—" They shut their mouth with a snap. "Forgive me. Truthspoken." They bowed deeply and without irony, but absolutely not without fury.

"Yes, Truthspoken," Jalava said, and spoke into their ring comm.

In moments, Bozde had knocked and was escorting Tavven out.

Iata wondered, briefly, if he might start shaking again. But no, he sat completely still. Absolutely sure of the rightness of what he'd just done. He'd done a lot of things in the last two days, but this was the first time he'd felt like he was taking actual steps to secure the kingdom.

Lodri shifted. Adeius, she hadn't disappeared, but she'd backed into the far corner nearest the door, and she'd been so still he'd mostly forgotten she was there.

"You'll need to make a public statement, I think," she said. "To reassure that you're still alive, and to announce that you've dismissed the commander and appointed a new one."

Jalava, coming back from the door, eyed Lodri with a scowl. But it faded as they approached him. "This shouldn't be my job. Please."

"If you're thinking I've given you too great an honor—I'm sorry, Jalava. I trust you. Homaj trusts you, and I know you would have been his choice, too. Log into Tavven's comm—please verify you have a commander's palace access."

Jalava tapped on the comm with shaking hands, logged it out, then used their own login.

"Fuck," they muttered. "Yes. I—I have access to your pass-code, don't I?"

"You can't use it, but yes. Only to show it to me, if needed. The system resets it every day. Or, well, show it to Homaj."

And what would Homaj think of this? Would he think Iata

was getting too comfortable with this power? Yes, Iata knew that presented with all the same facts, Homaj would likely have done the same thing he'd just done. Maybe not quite in the same way.

But Homaj had still left his life in Iata's hands, even with a chance earlier to take it back.

So it was done.

"Jalava," Iata said, and Jalava looked up. "Find the shooter. And do whatever you need to do to arrange security so that Homaj is safe. And Vatrin."

"And yourself," Jalava said adamantly. "Yes, Truthspoken."

They snapped into a tight salute and strode out.

83

EVENING

The very worst betrayals are the ones you see coming.

— HOMAJ RHIALDEN, SERITARCHUS IX IN A
PRIVATE LETTER, NEVER SENT; AS QUOTED IN
THE CHANGE DIALOGUES

Homaj woke to someone shaking his shoulder. He started, sitting straight up, taking in his surroundings.

Zhang. Zhang sat on the bed beside him, propped up against the headboard with a mountain of pillows, reading her comm, absolutely alert.

He was in an unfamiliar room—no. No, this was Eyras's room. Eyras's bed.

The lights were dimmed, but Eyras's room had no windows or clock display.

"It's evening," Zhang said quietly. "How are you feeling?"

Adeius, yes. The poison. He wiped his face and closed his eyes.

A delve into his body showed some residual damage,

mostly in his nervous system. He'd need to heal that before getting up.

"I need to heal again. I think a half hour at least. Maybe more."

Her mouth pulled tight. "You might not have that. I just got a priority on Guard channel, the palace is on lockdown again. Someone made an attempt on—on the interim ruler's life."

He spiked to full alertness. Iata. "Is he—"

"He wasn't harmed. That's all I know. We might need to move, and you might be in danger."

He'd already been in danger. Tingling pain in his arms, his legs, was a testament to that danger.

"All right," he said.

Carefully, he stood. Yes, there was pain. He stretched, moving silently through part of a martial arts sequence. He hadn't practiced as much lately as he should have, and the movements did not come as naturally as they might. And they brought pain, spiking at certain angles.

"I really do need to heal. But I can block the pain." He cleared his throat—it was a little raw. More gifts of the poisoning.

He glanced back at Zhang, whose brow was drawn as she studied him.

She opened her mouth—

The door banged open.

Homaj jumped, tripping backwards, just catching himself on the side of the bed. He stifled a cry as fiery pain shot through his right leg.

"Iata!"

Vatrin, as Seyra, stood in the doorway. They were the very *last* person Homaj wanted to see right now.

"Good, you're awake. The palace is on lockdown. We will need to speak with Commander Tavven about what they're doing to catch the culprit."

There was something off about that statement, but Homaj was too busy trying to pull Iata back around himself, rattled as he was with the nerve pain.

"Yes," he said through clenched teeth. "Okay."

Vatrin's gaze sharpened. "Haven't you healed yet?"

"I'm not—" Homaj gasped, and he gave up for the moment, sank back onto the bed. "I'm not Truthspoken. I don't heal as fast as you do."

Tears were stinging his eyes, and he did smooth those back. That he could do.

Vatrin hesitated. And Homaj had no spare thoughts just then to try and parse out what they were thinking.

"Whatever we do," they said, "it can wait until you trance. Make it quick, Iata. I can't have you showing that kind of pain if you're me."

Homaj nodded, and Vatrin withdrew, wonder of wonders. Completely self-serving, but it was enough.

He gasped back onto his pillow, and Zhang helped him scoot around to comfortably—*ha,* there was no comfortably—lay still.

"Will be a minute," he said, and sank into a trance.

When he came back to himself, Zhang was still there.

The pain was gone, and he did an internal inventory—the damage was, mostly, gone. Did he have time to heal it completely?

"How long?" he asked. His throat was dry, and he reached to the bedside cabinet, but there was no cup like he usually had beside him for a Change. Iata would usually manage such things, but, well.

"Eighteen minutes."

He tried to swallow, and Zhang reached to the cabinet on her side, came back with a water bottle and an energy bar.

"Thank you," he said with fervor, cracking the lid seal on the bottle. He tore open the energy bar as well—he'd purged any nutrients he'd gained from the meal earlier and had used up all the reserves he'd had to heal.

Homaj suppressed a shudder. "Any news? Are there more energy bars?"

Zhang handed him two more, a bag of snack cakes, and a sealed bag of nuts. She wasn't taking chances with more poisoned food. "No news yet. Palace is still on lockdown."

"Okay. Going back under." He downed another energy bar, handed back the water bottle and put the rest of the food beside him for when he woke again, then pushed himself back into trance.

This time when he came out, he felt no lingering damage. He swept through every corner of his body, his brain, his nervous system. But he had taken care of it. And that quick healing had left him feeling strained and desperately in need of food.

He sat up again, and Zhang handed him the water.

"Another thirty-six minutes." Zhang was looking grim, and he paused mid-swig.

"What happened?"

"Homaj dismissed Commander Tavven," she said.

He choked, capped the bottle, coughed. Oh. *Oh.* Iata would not have done that without good reason.

Homaj pushed out of bed, grabbing the last of the energy bars. "Was Vatrin back?"

"Once. They are impatient."

He shrugged, sat on the edge of the bed, and attacked the rest of the food. It wasn't much, wasn't enough when his body required resources after such abuse.

"Do you have any more energy bars or snacks? I need more to eat, and—" He opened his hands. He didn't trust the food from the kitchens, either. And didn't have time to have anyone test it—or the will, truly, if another tester couldn't Change to heal themself from poison.

"I have two more," she said, and pulled those from her pocket, handed them over. "I thought I should save them, but if you need them now, then you need them. I can see if there's more packaged food in the night kitchen."

"Vatrin might have more in their bedside cabinet."

She gave him a look that said she hadn't quite dared to look there. And wasn't sure she should—if there was any chance at all that it was Vatrin who'd poisoned him. Which, he didn't think so. But he couldn't be sure.

Homaj stripped off the wrappings on the two bars she gave him and ate them both in several bites, pausing only long enough to chew. It still wasn't enough, not when his body felt weaker than it should. But he directed the resources of the bars to where they'd do the most good. Steadied himself, and felt a little better.

"Should I tell the Truthspoken you're up?" Zhang asked.

He hesitated. He hadn't had time yet to think through exactly what had happened the day before—who could have poisoned him, and why.

He blinked. "Who is the new Guard Commander?"

"Jalava."

Homaj grinned, which he quickly tamped back down—Iata wasn't big on grins.

"Good." Jalava—Jalava he could tell about the poisoning, when he had the chance. He had to talk to Iata, but if Iata was locked down, he doubted he would get the chance soon. Did he dare try to communicate over comms?

He didn't want to risk it.

"Yes," he said, "tell Vatrin. I'm going to splash my face, I'll be fine. I'm up."

84

THE PATTERN

Knowing how the pattern feels is one thing; knowing what to do about it is another.

— HOMAJ RHIALDEN, SERITARCHUS IX IN A
PRIVATE LETTER, NEVER SENT; AS QUOTED IN
THE CHANGE DIALOGUES

When Zhang came back with Vatrin on her heels, Homaj had washed and dried his face, and pulled himself firmly back to Iata being Vatrin.

"I need to make a statement," Vatrin said. "Homaj has already made a statement that he has the situation in hand, and that he has dismissed Tavven. You took too long, Iata."

Homaj glared back with Vatrin's own glare. "I'm well, thank you."

Vatrin's face contorted. "You're not dressed, and you washed off the cosmetics."

He'd taken *poison* meant for Vatrin. Did they expect him to just spring up from that, no trouble?

"I have clothes laid out. I will do your cosmetics again this time, until you are capable of replicating my style—"

"Where's Eyras?" he asked.

Vatrin hesitated, just a breath. "She's in the city. Taking care of things I need."

Homaj nodded. That had been a lie. And maybe a reckless question on his part, because Vatrin's body language had gone stiffer.

He spread his hands. "If I'm still supposed to be you, I need a bloodservant, and not you doing all of this. You have more important things to do than dress me, Vatrin."

Vatrin still didn't like that, but they shrugged. "Eyras will come back when she's finished with her tasks. In any case, I already have a script for your statement. I have the lighting set up in the sitting room and the camera drone on standby."

Homaj mentally fortified himself. Adeius, he did not want to do this.

But he nodded and let Vatrin pick out which clothes to wear, let them do his makeup.

Vatrin gave him a tablet with the script to memorize while they worked on his face.

He memorized it in the first ten minutes, then spent the rest of the time pretending like he was still working on it, trying to think through what had happened. With the attempt on Iata's life—well, *his* life, with Iata in it—did this tell him anything new? Were they any closer at all to understanding just who the hell had decided it was a good idea to kill his parents?

He desperately needed to talk to Iata. Could he find a way to do that without Vatrin becoming suspicious? He didn't even have access to Vatrin's comm. Any comm. And had Lodri made contact with Iata? She hadn't come back to Vatrin's apartment, and for that, he certainly couldn't blame her.

What he knew:

The Truthspeaker was rotten. That was a given. He'd been

blackmailing Eyras, tried to blackmail or threaten Iata, and had something over Vatrin as well—either what Vatrin had said about the marriage to Lord Birka, or something more. Aduwel wanted power. Homaj was certain he'd kill to gain it.

But that didn't entirely fit with what Admiral Laguaya had said about who'd shot down Lord Birka. That had to have been either Vatrin or Eyras who'd purchased the weapon. Vatrin said Eyras was in the city—if that was true, was she trying to set up Homaj with further evidence against him? Laguaya hadn't made their discovery public, but they could. So someone— Vatrin, Eyras, or possibly the Truthspeaker—wanted to pin that murder on him. Why?

To discredit him, certainly. To sabotage his bid to rule—but the evidence had been planted, his biometrics had been used, before he'd made his formal bid. His gut was still saying that was a snap, panicked decision, and still saying that person who'd bought the gun had been Vatrin.

Who was currently touching his face to slick down his eyebrows.

Whose body and face and persona he still inhabited.

And who'd almost been poisoned earlier, if Homaj hadn't been there to be poisoned for them.

Had Vatrin tried to poison him? Did Vatrin know he wasn't Iata?

He still didn't think so. Vatrin was sharp, oh they were sharp, but they were just too full of their own place in the universe to see this. And he didn't immediately see Vatrin's motive in killing him as Iata, either. Vatrin was using him as a shield just now, and they seemed genuinely terrified that he'd been poisoned. Not terrified for him, most likely, but that it would happen again to them.

Who, then, would try to poison Vatrin? Who would have that kind of access?

The Truthspeaker was the obvious answer. And the deed

itself carried out by someone among the kitchen staff or the guards.

Iata had dismissed Tavven. Did he have proof that Tavven had a hand in the attempt on his life, or had he dismissed them because they hadn't done their job? And they hadn't. Homaj would likely have done the same. They knew Tavven, though their opinion of them had been fairly neutral until the day before. Tavven had let his parents die on their watch. And now Tavven had let an attempt happen on the interim ruler's life, and whether Tavven knew it or not, Vatrin's life as well.

Would the Truthspeaker take out both the heirs so he could abolish the balance of the Truthspoken system? That had been attempted once before, centuries ago. The attempt had failed. All the perpetrators had been executed. The remaining Heir had reigned with a holy terror and a cowed replacement Truthspeaker. Homaj didn't think Aduwel was that stupid.

Could Eyras have agreed to be Aduwel's puppet sometime in the last day and shifted the balance again? He'd asked Iata to play that out, but maybe it hadn't worked.

Fuck. Fuck, he had so many threads, and he was seeing the shape of the pattern, but not quite the picture it told. And he had the nagging feeling that it wasn't just one pattern involved here, not just one motive, but an intertangled web. Two wills, at very least.

"Do you have it memorized now?"

Vatrin didn't bother to hide the sneer in their voice. So he didn't bother to hide his own disdain. Which—*sigh*—was a very Vatrin thing to do.

"Almost."

"Well, I'm finished. You need to be done."

He made a show of rereading the last few lines of the script, then clicked the tablet off.

"I'm done." He glanced at himself in the mirror, almost

flinching at Vatrin's angry glare in the mirror back at him. His own glare.

"How do you want me to play the emotions?" he asked. "Because just now, I am absolutely pissed that someone tried to kill Homaj. And you."

Vatrin nodded. "That's good. Maybe more than I would usually show, but it's authentic. Yes, use that."

He closed his eyes—one moment, just one moment, to settle and not throttle Vatrin.

"Truthspoken," Zhang said, and Homaj let out an explosive, "Yes?" Just as Vatrin said the same.

They looked at each other, and Vatrin made a mocking bow to him.

"What?" he asked.

"Commander Jalava is here to see you, ser."

85

INVESTIGATIONS

The Palace Guard are supposed to be incorruptible—
but I suspect the reality is far worse than that.

— RUNA YAYAR IN AN ADDRESS TO THE
GENERAL ASSEMBLY

"Let them in," Homaj said, showing outward calm while absolutely panicking, and also cheering that either Iata or Jalava had seen fit to fill him in. Of course the Commander of the Palace Guard should visit both Truthspoken heirs after an attempt on one of their lives. But Homaj knew that this visit had also absolutely been meant for him. This was Iata's bridge of communication.

Jalava had said that they weren't very good at cloak and dagger. He had to hope, oh he had to hope, that Jalava could handle the situation. Jalava would know who he was. And he wouldn't be able to be kind, because Vatrin absolutely wouldn't be kind just now. Not that he himself as Homaj was overly kind.

Vatrin stiffened back into their guard persona as Zhang opened the door and Jalava stepped into the prep room. Jalava spared only a glance for Vatrin, and good. Homaj was fairly certain that Jalava knew who Vatrin currently was, and while Jalava did look nervous, their duty face was overruling their anxiety.

Jalava bowed a guard's bow to him, and while it was a little deeper than it should have been with them being the commander now, it was passable enough.

"Truthspoken."

"What has happened?" Homaj demanded. "Who tried to kill my brother, and has this person been found?"

Jalava rocked back at the onslaught, held up a hand.

"Ser Truthspoken, there was a shooting in the courtyard while the interim ruler crossed from the guest wing. I was there when it happened—a sniper from the direction of the Adeium. Several shots hit the palace wall, but there were no casualties or injuries. Truthspoken Homaj has dismissed Commander Tavven and appointed me as Commander of the Palace Guard. Ser."

Jalava stood, waiting, posture stiff.

"And what are you doing now to make sure I and my brother are safe from any more attacks?" He'd made his voice more mild, but he knew the bite was in his eyes.

Jalava met them, and points for Jalava.

"I have teams that I personally trust checking surveillance for the courtyard, checking every related record. Searching the premises. I've posted extra guards outside your apartment and the interim ruler's." They hesitated. "There is a possibility that the shooter was a guard."

Vatrin as Seyra shifted as if they wanted to protest. Jalava glanced at them, their pale face blotching—Homaj needed to redirect, fast.

He stepped forward. "Commander, you don't know this, but I was poisoned earlier. I was able to neutralize the poisons, but not without difficulty. There were two—one fast-acting in a high dose, which I caught quickly, and the other meant to be a subtle kill."

Jalava was well and truly pale now. "Truthspoken. I—I will have people I trust investigate. What do you need? Do you need the physicians, should I send for them? Uh, and do you still have the poisoned food or drink?"

"No," Vatrin snapped. "Of course we threw it out."

Homaj held up his hands, trying to quell Vatrin, who glared at him, but subsided into a scowl. He turned back to Jalava.

"Commander, I know the poisons used—at least the first one, and I'm fairly certain of the second. And both Lt. Seyra and Sgt. Zhang were witnesses. We don't need the physicians—I've already purged the poison and healed myself from the poisoning."

Jalava gave a tight nod, catching Zhang's eye.

"What I need is sealed rations," Homaj went on. "Any packaged food. High calorie, high protein. Anything my staff can heat up and that we can guarantee hasn't been tampered with."

Vatrin was nodding now. Vatrin, at least, knew how to cook, and they were an excellent chef. Their one redeeming quality.

"I'll prepare a list of what we need," they said. And added a belated, "Sir."

Jalava shifted. "Yes, uh, thank you. Lieutenant."

And that was getting dangerously awkward again. No, Jalava really wasn't great at cloak and dagger games.

"I want to investigate this personally," Homaj said. "No offense to you, Commander, but I don't know you, and I didn't appoint you. You report to me." And there, that was a solid link between himself and Iata.

Jalava shifted, face taking on a stubborn cast. "Yes, ser, I can report to you. But I do take my orders only from the interim ruler. At his explicit command."

Homaj narrowed his eyes, as Vatrin would do. As Vatrin—truly—was doing now.

Then Iata had prepped Jalava for this, had told them how he might respond as Vatrin. That he'd try to take control.

Good. So very good. Iata might have been shot at, but he wasn't fully rattled. And he might have been to the Truthspeaker, but he still had agency.

"Then yes, Commander," he said mildly, with a smile, "do report your findings to me the moment you have them."

86

IDENTICAL

They're identical, born three years apart—does the bond of twins still hold true? We'll find out after a word from our sponsors.

— INTRODUCTION FROM THE POPULAR VID SHOW *VARIANT STARS,* SEASON 3, EPISODE 24

"He was poisoned?" Iata barked at Jalava. They were back in his own prep room, which felt infinitely better than trying to inhabit the Seritarchus's apartment.

Adeius. The Truthspeaker had handed him vials of poison earlier—had it been those same poisons used to try to kill Vatrin? Was the Truthspeaker not even trying to hide it—was he showing Iata he was all in?

Was it even the Truthspeaker at all?

He had to get Homaj out of there, have him do anything other than be Vatrin just now. Or even being himself. It was too dangerous to be Truthspoken in this palace.

He wanted to run a hand through his hair, one of Homaj's

gestures that was fast becoming habitual, but he'd just fixed it again from its fraying after the shooting. He wasn't sure he had the energy for anything public yet tonight, but also, wasn't sure what else would come up. He had to remain presentable.

"Yes, ser," Jalava said, closing and slowly opening their fists. Their face was mottled red, their short hair mussed, their uniform slightly askew. But then, it had been a day, and a night.

"This whole palace staff is rotten to the core," Jalava ground out.

"Maybe. They will all need to be questioned, more quietly than I'd like right now." He wanted to turn the staff over, Adeius, force them all to be read by magickers if he had to.

But that wasn't the right way through this.

Jalava nodded, and Iata saw the frustration there as well.

"These assassins will be found," Jalava said, their voice a low growl. It had become a personal quest for them now, a point of pride and honor, and Iata had definitely made the right choice in boosting Jalava far past their normal duty rank. Not that he'd had a choice beyond Jalava for the job.

If he could get a message to Homaj through Jalava, could he manage to convince Homaj to get the hell out of there?

What would Vatrin be holding over him as Iata, though? Would Vatrin try to pin blame for the assassinations—or even this poisoning—on Iata when the person they thought was Iata stopped following their orders?

That was a problem for another time. Homaj just had to live through the next few days, and Iata wasn't at all sure he would, staying where he was right now.

And the longer a mission ran, the greater chances of a slip. What would Vatrin do if they found out it was Homaj who had been playing them all along?

"How was he, beyond that?" he asked.

Jalava shook their head. "He was the Truthspoken Vatrin, fully. I don't know how to read more than that. Lt. Seyra, who you said is actually Vatrin, was more visibly agitated by all of this."

They gave a stiff shrug. "Ser Truthspoken, I'm happy to debrief you, I know it's necessary, but you gave me a job to command the Palace Guard, and there is a lot to sort out just now, and potentially two assassins at large in the palace—"

Iata held up his hands. "Yes. Go."

Jalava hurried out—and Iata had only been holding them back.

There was too much to do. So much to do, and he'd been doing what the Truthspeaker wanted all day and not actually tending to the day-to-day fires in the palace, let alone these new catastrophes that needed handling—

Iata slowly sank down onto Homaj's vanity chair.

His own security here, he knew, was the best in the palace, the best Jalava could currently give him. And Jalava was doing their best just now to make sure Vatrin's apartment was just as secure. They'd called in every favor and colleague they knew they could trust, even calling some people in from retirement in the city who'd be bolstering the Guard ranks shortly.

Lodri was in his own bloodservant's washroom, taking a quick shower—she'd said she hadn't had the time the last two days and wanted to be clean before the next crisis.

Well, and he certainly understood that.

Was he safe just now? Was a Truthspoken ever safe?

Should he even be calling himself that, even if he was still Homaj? It was dangerous to think of himself as a Truthspoken.

The quiet of the room hummed in his ears, though he'd been longing for enough quiet to think for most of the day. He'd started this day with a crisis and hadn't yet had time to catch his breath.

Iata looked up at himself in the mirror. His appearance was Homaj's, but his body was his own. Just now, this was his appearance, too. His face, his hair, his muscles, his bones. His voice and his breath.

What if he had to live as Homaj? The rest of his life, as Homaj? If the worst happened, and he had no other choice?

How would he break the hold of the Truthspeaker if that happened? How was he going to break that hold now?

Lodri had said she would witness for him, but he didn't see how that would actually help him. Beyond maybe being a path through chaos. It was, at least, a weapon to use if weapons were spare.

He grabbed a makeup sponge and began touching up a few spots where it had smudged, when Jalava had pushed him to the stones.

He'd almost died today.

And no one would have known it was him who'd died.

Iata stopped again, studying himself. Really looking, not for flaws, not trying to reconcile his appearance, but looking at...himself.

He was identical to Homaj. Same sharp brown eyes. Same long, fine hair. Same facial shape, set of his jaw, pattern of moles. And with Homaj himself not being Homaj, he was the only Homaj Rhialden just now. He was already starting to bend the persona and personality of Homaj Rhialden toward a Seritarchus rulership. Two days, and he was becoming far more comfortable in this persona than he should be.

Homaj didn't want to rule. Iata...he couldn't say he wanted all of that weight on his shoulders, but he also knew he could do the job and do it well. He knew that. He was doing it now, and he was scared out of his mind, but he also was trained to administrate an heir's life. It wasn't that different than administrating a kingdom.

He set the sponge back down. Yes, the Truthspeaker had accepted his own bid to rule. But he wasn't a sanctioned Truth-spoken, no matter that he could Change. He was a bloodservant. His place was service to a Truthspoken, not being a Truthspoken himself. His place was to help his Truthspoken from the shadows, not to rule the whole damn kingdom. That would always be his place.

If they both lived through this.

He was Homaj's brother. Just now, his identical twin, if a year apart—and it was a year, not the almost two he'd thought. He was even closer in age to Homaj than he'd thought.

He had close family. He'd had fathers—Adeius—though he'd only found out after they were gone.

Could that be enough? Knowing that Homaj was his brother? That he wasn't as outside of it all as he'd been taught? As he'd been forced to think?

He'd been lied to. He'd been lied to all of his life by people who should have cared enough to tell him.

Iata could Change, and Homaj had said there would be more training. He did want that. He wanted that with an intensity that had cracked open along with the other damning truths he'd pulled out of his soul for the Truthspeaker.

He heard Lodri moving around in the other room, straightened, pulled Homaj back around himself. It wasn't hard at all this time.

His problem wasn't that he was uncomfortable being Homaj—he wasn't. His problem was that he was growing too comfortable. But that wasn't a problem he could solve just now.

87

LETTING GO

> *Knowing who you are and what you want is essential for a Truthspoken. It's entirely too easy to get lost in another personality's desires, or let your own overtake a personality you're supposed to be inhabiting as themself.*
>
> — HOMAJ RHIALDEN, SERITARCHUS IX IN A
> PRIVATE LETTER, NEVER SENT; AS QUOTED IN
> *THE CHANGE DIALOGUES*

Lodri came back out into the prep room, toweling off damp hair. He still didn't know her. He doubted Homaj had even had time to get to know her. But he trusted her enough from experiencing her truths and her emotions. And that would have to do for now.

Iata needed to see Homaj. He needed to meet with him, to pull everything they both knew together—earlier had not been nearly enough time. He really needed to convince Homaj to stop being Vatrin, but he knew his brother too well to think Homaj would leave his current mission.

With the personality Homaj had cultivated at court, with Homaj's intense desire to avoid Truthspoken responsibility, people thought he was lazy. Iata knew he was just, usually, anxious. And unwilling to be bent into a shape he couldn't fit into. But Homaj, when he had a mission he believed in, would see it all the way through, no matter the cost.

"You made me invisible earlier," he said to Lodri.

She stopped in the center of the prep room, a private room that had seen far too much traffic in the last two days. Lodri slung the towel around her neck, frowning. "That's not something I'd care to do again. It's incredibly dangerous, especially for someone who's not a magicker."

What he'd felt from her when she'd made them invisible, the intensity of her self-loathing, made him want to shiver. But he said, "Can you do it again, if you have to? For me, or for Homaj?"

She considered him. Not happy, but she nodded. "If it will save your lives, yes."

Iata stood, but he wasn't sure where to go. He truly had to talk to Homaj. Because this game they were caught in had to end soon. And maybe, between what they both knew now, they would be able to make a plan.

Firing Tavven was a start. Sending Jalava to be the bridge between himself and Homaj was another start. Putting his own lot in with the Truthspeaker was...something.

Tonight. He would find a way to meet with Homaj tonight.

"Can you go back to Homaj?" he asked Lodri. And he knew what he was asking—Vatrin had been exploiting her, threatening her with her unsealed status.

She met his eyes, and he wished he couldn't sense the urgency of her apprehension in that look. "If that's where you think I can best help."

He swallowed. "Keep him safe. You kept me safe. And right now, I am a lot safer than he is."

But she wouldn't be. She wouldn't be safe at all.

Lodri stepped closer, studying him, and he braced against the feeling of someone peering into his soul. He knew she was reading him, reading whatever emotions were showing, what he couldn't hide.

She'd as much as implied earlier that if it came to it, she'd support him as the ruler, too.

Lodri held out her hands. Said quietly, "Iata. I know you're conflicted. I know you think you're doing wrong here in how you feel, what you've had to embrace in yourself to make this all work. Am I reading that right? Can I help you sort it? Before I go?"

He swallowed. What she was offering was a vulnerability he wasn't sure he could give. Not now, when all his nerves were so raw and tangled.

But he had to know. He had to know what he'd do, if this all did go as he hoped and Homaj reclaimed his life. He thought he knew—he would go back to being Iata, the bloodservant.

Yes, of course he would do that. That was the only choice he had.

He clamped his hands over Lodri's, her palms still warm and damp from the shower. He closed his eyes so he didn't have to meet hers.

"Ask yourself the questions you need to know," Lodri said. "Out loud, if that's easier."

He couldn't voice the depth of his betrayal.

But then, he would have no secrets from her just now.

"Can I—can I give up the power?"

He waited. There was a knot of emotions he was sure were Lodri's—anxiety, fear, angst. He felt his own emotions, a turbulent mass of fear and determination and a deep wound of grief he wasn't yet ready to handle. All of it bundled up in his own rigid control. He listened for an answer. Listened in his bones, in any truth he could find.

"Yes," he finally said.

True.

But did he want to give up the power?

No.

And would he resent Homaj for taking back his own life?

Yes. Because no, Homaj wasn't suited to this nearly as well as Iata was.

True all the way.

But he would step aside. He would give it up. For the good of his brother, more than the good of the kingdom.

No, not true. For the good of the kingdom, too. Homaj might not be a Seritarchus, but he wasn't going to be a bad ruler. Iata would give him all the support he could. That was how he would serve this kingdom. That was the place that had been given to him, no matter his bloodline. No matter his training.

He had a brother. Adeius, he had a brother. He had a sister a sibling, too, but—he would truly do anything for his brother. Even embracing his darkest, most terrifying ambitions. And then, when it was time, letting them go.

Lodri released his hands and pressed her hands instead to his shoulders. He'd been swaying, he realized.

He straightened, but nodded to her.

He did feel clearer. His path more solid. And maybe that wouldn't help him with the Truthspeaker, knowing his own truths like this. But he'd needed it. And he was the one who had to get the kingdom through these next few days.

"Find a way," he said, "to get him out tonight. Through the back corridors, back to here."

He would do his best to keep Homaj from going back into danger. Whether Homaj listened was on Homaj, but he would do his best.

Lodri stepped back, tossed her towel over the back of Iata's vanity chair, and gave a small bow.

"Truthspoken. I will."

88

FRAYED NERVES

> *Paranoia is the drug the Rhialdens sell to the masses.*
>
> — LORD IVARI DEN EMIR IN A POST ON THEIR
> PERSONAL FEED

Homaj was eating several ration packs and the heaviest calorie snacks Zhang could come up with when one of Vatrin's people brought Lodri into the prep room.

He stood, his already frayed nerves spiking again.

"Magicker," Vatrin said, even before his guard had closed the prep room door behind Lodri.

Homaj watched Lodri stiffen—not obvious, but Vatrin would have marked that, too.

Did they enjoy watching her distress? Homaj was starting to think so.

"I saved your brother's life tonight," Lodri said to Vatrin, not to him. She waved at the packages of food on the table, which had been divided between Homaj and Vatrin. Zhang, because Vatrin was at the table, had been relegated to watching from the edge of the room. And Homaj had definitely had enough of hearing Vatrin's condescending plans for the next day.

In those plans, he was to continue to be Vatrin's full-blooded shield and magnet for any fire he might draw. In Vatrin's eyes, this was perfectly acceptable.

Homaj had made the public statement Vatrin wished him to, and he'd done it well, giving solemn promises and platitudes to a people who knew nothing about the integrity of the person who was saying them. Truly, in this case, nothing at all.

"Sit and eat, by all means," Vatrin said, but the words had a cruel edge, and Homaj was growing tenser by the minute.

At least, with a solid meal now fully replenishing his body's reserves, he was feeling much steadier.

Lodri sat. The table and chairs still smelled like the strong cleaners Vatrin had corralled one of their people to use to clean up Homaj's mess earlier.

Lodri eyed him, grabbed a meal bar, and unwrapped it.

"So you saved my brother," Vatrin said, and warning bells were going off in Homaj's head. He didn't at all like that tone. "Did anyone see you were a magicker?"

"The interim ruler did. And his guards."

Homaj got where Vatrin was angling with that—if they'd had Lodri nearby when they'd made their bid to rule, and it came out publicly that she was an unsealed magicker before Vatrin had a chance to spin that how they wanted, that would hurt Vatrin's position. So was Vatrin trying to say Lodri *shouldn't* have saved their brother?

Homaj carefully spread one hand across his thigh beneath the table, a vent of as much tension as he dared. A distraction to keep from screaming.

"I'm alive and unsealed," Lodri said, facing Vatrin. "There's a reason for that."

"Don't speak to me with that kind of swagger," Vatrin growled. "You know your place here, and it's to do as I tell you.

You should have come to my apartment, not wandered the palace. You will do as I say, is that clear?"

Never mind that Vatrin hadn't actually given her solid instructions before they'd taken off earlier but left her to Homaj. And Homaj, being Vatrin at the time, had left her again.

He met Lodri's eyes, and she smiled tightly.

If she'd been with Iata, and he had to assume they'd had a chance to talk and get the vital details straight, then she'd come back with more than just herself and her service. If he was her, he might not have come back at all with Vatrin's threat hanging over her. So, she'd returned at Iata's bidding? Or had she come back for him?

Vatrin pushed back their chair. "I have work to do. And apparently my brother hasn't approved me to wander the palace as he's approved you." They glared at Lodri. "Go into the bedroom, all of you—it's night, anyway. Don't come out without knocking. I'll do my work out here for now."

Homaj gathered up some more of the food, just to have a reserve, and Lodri grabbed what she needed, too. Zhang detached herself from where she was doing her best impression of a statue near the closet.

Homaj hesitated before going back into the bedroom. He didn't know what Vatrin was currently considering "work"— whether that was scheming, schmoozing, or actually trying to give Iata some help in running the kingdom. Vatrin had their own vital duties as the Truthspoken Heir—those hadn't become less vital with the reshuffling of power.

Vatrin didn't pull out their comm, though, to give any clue to what they'd be doing. They just sat at the table and looked up at Homaj impatiently.

He shrugged one of Iata's shrugs, when Iata was being too precious about the rules of things and trying to get him to care a bit more.

"Just be careful, Vatrin. Please," he said.

He meant that. Despite everything, he didn't want to see his sibling dead from carelessness.

And Vatrin, he was coming to see, was functioning on a lot more fear and a lot less reason than he was right now. Had Vatrin even allowed themself to grieve? They'd lost two parents and their lover in the span of hours.

And if they'd had a hand in all of those deaths?

Vatrin's eyes narrowed. "You'll have more to do later, Iata. Rest, but be ready to move when I say."

Homaj bowed Iata's bow and retreated into the bedroom. He shut the door behind him, and as much as he wanted to lock it, he didn't. It wouldn't be of any use anyway if Vatrin decided to come in. It was their bedroom after all.

His stomach, full of food, felt like he'd eaten stones. He brushed his curly hair back from his eyes and itched to let his own mannerisms show through, to be done with being Vatrin, or even Iata, but he couldn't. Not even here.

Lodri held out a hand to him and, frowning, he took it.

"May I?" she asked.

He wasn't entirely sure what she was asking, but when he nodded, warmth flooded into him. Like the First Magicker had done, when he'd made his bid. It was like emerging from a dark room into daylight, warmth on his skin, fortifying his soul.

He let out a jagged sob he hadn't been expecting.

Zhang hovered, concerned but not approaching.

Lodri tugged him closer, then embraced him, and he felt her radiating strength at him. Adeius, he was trying so hard to keep it together. He had to keep it together.

She leaned to his ear. "Can we talk tonight? All of us?"

She meant more than her and him and Zhang. She meant Iata, and likely Jalava, too.

He glanced at the closed but not locked bedroom door. They could go now. Vatrin tended to hyperfocus when they worked, whatever it was they were doing.

Would Vatrin expect them to go out through the back corridors? Had that been too easy an opening?

But he couldn't stand another moment in this apartment. He had almost died here today, and he wasn't sure his sibling cared. Not for his own life, anyway. At least, not nearly as much as theirs.

Even not knowing he was Homaj, even thinking he was Iata, Iata should have counted for so much more than the disregard Vatrin gave him.

He sniffed, wiped at his eyes rather than smoothing the tears away with Change, and moved to the panel door beside the bed. He pressed the wall to open it.

Homaj felt the light tingle in his fingertips of granted entry, but the door caught on something as he pushed it inward.

"What the hell?" he whispered.

Lodri moved closer. Touched the wall beside his hand. Then followed it down to a bolt newly fastened to the bottom of the panel and the wall beside it, where it would be mostly hidden by the bedside cabinet.

At least—at least it wasn't on the outside of the door. This felt like Vatrin's paranoia of someone coming in, not going out.

Lodri raised her brows at him, motioning toward the bolt. She could crumble the metal of the bolt.

And if she did, and Vatrin saw it, there would be hell to pay.

But they *had* to talk to Iata. Had to. This all had to end soon.

Homaj nodded. The bolt dissolved rapidly into flakes of rust, which Lodri scooped up and dumped in a trash bin.

"We'll hope Iata can find another bolt for us to fasten there," she said.

But he heard the implication in her dry tone: if they even came back.

He wasn't at all sure that he could.

The panel door finally opened, and they all slipped into the back corridors.

89

ALL THE PIECES

I have spoken with Truthspoken several times myself. In each instance, I observed perfect control and absolute flawless emotional projection. One of these times, however, was when a Truthspoken would have otherwise been in extreme emotional distress.

— DR. IGNI CHANG IN "TRUTHSPOKEN CONTROL IN THE CONTEXT OF EMOTIONAL INTELLIGENCE"

Homaj pushed open the door to his own bedroom, and Iata was there. Arms crossed and glowering to hide his fear.

Iata's face cleared as they entered, and he came straight for Homaj when the door closed.

"Are you all right? Jalava said you were poisoned—" Iata's eyes darted all over, checking for lingering signs.

Homaj held up his hands. "I'm fine. I'm tired, but I purged it all."

Iata turned to Zhang, who nodded confirmation.

Homaj sighed.

"Truly, Iata, you can actually take my word for that."

He got a small smile out of that.

Jalava was also in the bedroom, standing near the door to the prep room. The door was just slightly ajar.

Homaj took the barest moment to look around, see the neat and familiar space of his own bedroom, so different from Vatrin's sprawl. Even the bed was made.

Home. *Home.*

"I don't know how much time we have," Homaj said. "Let's talk in the prep room, there's more light."

He wanted light. Vatrin kept their apartment dimmer than he liked, they'd always had sensitive vision, and he was sick to death of being in twilight as well. He needed to see his own things, his own familiar spaces.

He touched the bed covers as they all filed out to the prep room, touched a chair near the door, touched a framed portrait on one wall.

"You shouldn't go back," Iata said. "Though I know you're going to say you have to."

"If you have a convincing reason for me not to, other than that it's dangerous, and I don't want to..."

He sighed. He truly did not want to.

Iata frowned at him, but didn't produce a more convincing reason. Those two reasons should have been good enough, he knew.

"I'm worried, Maja," Iata said. "Very worried."

Iata took his seat in Homaj's vanity chair, and when he noticed and started to rise, Homaj waved him back down and took the other. Jalava sat on the low couch on the far wall, and Zhang and Lodri with them. The dampening and scrambling systems were active—Homaj's ears had popped on entering the room.

"Okay," Iata said. "What's happened? Everything, please.

And I'll tell everything. We need to pull our information together. And hope there's enough for a plan."

So Homaj started from when he left the palace, going step by step through their search in the city, up until the point where Vatrin had found him again. Then, his agreeing to be Vatrin and coming to the palace.

Iata listened with few interruptions, as did Jalava, though Iata twitched when Homaj told of Laguaya's warning. And he grew stormy again when Homaj described the poisoning.

Homaj caught everyone up until the last minutes where he'd left Vatrin in their prep room. And then, it was Iata's turn.

Homaj listened intently as Iata described meeting with Laguaya and Abret and how he'd handled it, running into Eyras in her bedroom, falling asleep in the Seritarchus's study, and meeting with the Truthspeaker today.

Iata paused there, looking flushed. He met Homaj's eyes, looked away, met them again. Which was a sign of extreme distress for Iata.

"Maja. He accepted my bid to rule. My own. Legally— though I'm less sure now that I've had time to think about it that it's an actual legal bid."

"It could be," Homaj said.

Iata's distress visibly deepened, and Homaj held up his hands. "Sorry. I know—I shouldn't have asked that of you."

And he wasn't sure of the hollow feeling in his stomach as Iata had recounted it. He knew Iata must have overturned his soul to convince the Truthspeaker he was sincere—if he even had.

Homaj shook his head. "I shouldn't have asked any of this from you. Adeius—you were *shot at*."

"You were poisoned," Iata countered.

"Yes, but I knew what I was doing was dangerous—"

"So did I." Iata's jaw was tight, his whole posture a challenge. "Maja. I should be the one taking the risks, not you."

He opened his hands. He knew Iata was right. Which didn't make anything easier. But he'd been right, too, in thinking that agreeing to be Vatrin would yield information he needed. It had given him a lot of pieces to all of this that he wouldn't have had otherwise.

"Go on, please," he said, and leaned back in the vanity chair. He eyed the couch with its much more comfortable cushions, but he was feeling the exhaustion from all the tension, and from his poisoning and needing to heal, and from going two deep—Adeius, had that all been in one day? He'd slept earlier, but that had been more necessity than true rest. He was afraid if he sat on the couch, he might fall asleep, and he couldn't afford to.

Iata recounted the meetings the Truthspeaker had arranged for him that day, then his meeting Lodri, and the shooting. It was Homaj's turn to start with a boiling rage. Vatrin had just dismissed the shooting like...Adeius, Vatrin had implied that Lodri should have let him die. And Vatrin had been saying that for him, for Homaj, for their brother.

Iata was their brother, too. Vatrin knew that.

Iata wrapped everything up with how he'd fired Tavven—which Homaj was absolutely in line with, yes—and promoted Jalava. At which, Jalava sat stiffly and tried not to look like they were waiting for a blow.

"Jalava, I approve," Homaj said, too tired to try to soften anything anymore. "If I make it through this as the ruler, you're still the Guard Commander."

Jalava looked up, straightened. "Yes, Ser Truthspoken."

"Then," Iata said, "I sent Lodri to you. So now you're here."

Now he was here. All of them—maybe the only five people in this palace and on this planet who actually wanted him to rule and not Vatrin. Well, and maybe the First Magicker could be included in that, but she wasn't here.

"Okay," Iata said, "now we have everything we've gathered

in the open. We should pull it all together and decide what we're going to do with it."

Which was interesting, because Iata didn't usually take this much initiative. Iata usually waited for him.

But then, Iata had been ruling the kingdom since late yesterday morning. And Homaj—Homaj had been bumping into things around the city until they'd bumped back.

90

DRAWN PISTOLS

> *We have no idea what goes on in the private lives of Truthspoken, right? Like, we know what they show us, but they're literally trained to lie with every breath.*

— ANONYMOUS74451-Q3 IN THE CHATSPHERE
VALON CITY HOUSE STAFF/DEEP MUSINGS

Homaj cleared his throat, and Iata stiffened, chagrined.

Homaj quickly waved him down. "No. At the moment, you are the interim ruler. You called this meeting. If I gave you the responsibility, the least I can give you is the respect of carrying it out."

Iata was looking distinctly uncomfortable.

"I promise you, Maja, I will give all of this back as soon as you say—"

Homaj gripped the edge of his seat, rocked forward. "I was running, and it was supremely unfair."

Iata's gaze dropped to the floor, his near-perfect illusion of being Homaj fully shattered, his posture cowed.

Adeius, Homaj hadn't meant to do that.

He stood, moving carefully toward Iata, who was caving in on himself with every step Homaj took.

"Brother," Homaj said, and Iata's head snapped up. "By rights, if either of us is going to try to rule, this rulership should be yours. Not mine, and certainly not Vatrin's. But I know that's not how things work. I know, Brother. I know."

Iata's eyes filled, and he bit his lip. "I'm not trying to take it from you."

"I don't want it! You do—and we will work that out, okay? If we get through this, if we do end up ruling, it's going to be the both of us, okay? You handled all of this, *all* of this, and I did what I do, which is go find the problems and try to fix them. We'll work it out. But don't for a moment think you shouldn't look at me as an equal."

Iata's breath caught. And Homaj was feeling unsteady, too, because this was all uncharted space. He wasn't at all used to having a brother. Not especially the one he'd already had.

Slowly, Iata nodded. And he didn't drop his chin again. And his mannerisms didn't go back to Homaj's yet, either, but stayed solidly his own.

Homaj nodded, and, feeling lightheaded, he backtracked to the vanity chair and sat down again.

"All right. Yes," he said. "We need a plan."

There was a soft chime, an alert from the prep room's security system.

Iata pulled out his comm. "Someone's in the bedroom."

Jalava and Zhang were up first, taking positions to cover the bedroom door.

"It's Eyras," Iata said, and was striding toward the door himself. "She touched the door handle, it's reading as her. Though it might not be—"

Jalava held out their arm to bar him. "Back, Truthspoken!"

Homaj's brows shot up, but then...but then, Iata was still

him. Was still, until Homaj took his own identity back, the interim ruler.

Iata drew up short, glanced at Homaj, looked like he wanted to be chagrined again. But he set his jaw and apparently decided not to be.

Iata was the Seritarchus personality, not him.

Zhang opened the door.

Eyras froze mid-knock, taking all of them in at a glance.

Her gaze riveted to Homaj—but he wasn't carrying Vatrin's or Iata's mannerisms just now. And he rippled through a short series of his own tells.

Her shoulders relaxed, just a fraction. Her hand, which had been hovering near a hip holster, eased down as she noted Jalava's and Zhang's drawn pistols.

"It looks like I came at a good time," she said.

She was, mostly, herself, with some of her more notable features pushed farther away from her usual preferences. She looked like Eyras to his eyes, but not necessarily a Rhialden.

And what did a Rhialden look like, really, but what they all agreed a Rhialden should look like and then Changed themselves to fit?

"May I come in?" Eyras asked, gesturing inside.

"Yes, yes," Iata said, back to being Homaj again, and waved Jalava and Zhang back.

Eyras stepped inside, this time focusing on Jalava.

"You're the new Palace Guard Commander?"

Jalava jerked a nod. "Yes. Truthspok—"

Eyras made a warding gesture. "No, do *not* call me that."

She rounded on Homaj, advancing, and Zhang pulled up her pistol again, though she didn't quite aim it. She'd be aiming in his direction.

"What are you doing, Maja? Adeius, what are you *possibly* doing as Vatrin? Was that you at the palace all day today?" Her voice rose at this, nearly hysterical. She brushed her bright blonde hair behind her ear, gripped the back of her neck in obvious distress. "And where's Vatrin—"

"Their guard, Lt. Seyra."

Eyras flinched at that, sucked in a sharp breath.

Iata stepped closer to Homaj, too, his posture protective. "What? What about Lt. Seyra?"

Eyras bottled up. Homaj watched her zip up her emotions, letting none of them show, even to Truthspoken-trained senses.

Then she let it all out again.

He had a premonition of disaster, a rippling chill up his arms. And he almost—almost—told her to stop. Begged her not to tell him what he didn't want to know.

Eyras said, "Vatrin killed Jina Seyra yesterday morning. It's what made Xavi Birka bolt."

And saying this, she deflated. She looked around her, pulled over a dressing stool, and sat, face in her hands.

Homaj turned to Iata, who was looking back, eyes sharp and bright. They both, slowly, approached Eyras.

91

ARREST ME

> *The checks and balances in the Truthspoken system are vital to the functioning of the kingdom. If a Truthspoken does something unconscionable, the Truthspeaker can remove them, and the same for a Truthspeaker.*

— DR. T. DOSELA IN *THE TRUTHSPOKEN SYSTEM: A VARIED ANALYSIS*

"What happened?" Iata asked softly. "Eyras?"

She sat up straight, pointed at Iata. "Don't you dare ask if I'm okay. Either of you."

"I wasn't going to," Homaj said, but there was too much of Vatrin's tone lingering in his voice—and his voice itself was still Vatrin's. Eyras flinched back.

"Adeius, Maja, do something different," she said. "Something distinctive. I can't—"

He shared another look with Iata. He'd known Vatrin didn't get along with Eyras, and he'd experienced how Vatrin related to Iata as a bloodservant. But this kind of reaction, this was a trauma reaction. An abuse reaction.

Yeah. Yeah, that did square.

Homaj strode into the closet, quickly rummaging through racks until he pulled out a black embroidered coat that Vatrin would never wear but was all him. Then he reached for a hat that was on a rack used for various personas—it was a bright orange ridiculous thing, something one of the more ostentatious nobles might wear. He'd never found an occasion to wear it, but it made him smile.

He put it on and was rewarded by a choke of laughter from Eyras as he walked out, even as she looked to be biting back tears.

Homaj picked through pieces of various personas as he retrieved the vanity chair to sit closer to Eyras. He shifted his bearing and walk accordingly. Everything, absolutely everything non-threatening. He shifted his accent to the one he'd used yesterday as Lt. Reyin, because he was still tired, it was at hand, and it was a familiar enough accent in the palace.

Eyras watched him, and finally nodded.

Then she swiveled around to Jalava.

"You're going to arrest me for this."

Jalava looked grim. "Ser, I'll reserve judgment until I have all the facts."

Jalava had come closer now, too, as had Zhang. Lodri was still hanging back, but now Eyras pointed to her.

"And them? I don't know them, though if they're here and inside a dampening field, I assume you think they're trustworthy."

"Magicker Aminatra, she and her," Lodri said quietly, and stood. "I can witness for you, if you'd like."

Eyras's breath caught. But she shook her head. "No...let me get this out first."

Lodri nodded and sat back down.

"Eyras," Iata said, "why would Vatrin kill one of their guards?"

She closed her eyes, her hands slowly kneading together. "I told you the Truthspeaker was blackmailing me. I told Vatrin this five days ago, hoping for an ally. I'd debated on if I should take this to them or the Seritarchus..." She opened her eyes. "Vatrin was livid, but for all the wrong reasons. They were absolutely *furious* that I was their sibling." Her mouth pulled tight. "That fight wasn't pretty. I did heal the bruises."

"Adeius," Homaj said, then shut his mouth as she flinched again. He might be using a different accent, but his voice was still Vatrin's. And he wished desperately just now that it was not, but he didn't dare try to dip into a trance and miss what Eyras was saying, not with something as delicate as a voice.

"So—" Eyras said, gathering herself, "so, Vatrin decided that they were going to use the fact that the Truthspeaker was blackmailing me to blackmail the Truthspeaker into supporting their marriage to Lord Birka. This, of course, backfired.

"The Truthspeaker had been trying to maneuver Vatrin for a while now to move up their agenda for social reforms. Trying to convince Vatrin that they needed to marry and then force the Seritarchus to retire, with the goal that Vatrin would be ever more under the Truthspeaker's control. I don't know how far Vatrin got with all of this. They had been getting more aggressive with their push for social reforms, and meeting with Aduwel more often. But they disagreed strongly over Vatrin's need to marry and have heirs—Vatrin wanted to marry Lord Birka, while Aduwel was pushing for them to marry the Javieri prince, Yroikan."

Eyras's voice grew hoarse, and she paused. "I need something to drink—"

Zhang retrieved a water bottle from a cabinet and Eyras took it, taking a long swig that Homaj suspected was to stall more than anything else.

But he didn't press. Neither did Iata. They all waited until Eyras capped the lid again. Took a breath.

"So, Vatrin thought in this whole scheme with Aduwel that they could use my new information as leverage. What actually happened, I think, was Aduwel realized that he wouldn't be able to control Vatrin."

"So Aduwel killed the—our parents?" Iata asked.

She looked away. "That's my guess, though I don't have proof or know for sure. But if he was trying to escalate, to either force Vatrin to fall into line and become his puppet out of fear, or maybe eliminate Vatrin as well and then try to control one of us..." She shrugged. "The results are the same."

"Vatrin said Aduwel was trying to kill them," Homaj said. Eyras didn't flinch this time, but she turned her hard stare on him.

"Why are you Vatrin, Maja? That is the very last person you should be."

92

THE CONFESSION

I was never taught compassion. Not by my fathers, not by the Truthspeaker, not by the guards or the nobility or anyone around me. Kindness, sometimes, but not compassion. Truthspoken aren't supposed to need or want compassion. Why, after all, would we want for anything?

— HOMAJ RHIALDEN, SERITARCHUS IX IN A PRIVATE LETTER, NEVER SENT; AS QUOTED IN *THE CHANGE DIALOGUES*

"I'm Vatrin because I wanted answers," Homaj said. And then shrugged. "And, it sort of accidentally happened, and I ran with it."

Eyras sighed. "Ialorius, yeah. Change, as soon as you can. I am fairly sure Aduwel wants Vatrin dead. They aren't wrong to be afraid."

"But does Aduwel want me dead?" Iata asked. "I'm playing into his hands."

"Yes, and Adeius, why? Iata, that's why I came, to warn you —I thought I *had* warned you—"

"I was trying to find out more," Iata said, catching Homaj's eye. He rubbed at his own eyes. "All right. So, Aduwel probably killed our parents—or, had them killed. He has any number of the staff under his extortion, he wants power for himself, likely wants Vatrin dead because they weren't controllable like he thought. Yes?"

"Yes," Eyras agreed. "And...when we went to Aduwel yesterday morning, it was Vatrin, me, Xavi, and Lt. Seyra as guard." She shook her head. "No, wait, I should back up. When I came to Vatrin with my information, Xavi was there. I tried to get Vatrin alone, to talk alone, but they wouldn't have it, and they insisted I tell them what'd I'd come to talk about. They knew it was important, they could read that in me. I know I shouldn't have, but—you know Vatrin. So I said what I needed to say in front of Lord Birka."

The pieces he'd been missing, that had been hovering just out of grasp, were starting to fit into place. And Homaj felt sick at the picture they were painting.

Eyras twisted the water bottle between her hands. "So when we went to the Truthspeaker, Vatrin insisted that Lord Birka be there as both participant and witness, and Lt. Seyra be there for protection. They knew they were on dangerous ground—they just thought they could outsmart Aduwel at his own game. And maybe if it had been anyone other than Aduwel, they could have.

"And then...it more imploded than exploded. Vatrin made their threats, and Aduwel countered them. Aduwel listed a lot of small things Vatrin had been doing to hone in on the Seritarchus's power, and together, it was all very damning. Lord Birka wanted to go, I wanted to go, and Seyra was just doing their duty, but Vatrin said we should stay and all be witnesses to this wreck of a conversation. Then maybe they realized they were outclassed, because they suddenly pulled back, hustled us all out and into the back corridors."

She swallowed, looked up.

"We went to a safe house in the city. So Vatrin could think, because they knew the Truthspeaker would try to escalate somehow. I knew that, too. We were all in trouble. I wanted to go to the Seritarchus, but Vatrin didn't. Mostly because their own scheming would come out. And then—Seyra got the news about—the assassinations. Adeius, it was just...it was bad."

Homaj's throat had been closing all throughout this account, but he choked now, went for water of his own.

Eyras hadn't wanted Lodri to witness her truth. Did that mean she was spinning this the way she wanted? Was that possible?

The pain in her voice was there, oh Adeius it was there. From every sign he could see, she was sincere. And normally, his own training and gut on this would be enough.

But Eyras was evaku-trained. Eyras was older, even, more experienced. And she was obviously not a fan of Vatrin. Was she trying to bring them down the only way she could? Could *she* have possibly killed their parents, all just to set Vatrin up to fall, had it been that bad?

He glanced at Iata, whose face was openly troubled.

Homaj asked, "Who bought the gun? You or Vatrin?"

Eyras stilled. Just for a heartbeat, and she recovered quickly, but it was there. She looked around at them all, her face hardening again, then pointed to Lodri. "You. You have an aura?"

Lodri's expression was unyielding, but she stood, green rippling around her as she joined them all standing around Eyras. She held out her hand. This time, Eyras took it, eyes locked on Lodri's.

Lodri's whole body tensed, and Homaj wondered just what she was sensing from Eyras. It couldn't be good. But Lodri's brow crinkled, too, and that was empathy.

Eyras said, "Vatrin bought the gun. I fired it, on their orders. Fuck the stars, but yes, they did order the death of the person they wanted to marry."

Homaj swallowed convulsively before he got ahold of his body's reactions again.

"Why?" Iata asked. He was holding his arms tightly to himself now, and Homaj wasn't much better. "Why would they kill—that was their entire point with Aduwel, wasn't it? That they wanted to marry Lord Birka—"

Eyras nodded. "But in the Truthspeaker's office, Xavi heard too much. And when the Seritarchus was assassinated, Lt. Seyra wanted Vatrin to go back to the palace, tell everything to Commander Tavven, and have the Truthspeaker arrested. Which would have been a good plan, maybe, except Vatrin was sure the Truthspeaker would make it look like Vatrin had killed the Seritarchus, and present the proof of all the little things they and the Truthspeaker had been leading up to—leaving out, of course, the Truthspeaker's part in it. Aduwel wasn't the only one with staff on his payroll—he taught Vatrin how to use the staff, too, and even some of the guards."

Every word was a stab. Every word. Truth tumbling out, and a look to Lodri verified that with her nod.

"So Vatrin couldn't go to Tavven," Eyras said, her voice tight and pained. "And I'm not sure Tavven isn't—wasn't—on Aduwel's payroll, too. Well, or blackmail list. Either or. Maybe even Vatrin's. Tavven does have a family. Two spouses and three children between them."

"So Vatrin killed Lt. Seyra, to prevent them from going to Tavven?" Iata asked.

Eyras looked down. "Yes. And—Lord Birka wasn't a fool. He knew he was in over his head from the moment I told Vatrin what I knew. Adeius, if I had only kept my mouth shut. Or gone to the Seritarchus with this instead."

"Our father knew someone was working against him at the

palace," Homaj said. "I met—I met a source in the city. Who said that the Seritarchus suspected someone."

He briefly debated telling her about Weyan, but held back. Despite what she was saying now, despite Lodri verifying it as true, he wasn't sure he could trust Eyras. Not with someone else's life. She was desperate, and he knew not to trust desperation.

"Two someones," Eyras agreed. "To start with. Dozens or hundreds of someones when you count who they have under their control."

"And you?" Iata asked. "What did you want to do? Go to Tavven?"

She looked exhausted. Slumping in her seat, tapping the half-empty water bottle against her knee. Her hand still gripped Lodri's, but the tension had gone slack.

"I couldn't. I would have had to explain what started this all, and that—that would implicate me as well, wouldn't it? As the oldest."

Homaj wanted to march to the Adeium right now and haul Aduwel out by his throat.

Or to Vatrin's apartment and do the same.

No. No, he wasn't a violent person. And this would certainly not be solved with more violence.

"Lord Birka fled the safe house after Vatrin shot Seyra. But...Xavi wasn't going to get out of there alive even if he hadn't fled. I knew that when Vatrin bought the gun. They said it was for protection, but I knew it was more. Adeius, I just knew. Then they ordered me to—they threatened me—"

She shook her head. Held up her free hand. "It was a short fight. I caught up to Xavi, and I did it. Because Xavi knew about me, too. And you probably should arrest me for that, Commander Jalava."

93

ADAPTING IN THE MOMENT

A comedy unending
The ever-present vector
The motion is what killed you
The motion is what killed you

— THE ANTI-SPIN CONNECTION IN THEIR
HIT SINGLE "THE MOTION IS WHAT
KILLED YOU"

"You were given an order," Homaj said.

Eyras shifted. "Yes. But I'm as like to Truthspoken, and you know that. We were in the city. I could have found a way to disappear."

Iata cocked his head. "Why didn't you?"

"I was going to. I really was, after Xavi's—" She stopped, and it was Lodri who drew a sharp breath.

"She needs a minute."

Yeah, Homaj could guess she did. He rubbed at his face, and it didn't help. Didn't help any of this.

"True?" he asked. He didn't want to, but he had to.

"Yes," Lodri said. "To the best of her knowledge. There is some variance, but that's normal Human perception. I witness this as her truth."

"Will you witness it again?" Eyras asked, staring up at Lodri. "In public? Legal and admissible?"

"I'm not sealed," Lodri said. "I'm not registered, and I'm not even a citizen—I manifested young, and my mother—" She stopped, shaking her head. "I can't. I can't do this for you legally, but my mother would. Onya Norren."

Eyras's expression rippled through annoyance, disappointment, and settled on hope. If some of the bleakest hope Homaj had ever seen.

"Sister," Homaj ventured, and she held up a sharp hand. "Don't."

He shut his mouth. He didn't know if it was still his Vatrinness, or just too many wounds around all of this. He didn't want to add to them.

She locked eyes with Iata. "I came back, I told myself, to get my comm. I just wanted to take some of the good memories with me. I'd just lost my parents, too, even though they never—"

She shivered with a sob, gulped, went on. "Iata, when I saw you, I knew you were getting caught in Aduwel's web. So I warned you, but you didn't listen—"

"That was my fault," Homaj said. "And I am sorry for it."

Iata's lips were pulled tight. "Aduwel formally witnessed my own bid to rule."

Eyras swore, swiping at her eyes. She jumped off the stool, shaking her hand free from Lodri's.

"Then I don't know if I can help you. Either of you. Any of us—"

"You can," Iata said. "I think we have all the information we need now, enough at least to discredit both Vatrin and the Truthspeaker if not outright arrest them—and maybe we can, if

Jalava's the Commander of the Palace Guard—though making it stick without an outcry will be hard. But we can verify all of this through the First Magicker—at least, as much as we're able to, I don't think we should say anything about who you and I are, that we're full siblings—"

"Magicker testimony can't overthrow Aduwel or Vatrin. It's not enough," Eyras said, and she just sounded tired now. "You can't go up against Aduwel. He will win. He's already winning —Iata, everything you did today, everything public that made it into the feeds, he will use that. Whatever you've said to him— he will use that. All of it."

"But Vatrin doesn't know who I am," Homaj said. "They think I'm Iata."

Eyras spread her arms wide, in defeat or exasperation, he didn't know.

"All right," she said. "Yeah. That is making more sense now. Hell and all the holy mandates, Homaj."

"We can win this," Iata said, standing too, and so did Homaj. "We have to. And I think we can win this by playing Vatrin and Aduwel against each other. I have Aduwel's ear at the moment—I'm not sure I actually have his trust, but I at least have his ear. Maja, you have Vatrin's. We tell each of them something implicating the other. We bring everyone together, get the First Magicker to witness. We record what we can, if we can, though that might not be possible. We get one of them to break and implicate the other, then it will all spiral down."

"That won't happen," Eyras said. "Aduwel won't break, anyway."

"Vatrin might," Homaj said. "They've been showing signs of extreme strain."

Eyras nodded. "Yeah. Yeah, they would be." Some heat was coming back into her voice again now, and it was so much better than all the pain.

Homaj nodded as he thought this through, let the idea continue to bloom.

Nothing too public. Intimate, only with those already involved. That would make tempers more likely to flare, tongues to loosen.

And if no one broke? If they gave up their only advantages and this all spiraled out of control?

Well, at the rate things were going, neither he nor Iata would live through the week unless they also fled for their own lives. In which case, Aduwel and Vatrin would still win. Or one would kill the other. All of which was chaos for the kingdom. It would certainly cause economic upheaval, political upheaval, and might even bleed into civil war.

"Tomorrow," he said. "At ten. In the North Hall. It's small enough to be intimate, big enough to seem more official all around and play to big egos."

Eyras snorted.

"Can you be there?" Iata asked Eyras. "Can you Change, maybe, into one of my guards?"

Eyras narrowed her eyes. "I'm not sure that is a good idea. Vatrin would be able to spot me, certainly. And Aduwel. But I will Change anyway."

Homaj nodded. "I'd better get back." He still didn't know if Vatrin had set a trap for him, wanting him to leave. Adeius, he didn't know what would be waiting for him when he returned, and his mind was so stuffed and so tired that he wasn't sure how well he could improvise if he had to.

But he had to go. This didn't have a chance if he wasn't there to get Vatrin to come to the North Hall. If Iata tried to summon Vatrin as the ruler, they might ignore it as a power move, or avoid it as an assassination attempt.

Iata looked like he wanted to argue. He so badly looked like he wanted to grab Homaj and stuff him into a closet and not let him go back to Vatrin. Or to being Vatrin. Homaj would agree to something like that, Adeius, he so badly didn't want to go back, too. Especially with what he knew now.

But he *had* to go.

"Yes—go," Iata said, deliberately pressing open palms to his sides. One of Homaj's calming gestures. "Jalava and I will keep working this out." He stepped toward Homaj, lifted off the ridiculous orange hat, didn't quite smile. Homaj shrugged out of the coat and handed it over as well.

"Ruler's passcode," Iata said. "I gave you yesterday's this morning." He leaned forward and repeated what they'd done earlier that day, with Homaj memorizing the code.

Iata nodded and stepped back. "Be careful, Maja."

"Adeius. You too."

Motion. They were in some kind of motion, and if it wasn't yet a solid plan—well, he was an Ialorius personality. He thrived on adapting in the moment.

So maybe he would be okay. He could lean into that, pivot as needed.

"Tomorrow at ten, then," he said. If nothing drastic happened to stop it.

Adeius help them all.

94

THE HOUSING BLOCK

I'd swear there are places in the palace courtyard where the ground feels more hollow than others.

— ANONYMOUS03487-J5 IN THE CHATSPHERE
I'M AT THE PALACE, NOW WHAT?

In the back corridors outside his apartment, Homaj stopped Lodri and Zhang.

"I want to go to the Adeium," he said in a low voice.

Zhang exchanged glances with Lodri.

"I want to talk to Ceorre Gatri," he said. "I know—I know we should get back. But we need more help than this. I'm not intending to take on the Truthspeaker tonight, if that's what you're wondering. And if I'm seen by the Truthspeaker—then let him think Vatrin is plotting against him."

"And if he knows who you are and outs you?" Zhang asked, her voice equally low. "Like he did before?"

He opened his hands, closed them again.

"You're talking about the assistant Truthspeaker?" Lodri asked.

"Truthspeaker in training, yes. She seemed to be on our side before—my side, at least. She wasn't happy that Aduwel outed me in public."

"But you want me to read her?" Lodri asked. "I'm happy to help, but the more people who know I'm a magicker—"

He moved closer to her, because he knew his voice would want to rise, and he could not afford that here in the back corridors. Speaking even now was a risk.

"I know. Lodri, I know. But if we take Aduwel down, Ceorre is it. She's the only Truthspeaker in training we have—beyond her, *I* will need to help train the new Truthspeaker, because no one else in the kingdom knows more about evaku than Aduwel. Even the head speakers in other cities and other worlds."

"I don't like this," Zhang whispered. "We're already risking much by being away from Vatrin's room. They might find the crumbled bolt. They might have planted it just to see what we'd do with it. Is there any other way you can get Vatrin to come tomorrow without going back?"

Homaj's brows twitched. He'd forgotten to ask Iata if he had another bolt—no. No, of course Iata didn't have a bolt. Homaj knew every centimeter of that apartment and knew there were no analog bolts anywhere in it. That was Vatrin's paranoia, not his own.

Fuck.

And he knew Zhang was right. But he also knew this needed to be done. He had to know if he could trust Ceorre or not. And trust her, too, to witness that the Truthspeaker was corrupt. If he didn't have that from her...maybe none of this would work.

"I'll go with you," Lodri said, watching him. And she wasn't asking, but he knew that all of her help was contingent on him making some drastic reforms around magicker quality of life.

No, not contingent. She wasn't holding this over him. She

was pleading for him to win this bid. She was giving him every chance she could, all of it at high risk to herself.

He nodded, glanced to Zhang, who grudgingly nodded. He led them all through the back corridors, to the tunnels beneath the courtyard that would take them to the Adeium.

Zhang had her pistol out the whole way. Whether she thought they might run into Eyras again, or...someone else...he wasn't sure. But he didn't tell her to put it away.

In the tunnels under the Adeium, Homaj had to stop and get his bearings for where Ceorre would be staying. The Truthspeaker himself had a separate residence behind the Adeium, and then there was the housing block for the speakers. Ceorre was a speaker, yes, but the highest ranking among them. He'd never needed to seek out her personal quarters before, though. And was there a possibility Ceorre wouldn't be there, would still be at the Adeium? Either in meetings with Aduwel or doing her own work?

"Lodri," he said softly as he guided them toward the housing block. "We're behind the Adeium, we're headed to another building where the speakers live. There's an exit in a maintenance closet. If you go out through the exit, do you think you can detect where Ceorre is, if she has as much command of evaku as I do? Would she read as Truthspoken to your senses?"

Lodri tilted her head back and forth. Weighing his words, maybe, or maybe trying to sense from here.

She pointed ahead. Adeius, she had range.

"She's in that direction. Unless that's the Truthspeaker—"

"No, that is the housing block. Okay. There's another exit that's on that other side of the building, in a bathroom. We'll use that one. I'd like you to please go to her room and knock on her door and say—say that Homaj wishes to see her, and you'll bring her back to the palace. She will be able to read that the first statement is true, and the second is not."

"So then where will you take her?" Lodri asked.

"There's an underground garage on the other side of the courtyard tunnels, accessible only to Truthspoken and blood-servants. We'll go there—it's the safest place I can think of at the moment to talk."

Lodri nodded, then passed him between the narrow concrete walls and began leading the way. He had to unlock a door going up into the housing block, but he followed her up a steep flight of stairs to the entirely other side of the housing block he'd thought Ceorre would be.

Beside him, Zhang's tension was mounting. So was his own. He'd go get Ceorre himself, but he knew Vatrin showing up here just now would be a disaster, especially if Ceorre wasn't, after all, on his side. If he'd read her wrong. Or if the Truthspeaker had threatened her in the meantime, and she couldn't go against Aduwel.

They reached a narrow landing with a locked panel door at the end, the space just big enough for the three of them if they pressed close together. Homaj stretched around Lodri to touch the scan plate. He wondered if he'd need Iata's ruler's code, and if he'd need to Change his hand back to his own DNA—but no, the door unlocked.

The dim back corridor lights went out when the door opened, leaving them in the dark, save for a crack of light around the panel door.

He held up a hand before he pushed the door open. It would lead to a stall in a communal bathroom.

Lodri said, "No one's in there."

He nodded, and pushed in the panel door.

Lodri slipped through the narrow door into the empty stall, edging past the toilet. The bathroom lights were dim for the night. "She's one room over. I'll come back quickly if I can."

Homaj nodded, then retreated and pulled the panel door as shut as he could and still have it open for Lodri to return. If someone came inside in the meantime, he'd close it and let

Lodri knock—but this was better if she had to come back through quickly.

They waited.

Zhang shifted beside him, restless but alert. His fingers fidgeted with the hem of the long tunic he wore, playing with the beaded trim. Then turned one of Vatrin's rings over and over on his finger.

He wanted that coat and orange hat again. Anything—absolutely anything—to push him away from Vatrin.

Adeius, he wanted this to be over.

Zhang's breaths seemed too loud in the cramped, dark space. His own weren't much better, and he consciously slowed his heart rate, slowed and steadied his breathing.

He heard the outer bathroom door bang open, and he tensed.

Two sets of footsteps.

He didn't know Lodri well enough yet to identify her walk, but he did know Ceorre. And was that walk hers? The steps echoed on the tiled floor, both sets running together.

Then the stall with the panel door opened. The steps came straight for the door he stood behind, and that had to be Lodri.

Zhang holstered her pistol—it would do no good in this tight space. He saw the barest glint of her uniform buttons, the blue of her hair, in the sliver of light from the edge of the panel door. She moved toward the door, pushing him back, and he didn't protest.

He himself tensed to run back down the stairs behind them, knowing Zhang would buy him time.

He hated the thought, but knew its necessity. He knew what hung on his survival.

The door swung open.

95

LIVE

> *The regard of someone who trusts you is worth a thousand times more than the regard of someone who doesn't.*

> — UNKNOWN, COLLOQUIAL SAYING

Homaj caught Lodri's scent as she stepped onto the cramped landing—Iata's shampoo, she must have showered in his washroom. And then he saw a glimpse of Ceorre's dark, glossy hair pulled up into a tail before the panel door shut behind her.

He had to take a step back onto the stairs so they all could fit.

The dim lights in the back corridors flickered on.

Ceorre stared down at him, and he stared back up at her. He wasn't trying to be Vatrin just now, but he also wasn't broadcasting his own tells. He was almost certain Lodri hadn't told Ceorre he'd be Vatrin.

Did she already know? Did the Truthspeaker?

But he saw the subtle signs of Ceorre's tension easing as she marked who he was. No, she hadn't known.

And that was step one accomplished.

He led them all back down into the tunnels beneath the Adeium complex, then under the courtyard, and to a small underground garage with electric bikes in racks. Not the same one he'd taken Zhang to the day before.

Zhang looked around as they entered the garage, eyes sweeping everything.

"No one here," Lodri said. "Can we talk?"

Ceorre reached for a pocket on her shirt—Zhang's hand twitched toward her pistol, and Ceorre paused.

"A dampener. I've been carrying one since yesterday, anticipating you'd track me down at some point."

Adeius, had she?

Homaj, momentarily thrown, surveyed Ceorre's appearance —dressed down for the night, yes, but not in any way disheveled. It was late, but she hadn't been disrupted from sleep.

"You have one of the smaller apartments?" he asked. "You could have one of the much larger ones on the other side of the building."

She shrugged. "I don't like moving. I stayed where I first started. It suits me fine."

She clicked on the dampener, and Homaj's ears pressurized, then popped as the field went up around them.

If Aduwel had managed to gain access to the back corridors, through coercing Eyras or Vatrin or even Tavven, he could have bugs here, his own cameras. Or Vatrin could have their own bugs—that was certainly possible.

He didn't have his bug-sniffing lip gloss with him.

But Homaj needed to not be Vatrin just now, not for this. He had to take the risk.

"You're in danger," Ceorre said. "A lot of danger. You and Iata both—I'm assuming you know what he's been doing and approve? Yes, right. But you're in the most danger just now, I think. I didn't know that you were Vatrin. Have you been all day?"

"Yes. I was Vatrin in truth at their bid. At their request. They think I'm Iata."

Ceorre swore softly, her brow furrowing as she studied him. "I don't think Aduwel knows—you haven't been in his sight yet, and you exited the Reception Hall this morning before he came in."

Her gaze flicked to Lodri. "I don't know your companion."

"Lodri ver Aminatra," Lodri said. "I'm a magicker."

"She is the daughter of the First Magicker," Homaj added. "They support me in my bid."

Lodri didn't let her aura flare, but she did hold out her hand.

Ceorre took it, no hesitation.

"Where are your loyalties, Ceorre Gatri?" Lodri asked, before he could more diplomatically get around to asking the same thing.

"To the kingdom," Ceorre said promptly. "To those sanctioned by Adeius to rule it. And no, that is not Aduwel. He has broken that sanction and that trust. I have suspicions—"

"We have confirmations," Homaj broke in, and Ceorre's gaze snapped back to him.

"Do you," she said, and there was a dangerous edge there. Not, he thought, aimed at him.

"No tangible proof," he said, "yet, but we have a witness around that proof, enough to have Aduwel arrested. And Jalava will certainly arrest him."

"Enough to make that arrest stick?" Ceorre asked. "If the high houses and the General Assembly demand his release?"

"I think so. Maybe." Adeius, if Aduwel had some of the

heads of high houses under his blackmail control, too, that could get ugly.

Homaj couldn't think about that now. There was nothing he could do about that now.

"Arresting Vatrin might be...trickier," he said. "But also, I think, not impossible."

Vatrin had their own allies among the high houses. And would that be a problem?

Almost certainly.

But Homaj was an Ialorius personality. He would assess and adapt. He would find a way, he had to.

Ceorre slowly nodded. Emotions, briefly, flickered across her features, too fast to fully read, and then her face showed the emotion he knew she wanted it to show: rage. A righteous fury.

"You have my loyalty, Homaj," she said. "You've had it all along. All of it that I can give that isn't fully given to Adeius. I'll be your balance, you be mine."

He swallowed, but nodded. The Truthspoken ruler wasn't positioned over the Truthspeaker—they were a balance to each other. Secular ruler and religious ruler. Ceorre was as much as making her own bid to rule just now.

"True," Lodri said. "You have my witness." And she let go of Ceorre's hand.

That letting go was as much a witness as anything else—Lodri didn't feel she needed to read Ceorre any further.

"Then you have my loyalty as well, Ceorre Gatri," he said. "I'll be your balance, too. You'll be mine." He paused, letting his own rage, for just at moment, surge. "And we'll take down these fuckers who killed my parents. We'll take them down."

Ceorre gave a small smile.

And that was done. Not an official ceremony, not officially sanctioned words. But he had his Truthspeaker, if he could take down the old one.

And she had her Seritarchus, if he could manage that, too.

"What do you need from me?" she asked.

He thought quickly. "Iata and I are both going to maneuver Aduwel and Vatrin to the North Hall tomorrow morning at ten. If for some reason Aduwel doesn't want to come from Iata's prompting—make sure he comes. On my end, I—I don't know how it will go with Vatrin yet tonight, if they'll discover I've been out."

"Then don't go back—"

"I have to, Ceorre. I have to. I haven't figured out any other way that Vatrin wouldn't discard. This doesn't work if Vatrin thinks I'm working against them."

"And what excuse will you give if they find you're not there? They're expecting you to be there? How long have you been gone?"

He shrugged. "Too long. They might already be searching for me. I'll tell them that Iata—well, Homaj—summoned me, or maybe that I was worried and wanted to see him after the attack on his life—"

"Adeius, Maja." Her voice cracked, and that break in her normally rigid control nearly broke him.

"I'll figure it out, Ceorre. I can adapt. And I have Zhang and Lodri with me if I need to escape."

Ceorre gripped his shoulder, gave a fortifying squeeze. For him or for her, he wasn't sure.

"And if Vatrin panics and flees tonight?" she asked. "Will that change your plans?"

He glanced to Zhang, and she looked expectantly back.

He was still not used to having to make decisions that broadly changed lives, not on this sort of scale. He'd been trying not to do that these last few years.

"Yes," he said. "If that happens, we'll figure it out." He shifted, and Ceorre let go. "Okay. Then, if you're with us, we should go. Be there at ten tomorrow."

She nodded once. "We will be. But if we're not—do you

have a second time to meet?"

"Uh—" They hadn't thought of that. "Four in the afternoon. And I guess we should change the location if that happens— the Lavender Hall. If we miss ten." That time before dinner would likely hold the least amount of scheduling overlap. He would have to stop by Iata's—Adeius, *his*—apartment again to quickly coordinate that.

But he knew, he knew to his bones that they would only have one chance at this. Everything else was moving too fast, and the assassins had already made their second and third moves.

Ceorre bowed a shallow bow to him, and he returned it.

"Be careful, Maja," she said. "I'd very much like you to live to actually rule. I'll see you tomorrow."

How do Truthspoken deal with their own pains? Do they have vices? Surely some of them have vices.

— XINANDER, VID COMMENTATOR, IN A VIRAL VID ON THEIR FEED

His second meeting with Iata that night was a terse conversation held just inside his bedroom, facts exchanged, anxious looks hidden as well as they could be. Iata was fully Homaj again now, Homaj easing himself back into Iata-being-Vatrin.

One last night. One last night, and then whatever happened tomorrow would happen.

But Adeius, he did have to get through the rest of this night.

He had to get past whatever would happen next with Vatrin.

"I sent Jalava to Vatrin," Iata said. "Just after you left—I had a feeling you would go to Ceorre."

"Sent Jalava to do what?" Homaj asked, his tone waspishly Vatrin's.

He closed his eyes. Opened them to Iata's tight and knowing smile.

"To interrogate Lt. Seyra about your poisoning."

"That was, what, an hour and a half ago? They haven't come back?"

Iata opened his hands. "You might need to rescue them."

And that was an unsettling thought.

Now, Homaj slowly opened the panel door into Vatrin's bedroom. He waited, listening. Behind him, Zhang pressed close, trying to see around him—she hadn't won the argument to go first this time, either. Vatrin was much more likely to shoot her than they were to shoot him. He was mostly sure of that.

But he heard nothing. The bedroom was still night-dim, still messy. Had he really been gone an hour and a half—no, more—and Vatrin hadn't noticed? Was Jalava still out there, had Jalava taken Lt. Seyra somewhere else?

Surely Vatrin would protest, or be suspicious, if Jalava marched them off. Adeius, surely Jalava wouldn't even attempt it, knowing who Vatrin really was.

Jalava was *not* good at this sort of pageantry. But Jalava was, he'd seen, good at moving into Job Mode.

Would he step into the prep room and find—what?

He paused, listening again. Zhang and Lodri entered the bedroom behind him, Lodri silently shutting the panel door.

He heard nothing.

He leaned close to Lodri. "Is anyone in the apartment? How many?"

"Two," she said. "They're not in the prep room, though, but farther out."

The sitting room, then? That would be smart on Jalava's part. If Vatrin had gone out to meet Jalava, and they would have been curious for news themself, so that was likely, meeting in the sitting room wouldn't have allowed Vatrin to call for or try to wake their Truthspoken without arousing suspicion of their own guilt and wanting to dodge the interrogation. It was, after all, an investigation into an assassination attempt by someone who'd had access to the Truthspoken.

And Jalava was the Commander of the Palace Guard and had that right to question. It might not be standard practice for Jalava to interrogate a guard in a Truthspoken's apartment, but there were a lot of reasons why they could justify that right now.

"It is Vatrin and Jalava? Can you tell for sure?" he asked.

"A Truthspoken—yes, Vatrin—and a non-Truthspoken. Who feels like Jalava. There is a directness to their soul essence that isn't common."

"Good." Adeius. So Jalava was still doing what they'd come to do. Had they been out there grilling Vatrin as Seyra all this time, with Vatrin unable to shake them off without breaking character?

Homaj took a breath, checked Iata's personality around himself, and checked Vatrin's own personality. He'd let it slip a little in the time it had taken to come back here from talking with Iata. Pulling Vatrin back around himself was just that unpalatable.

He moved around the bed, opened a dresser that he knew would hold underwear and night clothes, and pulled out a knee-length satin night gown.

He shrugged out of his coat and started to undress, then stopped when he remembered the impossible row of buttons up the back of his tunic.

"Zhang," he said quietly, "help me out of this monstrosity of a tunic."

She moved and fumbled at the buttons, finally finding a flow. Lodri stepped up and started undoing them downward as Zhang went upward.

Out of the tunic, he stripped quickly from there and dressed in the night clothes.

"Lodri, go to bed in Eyras's room. You were asleep. Zhang, you were guarding me, so you were awake. You knew the commander was here, but were under orders not to wake me because of the poisoning earlier. Me—I was restless and demanded to know what was happening, and you told me. I'm going to make sure nothing is wrong, because as Iata, I'm concerned about Vatrin's safety—and as Vatrin, about the new Guard Commander grilling one of my guards."

It was a complex flow of motivations, but they both nodded, and Lodri strode toward the bloodservant's bedroom.

Homaj checked his body and carefully let more of the exhaustion he'd been keeping at bay show, let it thicken his voice. He ran both hands through his hair to muss it before trying hastily to fix it again.

He glanced at Zhang in the dim light.

She nodded.

He moved with sleep-clumsiness toward the door and flung it open, then strode through the prep room and flung that door open as well.

"What's going on?" he demanded, crossing the hall to the sitting room beyond it. He squinted for real into the brighter light of the sitting room lamps. The air was cool on his bare legs beneath the knees.

Jalava, who'd been sitting in a wingback chair across from a very angry Vatrin on the couch, stood.

"Truthspoken. Forgive me, I was hoping not to wake you."

"Well, you did." Homaj strode over to them, peering down at Vatrin, not bothering to hide his annoyance.

Vatrin stood as well, mostly failing at keeping their own temper from showing. They hadn't been able to break character even a little here, not when the sitting room was under surveillance. Not if they wanted everyone to continue to believe that Homaj was Vatrin. And that had meant obeying the Commander of the Palace Guard's orders and letting themself be questioned.

He was witnessing a deadlocked war zone here.

"Commander Jalava has been questioning me—at length— about the poisoning, and about anything I knew about the assassinations. Ser Truthspoken. Which of course I knew nothing. They would not let me wake you."

Homaj inwardly winced at this speech—that was coming dangerously close, on Vatrin's part, to gross insubordination, to breaking their character, and to implicating some kind of guilt from their choice of words. Had this interrogation thrown them that far off their control?

Homaj turned to Jalava. "Lt. Seyra is loyal to me. When I said keep me informed of the investigation, I didn't mean start grilling my personal guard *in my own sitting room.*"

Jalava's chin went up. "Ser Truthspoken. With all respect, Lt. Seyra is not your sworn guard, but a rotation guard. I intend to be thorough in this investigation and interview all rotation guards—"

"Well you don't have to be thorough here, tonight."

Jalava's eyes flashed, but then they took a wise breath, took a step back, gave a shallower bow than they had earlier. They were learning. "Truthspoken. I will finish questioning Lt. Seyra another time."

"Yes, and not here, where it can disturb my sleep. You are out of line, Commander. Please leave."

The "please" was probably a mistake, Vatrin seldom said please, especially when they were upset. And Vatrin would have little intention of ingratiating themself to Jalava, because they'd absolutely intend to replace Jalava as soon as they were the ruler.

But he knew he was taking the right overall tone, because Vatrin as Seyra had drawn themself up and was looking self-righteous. Which was also out of line for what was happening just now.

And he couldn't think, not at all, about how the real Lt. Seyra was dead at the hands of the person who now wore their body.

"Of course, Truthspoken," Jalava said stiffly, and smartly turned, striding out.

When they heard the main apartment doors close, Vatrin rounded on Homaj, glaring until he motioned them back toward the prep room.

The prep room door closed behind them, and Zhang took up position by it.

"Why did you wait so long—"

Homaj held up his hands. "I was asleep, Vatrin! Zhang woke me—"

Adeius, he shouldn't have put that on her, but the lower down the social order, the less competence Vatrin expected from people.

"I told her not to disturb me," he said. "I needed to sleep after the poisoning—"

Vatrin pinched the bridge of their nose. Not their own gesture. It had to be one of Seyra's. Which did not settle well at all.

"Fine—fine. Fuck it all. Adeius fuck it all. I'll charge Jalava for that—that—gross breech of protocol. They won't last a day past my confirmation as ruler. They are an insufferable prick, invading my apartment to interrogate my guards."

But Vatrin had let them in. Jalava wouldn't have come in without permission from someone in the household.

"Fuck," Vatrin said again, and wiped at their eyes. "I should sleep. I got very little work done tonight."

Implying it was Homaj's fault, or Iata's in their eyes.

Had they truly not known Homaj was gone? Had it not been a setup?

And they weren't suspicious of Jalava now?

He saw no signs, and he was searching as hard as he could.

What he saw was eyes a little bloodshot around the edges. What he smelled were traces of alcohol on Vatrin's breath—the effects of which they would have smoothed away when they went to meet Jalava. But they couldn't totally eliminate the smell, and they had been drinking. He saw the bottle now, stashed away again on Vatrin's vanity beside the various colognes and perfumes.

Homaj didn't know whether to laugh or to cry. He had the manic urge to hug his sibling, to completely deny everything, because they had just lost their fathers. Couldn't he take a moment, just this moment, to grieve with someone else who understood?

But Iata also understood. Eyras understood.

Vatrin's gaze on him sharpened, their posture just this side of defensive, but they said nothing.

"I'll sleep in the guards' bunk room," they said. "I'm due an off-shift." A sour smile at that. "Go back to sleep, Iata. You're getting up early—we have much to do tomorrow."

Homaj nodded, just deeply enough to be a bow. "Yes, of course, Truthspoken."

Vatrin growled something incoherent, left, and Homaj didn't say another word until he was back in the bedroom, the door shut and locked behind him. And he still wasn't sure if he should speak. If Vatrin had thought he was still here, did that mean Vatrin didn't have their own bedroom under surveillance? Or that they hoped Homaj would go talk now and reveal information that Vatrin wanted?

He was too tired for this yet tonight, and shaky at the close call. And wary, too, that Vatrin hadn't been as vigilant as he'd thought they'd be.

Vatrin had wanted time to be alone to get drunk. That's why they'd pushed them all out to the bedroom.

Vatrin so rarely drank at all that Homaj was rattled by Vatrin's need, and their negligence. He'd been running circles around Vatrin, not the other way around.

But Vatrin had killed their lover the day before. Vatrin had killed the man they'd risked so much to marry—not by their hand, no, but they'd ordered the strike.

Vatrin had hit Eyras hard enough to bruise.

He swallowed, tasting the edge of bile.

Letting out his exhaustion to fool Vatrin had truly let out the exhaustion.

He wanted to cry. He just wanted to cry. But at that moment, he felt all dried up, his soul a tightened knot within him.

He waved to the bed beside him. There was more than enough room for two people to sleep without even a hope of touching.

"Sleep, Zhang. You have been up most of the last two days. I need you sharp tomorrow. We both do."

That last for Vatrin's benefit, if they were listening. Which he was almost certain now that they weren't, but he couldn't count on that, not even a little.

It gutted him more than a little that his sibling was falling apart. It gave him hope, yes—hope for a resolution tomorrow. But it cut him to his core.

Zhang frowned, but exhaustion was written on her face, too. And if Vatrin wanted him dead—well, Vatrin would have already killed him. There had been plenty of chances so far.

Zhang nodded and carefully got into the other side of the bed, far from him. She'd sat beside him in Eyras's bed earlier, propped up on the pillows, but that had been on medical watch. He sensed she thought this was different.

And he knew—he *knew* some of her discomfort was his reputation as a player at court. Yes, he preferred men and masc people, but he did sometimes sleep with women, too.

And maybe she still had Eyras's reality of the horrors of living with Vatrin in mind.

He wasn't Vatrin. He had his faults, yes, but he would *never* be like Vatrin.

He held up his palms, held her gaze. "I'm going to sleep. That is all." And he hoped she saw that was all he'd ever do around her.

And maybe he'd been reading too much into her hesitation, because she shrugged and said, "Of course."

97

THE SERITARCHUS

That saying's been going around a lot lately, and I'll add to it: The regard of someone who wants to use you, however, is something you can use in return.

— KIR MTALOR, SOCIAL COMMENTATOR, IN A
POST ON THEIR PERSONAL FEED

In his prep room, Iata centered himself. His hair was impeccable, done up in looping braids today with interwoven strands of pink nova heart gems. His gray jacket—more sober than usual—covered a flowing cream knee-length tunic. High boots with the barest hint of pale pink filigree around the top. Gray suede leggings. He knew his makeup was entirely on point.

His armor.

His weapons.

He was about to give the performance of his lifetime. And when it was all done—wherever he ended up when it all fell down—he knew he would have done his best.

He was a Rhialden.

He was a *Rhialden.*

And today, the kingdom was his.

"Truthspoken?" Jalava asked, stiff and formal.

Chadrikour had taken over immediate command of his personal guard, which Jalava had filled out with a few more people they trusted. While Iata regretted that he wouldn't always have Jalava close at hand, having decided not to relax his persona at all around Chadrikour, Bozde, and Ehj, he felt much safer with Jalava running palace security. Much safer.

But Jalava was still here now, at the start of this most important day. He nodded to them, and they both stepped out into the hallway. They collected Chadrikour and the rest of his guards, then set out on the walk through the palace to the Adeium.

On the way, Jalava's eyes roamed everywhere, head tilted as they listened to their ring comm.

Jalava had released the palace lockdown early that morning —the palace couldn't function, the kingdom couldn't function, under sustained lockdown.

They hadn't yet found the assassins. But Iata was fairly sure he was now walking toward one of them—at least, the person who'd given the order.

And Homaj, still back in Vatrin's apartment? Jalava had said that their intervention with Vatrin looked to be successful. Iata knew, though, that they hadn't been happy about gaining that powerful of an enemy.

He would do what he could. If this didn't shake out the way they all hoped, he would do what he could to protect Jalava.

Iata could only hope Homaj was faring well. And that Jalava's worries wouldn't be valid worries much longer.

Crisp morning air met him in the courtyard. And people were looking at him differently now. Did Homaj suddenly become a person of note once he'd proven that he was worth trying to assassinate?

The Truthspeaker was in his office, as Iata had known he would be. Aduwel had given him the command the day before to show up early—they had rounds to make again. It had absolutely been a command.

"I see you're alive," Aduwel said, not bothering to stand as Iata entered.

"You are, too," he snapped back.

Aduwel's dark brows rose. "Oh, are we sharp this morning?"

Iata took a seat across from the Truthspeaker's desk, which the Truthspeaker didn't offer. "Did you poison Vatrin yesterday?"

"Of course not," Aduwel said immediately, and with perfect sincerity, as far as Iata could tell.

"Because if you did," Iata said—and stopped. Sat back. Took a breath.

Aduwel smiled.

Iata could make no threats here.

And the ground they were on was re-established.

Iata waved a hand glittering with rings. "What do we have today?"

Aduwel pulled up a holo window and turned it around, pointing out various items on a very tight schedule. Was Aduwel trying to kill him from sheer exhaustion? But it was more of the same from the day before, this time built around Aduwel's insistence that Iata as Homaj should be paraded around.

"They need to see you're not only alive but thriving."

Iata began to wonder if Aduwel had in fact arranged that assassination only for it to be botched, so he could use it politically.

But those holes in the wall had been aligned with Iata's head.

He shivered, which Aduwel noticed.

The Truthspeaker smiled, which Iata definitely noticed.

Iata pointed at the ten o'clock block in the schedule. "This. I want to be in the North Hall at ten. Vatrin will be there. I want them to see I have your support."

Aduwel sat back, regarding him. All of those statements could be true. Iata held his sincerity with those statements at his core. He met the Truthspeaker's eyes.

"My sibling has ignored me all of my life," Iata said. "Worse than that. They dismissed Homaj, too, as someone who couldn't dream of ruling this kingdom. Give me one moment of vanity, Aduwel, just one. I know—I know, if I'm going to rule this kingdom, then my sibling has to fall. I don't want that, but they can't rule the kingdom."

He gestured in the general direction of the palace. "You've seen how they are. They think power is their right. Yes, they were born into it, but they look at everyone else around them as if they're less than. Me, certainly. Even you, I think."

"Homaj," Aduwel said in his deceptively smooth tone, "you're trying to push me."

"Yes!" Iata exploded. "Because I might not have another chance, if I'm being shot at, and Vatrin's being poisoned— Adeius—I just want to see them, once more. And whether they know it's me, or think I'm still Homaj, because they can't get it out of their head that anyone other than themself could possibly impersonate Homaj well enough to pull this off—let me have that, Aduwel. If all my siblings will be gone, and my parents that I didn't even know were—and they're gone—if this is to be my life, if this is what's needed for the good of the kingdom, then please let me have that satisfaction. Just for myself, just this once."

He sat back, muscles tight, looking to Aduwel, looking away, forcing his gaze back again. His eyes stung with tears he was trying to hold back, and he tried to smooth them away. Mostly succeeded. He forced his gaze on Aduwel's to hold, to gain presence. He let himself fully inhabit the Seritarchus he could become.

Could become. Homaj had said they would do this together. This moment, he would choose to believe that.

Aduwel's face turned pensive. But he nodded.

"At ten, you said? Yes, we'll divert there. A short diversion, mind you." He paused, still studying Iata. "Some might call this petty, but I do see it for what it is. Those of us who live close to power and never fully see its light on our own faces crave to have those moments where we can be the suns ourselves."

Iata nodded. His eyes were still shining with the fervor of his request. "Yes. Thank you. Yes."

"You will make a good ruler, Iata. An excellent Seritarchus. Now, come. Let's review what must be said at our first meeting this morning."

98

FLAWLESS

A perfect performance isn't just something we strive for, it's required in almost every situation. If we slip, we fall. And so the kingdom might fall, too.

— HOMAJ RHIALDEN, SERITARCHUS IX IN A
PRIVATE LETTER, NEVER SENT; AS QUOTED IN
THE CHANGE DIALOGUES

Homaj had decided, when he woke that morning, that the best lure to get Vatrin to the North Hall at ten was the prospect of outmaneuvering their younger brother, and chipping away at his support while bolstering their own platform. The plan was for Vatrin to show their outrage that Homaj had been shot at the day before—all the while subtly undermining everything Homaj was doing. The chance to goad their younger brother in public was not to be missed, especially after his minion had grilled Vatrin for over an hour the night before.

Outshine the enemy, and your work will be done for you.

"And you're sure that Aduwel won't be there in the North

Hall?" Vatrin asked for the second time. Which was a mark of just how nervous they really were. "You've been doing well enough, Iata, but I don't think you're that good. Certainly not that good. If Aduwel knows that the person the palace sees as me is not me, he'll try to find out who I am and kill me that way. Not poison this time, I'm sure."

"Homaj will have his guards, they'll protect you as well—"

"They'll protect *you*, not me. I'm supposed to be one of them. And I don't trust Jalava at all."

Vatrin straightened Homaj's collar. At least the tailored suit for today was something he could put on and take off on his own. But it was tight, so tight. Did Vatrin ever like to breathe?

Homaj glanced at Vatrin in the mirror as they fussed with his hair. "Have you found out anything more about the assassinations of the Seritarchus and—"

"I have leads," Vatrin said shortly. "Right now, I'm more concerned with staying alive. If you're worried that Homaj might usurp my bid to rule, don't be. He doesn't have the approval of the people. If the high houses and the General Assembly go to a vote—and Homaj should see he won't win, or give up this game and concede long before then—they will certainly choose me. You don't need to worry. He won't be the next ruler."

That Vatrin thought Iata was worried that Homaj would rule was...illuminating. They truly could not see beyond their own inflated sense of greatness. And maybe they thought that Homaj treated Iata as badly as they treated Eyras, and that they were an improvement.

Adeius, how *did* they think he treated Iata if they considered themself an improvement?

They truly thought they were doing what was best for the kingdom, didn't they? Their reforms, their projects. But it wasn't about that at all. Did Vatrin even care if the Blue District education system got an overhaul? Or if hospitals around the kingdom had enough funding to cover the influx of patients with the spread and growing concern of the Bruising Sleep?

That was all beneath Vatrin. Vatrin used those things as a means to let the people adore them. They didn't actually care about those people who did, though.

They'd killed their lover, the man they'd wanted to marry. He had to keep reminding himself of that. That was who he was dealing with.

Homaj would do anything to keep Vatrin from taking the rulership.

Vatrin ran lipstick over his lips. It tasted vaguely of cherries, and he wanted to gag.

"You're ready. The schedule is full today—and yes, we will make a detour to the North Hall if my brother will be there. And if my brother *will* be there, I want you to be me in truth today. That is safest for us all."

Safest for Vatrin, surely.

"We've gone over everything you need to say, all the points you'll wish to make, build that all in. You are very upset that anyone would make an attempt on a Truthspoken's life, you are personally handling the situation—"

"Yes," Homaj said. "I'll submerge."

"You are getting good at that," Vatrin said, as if that was high praise.

He nodded, held up a hand, closed his eyes.

He was already most of the way toward Iata's personality, his own hovering just outside himself. Now, he made sure Vatrin's personality shifted to the center. His performance must be absolutely *flawless*.

Because he didn't submerge.

He opened his eyes, blinked. Refocused. Stood, and Vatrin stepped back to give him space.

"Seyra. Why are you standing there? Get the rest of my

guard, we're due for my first appointment. Zhang, Lodri —come."

Vatrin's brow creased, but they didn't question as he gathered his two allies with him. Vatrin would assume that he as Vatrin would have found value in Zhang and Lodri.

Vatrin would be right. For the wrong reasons.

99

THE NORTH HALL AT TEN

> *It's not just our duty in the eyes of Adeius, but our duty to humanity as well.*

— TRUTHSPEAKER ADUWEL SHIN MERNA IN
"STRIVING FOR PROSPERITY"

The Truthspeaker walked beside him. Not before, or behind, but beside. The Truthspeaker had never walked beside Anatharie Rhialden, but always a step behind, though they were technically equals.

Iata had no illusions that the Truthspeaker thought he was an equal.

Ceorre was at his back, though, and she'd given him a look when she'd joined them, and a small, gracious bow. As befitted both of their stations.

It was nearly ten.

Their steps echoed down the long corridor that ran between Lavender Hall, where he'd last met with a group of Valon billionaires, and the North Hall. Where Aduwel was about to grant him his request.

HOMAJ HAD BEEN HOLDING Vatrin's personality all morning, adapting and flowing with Vatrin's inherent momentum. Vatrin was a Melesorie personality and functioned on being in motion, being visible, carrying their thoughts and ideas from person to person in a charismatic whirlwind so people didn't look too closely.

He hadn't broken character once, not at all. He was supposed to be submerged.

As they neared North Hall, coming from one of the antechambers of Rose Hall across the corridor, where he'd been meeting with a cadre of mid-nobility sycophants, he said, "My brother will need an example of what a ruler should be. He's certainly not making a good show of it now, with the palace just out of lockdown again and everything in disarray. Which I've spent all morning cleaning up."

The running monologues were killing him. But Seyra's satisfied nodding just behind him kept him going.

This day had an end. And it would be soon.

JALAVA, ahead of Iata, pushed open only one of the double doors to the North Hall, waving two more guards inside. They'd been doing that all day, checking ahead. And though the Truthspeaker seemed vaguely annoyed at the new security procedures—and the new Guard Commander in general—there was no reason to protest now as Jalava blocked the view into North Hall with their body.

The lights were on in the hall.

Iata lifted his chin in anticipation, glancing aside at Aduwel, who'd raised a brow at him. He smiled one of Homaj's edged smiles in return.

Because they couldn't both fit through the single doorway, it was Aduwel who gave way to Iata entering first. Because whatever other power games they'd been playing all day, the people still saw the Truthspoken ruler as a higher position than the Truthspeaker.

Iata stepped into the hall, glancing at the doors across from him, which were still closed. The North Hall had doors on each wall, but only these two facing walls were the main entrances—Vatrin would certainly wish to make an entrance.

But it was ten. It was *ten.*

On the other side, both doors opened, and Vatrin and their retinue swept in—and froze, as Aduwel entered behind Iata.

Aduwel, too, stilled, staring at Vatrin.

Then the hall's third door to the right side opened, and a third person stepped inside, completing their triangle: First Magicker Onya Norren.

Aduwel leaned to Iata. "You said this was a reception—"

Iata held himself stiffly. "I thought it would be."

He didn't know if Aduwel believed him, but Aduwel was at least distracted.

"What is this?" Vatrin called, striding toward the center of the room. "This was supposed to be a reception. I don't see a reception here. Good morning, Aduwel." A very slight bow. Absolutely not mocking.

Iata couldn't see a flaw in Vatrin, absolutely saw nothing of Homaj. For a moment, his mind stuttered, and he searched the other faces. But Lt. Seyra was there, eyes locked on the Truthspeaker. But then Seyra glanced toward him, and he looked on to Zhang beside them, to Lodri.

Adeius. Lodri.

He let the storm build in his own eyes, brought his gaze back to Vatrin. To the person who was currently wholly Vatrin, and Iata hoped to Adeius that Homaj hadn't actually submerged.

"Why is the First Magicker here?" Vatrin continued. "She witnessed my bid, that is all I needed."

"Good morning, Truthspoken," Onya Norren called, walking across the hall. "Good morning, Aduwel. I was told there would be a reception as well."

"Then we should find who has done the telling," Aduwel said, glancing at Iata. But Iata was busy glaring at Vatrin.

His turn to say something. "Vatrin, have you—"

Lodri tensed.

First Magicker Onya Norren paused, glanced back behind her.

The door the First Magicker had entered through banged open again, and they all turned.

Commander Tavven—*former* Commander Tavven— stepped through. And that was not planned. Oh Adeius, that was not planned.

Because Tavven had a gun.

100

THE USURPER

> *When we see what's truly there is when we see for the first time.*
>
> — CEORRE GATRI, AS QUOTED IN *THE CHANGE DIALOGUES*

Tavven limped into the North Hall, their pistol aimed straight at Homaj's head.

His heart jumped into his throat. But he didn't lose his focus as Vatrin. He *could not* lose his focus.

"Commander Tavven," he said, stepping forward, as both Zhang and Seyra grabbed his arms to pull him back.

"We need to go," Vatrin hissed into his ear. "Truthspoken, we really need to go."

"No shit," he shot back. "Let go of me, Lieutenant."

"I'm done with your games," Tavven announced. Their voice was unsteady, but their aim was not. They were still advancing. "If I'm going to go down, then it will be with my honor intact. What little I have left."

Jalava, across the hall, had fanned out their own guards

around Iata and the Truthspeaker, sending two more along the perimeter of the room to shore up Zhang and Seyra, and Vatrin's other two unfamiliar guards. All of the guards had weapons out and aimed at Tavven, though Homaj saw the conflict in some of their eyes. The anger in others. Tavven had been their commander, and now Tavven held a gun to a Truthspoken.

"Tavven, put down your weapon!" Jalava called. "Surrender and you will have a trial—"

Tavven laughed, a sound so wrenching it made Homaj flinch. "I won't survive until a trial," they said. "Ask the Truthspeaker. Ask the Truthspoken here."

Oh Adeius. Oh *Adeius.* Was Tavven the witness they'd needed all along?

Tavven continued to advance on him.

"I've done nothing," Homaj said, hands out. "You are covering your own incompetencies, *you* let *my* parents die on your watch, or did you kill them—"

"And you just tried to assassinate—"

Tavven fell with a cry. Homaj jumped back, feeling heat sear his left side. Where Seyra was.

He whirled. Seyra held a pistol out and put two more shots into Tavven's chest.

Homaj opened his mouth to protest, because he was fairly sure he knew what Tavven had been about to say, and of course Vatrin wouldn't want anyone to hear that.

And he was reasonably sure, too, what Vatrin was about to do next.

Tavven—he had not expected Tavven to show up. The former commander had to have been watching and waiting for an opportunity like this. Had they bribed the staff not to report them? Was this a last revenge? An attempt at redemption?

He looked down at Tavven crumpled on the floor with outward contempt. And had to smooth hard to shove down the bile that wanted to claw up his throat. Tavven was a villain here. But they'd known they weren't coming back from this meeting alive. And yet they'd still come.

"I've been usurped!" Vatrin as Seyra yelled.

Homaj pulled in a sharp breath. Yes. He'd thought—yes. Vatrin couldn't just erase the witness. That had been impulsive enough. And so fucking dangerous—if Tavven had seen the shot coming and fired at Homaj—

"This person"—they stabbed a finger at Homaj—"has been impersonating me for the last two days. I have been coerced and threatened—"

Vatrin had erased the witness. And now they were trying to pin someone else with their crimes.

It wasn't a bad spur-of-the-moment plan.

If Homaj had actually been Iata, he would have had little recourse. The First Magicker was here—and he thanked Lodri deeply for that connection—and could verify that he wasn't Vatrin. And could verify what Vatrin would say next—

"Iata byr Rhialden is trying to usurp the Rhialden rulership. He can Change, and he has decided to rule by usurping my life —he tried to kill Homaj—witness, First Magicker. Witness that he is not Vatrin Rhialden, I am!"

It wasn't a horrible spur-of-the-moment plan. But Vatrin didn't have all the facts.

Homaj glanced across the hall to his brother and smiled.

IATA SAW the moment that the Truthspeaker got it. Aduwel glanced to him, back to the person who was visibly Vatrin, to Vatrin's guard, Seyra—who was claiming to be Vatrin. His nostrils flared, his only visible sign of rage.

"We are done here," he said, and turned to go.

Iata caught his arm. "No. We're not."

He was near quivering at the audacity of that move. But he held Aduwel's arm, though Aduwel tried to shake him off.

"No, we're not," Seyra said, advancing. "You're the one who planted Iata to usurp my life—"

"No one here believes that," Aduwel growled, turning back to face the oncoming Vatrin. Who was still, apparently, oblivious to what was actually going on.

Iata saw the burning, manic look in their eyes. Fear, or grief, maybe. A rage that looked like it might consume them.

"So you side with my brother," Vatrin said. "You told me we would make a better kingdom! You told me! You promised that to me!"

Iata stepped back, eyeing Vatrin's pistol, which was coming up again.

Vatrin was an excellent shot. He knew that. They'd always been. And they'd just demonstrated they were a lightning quick shot, too.

Jalava's people had their guns up again, pointed at Vatrin this time.

Vatrin jerked to a stop. "Don't aim your weapons at me! Arrest the Truthspeaker! I *have* been usurped, he's the one who—"

"If you are Vatrin," Aduwel said calmly, "then you'll submit to the authority of the Palace Guard until we sort this out—"

"I will have my truth witnessed!" Vatrin screeched. "First Magicker—"

Iata saw a rustle in Aduwel's formal red and purple robes. A glint of metal. Aduwel had his own pistol, didn't he? And with Vatrin as crazed as they were at this moment, few would blame the Truthspeaker for shooting them. At least, not enough to make a conviction stick. And the Truthspeaker would come away from this free. He'd spin it all, he had too much power, he'd hold what Iata had done and what Homaj had done in impersonating Vatrin over them—

Iata strode forward, stepped between Vatrin and the Truth-speaker.

Jalava lunged to stop him, but he was already moving.

"Vatrin," he said. "I believe you. We will work this out."

"Brother," Vatrin snarled, then hesitated. Their eyes flicked over him, and though he was still holding his persona as Homaj as tightly as he could, he knew the edges were frayed.

Vatrin looked back to Homaj, to the person who was still visibly them, and the look of naked betrayal on their face was wrenching.

"You!" they shouted. "Oh Adeius, you—"

The Truthspeaker's pistol arm shot up.

Iata jerked to jump forward and push Vatrin out of the way, but Vatrin saw and whipped around.

Vatrin's shots hit Aduwel with the same unerring accuracy as they'd hit Tavven.

Everyone froze, just a heartbeat.

"Do you see?" Vatrin shouted. "Do you see how they're all trying to take me down?"

Then they swiveled again, their pistol this time aiming at... themself. Visibly themself. At Homaj.

101

STRICKEN

> *Time does slow, when a moment is all you have.*
>
> — HOMAJ RHIALDEN, SERITARCHUS IX IN A
> PRIVATE LETTER, NEVER SENT; AS QUOTED IN
> *THE CHANGE DIALOGUES*

Homaj watched Vatrin whip up their pistol, aimed at him. He was their brother. He shouldn't be looking at that kind of rage, that kind of hatred aimed at him. He watched with a horror that rooted him in place.

He'd known. He'd known even before Eyras had come to them that Vatrin was rotten to the core. That Vatrin shouldn't be the one to rule the kingdom. That Vatrin had, in fact, had something to do with the murder of their parents.

He had known. And that was why he was where he was right now, who he was right now.

And why Vatrin's finger was pulling the trigger.

He unfroze enough to try to dodge, to drop to the floor, but he knew he wouldn't be fast enough. He didn't even have time to close his eyes. Vatrin's face, the face of yet another person they'd murdered, leered at him from behind the aim of their gun arm.

Then—it didn't. The light went out of Vatrin's eyes. Vatrin fell, roughly hitting the mosaic tiled floor, their pistol clattering, sliding away from them.

A shot rang out—Homaj did drop to the floor now. And looked up, looked around frantically for who'd shot Vatrin. Who'd been fast enough. Jalava?

Jalava was charging toward him.

But no, the shot had come after Vatrin had crumpled, and from behind him, not the direction Jalava had been standing. And Homaj had never seen—he'd never seen life leave someone's eyes like that before. There had been no space between one moment and the next. Vatrin was there in their own body; Vatrin was gone.

He heard a scream beside him, and footsteps running.

A woman's scream.

Homaj shook off Jalava, who was trying to pull him up, and turned to see First Magicker Onya Norren skid to a stop on her knees beside...her daughter.

What? Adeius, had Lodri been shot?

But Homaj watched in a new and entirely different horror as Lodri flickered once, twice. She looked up at him, met his eyes.

And then she vanished.

He waited. He waited, his heart hammering in his throat, but she didn't appear again.

What—what had just happened?

He turned back to Vatrin, crumpled on the floor.

Looked up at Iata, who stood rooted a few paces away, hands out, mouth open in an echo of his own horror.

"Truthspoken," Jalava said, trying to haul him up. "Please—"

Zhang, who'd been beside Lodri, shook herself enough to

join them. But she kept looking back at where Lodri had been.

And so did he.

Homaj yanked himself out of Jalava's grip. Crawled over to where Onya Norren sat with her face in her hands, rocking, her voice a thready keen.

He knew what that posture meant. He felt it rising in himself. He'd lost his fathers the day before. He'd just seen a person who he'd thought a permanent fixture in his life—Tavven—shot. And Aduwel, who'd helped teach him much of what he knew. Despite everything, it still gutted him to see the Truthspeaker also laid out on the mosaic floor.

And then—his sibling.

Vatrin, lying still and undignified. Not even, in this moment, themself. And he knew, with everything else he knew, that he shouldn't be feeling a keening rising up in himself.

He shoved it back down.

He shoved it down deep. Because he knew—he *knew* what he had to do from here, as people who'd heard the shots and other Palace Guard finally pushed inside past the bubble that Jalava had given them.

He knew he had to be Vatrin just a little while longer. Just a little.

He reached for Onya, gripped her shoulder, leaned close.

"She killed?" he asked. "With her magics?"

A nod was her only answer.

He squeezed her shoulder again and used his other hand to push himself up. Zhang was there, steadying him, her eyes wide. But she was there, she was alert, and scanning the growing crowd for further dangers.

"My people!" he called, holding up his hands.

The murmurings around him died down as more and more courtiers and staff and guards spilled in. Jalava's guards were trying to corral them back, but the press was inward and inevitable. Everyone knew something momentous had just happened.

"My people—the person who arranged the murder of my parents has revealed himself, along with one of his conspirators. The conspirator murdered one of my guards, who tried to stop them from harming me. I will be forever indebted to Lt. Seyra, and I honor them for their sacrifice. And I will not dignify the acts of those who betrayed us all by saying their names."

He had debated, in that last second, on pinning this all on Tavven. Tavven wasn't innocent, and they may have well been the one to order his fathers' assassination, on the Truthspeaker's command. On Vatrin's command, they had tried to kill Iata as the interim ruler, and they might have succeeded there, too. But they had a family. And they'd been trying, for whatever value that trying was worth, to make something right in the end. The Truthspeaker would make the much flashier villain, overshadowing Tavven's part in this.

And too many people, too, knew how rotten the Truthspeaker was. The Truthspeaker's hand in this wasn't something he could neatly cover up. He hoped the high houses would see this as a warning, though, if they ever wanted to take power for themselves. The Truthspoken saw, and the Truthspoken took down their enemies. No matter how high the position.

The Truthspoken saw everything—and acted on it.

He only wished he'd known any of this sooner. Been more aware. Had even tried to see what was going on for weeks—or months—or years beneath the surface of his life in the palace.

Homaj looked up.

He expected gasps, the drama of the court. Instead, there was utter, intense silence. As people took in those lying on the floor. Tavven. A guard lieutenant. The Truthspeaker.

"They have been—" his voice broke, and he let it. "They have been stopped. And I have failed you, my people."

He dropped to his knees. Looked up to Iata, who still stood frozen, now for a different reason.

"My brother was the one who discovered the root of this plot," he said. "I—I didn't believe it was possible. How could a Truthspeaker turn against his Truthspoken? I believed—and he killed my lover—"

He let out a sob. A genuine sob. Because fuck. Fuck it all.

Iata unfroze and reached him, nudging out Jalava to stand by his side.

Homaj held up his hands again. "I am stricken with grief. I cannot rule in this state. I didn't see the danger." He swept his gaze around the crowd, stopped when his eyes caught on a guard he didn't recognize. But the tells, the broadcast tells, he absolutely did.

Eyras. She was cradling a pistol.

He knew. He knew now where that last shot had come from. The one that had hit Vatrin while they were already dead.

Her eyes were red, but not streaming tears. She met his gaze, bowed her head, then pushed back through the crowd.

Homaj swallowed. He wanted to go after her, but he had to finish this. He had to.

He swept the crowd again until he found Ceorre, who'd moved a distance from where she'd first entered with Iata and the Truthspeaker.

Well. She was the Truthspeaker now.

"Truthspeaker!" he called to Ceorre. "Witness: I, Vatrin Rhialden, abdicate all claim to my title and the rulership, under the eyes of Adeius. I foreswear Change. You will not see me again. For the good of the kingdom."

And then, waving away both Iata and Zhang, he slowly made his way out, head held high. The people parted as he passed, and no one stopped him.

102

CHEERING

The eyes once open have been closed
The breath once spoken has returned to the first breath
The heart has returned to the whole
To await She Who Wakes

— TRADITIONAL GREEN MAGICKER
MEMORIAL RITE

Iata watched his brother go. Adeius, like an angel from the stars, parting the crowds.

He knew what Homaj was doing. Saving the Rhialden name and pinning the blame where it couldn't be denied, with how many people Aduwel had bribed and coerced in the palace, and who knew how many in the city and the rest of the kingdom. It had to be done, Homaj wasn't wrong. And he wasn't wrong that implicating Vatrin would crack the kingdom just now. Especially with how much Vatrin was loved.

Vatrin would be mourned as a hero. A martyr, even. Homaj himself would get a boost in public opinion from Vatrin's endorsement.

It had to be done.

But it hurt with a force that tore at his soul.

"Truthspoken," Zhang said quietly, coming up beside him.

She hadn't gone with Homaj. Hadn't departed in Homaj-as-Vatrin's wake. That had to be done alone.

He hoped—oh Adeius, he hoped that Homaj hadn't just made a grand gesture of his own and would truly disappear, run away from all of this for good.

But—no. He knew he'd find Homaj in their apartment, he knew how life must go on from here. Homaj knew, too.

Iata nodded to Zhang, looked up at the people watching him now, watching what he would do.

He straightened. Pulled from his body's waning reserves to put strength into his posture, into his voice.

"People of Valoris," he said. "I am—" He looked at where Homaj had just gone, back at the people watching him now. Waiting. He bowed, low and deep, then straightened back into his full strength.

Homaj had wanted to be a Seritarchus. That was the style of rule needed just now. So Iata would fully inhabit the Seritarchus that was needed. The Seritarchus that he himself was.

"I honor my sibling and their sacrifice," he said. "And I grieve with you at the loss of my parents, at the betrayal of the Truthspeaker, who has betrayed us all. But I promised you that I would find who had done this to our kingdom and would make them pay. And—they have. They have. We can rest now. We can move forward now, in strength, in the breath and will of Adeius."

He beckoned to Ceorre.

"My sibling, Vatrin, saw fit to name Ceorre Gatri as the next Truthspeaker. I have already witnessed the truth and sincerity of her service—she will not betray our people like Aduwel. She helped me expose his crimes for what they are. And for that, Ceorre, you have all of my gratitude."

He bowed to her, again deeply, and she bowed back, just as deeply.

"Truthspeaker," he said. "I appoint you, in the eyes of Adeius. Watch over our people. Be my balance. I will be yours."

Homaj had told him the informal vows they'd given each other the night before. His throat wanted to tighten now at echoing them, but she smiled slightly, nodded.

"Seritarchus," she said. "I appoint you, in the eyes of Adeius, and accept your bid to rule. Watch over our people and be my balance. I will be yours."

There would be formal investitures later. Because ceremony must be followed. But now—now, the energy in the hall was changing, from one of chaos and despair to one of excitement and hope.

This had been the right choice. The security and control of a Seritarchus rule had been the right choice.

"We will move forward," Iata said, and the crowd quieted again. "We will go forward in strength. Those who sought to bring us down will only make us rise higher. I know I wasn't your first choice to rule this kingdom, but I will rule fairly and with strength, and we will flourish, under the eyes and will of Adeius. This I promise you, with the same strength and fervor that I promised I would avenge you. The Kingdom of Valoris will only grow stronger!"

Iata rocked back as the people cheered. They actually *cheered.*

He did not look at the bodies still lying on the floor.

He wanted to go to the First Magicker and do...something... Adeius, and he would have to process what had happened there later. But Jalava saw where he was looking and pointed Ehj toward helping the First Magicker.

And now Iata needed to make his exit, with as much if not more style than Homaj had just done as Vatrin.

He decided, because Homaj was going to have to inhabit this persona he was rapidly creating, that he would keep that edge of sarcasm, transform the don't-care attitude into a you-can't-disrupt-my-strength attitude. So he smiled, made a flourishing bow to the crowd that was just a hair's breadth from mocking, then dipped further into a true bow and held it, while they continued to cheer.

Then he rose, looked at no one in particular, and left the opposite way Homaj had just gone. Back through the way Homaj had originally come in, posture casual, sardonic smile in place, head held high.

He held that all the way back to the royal residence, and even then, the staff who had access followed him into the wide corridor, still cheering him on.

103

PROMISES

A legend is never to be discounted. A legend is a tool, a weapon. Each ruler is their own legend.

— ANATHARIE RHIALDEN, SERITARCHUS VIII
AS QUOTED IN *THE CHANGE DIALOGUES*

Homaj shuddered out of his Change trance. He didn't look down at himself, didn't test the bounds of his body. He just tumbled straight out of bed, grabbed a dressing robe and wrapped it around himself, and headed for the washroom.

Zhang, who he was vaguely aware had been sitting in a chair near his bedroom door, followed him.

"Truthspoken—"

He looked in the mirror and saw himself. Tan skin, long black hair, his own familiar features. And Adeius, he'd never been so glad to see his own face.

He put his face in his hands, his shoulders shaking as emotions he'd been shoving down caught up with him.

Zhang, hovering near the door, said after a minute, "Homaj?"

He laughed, because fuck, it was good to hear his own name. He didn't usually get dysphoria through a Change, slipping in and out of personas was breath to him. But this time —*this time*—had been drastically different.

He glanced at himself again, recentering in himself, not Iata, not Vatrin—not ever Vatrin again. Vatrin had made their exit, and now they would disappear. He would never have to see—or be—Vatrin again.

He leaned over the sink, swallowing as he worked to calm a sudden surge of nausea.

"Oh Adeius, Zhang."

She stepped closer. "Is it still the poison?"

He shook his head. Wiped his beading brow, then reabsorbed the remaining cold sweat.

"No, not...not that kind of poison."

"What do you need, ser?" she asked, and he was aware of her being there, and aware of the small distances she was putting between them again. Distances that needed to be there.

He was the ruler now, not just the interim ruler. He knew Iata would have finished that for him, even as he'd stumbled his way back into his apartment through the back corridors, crashed into his own bed, and threw himself into a fast Change. How long had it been?

He didn't have a comm.

"How long was I—"

"Forty minutes, I think. We arrived twenty-five minutes ago, and that was Iata's best guess. Do you need to eat?"

She pulled two energy bars from her pocket. Adeius, he could hug her.

He tore one open.

"And Iata—"

"Is in the prep room."

"And—"

He stopped on a mouthful of energy bar. Too many questions could follow, and none he really wanted to ask just now.

He finished the first bar, grabbed a cup by the sink and filled it for a drink, straightened.

"What I need from you, Zhang, is to be the captain of my guard. And call me Homaj, or Maja, in private. I need—I need someone to see me, and know me for who I am, and you have, through all of this."

She straightened, too, stiffening way up.

Shit, he'd gone too far. He wasn't fully present yet, his thoughts still jangling, he had to clear his mind fully from his trance.

But she nodded. Her eyes filling. "I will. Thank you, Homaj."

She looked at him in a way that made him think that maybe he wasn't the only one who'd been seen today.

He offered her a smile, the first genuine smile he'd felt in what seemed like years now.

IATA LOOKED up from his place at the vanity, where he'd set down his comm and put it into projection mode. He was rapidly sorting through holo windows of the messages pouring into the ruler's inbox.

Homaj entered, fully himself, hair damp from a shower, dressed in loose jogging pants and a sweatshirt. Something he might typically wear before dressing for the day. It felt jarringly...normal.

Iata's fingers stopped midair, the window he'd been about to flick away blinking in his indecision.

This was Homaj's chair. Homaj's comm. Homaj's inbox—he shouldn't be sitting here. He shouldn't be making decisions on which urgent matters to address and which to set aside for later.

He stood, knocking the comm off the vanity, and bent to pick it up. With shaking hands, he straightened, held the comm out as if it would burn his hand.

"Take it," he hissed. And couldn't meet Homaj's eyes.

Homaj did take the comm. But then Homaj's hands pressed lightly on his shoulders.

"Iata. Yan."

Iata's chin snapped up. "That's not my—"

"You need a private name."

"But that's only for Truthspoken—"

"Does it suit?"

Did it? He was having trouble thinking through the fact that Homaj was himself again, and the ruler, and Iata—Vatrin hadn't been wrong about Iata being a usurper.

Iata took a gathering breath.

No. Homaj had told him the day before that they were equals. They were brothers.

He met Homaj's eyes. Blinked several times until he reoriented himself to not *being* Homaj. At the moment, he was merely Homaj's twin. His own self. He let his own mannerisms flow back over himself, shuddered through a series of his own tells to reground again into himself, as Iata.

Yan. Did it suit?

"Yes."

Homaj grinned. No, *Maja* grinned. This person who he'd thought had slowly succumbed to the pressures of the Rhialden Court, but who he'd seen again these last few days. Who was here again now.

His brother.

Iata jerked forward and embraced him, holding tight. So

tight. Adeius, he'd been sure he would lose his brother to Vatrin's unerring aim.

Homaj crushed him back just as tightly. "Don't you ever stand between me and a gun again. That is not your job anymore."

Iata didn't agree. But he didn't disagree, either.

Homaj pulled back. "Yan." He held up the comm. "This is the Seritarchus's comm. Not mine. When you're—"

But Iata was shaking his head. He glanced around them. He'd been alone, and Zhang, who'd been guarding Homaj while he'd Changed, nodded at Iata and retreated again to the bedroom. The door shut quietly behind her.

They were alone.

Iata brushed stray hair out of his eyes. "Maja. I can't be you again—"

"Iata, I can't do this alone. I can't. Not to start with now, maybe not ever—"

Iata hissed. "Maja, what I told the Truthspeaker—I want it too much—"

"I trust you, Yan."

Adeius, but those words cut. Because he shouldn't. Because Homaj didn't know all the things Iata had been fighting not to feel for the last few days.

"I *trust* you," Homaj said again, but weighted the words this time, his eyes locked on Iata's. "I trusted you with the kingdom, and it's intact. I trusted you with my life, and I'm pretty sure it's in a better place than where I started from, isn't it?" He shifted. "You don't have to push your ambitions aside. Use them. I'm going to need them. I don't know how to run this kingdom the way you do."

Iata closed his eyes. "Maja—"

"Yan."

So much in that one word. A private name. A Truthspoken's name.

Iata, slowly, nodded. "But I need to Change now. I can't be you for the confirmation, for your formal oaths—"

"Agreed. Very much agreed. But when I need a break, or when there's something that is best suited to you—"

It was so much. And not enough. And too much all at once.

But Iata nodded. Because it was more than he would ever have hoped. More than he likely deserved.

Or maybe not.

He dipped his head in a bow, but not a deep one.

He looked up to see Homaj smiling in a face that was crumpling.

"We lost a sibling today," Homaj said. "But, I didn't lose you. I didn't lose my brother."

"I'll Change," Iata said, and knew he'd better flee now before everything poured out. All the grief, all the joy, all the anger, all the pain.

He whipped past Zhang waiting in the bedroom, then stopped, glancing at the prep room door, back to her.

"He asked you to be his guard captain?"

She nodded.

"Good. Keep him safe."

"And you," she said.

He stopped short.

"When you are Homaj, I will keep you safe as well."

She got it. She understood every nuance going on here, all of them.

"Thank you," he whispered, and fled into his own bedroom.

It wasn't that the room seemed smaller—it didn't, and it wasn't.

But he felt like he'd expanded beyond it. He would have to learn to re-inhabit Iata the bloodservant again.

But then, that wouldn't be his only role, would it?

Homaj would have his formal confirmation ceremony later today, but Iata had been the one who'd actually, in the moment, sworn himself to the kingdom as the Seritarchus. And Ceorre hadn't said Homaj's name in that oath—had that been on purpose?

He tugged at his braids until they came loose. Carefully loosened his clothes all around, then lay down to Change.

104

BUTTERFLIES DRIFTING ON
THE WIND

I know that becoming the ruler never happened to you, Uncle. And maybe growing up, you knew it was a possibility, like I did. But did you ever fear, secretly, that if it happened it might consume you? That, I think, is my greatest nightmare. I throw my whole self into every role I assume. I have to, it's who I am. So what if my role is the kingdom? Where does that end, where does it stop siphoning off all of my life force until my only name is the kingdom and my only identity is the kingdom? Isn't that terrifying?

— HOMAJ RHIALDEN, SERITARCHUS IX IN A
PRIVATE LETTER, NEVER SENT; AS QUOTED IN
THE CHANGE DIALOGUES

The city air that morning was chill and bracing, the sounds of the port controlled chaos.

Homaj wasn't himself. He wasn't Tanarin, like he'd been the last time he was in the city. He wasn't anyone he had a name for unless someone asked him in the moment.

He hadn't come with Zhang, though she'd protested. Iata had protested, too—but Iata had Changed again and was holding the palace while Homaj was out.

It was three days after his confirmation as Seritarchus. And it would have been two days too late if he hadn't begged his uncle to stay until he could see him. Until he could manage a moment away from the palace. The comm code Iata had found in their father's desk, at least, had worked.

Now, he stood in the busy city spaceport, watching for Weyan Odeya's tall frame. Watching, too, for someone he didn't know who wouldn't be a stranger.

He spotted Weyan a distance away and started toward him, letting himself be jostled in the crowd.

The last few days had been...intense. Learning to shape himself into a persona that was both himself and moving further from himself by the moment was hardly easy. He hadn't yet had a breakdown, but he was sure it was coming.

And now, the wind blowing his short, bright red hair, he just let himself feel this moment away from everything.

The people had slid from the mythos of Vatrin right into his own. And he'd been hard at work, with Iata's help, crafting exactly how that should play out.

Ceorre had also moved gracefully into the role of Truths-speaker, and she was self-possessed enough to know that she did have all the training she needed, if not all the experience.

But then, that was where they were both starting from—training without experience. It wasn't a horrible place to start.

The state memorial for his fathers was yet to come. The heads of high houses and the various nobility had to travel inward from the farthest worlds in Valoris, and that would take weeks.

There would be no memorial for Aduwel. His ashes weren't to be sent into the sun, like every other Truthspeaker before him.

Vatrin would have no memorial at all—they weren't, legally, dead. Though he would say a quiet prayer for them, even still, in his heart.

And Tavven?

Tavven had left a fully signed and sealed paper confession in their palace apartment, as well as details on everything they knew about Aduwel's activities in the palace and city, including names of people they knew Aduwel had blackmailed or bribed.

They made absolutely sure to mark that distinction—they themself had been blackmailed. Though they confessed that it had turned into bribes as well. It was how they'd gotten the job as Commander of the Palace Guard to begin with, on Aduwel's recommendation to the Seritarchus.

They'd also listed the locations of every bug they'd personally installed at Aduwel's request. Or command, however you looked at it. None of them, thankfully, were in the residence— Tavven had emphasized their refusal in that as well.

They'd asked that their family not be punished for their own sins—and yes, Homaj would honor that. Though Tavven had, in the end, confessed to looking away when Aduwel had inserted his own people among the Seritarchus's guards on the day of the assassination. People, it had turned out, who were carrying chemical explosives. And Tavven themself had, under Vatrin's command, given orders to the sniper who'd shot at Iata, so that was confirmed. That sniper would have killed Iata if not for Lodri. Jalava had caught and arrested the sniper that morning.

But Tavven was dead. And their family was not. And Homaj was feeling very much like the sins of one family member shouldn't touch the innocent. If they should, Vatrin's would surely have stained him.

Weyan spotted him in the crowd and waved. Homaj was no one recognizable and Weyan hadn't been Truthspoken in years, but evaku training still held true.

Weyan's smile was a somber sort of smile. Everyone's was, these days.

"Hello, Nephew," he said, and pulled Homaj into a hug.

Homaj caught his breath. The last three days had been full of a lot of things, but familiar affection wasn't one of them.

He blinked hard, but didn't try to smooth away the sudden sting in his eyes. He also wanted, for just a few hours, to not be Truthspoken. To not have the strain of being *on* every moment of every hour.

He pulled back and saw the petite woman standing beside Weyan. She didn't look anything like Eyras, but he knew the tells. He knew...knew his sister's tight smile for the pain it was.

"Sister," he said, reaching for her.

She shook her head, stepped back. "No. I—no."

It hurt. Adeius, it hurt. But he nodded. This was the family she'd been born into, but it had hardly been that, too. Two fathers who'd never once told her she was theirs. A Truthspoken sibling who had been horrible to her. And himself? He knew he hadn't exactly been kind.

His deepest regret was that he hadn't seen what was happening sooner. And he might have, if he'd had any interest at all in paying attention.

"Will you be staying with Weyan?" he asked.

She glanced up at Weyan. "For a little while, I think. Then —" She shrugged. And let out a strangled laugh. "It's weird, isn't it? Having no choices at all, and then suddenly having all of them? Don't ever ask me to come back, okay?"

He bit his lip, glanced at Weyan's hardening face before saying, "I won't. Unless you want to."

"I won't," she said, with absolute finality. Her smile didn't reach her eyes. "Goodbye."

She turned, started walking toward the gathering line into the commercial shuttle.

Weyan glanced over his shoulder at her, then stepped closer and gave Homaj another hug.

"She's hurt. Adeius knows I know a bit about that, if not nearly what she's gone through."

"Take care of her," Homaj said into his shoulder, holding tighter than he would have wished to admit. Weyan wasn't his fathers. Wasn't anything like. But—but he was a connection, a door that was fast closing.

"I will, as best I can. But I think she'll mostly be taking care of herself, and that will be good."

He let go, surveying Homaj closely. Not remembering what he looked like, Homaj knew, but his tics, his tells, his posture, his demeanor. And even all of those right now were mostly not his own.

Weyan leaned close. "I hope your rule is long and uneventful."

He leaned back, smiling. A sad smile that crinkled his eyes, even though, with Truthspoken genes, he still didn't look the age he should be. "If you ever have need—and mind you, only dire need, but if you do—find me. You have my comm code. And I'm not terribly hard to find if you know where to look."

Homaj stepped back, suddenly feeling more awkward than he should. "Do you want me to write, like my father—"

"No. No, I think it will be better if you don't." Then he shrugged. "But maybe, when your children are born. That would be a good day to write."

He nodded.

Weyan nodded, too, then hesitated.

"What you have with your brother—I never had that. I wish I'd had. My"—He looked around at the people around them and couldn't say "bloodservant"—"my sibling, I see them occasionally, but we're not close now. What you have is good. Do everything you can to maintain it."

"I will."

"Then...goodbye. I'm sorry I couldn't have been more help."

"You were, though," Homaj said. And wanted to go on, to draw the moment out.

But Weyan just patted his arm and walked away. Weyan caught up with Eyras, who'd already found a place in line.

What was the world Homaj lived in that his family, his blood, had to scatter like this? Had to kill each other, had to die?

He turned and walked slowly out of the port, letting the ordinary sounds of loading, of boarding, surround him. The ordinary people. Did they have families like his? Did anyone?

Well, maybe the high houses.

And that was his family before, he decided. But it wouldn't be that way with his brother, or his own children, when he had them. He would make sure of that.

GREEN HALL SAT at the edge of Portside District, just next to Financial. Homaj craned his neck to take in the imposing, six-story carved gray stone building. He'd known he would come here after seeing Weyan and Eyras off. He'd known he'd have to.

And he could have just summoned Onya Norren to the palace, he knew that—but also, he couldn't have.

He climbed the stairs and was challenged at the door.

"I'm here to see First Magicker Norren."

"The First Magicker is not taking any appointments right now," the door guard said. "You'll need to leave."

"Tell her Homaj wishes to see her."

And he let a little more presence into his stance. Let a sardonic smile tug at the side of his mouth.

The guard stiffened. "If this is a prank—"

"It's not," he said, and let steel enter his voice, too.

The guard slipped inside, came back a moment later with two more. They escorted him in silence into the marble-tiled entryway, into the elevators, up to the top floor where the First Magicker had her office. He'd never been here before, though he knew his father had, once.

She wasn't at her desk when they entered but to the side of a room that was more greenhouse than office, windows high overhead letting in rays of sunlight, plants covering every available surface around the walls and only marginally leaving space to walk along the floor.

The First Magicker looked up, *looked* at him, and pointed to the procession of guards. "Out. I'll see him."

The guards blinked, but didn't protest.

Homaj approached her carefully, posture non-threatening.

She snorted. "I know you're not going to harm me. You have no reason to do so. Sit, please." She waved at a chair across from the one she was sitting in. She was nursing a steaming mug, one of the kind that stayed hot until you turned it off. He wondered how long she'd been holding it without drinking.

She glanced down at her mug, gave a small shrug, set it down.

"Why are you here, Homaj? Why have you, the Seritarchus, deigned to come visit me here in this humble hall of magickers?"

"Don't patronize me, Onya," he said without heat, and sat across from her. "I'm here as your ally."

He spread his hands. "I have a debt. Twice over. Maybe more than twice."

She nodded. Then looked away, sighed.

"You want to know what happened."

"Yes," he said, choking on the word. "I thought—"

"You thought magickers couldn't kill. We can't. Not usually without also harming ourselves. Usually dying ourselves." Her eyes were like diamonds, refracted in the deep green light of her aura. A beam of sunlight through the high windows glittered the dense holographic rank seal on her cheek.

"Why did my daughter, who grew up as a non-person, who has hid who she was every moment of her life from your family, from people like you—why did she kill to protect you? Knowing what it would cost?"

He nodded. His throat was too tight to do more. Yes, that was his true question.

Onya opened one hand. "Forgive me. Even those words, to you, are violence. If you're truly an ally, then I welcome you. If you feel you're indebted—it's a debt you owe to your fellow Humans who are magickers, not me. That's why. My daughter believed, and I believe, that you are our best chance at safety, at freedom, at basic Human rights.

"Homaj, I know you aren't the person you project. Your truth clashes with the image you show the worlds. You know the conditions we magickers live under—you know. I know you tried to fight for us with the last Seritarchus, your father, and were shot down. I do know that." Her mouth pulled tight. "Lodri knew. And yes, that's why. If you had died—"

He sat forward, feeling upended and raw. "There would have been Iata. He's a better man than I am in almost every way—"

"Maybe," she said. "Though I don't believe that. Everyone is equally their own person."

He ran his hands through his hair. "Please, please don't try to give me that bullshit—"

"She gave her life for you," Onya said, her voice ringing throughout the room, shivering the plants. "She saw you were worth saving that much. Enough to give her life. For you. Don't you dare waste that gift."

He sniffed hard through tear-blurred vision.

After a moment, Onya handed him a tissue.

"By She Who Wakes—blow your nose, it's running everywhere. I thought you Truthspoken were supposed to be able to keep your noses from running."

He blew hard into the tissue and had to reach for another.

"We—yes. But—"

He waved at the words that would not come.

She sat forward in her chair, held out her hand. He'd just blown his nose, but that didn't seem to matter to her. He wiped his hand on his pants anyway before stretching out to take hers.

Warmth flooded into him, like a summer morning. Meadows blooming and butterflies drifting on the wind.

She saw him. He felt it in her clarity, sweet and stable. She saw him now and had still decided—was still deciding—that he was the ruler she wished to follow.

"You're here as an ally? You have allies, too. Never forget that. I will honor my daughter's choice, too, and make it my own."

He sighed as a chill that had settled into his bones these last few days eased.

He'd thought—he was sure he'd only find recrimination here. Maybe he'd wanted it. It might have been easier to believe that he'd failed and would continue to fail.

But he only felt warmth and approval from Onya. And a sadness, a depth of grief that they both shared, in their own separate losses.

She patted his hand, then let go.

"Now, while you're here, I'd like to go over some of the ways you'll be making our lives better."

And he would. He promised himself, he would.

Thanks so much for reading! I hope you enjoyed *A Bid to Rule*, and if you did, please consider leaving a review! If you read this book as Book 3 in the numbered series order, the story continues with Homaj, Iata, Dressa, Ari, and Rhys in *Court of Magickers,* Book 4.

Want to stay up to date on the latest books? Sign up for Novae Caelum's newsletter!

https://novaecaelum.com/pages/newsletter

THE CAST

Note: Because this future universe has full gender equality, binary gender characters (male, female) may be cis or may be trans. I've only stated if they're trans if it comes up within the story itself.

Homaj Rhialden (Maja): The second Truthspoken heir to the Kingdom of Valoris, soon to be ruler. Suave, snarky, scared AF. Genderfluid, pan (mostly gay). he/him (usually)

Iata byr Rhialden: Bloodservant to Homaj. Always and ever more than he seems. Male, hetero. he/him

Vatrin Rhialden (Trin): Truthspoken Heir to the Kingdom of Valoris. Well loved by the public. Nonbinary, pan. they/them

Eyras byr Rhialden: Bloodservant to Vatrin. Has had a harder life than it seems. Female, bi. she/her

Vi Zhang: Sergeant in the Palace Guard. Learns quickly, has an excellent BS detector. Loyal. Female, gray ace. she/her

Jalava: Lieutenant in the Palace Guard. Gruff, no nonsense. Not so good at detecting BS, but mostly because they really just want to trust. Genderqueer, pan. they/them

Aduwel Shin Merna: Truthspeaker, the religious leader of Valoris. Likes to make the rules more than he likes to follow them. Male, pan. he/him

Ceorre Gatri: Truthspeaker in training. Takes no prisoners, knows no obstacles. Female, bi. she/her

Onya Norren: First Magicker of the Green Magickers. Likes to be an enigma. Cares to her core. Female, hetero. she/her

Lodri ver Aminatra: Daughter of Onya Norren, not a citizen, not a registered person. Incandescent for her cause. Female, bi. She/her

Sarin Tavven: Commander of the Palace Guard. Can access all the secret passageways. This may or may not be a good thing. Nonbinary, pan, poly. they/them

Weyan Odeya: Former Truthspoken, now a citizen of the Onabrii-Kast Dynasty. Is not a fan of the Truthspoken system. Trans male, pan, poly. he/him

Dassan Laguaya: Admiral of the Fleet of the Valoran Navy, tough as nails, loyal to the kingdom. Nonbinary, ace. they/them

Banamar Abret: High General of the Valoran Army. More politician than tactician. Always has an agenda. Agender, pan. e/eir

THE FACTIONS

Kingdom of Valoris: 187 worlds of theocratic goodness. Ruled by the Seritarchus. Bickered over by the high houses. Shares a border with Kidaa space.

The Kidaa: A species of quadruped sentients. Organized into clans, occupy a large portion of space. Far more technologically advanced than Humans. Hard to talk to. Pacifists (theoretically).

The Onabrii-Kast Dynasty: Former territory of Valoris, now their own empire. Also share the border with the Kidaa. Not super interested in sharing anything else.

Green Magickers: Organized sub-culture of people who manifest the ability to use Green Magics. Marginalized. Can't do violence.

The Adeium: Religion at the heart of Valoris. Genderfluid god. Oversees the Truthspeaker and the Truthspoken.

ABOUT THE AUTHOR

Novae Caelum is an author, illustrator, and designer with a love of spaceships and a tendency to quote Monty Python. Star is the author of *The Stars and Green Magics* (a winner of the 2022 Laterpress Genre Fiction Contest Fellowship), *The Emperor of Time* (a Wattpad Featured novel), *Good King Lyr*, and *Magnificent*. Stars short fiction has appeared in *Intergalactic Medicine Show*, *Escape Pod*, *Clockwork Phoenix 5*, and Lambda Award winning *Transcendent 2: The Year's Best Transgender Speculative Fiction*. Novae is nonbinary, starfluid, and uses star/stars/starself or they/them/their pronouns. Most days you can find Novae typing furiously away at stars queer serials, with which star hopes to take over the world. At least, that's the plan. You can find star online at novaecaelum.com

ALSO BY NOVAE CAELUM

∽

Visit Novae Caelum's website to find out where to read these titles on your favorite retailers or direct from the author!

https://novaecaelum.com

ALSO FROM ROBOT DINOSAUR PRESS

TERRA INCOGNITA BY MATI OCHA
Hiking in the Peak District at the moment Earth is—accidentally—infused with magic and thrown into an indifferent and muddled system, Will returns to his Derbyshire village to find a ghost town.

HOLLOW KING BY DANTE O. GREENE
Barridur finds himself in Hell where he meets the fabled Hollow King. A cruel and capricious god, the Hollow King offers Barridur a chance to return alive to the living world. All Barridur has to do is defeat the Nine Champions of Hell. No pressure.

YOU FED US TO THE ROSES: SHORT STORIES BY CARLIE ST. GEORGE
Final girls who team up. Dead boys still breathing. Ghosts who whisper secrets. Angels beyond the grave, yet not of heaven. Wolves who wear human skins. Ten disturbing, visceral, stories no horror fan will want to miss.

A WRECK OF WITCHES BY NIA QUINN
When you're a witch juggling a sentient house and a

magical plant nursery, you already think life is about as crazy as it can get. But scary things start happening in my mundane neighborhood when my friend goes missing. It's up to me and my ragtag group of witches—oh, and the ghost dogs—to get things under control before the Unawares figure out magic's real.

THESE IMPERFECT REFLECTIONS: SHORT STORIES BY MERC FENN WOLFMOOR
From living trains to space stations populated with monsters, these eleven fantasy and science fiction stories from Merc Fenn Wolfmoor will take you on otherworldly adventures that are tethered to the heart.

FLOTSAM BY R J THEODORE
A scrappy group of outsiders take a job to salvage some old ring from Peridot's gravity-caught garbage layer, and land squarely in the middle of a plot to take over (and possibly destroy) what's left of the already tormented planet.

THE MIDNIGHT GAMES: SIX STORIES ABOUT GAMES YOU PLAY ONCE ED. BY RHIANNON RASMUSSEN
An anthology featuring six frightening tales illustrated by Andrey Garin await you inside, with step by step instructions for those brave—or desperate—enough to play.

SANCTUARY BY ANDI C. BUCHANAN
Morgan's home is a sanctuary for ghosts. When it is threatened they must fight for the queer, neurodivergent found-family they love and the home they've created.

A STARBOUND SOLSTICE BY JULIET KEMP

Celebrations, aliens, mistletoe, and a dangerous incident in the depths of mid-space. A sweet festive season space story with a touch of (queer) romance.

Find these great titles and more at your favorite ebook retailer!

Visit us at: www.robotdinosaurpress.com

RE - #0002 - 160524 - C0 - 216/140/32 - PB - 9781958696200 - Matt Lamination